Praise for *New York Times* bestselling author Tina Leonard

"Leonard's tough and stubborn characters make a vibrant impression and will stay with the readers long after the last page is turned."

—*RT Book Reviews* on *A Callahan Outlaw's Twins*

"[A] fun, fast-moving story with just enough seriousness to make it a delightfully heartwarming romance."

—*RT Book Reviews* on *Catching Calhoun*

"Leonard's penned the best and funniest so far in the Callahan family saga. Readers are in for a wild ride."

—*RT Book Reviews* on *The Bull Rider's Twins*

Praise for *USA TODAY* bestselling author Judy Duarte

"Duarte's fateful second-chance romance is amazing, starring a couple whose teenage love produced an adorable lad who is a testament to resilience. A tragic twist gives them all an opportunity to become a forever family."

—*RT Book Reviews* on *The Daddy Secret*

"Duarte's romance is part mystery and all drama when secrets, betrayals and feuds fill the pages, and the love story is refreshingly pure yet sensually stimulating."

—*RT Book Reviews* on *Tammy and the Doctor*

"Judy Duarte's superb *Their Unexpected Family* pulls the reader deeply and satisfyingly into the hearts and minds of the characters."

—*RT Book Reviews* on *Their Unexpected Family*, 4.5 stars

HOME ON THE RANCH:
FAMILY PLANS

———————— ✗ ————————

New York Times **Bestselling Author**
TINA LEONARD

USA TODAY **Bestselling Author**
JUDY DUARTE

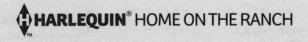

HARLEQUIN® HOME ON THE RANCH

ISBN-13: 978-1-335-02047-5

First published as The Rebel Cowboy's Quadruplets by Harlequin Books in 2014 and The Cowboy's Family Plan by Harlequin Books in 2012.

Home on the Ranch: Family Plans
Copyright © 2018 by Harlequin Books S.A.

The publisher acknowledges the copyright holders of the individual works as follows:

The Rebel Cowboy's Quadruplets
Copyright © 2014 by Tina Leonard

The Cowboy's Family Plan
Copyright © 2012 by Judy Duarte

Recycling programs for this product may not exist in your area.

Printed in U.S.A.

HARLEQUIN®
www.Harlequin.com

CONTENTS

Tina Leonard is a *New York Times* and *USA TODAY* bestselling and award-winning author of more than fifty projects, including several popular miniseries for the Harlequin American Romance line. Known for bad-boy heroes and smart, adventurous heroines, her books have made the *USA TODAY*, Waldenbooks, Ingram and Nielsen BookScan bestseller lists. Born on a military base, Tina lived in many states before eventually marrying the boy who did her crayon printing for her in the first grade. You can visit her at tinaleonard.com, and follow her on Facebook and Twitter.

Books by Tina Leonard

Harlequin American Romance

Bridesmaids Creek

The Rebel Cowboy's Quadruplets
The SEAL's Holiday Babies
The Twins' Rodeo Rider

Callahan Cowboys

A Callahan Wedding
The Renegade Cowboy Returns
The Cowboy Soldier's Sons
Christmas in Texas
"Christmas Baby Blessings"
A Callahan Outlaw's Twins
His Callahan Bride's Baby
Branded by a Callahan
Callahan Cowboy Triplets
A Callahan Christmas Miracle
Her Callahan Family Man
Sweet Callahan Homecoming

Visit the Author Profile page at Harlequin.com for more titles.

THE REBEL COWBOY'S QUADRUPLETS

TINA LEONARD

Much love and gratitude to the generous and supportive readers who have embraced my families and communities so enthusiastically—I have the best readers in the world.

Chapter 1

Justin Morant recognized trouble when his buddy Ty Spurlock texted him a link to a dating website. This was what happened when you had to leave the rodeo circuit thanks to a career-ending injury: your friends decided you needed a woman with whom to share your retirement, and maybe a spread to call your own because you were going to need something to do with your new spare time. The woman would run your life and the spread would rule your life, and maybe it was one and the same. You'd work hard, be tied to the land and the woman, never have two nickels to call your own. You'd have children and, suddenly, you were up to your neck in obligations and debt.

He'd seen it happen too many times. At twenty-seven, Justin was in no hurry to be fobbed off on a woman who was so desperate for a man that she'd use an online service.

He packed up his duffel, tossed it in his seen-better-days white truck and headed away from Montana, destination unknown, knee killing him this fine summer day.

His phone rang and Justin pulled over. This was a conversation that was going to follow him every step of his self-imposed sabbatical if he didn't stamp it out now.

"I'm not going to answer the ad, Ty," he said, skipping the greetings.

"Hear me out, big guy. I'm *from* Bridesmaids Creek. I know where the Hawthorne spread is. It's the Hanging H ranch, or, as we locals fondly call it, the Haunted H. Go check out the place. You've got nothing better to do, my friend."

"What kind of a name is Haunted H?"

"The Hawthornes used to run a yearly haunted house for kiddies there, and folks remember that. It was bad to the bone, and rug rats to small-fry attended like bees at a hive. Mackenzie's folks did everything they could to turn a dime with it. Her family raked in dough nine months a year with puppet shows, petting zoos, pony rides and lots of good treats."

"Nine months a year?"

"Well, three months a year it was turned into Winter Wonderland at the Haunted H, to go with the town's annual Christmastown on the square," Ty said, as if Justin didn't understand the importance of holidays. "You have to appreciate that a haunted house wouldn't be as much of a draw as Santa Claus for the youngsters."

"So what happened to the place?"

"Hard times hit us all, buddy," Ty said, a little mysteriously for Justin's radar. "Give Mackenzie a call. You're burning daylight on this deal. Someone's going to answer that ad, which will come as a shock to her because she doesn't know what's been done on her behalf." Ty laughed. "The only thing I haven't been able to figure out is why someone in Bridesmaids Creek hasn't already gotten her to the altar. I'm not suggesting you try to do that, of course. Small towns usually keep their own pretty well matched up, and judging by her profile on the dating site, that should happen soon enough. Good luck, my friend."

Ty hung up. Justin tossed his Stetson onto the seat with some righteous disgust and pulled back on the road.

He wasn't going to Texas. Not to Bridesmaids Creek to a woman whose family had operated a haunted house.

Just because a man could no longer ride didn't mean he had to make a laughingstock of himself.

Mackenzie Hawthorne smiled, looking at the four tiny babies finally sleeping in their white bassinets. "Whew," she said to Jade Harper. "Thanks for the help."

"That's what best friends are for." She arranged soft white blankets over each baby, protecting them from the cool drafts blowing from the air conditioner, which seemed to run almost constantly this baking-hot July. "Who would have ever thought Tommy possessed the swimmers to make four beautiful little girls?"

Mackenzie smiled at her adorable daughters, all scrunchy-faced in their tiny pink onesies. "Don't talk to me about my ex. Every time I think about him dating that twenty-year-old, I want to eat chocolate. I'm trying very hard not to do that. Your mother keeps me busy enough with desserts I can't resist."

Jade laughed. "Tommy Fields was never right for you. What you need is a real man." She hugged Mackenzie. "You rest while these little angels are asleep. Mom will be over this afternoon with dinner and to help out. I've got to get down to the peach stand and help make ice cream. 'Bye, darling."

"Thanks for everything."

Jade flopped a hand at her. Mackenzie was grateful for all the friends she had in Bridesmaids Creek. Everyone had been pitching in almost nonstop, bringing food, baby clothes, and giving their time so she could shower and even nap sometimes. She hated to be a burden, but when she mentioned that to anyone, she was reminded that she gave generously of her time to the community, as had her parents.

Mackenzie walked through the huge, heavily gingerbreaded old Victorian mansion, wondering how she was going to fix the fences that were rotting and sagging, not to mention the gutters on the house. Never mind run the horse operation. With four-month-old babies, she was constantly running, taking care of them.

But she wouldn't trade her babies for anything. Tommy might have turned out to be a zero as a husband, but Jade was right: he'd left her with four incredible gifts.

And a lot of bills.

But her parents had been entrepreneurs, smart with money. She had a small cushion, if she was very careful with those funds. She wasn't destitute, thank God. Raising four children was going to take everything she had and then some.

She needed a miracle to keep herself from going into debt, and with no income coming in and no way for her to work until the babies were older, things could get tight fast.

* * *

Justin was nobody's idea of a miracle, certainly not from his point of view. If the little lady was looking for one, she was doomed to disappointment. Yet here he stood on the porch of the strangest-looking house he'd ever seen two weeks after Ty had tweaked him about it, wondering what in the hell he was thinking by letting his curiosity get the best of him.

The house hovered tall and white on the green hilly land several miles outside Austin. Four tall turrets stretched to the sky, and mullioned windows sparkled on the upper floor. A wide wraparound porch painted sky-blue had a white wicker sofa with blue cushions on it, and a collection of wrought-iron roosters in a clutch near a bristly doormat with a big burgundy *II* on it.

Quaint. The place was homey in a well-worn sort of shabby way, and he'd be sure to tell Ty that he didn't appreciate him sending him out here to see a doll's house in the middle of nowhere. Miles and miles of green pastureland badly in need of mowing surrounded the house, wrapped by white-painted pipe fence so it wasn't totally hopeless, but still. No man would live here willingly.

The door opened, and a petite brunette stared out at him. She didn't come up to his chest, not totally. Brown eyes questioned why he was taking up space on her porch, and he asked himself the same. She was cute as a bunny with sweet features and a curvy body. The matchmaking ad had probably gotten hundreds of interested hits. Not to mention the nice breasts—and as she turned to answer someone who'd asked her something, he noted a seriously lush fanny—yeah, her ad would get hits. He wondered if she knew what Ty had done on her behalf with the dating ad and pulled off his hat, telling himself he'd just introduce himself and go.

This was no place for him.

"Can I help you?"

"I'm looking for Mackenzie Hawthorne. My name's Justin Morant. Ty Spurlock sent me by."

"I'm Mackenzie."

Her voice was as pretty as she was. Justin swallowed. "Ty said you might need some help around here."

Pink lips smiled at him; brown eyes sparkled. He drew back a little, astonished by how darling she was smiling at him like that. Like he was some kind of hero who'd just rolled up on his white steed.

And, damn, he was driving a white truck.

Which was kind of funny if you appreciated irony, and, right now, he felt like he was living it.

Sudden baby wails caught his attention, and hers, too.

"Come on in," she said. "You'll have to excuse me for just a moment. But make yourself at home in the kitchen. There's tea on the counter, and Mrs. Harper's put together a lovely chicken salad. After I feed the babies, we can talk about what kind of work you're looking for. Mrs. Harper will love to pull your life story from you while you eat."

She made fast introductions and then the tiny brunette disappeared, allowing him a better look at that full seat. Blue jeans accentuated the curves, and he figured she was so nicely full-figured because she'd just had a baby.

Damn Ty for pulling this prank on him. His buddy was probably laughing his fool ass off right about now, knowing how Justin felt about settling down and family ties in general. Justin was a loner, at least in spirit. He had lots of friends on the circuit, and he was from a huge family. He had three brothers, all as independent as he was, except for J.T., who liked to stay close to the family and the neighborhood he'd grown up in.

Justin was going to continue to ride alone.

Mrs. Harper smiled at him as he took a barstool at the wide kitchen island. "Welcome, Justin."

"Thank you," he replied, not about to let himself feel welcome. He needed to get out of there as fast as possible. The place was a honey trap of food and good intentions. Another baby wail joined the first, and Justin's ears perked up. Two? Maybe she was babysitting. He looked at Mrs. Harper, worried.

Mrs. Harper laughed. "Yes, she probably does need a hand," she said, misunderstanding the question on his face. "Run on in there and help her out for a second, and I'll serve up a lunch for you that'll take the edge off any hunger pangs you've got." She pulled a fragrant pie from the oven—an apple pie, he guessed—and his stomach rumbled.

Okay, he could go check on the little mother for the price of lunch. But then he was heading out, with a "Sorry—this job doesn't fit the description of my talents," or something equally polite.

He was going to kick Ty's butt hard, over the phone, which wouldn't be nearly as satisfying as doing it in person. He'd driven a day out of his way to apply for what he'd thought might be bona fide employment.

He walked into the den, guided by the baby cries. Mackenzie glanced at him from the sofa. "Don't be scared—they'll calm down in a moment," she said, but he was anyway, unable to stop staring at the four white bassinets, three babies tucked into them like pink-wrapped sausages working free of their casings. Mackenzie held a fourth writhing baby close to her chest, and Justin realized she was nursing.

Holy crap. She had four babies. He backed up a step, belatedly removed his hat. "I'm not scared. I'm something else, but I'm not sure I can identify the emotion." He looked at the three squalling babies, clearly deciding they all wanted their mother's attention at once. "What can I do?"

He hoped she'd say nothing, but instead she pointed him to a bottle. "If you're sincerely asking, Holly's next in line."

Holly? He glanced back at the baskets. Tiny nameplates adorned the bassinets, which for some reason reminded him of the carved beds of the seven dwarves. Only Mackenzie was no Snow White under an evil spell, and he was certainly no handsome prince.

But the lady did need help; that much was clear. She was in over her head by any reasonable metric, whether it was the ranch (which she probably would lose, if he were a betting man) or these tiny babies (which would require an army of assistants that he figured she couldn't afford—again, no hard bet for a man who liked betting on sure things). This would only take an hour, he figured, and an hour he certainly did have, damn his torn PCL.

Justin studied the nameplates to make certain he picked up the right baby. Holly, Hope, Haven and Heather. All chosen, no doubt, to go with the Hanging H of the ranch, which was sort of a hopeless exercise because they'd all get married one day and their last names would change. To Thomas or Smith or whatever. Then he remembered that Mackenzie's last name was Hawthorne, and she must not have ever changed her name when she got married.

If she'd been married.

Gingerly he picked up Holly, who had a pretty annoyed wail going, grabbed one of the bottles off a wooden tray and slipped it into her mouth. Oh, yeah, that was exactly what she wanted—food—and what he wanted—golden silence.

"Thank you," Mackenzie said. "They all decide they want to eat at once, every time."

He sank onto a sofa, carefully holding the baby. "My brothers and I were the same. It lasted through our teens and drove our parents nuts." He glanced at the other two babies, who were now occupying themselves with listening to the adult voices in the room. "I guess these are all yours."

She smiled, and he noticed she had very shapely lips. He avoided staring at the blanket at her breast, not wanting to catch an accidental glimpse of something he shouldn't see. He was a gentleman, even if he found himself at the moment feeling like a fish out of water.

"They're all mine." She smiled proudly at her children. "We're still working out some things, but the girls are coming along nicely now. They have a little better routine, and the health issues are more manageable."

He turned his gaze back to Holly so the doubt wouldn't show on his face. The overgrown paddocks, the sagging gutters and the chipping paint stayed on his mind. These four children—was the father totally useless? Did he not care about the state of his property? Or these four sweet-faced babies? Not to mention the sexy mother of his children.

"Their father is in Alaska," she said, somehow reading his thoughts. "Working on an oil rig. And when he's not working, he's otherwise engaged. We don't hear from him," she said. "Not before the divorce or after. I'd been on a drug to help me get pregnant, and he was unpleasantly surprised by the results." She put a now-content baby into the empty basket marked "Heather," diapered her, kissed her and picked up Hope. "This one was born with lung issues, but we're slowly getting past that. And Holly has struggled with being underweight, but time has been the healer for that, too." She smiled at Justin, and he saw how beautiful she was, especially when her face lit up as she talked about her children. "So tell me what kind of work you do, and we'll see if our needs match."

He held in a sigh, wondering how to extricate himself from this dilemma. He could help this woman and her brood, but he didn't want to. Justin glanced at the four babies. They had calmed some as they were getting either bottles or a breast—there was a thought he had to stay away from.

Mrs. Harper bustled in with a tray of food for him and took the baby he was holding. "I heard you say that you need to talk business. I'll feed this one, and you eat. Your plates say you're from Montana, so you've come a long way to talk about work. I know you're starved."

No, no, no. He needed a job, but not this job. And the last thing he wanted to do was work for a woman with soft doe eyes and a place that was teetering on becoming unmanageable. From the little he'd seen, there was a lot to do. He had a bum knee and a bad feeling about this. And no desire to be around children.

On the other hand, it couldn't hurt to help out for a week, maybe two, tops. Could it?

He ate a bite of Mrs. Harper's chicken salad, startled by how good it was. Maybe it had been too long since he'd had home cooking. He smelled the wonderful cinnamon aroma of apple pie, and his stomach jumped.

Mackenzie bent over to put the fed, diapered and happy baby she was holding back into the bassinet. He watched her move, looked at her smile, admired her full fanny and breasts—stopped himself cold.

He had no business looking at a new mother. He really had been on the road too long. Glancing around him, Justin took in the soft white-and-blue curtains, the tan sofas, the chairs in a gentle blue-and-white pattern that complemented the drapes. A tan wool rug lay under a blocky coffee table, the edges rounded and perfect for children who would be learning to pull themselves up in a few months.

Taking another bite of Mrs. Harper's delicious meal, he focused on the food and not the homey atmosphere. That's what was wrong: this felt like home. It could draw in a man who wasn't careful, who wasn't aware of the pitfalls.

Maybe Ty hadn't sent him here because of Mackenzie's ad. Maybe she simply needed a grievous amount of help, and Ty had known he needed employment.

He could do this job—or at least he was comfortable with the work he could see that needed to be done.

But he needed to know.

"So about your ad," he said, and Mackenzie and Mrs. Harper looked at him curiously. "On the dating website."

She shook her head. "What dating website? I didn't

advertise on a website. I talked to some friends about the position for ranch foreman." She straightened. "Are you saying you came all the way here from Montana because you think I'm looking for a man?"

Chapter 2

Mackenzie planned to give Ty a piece of her mind at the first opportunity. A phone call to express her dismay at his ham-handed matchmaking was tops on her list.

The cowboy who'd clearly been sent on a mercy mission seemed supremely uncomfortable at the outraged question.

"I thought you were looking for help around here," Justin said. "So, yes, I was under the impression you were looking for a man. Though not in the manner in which you may have mistaken."

"Ty put me in a dating website, and you show up here. How would you feel if you were me?"

Mrs. Harper drifted from the room with a baby in her arms. Mackenzie was too upset to cool her temper.

"Probably grateful that one of my friends cared enough to reach out to try to get me some help. Incidentally, I haven't seen the ad. Didn't look." He shrugged, dismissing it.

That was a man for you. It was all about the practicalities, when the mousetrap was perfectly clear to her. You didn't live in Bridesmaids Creek and not know that people plotted to get you married. Always done lovingly in your best interests, of course.

Which was how she'd ended up married the first time—not that Tommy hadn't been a sinfully gorgeous, totally lazy man more interested in pleasure than anything resembling work.

There was a lot of work to be done around the Hanging H, so named when one of the Hawthorne *H*'s had partially fallen off the sign. The name had stuck—though she knew very well that Daisy Donovan—one of the town's most notorious bad girls—liked to say the ranch was called the Hanging H because the Hawthornes were barely hanging on. Mackenzie did need help, which would have been quite obvious to the handsome cowboy meeting her gaze without hesitation. Tommy might have been handsome in a hedonistic sort of way, but this cowboy had him beat for raw sex appeal.

"You're right. If you're here just for work, and not because of a matchmaking website, I'd like to talk to you more about the position." She decided to give him the benefit of the doubt. Hazel eyes stared at her, unblinking. Justin didn't look like he had romance on the mind. Broad shoulders complemented a trim waist, the sinewy body of a man who spent his time actively. He had a square jaw that hadn't been shaved today—or maybe even yesterday—and shaggy dark hair that hadn't seen a barber in many months.

All in all, the kind of man who would turn women's heads.

"I'd be interested in hearing more about the kind of help you're looking for," he said.

She looked at her babies, tried to turn off the zip of sex appeal that was overruling her ability to think clearly. "Why would you want to work here? There must be a lot of ranches hiring."

He nodded. "I'm sure I can find a job if this doesn't work out. But Ty seemed to think you could use a foreman."

"A foreman position would be a long-term proposition." She looked at him, curious. "Somehow you don't strike me as a long-term kind of man."

"Things change."

Okay. She'd noticed he had a bit of a limp, and there was probably a story to that. In fact, there was no doubt a story to Justin in general, but she wasn't looking for a colorful background. She needed help here, and the fact was Ty's reference counted for a lot. There was no doubting that Justin didn't want to answer a lot of questions about himself, which was fine because she could ask Ty whatever she wanted to know. She could simply negotiate an open-ended employment offer with Justin.

"Yes, things do change. Thanks for helping out with the babies. If you give me ten minutes to get them settled and grab the books, I'll go over the job requirements with you."

He nodded. "Thanks."

She gazed into his hazel eyes, seeing nothing there but appreciation for a chance of employment. No attraction, no flirtation; just level honesty.

Whatever it was she'd felt from the moment he'd

walked into the room, he didn't seem to be affected by it.

Which was fine.

She went to find Mrs. Harper to watch the babies while she talked to Justin. If she hired him, she was going to call Ty.

Whether Mackenzie thanked him or yelled at him about the cowboy in the other room remained to be seen.

Two weeks had gone by, and Mackenzie hadn't seen much of Justin since he'd moved into the foreman's house. But evidence of his presence was obvious: the gutters no longer hung sad and neglected, the paint on the house gleamed, the paddocks were mown and hay was bundled into round bales that studded the landscape outside her window.

It was beginning to look like the Hanging H of old, which brought back a lot of happy memories.

Jade came into the kitchen, peering over her shoulder at the paddocks. "Looks like a postcard, doesn't it?"

Mackenzie nodded. "Maybe I should have thanked Ty for sending Justin my way."

Jade laughed. "You didn't thank him?"

"I was too annoyed when I found out he'd put my name in a dating registry."

"To be fair, that was a tiny fib on his part. He didn't really do that. It was just a little intrigue he threw in for Justin's sake."

Mackenzie shook her head and returned to the babies, who sat in carriers, all four of them, on top of the wide kitchen island. They gazed at different things around the room or their toes, content for the moment. "Ty can get a little crazy at times. But, yes, I should thank him now. The ranch looks like it's in recovery mode."

"And then there's other kinds of recovery," Jade said, still staring out the window. "Is this your daily view?"

Mackenzie turned to see what Jade was goggling at.

Justin. Hot, dark skin gleaming with sweat, bare to his blue-jeaned waist. Muscles for miles. Mackenzie stared at the man wearing a straw Resistol, amazed to feel her heart beating like mad. "Actually, no. That's never been the view."

"Too bad." Jade laughed. "If it was, I'd be eating lunch over here every day with you."

"You do eat lunch with me almost every day. You make the lunch." Mackenzie tore her gaze away from Justin and sat at the island. "I've been meaning to tell you that I feel like things are much more under control. You and your mom don't have to come over here every day anymore to help me out. I'm going to be okay." She smiled at Jade. "You've been amazing friends. You and everybody who's sent food over."

"Pooh," Jade said. "Don't think you're going to run me off now that you've got a bona fide beefcake on the ranch. I'm single, you know."

Mackenzie held Heather's tiny foot in her hand. "By all means, come by if you want to. I just hate to keep taking up your life."

"Believe me—this is a joy and pleasure. And it would kill Mom if you cut off her visiting privileges." Jade stood beside her. "She dotes on these babies. Says they may be the only grandchildren she has because I'm so slow about finding a husband."

"You could try Ty's matchmaking registry."

Jade laughed. "I'll meet my handsome prince when

it's meant to be." She went back to staring out the window. "Did you notice his limp?"

Mackenzie sighed. "Yes. It's more pronounced when he doesn't know I'm watching him, which tells me he doesn't want to talk about it. So I don't ask." She tucked the blankets around the babies and smiled. "He does his job. I don't see him. He came into the kitchen last Friday, and I handed him an envelope with his pay in it. Your mother gave him a lunchbox, so I think she's feeding him. That's the relationship we have, and now you know everything I know."

Maybe that would settle Jade's curiosity.

"You have to wonder about that matchmaking story, though. Something brought that handsome stud here. He could have gotten a job where he came from, right?" Jade asked, curiosity clearly not abated.

"Don't ask me. I took Ty's word as a reference and didn't ask too many questions. As you may have noticed, I needed help around here, and if he was looking for a job, I was happy to give him a try." It had nothing to do with the fact that he was, as Jade mentioned, quite handsome. Sexy. Breathtaking, if a woman was looking for a man.

But she wasn't.

"I had a husband," Mackenzie said, looking at her babies with adoring eyes. "And while I wouldn't say I wish I'd never met Tommy—I have him to thank for my sweet children—I can't say a husband is something I'm looking to put on my shopping list. But speaking of shopping, I'm taking you up on your offer to babysit while I go into town to grab some things."

Jade gave up watching Justin and picked up a baby. "I was hoping you were still going to let me babysit. An afternoon out will do you good. And my first-timer's nerves will be calmed."

"You'll do fine! You've helped me almost every day with the babies." Mackenzie hugged her friend.

"My nerves are due to my suspicion that you might not be able to leave your babies for the first time," Jade said, laughing. "Mom's coming by for backup. We have everything under control. Go."

A knock sounded on the kitchen door, and Jade pulled it open. "We don't knock on the back door— just come on in," Jade said, and Justin entered. Even a little sweaty and a bit dirty, he was a sexy, handsome man—just as Jade had noted.

"Ladies," he said, removing his hat.

"Hi," Jade said. She poured him a glass of tea from the pitcher on the counter. "I'm going to put these babies down for their nap."

She left the room carrying Hope. Mackenzie smiled at Justin as he put the empty glass back on the counter. "Would you like some more?"

"No, thank you."

He had the most amazing eyes, the nicest hands— Mackenzie pulled her gaze back where it belonged. "The house looks great. And it's nice to see the lawn mowed. Thank you."

He nodded. "I was going to head into town. I figure there's a hardware place and maybe a tractor supply in town so I can get some parts." He glanced at the remaining two babies on the kitchen island after Jade came in and removed Heather. "I thought I'd see if there was anything you need."

Him, maybe? "Thank you. Actually I'm being sent into town myself."

"That's right," Jade said, sailing into the kitchen to pick up Haven, cuddling the baby to her. "It's high time my friend got out. She's a wonderful mother, but everybody needs a break. Although I'll believe that she leaves these babies behind when I see it. Try to help ease her out the door, will you?" She grinned and left.

Justin shrugged. "I can drop you off in town."

Mackenzie hesitated. "That's all right. I can drive."

"I could use a tour."

She looked into his eyes, surprised. "Haven't you been into Bridesmaids Creek?"

"Just ran in to grab some feed for the horses."

There was a lot of lore in Bridesmaids Creek. She was half tempted to go with him so she could tell him all the wonderful stories.

On the other hand, she was tempted to go with him simply because he was the hottest man she'd ever laid eyes on.

Which wasn't the best reason, but it was a reason. She could feel herself melting under his gaze. He seemed so solid, so strong...so unlike Tommy.

"I really—"

"Go," Jade said, coming back into the kitchen to collect the final baby. She cradled Holly as Mrs. Harper came in the back door bearing a pie.

"Hello, everyone," Mrs. Harper said. "I brought something for Justin because I know how much he likes apple pie."

"Yes, ma'am," Justin said. "I can find room for that."

Jade handed Holly to her mother after she put the pie on the counter. "Justin and Mackenzie are just leaving."

"Oh, good," Mrs. Harper said. "That will give me

time to make up some fried chicken to go with it for later."

"I think we're not getting any of that pie until we get our chores done," Justin said, his gaze turning to Mackenzie again.

"I think you're right." She also sensed a heavy helping of matchmaking, too, but forewarned was forearmed. She gave Jade a wry look, who returned that with an innocent look. When Justin opened the kitchen door, Mackenzie went out, telling herself that all the matchmaking in the world wasn't going to make her fall in love again.

"After hearing Ty sell Bridesmaids Creek," Justin told Mackenzie as he drove into town, "I'm anxious to get the tour. Ty brags about the Bridesmaids Creek swim, he talks about the Best Man's Fork, and a few other bits of lore, but I was never sure if he was just pulling my leg or not. Ty likes to hear himself talk, and talk big."

"There's a lot of history in BC," Mackenzie said. "Some good, some bad. Just like any place, I guess."

He nodded, pulling his truck into a parking spot in the wide-set, clean town square. Families with kids milled in front of the shops, but not as many as one might expect to see if one were in a city.

Still, it felt like a comfortable town where everyone knew each other, celebrated each other's hopes and joys. "The Wedding Diner?" Justin peered at the white restaurant with its pink-and-white-striped awning, big windows and flashing pink Open sign.

"Home cooking, and, if you're interested, Mrs. Chatham will tell your fortune for you."

Justin grunted. "I don't believe in fortune-telling."

"Oh, she doesn't do read-your-palm kind of stuff. Mrs. Chatham has a completely different method." She got out of the truck and he followed suit, meeting her on the pavement.

"So, shall we meet back here at four?" Mackenzie asked. "I know you said you wanted to go to the feed store. By the way, Ralph Chatham, Jane Chatham's husband, runs that."

"Does he tell fortunes, too?" Justin asked, telling himself to relax and enjoy the small-town ambience.

"Not exactly. But he does do a Magic 8 Ball kind of thing where you pay a small fee, his steer drops a cowpat on a square for you and you win a prize. Or you can trade the prize for one of Mrs. Chatham's sessions."

Justin laughed. "Cow-pie-drop contests are done in lots of places."

"You laugh," Mackenzie said, "but Mr. Chatham's steer is well loved in this town. The steer's name is Target thanks to his aim and the fact that he's made some folks a good bundle of money. Target always hits a mark. See you at four." She smiled and walked away, stunning him when she walked into a shop with a bouquet-shaped shingle that read "Monsieur Unmatchmaker. Premier Unmatchmaking Service."

Was the whole town backward? Off its collective rocker?

It was none of his business why Mackenzie would need an unmatchmaking service. *Ugh.*

The unforgiving rodeo circuit had been more sane than this town.

Still, he'd been serious about getting a grand tour from Mackenzie, though she obviously hadn't thought he'd meant it. How better to learn about Bridesmaids Creek than from one of the town's favorite daughters?

He glanced toward the unmatchmaking service, seeing that next door to Monsieur Unmatchmaker's dove-gray-painted shop was a pink store with a cheery window and painted scrolling letters that read, "Madame Matchmaker. Premier Matchmaking Service. Where love comes true."

He laughed out loud, startling some passersby. Suddenly he understood why Ty had worked so hard to sell him on this town: the whole place was set up on gigs. Sleights of hand. Fairy tales. From the rumored special steer with excellent aim to The Wedding Diner with the fortune-teller owner to the matchmaking–unmatchmaking rivals—everybody had a gig.

So did Mackenzie, now that he thought about it. Her parents had run a successful haunted house for years, and, according to the talkative fellow at the feed store, parents from miles around had brought their very young kiddies to enjoy the place. No real spooky stuff was allowed. Just down-home bobbing-for-apples fun. Puppet shows, piñatas, a parade with characters.

Until a local murder near Mackenzie's place had spooked folks. That year, attendance had gone way down. So far down they'd had to close the haunted house. They'd been virtually bankrupted, or so the story went.

"You still here?" Mackenzie asked, shaking him out of his reverie.

He snapped his gaze to hers. "Yeah. Your errand was fast."

Mackenzie nodded. "I just wanted to check in on

Monsieur Lafleur. He had gall bladder surgery recently."

"Rough."

"It was rough." She started walking and he followed, more out of a desire to be with her than to hear about Mr. Lafleur's funky gall bladder. "It was gangrenous and they couldn't get to it laparoscopically, so they had to do it the old-fashioned way. Not much fun."

He felt a little sympathy for Mr. Lafleur after all.

"But his wife is wonderful and she took good care of him. They bicker like crazy, but they've been married for fifty years and love blooms in spite of the bickering." She looked up at him, and Justin felt something hit him somewhere near his gall bladder—not his heart—that felt suspiciously like something bordering on attraction.

All this talk of wonky gall bladders was stirring up his desire to eat. That was all it was. He glanced toward The Wedding Diner, wondering if it was safe to go inside and eat without prognostications of marital bliss being preached at him.

"Madame Lafleur runs the matchmaking service," Mackenzie said, snapping his attention back to her and away from the people filing inside the diner.

"The Lafleurs run rival businesses?"

"Complementary businesses. Some people want love, and some people want relationships ended. Monsieur Lafleur doesn't get as many clients as his wife, of course, so he teaches French at the high school and tutors privately in his shop."

"If the divorce rate is around fifty percent, how is it that Monsieur Lafleur has to supplement with teaching and tutoring and his wife doesn't?"

"Because this is Bridesmaids Creek. When matchmaking occurs here—and it occurs often—the relation-ships tend to stick. Madame Lafleur takes great pride in her ability to bring people together who are perfect soul mates."

He idly wondered if Mackenzie had utilized the services of Madame Lafleur. If so, she didn't seem bothered by the irony of her marriage not lasting. He looked away for a moment, trying to shake off the charm of the town. His rational side said it was just all so ludicrous, and the first chance he got he was going to tell Ty that he'd sent him to a place where people were clearly just one car short of a crazy train.

"Can I buy you a snack? Seems a shame not to take my boss to get a soda and a slice of pie, or whatever is served in The Wedding Diner."

"Sure." She looked at him curiously. "You realize you'll be setting yourself up for the gossip mill."

"Putting myself right in the line of fire." He opened the door for her. "After you."

Chapter 3

Mackenzie and Justin were greeted warmly by the proprietress of The Wedding Diner, an amply shaped woman with a big smile.

"Jane Chatham," Mackenzie said, "I'd like to introduce you to Justin Morant. He's been helping out at my place."

Jane's smile widened as she swept them over to a bright white booth inside the diner. "Welcome, Justin. Those four darlings running you off your boots over there?"

He removed his hat and took the seat she indicated. "It's a nice place."

"Sure it is." Jane laughed. She looked at Mackenzie with a fond smile. "I'm sure you're happy for the help."

"You have no idea."

Justin felt a slow warmth steal up the back of his

neck. It was just a job like any job. He rubbed his knee surreptitiously under the table, glad it wasn't aching much today. It wouldn't matter if Mackenzie had twelve kids—he was glad for the work.

And the chance to work for himself. Under a blue sky with no one talking to him.

"Still thinking about selling the place?" Jane asked Mackenzie, and Justin listened hard in spite of himself.

"We'll see what happens," Mackenzie murmured. "In the meantime, can we talk you out of some of that delicious pie I smell?" She looked at Justin, and he felt a tiny zap hit him around his chest cavity again. Really weird, because he'd never been much of a heartburn sufferer.

He told himself he'd grab some antacids later.

"You order what you like," Mackenzie told him, "but I'm not about to pass up that blackberry pie."

"I'll have a slice."

"Two, please," Mackenzie said, and Jane ambled off with a pleased nod.

"You didn't mention you were selling your ranch," Justin said, so startled by the news he forgot he'd intended to mind his own business.

She nodded. "It would probably be best. It's hard for me to keep up with on my own, to be honest, and since I'm not working, I need to keep my savings for my daughters." She smiled. "Selling the Hanging H would mean college educations and a few other things comfortably. I'd like to not stay awake at night worrying about money."

He cleared his throat. "Your ex doesn't pay any child support?"

She shook her head. "Hard to squeeze blood out of

a turnip, especially a turnip that stays on the move to avoid child support."

Ouch. Justin sipped the coffee Jane brought over, glad for the dark steaming brew. He then busied himself with the flaky, rich blackberry pie, delicious enough to draw a sigh of pleasure from him if he weren't so caught by Mackenzie's story.

Her plans made total sense. A woman with four brand-new babies, who'd been born with some challenges, was going to need cash. A lot of cash. She was being wise, had clearly given her situation a lot of thought. It was what he'd do were he in her boots.

Seemed a shame to sell a family home, though. He thought about his childhood home, and how much it had hurt when it was gone. He and his rowdy brothers had grown up there, enjoyed the benefits of living and working on a family ranch. When his father had taken up with another woman, scandalizing the town, his mother had booted him out of the house and sold the family ranch—her right as it was the home she'd grown up in. Though his father had tried to make amends, Dana Morant was made of sterner stuff. She'd taken her boys to Montana to be near her sister, and life had changed forever. Mainly for the better but always with the lingering shadows of what might have been. Jensen Morant now lived on a thousand acres of rich Montana ranchland. Justin didn't go near the place.

He looked at Mackenzie's soft hair and gentle smile.

"You were way far away," she said.

He took another bite of pie, sipped his coffee. "Let me know what I can do to help."

"You have already. I can put the ranch on the market now, thanks to the wonderful shape you're getting it in. I really appreciate it."

A sudden pound on his back had him looking over his shoulder. "Ty!"

"Me in the flesh." Ty slapped him on the back again and nodded at Mackenzie. "Jade told me I'd find this devil here."

"I have things to discuss with you, Ty," Mackenzie said, and he grinned.

"You can thank me later for sending you this guy," Ty said.

"That's just it," Mackenzie said. "You really shouldn't have."

"Getting attached to him?" Ty teased, and Justin decided the conversation had gone far enough.

"Join us," Justin said.

"No. No time." Ty looked at him. "I'm in town for one thing and one thing only. And that's to help you back to the rodeo circuit."

Justin frowned. "How am I going to do that? I'm a bit physically challenged at the moment."

"In a different capacity than riding," Ty said. "You and I are going to travel the country recruiting talent."

"Talent for what?" Justin didn't like the idea of that at all. Correction: once upon a time he might have jumped on it enthusiastically. Traveling the country with one of his best buddies, seeing his friends on the rodeo circuit, giving back to the sport he loved so much—dream-come-true stuff.

His gaze slid to Mackenzie, who watched him with gently smiling eyes as she listened to Ty go on and on with his plans. Justin couldn't work up the same excitement.

He felt like he had plenty to do here in Bridesmaids Creek that was important. Mackenzie smiled at him, a slow, sweet smile. Her big eyes were looking at him, so trusting, and that heartburn he'd been experiencing felt more like his heart was melting into a big soupy puddle.

Dang. This was new. Different.

Maybe hitting the road with Ty was the right idea.

He looked at his friend. "Why don't you stop by the house later and tell me about this harebrained plan of yours?"

Ty looked at Mackenzie. "Would you mind? I know you've got a lot going on over there."

"You're welcome anytime." Mackenzie got up. "Just know that if you take my cowboy, who has become indispensable to me, I'm going to offer you up as a candidate for the Best Man's Fork run. All in the name of charity, of course." She winked at Justin. "I'm going to talk to Jane for a moment."

She headed toward Jane at the cash register. Ty studied his friend.

"You've got the strangest look on your face," Ty said as Justin returned his gaze to Mackenzie. He just couldn't seem to get enough of looking at her. "I'd say you have indigestion, except you're smiling."

Justin relaxed his mouth so the smile would disappear. He *had* been smiling, because his muscles ached a bit. Like he'd been smiling a long time—watching Mackenzie walk and chatter with some friends who came over to talk to her.

"I'm not smiling, but I may have indigestion."

Ty snorted. "I see what's going on here."

"Do you." He made the comment as flat as possible.

His buddy's opinion didn't really matter. Ty had no idea what was going on, because Justin had no idea.

"You're tired," Ty said. "Being around those babies and that falling-down farm has worn you out. You better hit the road with me. You'll be back to your old self in no time."

"What was my old self?"

Ty put his hat on, prepared to leave, which was fine with Justin. Then he could go back to surreptitiously staring at Mackenzie. "Grumpy, cranky, annoying."

Justin grunted. "Thought that was you."

"Not me." He peered at Justin. "I really hope this wasn't too much for you, old buddy. I didn't mean to bring you down. Figured some time in a small town with a real job would do you good."

Justin put his hat on, too, because if he didn't get out of there, people were going to notice that he couldn't stop staring at his beautiful boss. "That's what you get for thinking. See you at the house. Don't get there too soon. I'm taking the boss lady shopping."

Ty stared at him, stunned. "What's happened to you?" he whispered. "You're a shadow of your former self!"

Well, that was a question he didn't care to ponder too much. Mackenzie came to stand beside him, smiling up into his face, and his poor stupid heart felt like it took the final dive into his stomach.

What had happened to him, indeed.

Mackenzie and four babies were happening to him, and they were going to require a great deal of consideration. This was a bad idea, this tiny woman with the big eyes and her sweet family. A very bad idea, because he wasn't a family man; he wasn't a staying man.

"You ready?" he asked Mackenzie, and she nodded.

"If you're not going to chicken out," she teased.

Oh, he might. He was thinking about it. Thinking about it hard.

But something told him he probably wouldn't.

Four hours later, when Ty stopped by the house, Mackenzie wondered what her old friend was really up to. Ty had sent Justin to her, now he wanted him to hit the road?

It all seemed very convenient. As if Justin might have conned his buddy into helping him escape the Hanging H with a good reason.

"Anyway," Ty said as the three of them sat at the wide wooden kitchen table, "the reason I stopped by is to get a game plan going with Mackenzie."

"Game plan?" Mackenzie glanced at Justin. If Justin had been part of Ty's game plan, she wasn't sure she wanted to know what the next play was.

"I wouldn't leave you here without backup," Ty said. "I know that in spite of his knee—"

"My knee's fine," Justin said, clearly annoyed.

Mackenzie glanced at him. Occasionally she saw Justin favor his knee, but it did seem as if he'd been limping less since he'd arrived at the Hanging H. The doctor in town had given him a soft knee brace, which he wore without hesitation. Now there were days when Justin walked like he wasn't in any discomfort at all.

"I know your knee's getting better," Ty said. "I'm just saying that in spite of your knee, you've been a big help here. I can see a lot of improvement." Ty shook his head. "Still, I wouldn't leave Mackenzie in the lurch, so I was wondering if you mind, Mackenzie, if I swap cowboys on you."

Mackenzie hesitated. "Swap cowboys?"

"Replace Justin, in a manner of speaking," Ty said. His words ceased entirely when the kitchen door opened and Jade walked in.

"Howdy," Ty said. He stood up to greet the tall, sexy redhead, removing his hat for a moment. "Jade Harper, long time, no see…and clearly I've been missing out."

Jade laughed. "No sweet talk from you, Ty." She gave him a hug and he might have tried to pinch her bottom, but Jade was too fast for him. "Hi, Justin. Mackenzie, who are the three hunky guys who just pulled up in the black truck outside?"

Mackenzie got up to look out the window.

"*That's* the game plan," Ty said with a glance at Justin. "I don't want you to miss my buddy Justin when I take him with me, so I thought I'd trade you, three for one."

"Wow," Jade said. "Grab this deal, is my advice, Mackenzie." She laughed at Justin's smirk.

"Ty, I don't know if I need three—" Mackenzie began.

"You need help out here," Ty said.

Justin didn't say anything, and a bit of unease began to hit Mackenzie. Did he want to leave? Maybe he'd told Ty that he wanted to. She looked at his face, hazel eyes giving away nothing, his dark hair awry as he ran a hand through it. He looked distinctly uncomfortable.

As Ty had noted, Justin's knee was better—not well enough to ride or run a fast race, maybe, but better— and the last place he wanted to be was stuck here with her and four little baby girls.

"I'll get that," Mackenzie said when knocking erupted on the front door. "Might as well give the candidates a grand tour, let them know what they're getting themselves into."

Justin glanced at her, his eyes widening like he was surprised by her comment. She went through the den, checking the babies quickly—still sound asleep, as was Mrs. Harper in the corner chair—and opened the front door.

Whoa. So much testosterone, so many muscles. "Hi," Mackenzie said, a little startled by all the masculinity crowded on the front porch.

They took off their hats.

"Ty sent us," the tallest one said with a rascally grin. "He said the Haunted H was looking for help to get ready for the county's biggest haunted house and pumpkin patch for miles around."

Mackenzie blinked. What had Ty meant by that? She was selling the place, not going back into business.

"Hello, fellows," Justin said from behind her. "If you're looking for Ty, you'll find him in the side paddock."

"Thanks."

They tipped their hats to Mackenzie and left the porch. Mackenzie turned to look at Justin.

"I don't want to get in the middle of things," Justin said, "but if you want me to leave, just say the word."

"I don't want you to leave." That was the last thing she wanted. "Do you want to go?"

"No. Not if you don't want me to." He shrugged as if he could go either way, whatever she decided. Still, she had the feeling her answers mattered. "I'm not going to say that I know everything about your town or your ranch. But so far things have been working pretty smooth. Or at least I thought they were."

"Ty seems to think he needs you with him." Mackenzie stepped off the porch.

"I'll make that decision." Justin followed her. "Or you will."

Something about this whole thing felt like a setup. Ty's story to the three hunks who'd come riding into town in their big black pickup, that she needed to restart the old family business, felt fishy. Never had she mentioned breathing life back into the haunted house to anyone. It was a dream she'd kept buried, knowing it wasn't practical. She couldn't run that kind of people-intensive business herself, and especially not with four newborns. The small remaining funds she had needed to go into their care—not the vague hope of bringing back the Haunted H.

And yet she had to admit restoring all her family traditions would be a wonderful way to raise her girls. She had had a storied childhood, full of wonder and magic and fairy tales.

But for a fairy tale, one needed a prince.

She looked at the five men leaning against the corral, studying her, waiting for something, some signal. Big, strong, handsome men. They all had rugged appeal, Justin most of all, in her opinion.

A prince had no reason to stay in Bridesmaids Creek—not unless there was a quest, something to make him stay and fight.

"So, Ty," Mackenzie said slowly as Jade came to put her arm through hers for support, "maybe you'd like to explain why you're offering me three cowboys for the price of the one I've already got?"

Chapter 4

"These fellows here," Ty said, grandly waving his arm to indicate his friends, "go by the names of Sam Barr, Squint Mathison and Frog Grant."

"I'm sorry." Mackenzie stared at the last big man who'd been introduced. He was a broad-shouldered man with bright blue eyes and a shock of saddle-brown hair that wouldn't lay flat even if he used molasses on it. "Frog?"

The men laughed. "Gets 'em every time," he said, not minding the attention. "That's not my real name."

"We call him Frog because he looks like he's hopping around like a frog on the back of a bronc." Ty slapped the man on the back. "Anyway, he kind of looks like an amphibian, so it fits."

"I don't see any frog about him," Jade said, and silently Mackenzie agreed.

"These gentlemen have come to apply for the position of hanny," Ty said, delighted to have a stage to sell his snake oil from.

"Hanny?" Mackenzie tried not to laugh. "Is that what you call a working hand now?"

"It means, Miss Mackenzie," Squint said, his brown eyes earnest, "that Ty tells us you need hands to work this place and sometimes some occasional babysitting."

"Oh, a *manny,*" Jade said.

"No." Ty shook his head. "A manny is a male nanny. These men are hands. They're also willing to help out with Mackenzie's munchkins."

"That wouldn't be necessary—" Mackenzie began, but Ty shook his head.

"These men haven't seen the inside of a home in so long that a little babysitting would make them happy as clams." He looked at his friends. "And they don't have any problems cleaning up stuff."

"Stuff?" Mackenzie echoed.

"Oh," Jade said. "You promised you wouldn't mention what I told you on the phone, Ty."

Mackenzie glanced at Justin, who shrugged, his whole demeanor screaming, *I had nothing to do with this.*

"Baby spit," Ty said helpfully.

"Upchuck," Squint elaborated.

"Hurl," Sam said.

"Giveback," Frog said, and Mackenzie held up a hand.

"Thank you, but I have it under control," she said with a glance at Jade.

Jade looked guilty. "She handles poo just fine. It's the other that gives her a little trouble."

Embarrassment swept Mackenzie. She couldn't meet

Justin's gaze, though she could feel him looking at her. "It was tough in the beginning, but I'm fine now. Anyway, I don't need help with my children."

"And I'm not going anywhere," Justin said.

Mackenzie glanced at him. "You don't have to stay if you need to go with Ty. I'll totally understand. But I haven't got a need for three hands, fellows. Sorry."

"Darn," Jade said. "I wish I'd known that all I had to do to get three handsome hunks to show up in their black truck was have babies. I'd have given that a shot."

The three newcomers seemed to appreciate Jade's comment. Some of the bravado had gone out of them at Mackenzie's refusal of their services, but at Jade's words their air of jauntiness returned.

"You could always give us a free trial," Frog said.

Mackenzie shook her head. "I don't need any help. But come into the kitchen. Let me at least feed you lunch before you go."

"That's an offer I won't refuse," Sam said.

All three gentlemen grouped close around her as she turned to walk to the house.

She looked at them. "I'm okay, guys, really I am."

"You should be resting," Squint said.

"We'll take care of you," Frog told her.

"Guess you're stuck with me, beautiful," Ty told Jade. He put his hand around Jade's arm as they walked.

"I've got some work to do," Justin said, and Mackenzie turned.

"Lunch first. Then you can work all you like." She didn't want him leaving her with Ty. His buddy was working on a plan—maybe big plans—and anyone from Bridesmaids Creek knew that when plans were afoot, you'd better have backup around.

Justin was really handsome backup.

"Sure. I'll come along."

She flashed him a grateful smile. The group went inside, crowding the kitchen, and Mrs. Harper smiled at them.

"Are these the hands Ty was telling me about?" she asked. "I'm Jade's mother, Betty Harper. It'll be nice having more help around here. Now sit down and eat before Mackenzie puts you to work."

Mackenzie started to say that she wasn't hiring anyone, but Jade gave her arm a light pinch.

"What?" Mackenzie said.

"Don't send them away yet," Jade whispered.

"It's not fair to keep them here when I don't have work for them!"

"You have work for them. You could hire a dozen of them and it wouldn't be enough."

Mackenzie looked at the five strong, large men sucking down huge quantities of food. "If I hire these hannies—really harebrained idea of Ty's, by the way—I'd have to pay them. And that's not in my budget."

"We'll figure something out. An idea will come to you," Jade said, comforting her.

"No, it won't." She went into the den to check on her babies, who were all asleep except Hope, who was gazing at the mobile over her playpen. Mackenzie picked her up. "If I had spare money, I'd be putting it away for college educations. Besides, I'm selling the Hanging H."

"Don't be so hasty." Jade took Hope from her. "Give Justin and Ty a chance to help you."

Mackenzie watched as Mrs. Harper fed the big men seated on the wooden barstools around the island. Her gaze wandered to Justin. "If I thought there was a way, I might give it a shot."

"You don't want to get rid of the family home, do you? Wouldn't you like the girls to grow up here?"

"It's just me and four babies," Mackenzie said. "I have to be practical. My folks were a team, and they only had me for many years before my sister was born. My focus needs to be on my children, not running a business and a ranch." She knew from experience that good times could be few and far between when it came to running what amounted to an amusement park.

"You're overlooking one small detail," Jade said. "According to Ty—"

"And that reminds me, you seem to be getting chatty with Ty."

"Not chatty. We talked once. I let slip about the baby spit-up bothering you. Sorry about that."

"I'm past that now," Mackenzie said. "I don't get queasy anymore. I think it just scared me because Hope did it so often."

"The thing you might not be aware of is that these men are looking for a place to stay," Jade said, glancing at the muscled hunks at the kitchen island. "Ty told them they had to pay rent. You'd essentially be a landlord. In other words, money coming in right away. They'd throw in some ranch work, some babysitting, for their meals."

Mackenzie looked at her. "Why is Ty so involved in my business?"

"He says you need help. He needs help. *They* need help." Jade went to the counter, then returned with two pieces of pumpkin spice cake in one hand and a baby in the other arm. She handed a plate to Mackenzie. "Ty says that if you sell, some developer is going to grab this place and cut it up into tiny lots for houses. I'm pretty sure he's right. You're sitting on five hundred acres, Mackenzie. If each house is put even on a large one-acre lot, that's five hundred homes. A thousand homes if they built smaller."

"Is that a bad thing? More housing for Bridesmaids Creek?" She got the image Jade was trying to draw.

"Not necessarily. You think about whether that's what you think should happen in our small, friendly community."

"We don't know that would happen." Mackenzie took a bite of the cake. As always, Mrs. Harper's cake was scrumptious. "The land might go to a hospital, or we could use a new elementary school. Something more beneficial than the Retirement Home for Beat-Up Riders Ty seems to have in mind." She studied the cowboys. Fit, handsome, hunky. But definitely not young enough to keep up on the circuit. And that's what this was really all about. "Justin says he's not going anywhere. So this is all really moot. I don't need help with the babies, and I don't need any more help than Justin." If he was planning on staying.

"Are you counting on him too much?" Jade asked.

Her gaze slid to Justin. She was startled to find his eyes on her. "I don't know," she murmured. "Maybe."

Jade had a good point. It was a mistake to count too much on another person. Witness her ex. She couldn't allow herself to get overly comfortable again.

She heard a motorcycle roar outside, glanced at Ty. Was he having yet another buddy come by? She looked at the cowboys having a great time eating Mrs. Harper's food and regaling her with rodeo stories. Maybe one couldn't have too much of a good thing.

A knock on the paned window of the back door sounded above the laughter. Jade opened the door and Daisy Donovan sashayed in, long brown hair spilling from her helmet, short black leather skirt swinging, black cowboy boots showing off shapely legs even Mackenzie had to admire.

Daisy Donovan had always had radar for hot guys.

"Hello, fellows," Daisy practically cooed. She basked in the sudden stares from the hunks. Ty's buddies had ceased eating, ceased talking and maybe ceased breathing, stunned by the wild-child vision that was Daisy Donovan.

"I brought you a baby gift, Mackenzie," she said, handing her a pink-and-silver wrapped box she pulled from the band of her skirt. The men's gazes never left her. "Hello, Mrs. Harper. Jade."

The guys jumped off their stools to allow Daisy to sit. She smiled and went to stand beside Justin. "I'd love a piece of your delicious cake, Mrs. Harper," Daisy said, her eyes on Justin. She then made certain every man in the room got the full benefit of her smile. Mackenzie was astonished that they all didn't faint from the feminine firepower launched at them.

"Thank you for the gift, Daisy," Mackenzie said. She unwrapped it to find four engraved silver teething rings. A very nice gift, indeed—for a woman who had never really been her friend. Daisy was a natural-born competitor for the male eye, and guys adored her.

"It's just a little something for those sweet babies of yours," Daisy said, smiling at the men. She took a bite of her cake, Marilyn Monroe–sexy, and Mackenzie imagined she heard hearts popping in the kitchen.

"Wonder what the Diva of Destruction wants?" Jade muttered under her breath.

The answer to that was obvious. Daisy was man-hunting. And by the looks of how she was staking her claim, she appeared to be hunting Justin.

Mackenzie told herself it didn't matter if Daisy was hunting Justin or not.

She didn't quite convince herself.

"What are you up to, buddy?" Justin had managed to catch Ty in an unguarded moment in the barn, where he was showing the three new guys the layout of the Hanging H. "It's time you share the plans that are buzzing around in that brain of yours."

"The plans are for you and me to hit the road," Ty said, giving him a genial thump on the back. "I told you—we're going to hunt up recruits."

"Yeah, but you didn't say what we're going to be recruiting talent for." Justin glanced toward Sam, Squint and Frog. "Did those guys make your recruitment list?"

Ty laughed. "Them? No way. They're just replacing you, which I think is fair, considering I brought you here. I couldn't leave Mackenzie without help."

Justin leaned against a post, crossed his arms. "Why are you so interested in Mackenzie's welfare?"

"It's not just her. It's you, too. And Bridesmaids Creek, if you really want to know."

"You're trying to bring men into Bridesmaids Creek." Justin shook his head. "They have a matchmaker here, you know. Aren't you kind of bumping the competition?"

"Just giving the matchmaker some material to work with."

"Why?" Justin's curiosity was getting the best of him.

"You'd had to have grown up here to understand." Ty shrugged. "The Haunted H was a great draw. Lots of jobs were lost when the Hawthornes had to close it down."

"That's what this is all about? Bringing jobs back to your hometown?"

"Not exactly." Ty wouldn't meet his gaze.

"Oh, I get it." Justin thought he suddenly saw into the cracks of his buddy's mercurial brain. "You're trying to find a man for *Mackenzie*."

Ty shrugged. "It's complicated."

"Not that complicated." Justin snorted. "When did you decide to play guardian angel to Mackenzie?"

"Since I was the guy with the not-too-swift idea of setting her up with her ex. My onetime good buddy, who turned out to be a weasel of epic proportions."

Justin stared at his friend. "Have you ever considered that maybe Mackenzie doesn't want another husband?"

Ty snorted. "Don't be silly. She's a woman. A woman needs a husband to feel complete."

"I'm not sure I ever saw this chauvinistic side of you before."

"Yes, you did. You just didn't recognize it, because you and I were thinking alike." Ty laughed. "Don't worry, good buddy. I'm not including you in my plan. Just the opposite. I'm clearing you out to make room for some cowboys who don't wear the rebel badge as enthusiastically as you do."

If being a hard-baked bachelor earned him that honor, he supposed he'd go with the rebel badge. "And that's why I'm being dragged on a recruiting tour? You want me out of the way so your matchmaking has a better chance of succeeding?"

"Look. The idea came to me after I'd sent you here." Ty looked at him patiently. "I realized that Mackenzie didn't just need help bringing back the old place—she needs a husband and a father to those children. I'm the man who fixed her up with the loser, so I'm going to put it right."

"Why don't you just put your own neck into the marriage noose and save everybody some agony if you feel so guilt-ridden?"

Ty put up his hands as if to ward off the very idea. "My conscience is guilty but not stupid."

Justin stared at his friend. It was true. Ty wasn't husband material.

Neither was he.

Justin sighed heavily. "I think you're nuts. But whatever. It's not my town. Nor are these my friends."

Ty brightened. "So you'll do it? The lead stallion agrees to head off and leave the pen to the lesser junior stallions?"

"You make it sound like Mackenzie's ever looked my way twice in a romantic way, which I can assure you she hasn't. We haven't spoken that much since I've been here."

"Call it a hunch. Clearing out the pen, as they say. The ladies always want the one they can't have. Mysterious types seem romantic. Like Zorro."

Justin shrugged. "I think you took one too many falls off the mechanical bull, Ty, but whatever. I'll go with you," he said, "but you better hope Mackenzie never finds out what you're up to. I have the feeling that little lady doesn't think she needs any man to rescue her."

"Mechanical bull! I was no dime-store cowboy," Ty said, following Justin as he headed back to work. Justin couldn't stand around examining the holes in his friend's head any longer. Mackenzie hadn't given one signal that she might be interested in him in more than a foreman–boss lady relationship.

Still, he had a slightly uneasy feeling about leaving her to the romancing of the Three Dating Daddies—a thought that totally brought him up short.

That's what one of those men might become: a dad to Mackenzie's four little girls.

Maybe the most troubling thought of all.

Chapter 5

"You're going to have to keep an eye on Daisy," Jade told her as Mackenzie settled her daughters down for an afternoon nap. Late-day sun filtered through the windows of the family room, twilight just arriving at nearly seven o'clock. Mackenzie loved summer days when there was so much cheery sunshine.

She couldn't be bothered to think about Daisy Donovan.

"I'm not going to keep an eye on Daisy. I don't care what she does."

"You do care. All of Bridesmaids Creek cares. Her and her band of rowdies are bent on making certain this town drops off the map for families. That way Daisy's father can keep buying up the land around here in his quest for mineral rights and selling huge land parcels to the government. Or worse." Jade flopped down onto a flowered sofa, fanning herself. "As our town bad girl, Daisy lives for herself. My guess is she didn't come here today to bring you a gift, but to check out the new foreman. Everyone is town has been chattering about the hot guy you've got working the place."

"It doesn't matter. I'm not even going to think about Daisy's shenanigans. Even if Justin decided to hop on the back of her motorcycle and roar off into the sunset, I wouldn't think about Daisy."

Jade laughed. "Methinks you protest a bit too much. So what did you think about the three new guys?"

"That Ty and I are going to have to talk. The men are welcome to stay here and bunk in the bunkhouse, but I don't know if I have enough work here for three more men."

"Not unless you reopen the haunted house."

"Which I'm not going to do."

"It's August. We have plenty of time until October," Jade said.

"I know. But my only priority right now is my babies. We'll do fine living in a small cottage in town."

"There might be a miracle. You never know." Jade got up to stare out the window. "She bugs me—I swear she does. Why are men always so blinded by Daisy?"

"Because she's beautiful and has a wild streak. There's nothing blinding about it. It's human nature." Mackenzie smiled at her babies. "You girls, however, must promise your mother to grow up to be teachers, nurses and librarians. No motorcycles for you!"

"My goddaughters won't be Daisies," Jade said, laughing. "However, I think Daisy may be about to kiss a frog."

"Not Frog?" Mackenzie hurried to the window. "Poor

Frog! Of all of the new cowboys, I'm pretty sure he's the least suited to Daisy's charms."

"Hate to watch a good man fall." Jade walked away from the window. "In fact, I can't look."

"Can't look at what?" Justin asked, entering the room.

Mackenzie glanced over her shoulder, struck again by how handsome Justin was. She'd gotten a little used to him at the Hanging H, even if she wouldn't share that with a soul. Still, if he wanted to move on with Ty, she'd understand. She'd be sorry—but she'd understand. "We're spying."

"I can see that." He joined her at the window, and Mackenzie was shaken by the sudden warmth of proximity. Almost intimate, their arms nearly touching. She smelled spicy cologne and strong male, felt body heat and strange sensations sweep over her.

She was awfully glad it wasn't Justin out there getting far too close to Daisy Donovan's heart-shaped lips.

"I'll take the night shift," Justin told Mackenzie as she finished bathing the girls. She put them into soft nighties and touched a towel gently to the light fuzz atop their heads. A little baby oil for the dry spots, and they were like angels ready to be tucked in for the night.

"You don't have to," Mackenzie said. "But thank you, Justin. Babysitting isn't part of your job description."

"I've been thinking about my job description." He carried Hope and Holly down the hall, so Mackenzie picked up Heather and Haven and followed. She watched the big man settle her daughters ever so gently into their white-ruffled cribs. "This business of Ty bringing on hannies for you, for example."

"Ty is nuts, and there'll be no hannies around here,

nor mannies. Silliest thing I've ever heard." Mackenzie covered her daughters with light pink blankets and
kissed each of them. "Ty doesn't want to bring those
cowboys here to help me as much as he's looking for a
place for some of his buddies to work. I'll ask around
town, see if anybody needs a couple of hands."

"You know I'm leaving with Ty. Probably day after
tomorrow."

She felt a slight prick at that news. "Then I'll only
need one of the men. Maybe Frog. He seems pretty
harmless." She sighed to herself. And maybe if he were
here he'd be less likely to fall into Daisy's clutches.

"Frog, is it?"

"I can't get used to a grown man being called Frog."

"Hiring him on here isn't going to save him from
Daisy."

She looked at Justin. "Who says I want to?"

"I know something about the female mind. And I
heard you and Jade talking about saving him."

"Jade was talking about it. I personally think Frog
can probably take care of himself just fine." She didn't
look at Justin directly. Just too much sex appeal, too
much closeness.

It was the babies. She loved the way he took care of
her daughters, handling them like they were delicate
treasures.

He moved a strand of hair away from her face, and
she tucked it up into her ponytail. "I should catch a
shower while they're down. We've hit the four-hour
mark at night now, and I take full advantage of those
four hours."

Justin moved away, sat in the rocker. "Go. Get some
rest. I'll keep an eye on them."

"There's no need," she said quickly. "The monitor is on, and I'll hear them—"

He waved a hand at her to leave. "You need four hours to yourself. I'll wake you when they start looking for dinner." A smile tugged at his lips. "Better take me up on my offer. Ty's taking me out of here tomorrow or the next day."

"Oh. Okay. Thank you." She backed up slowly, then turned to hurry down the hall. He was actually leaving. She'd always known he would, and yet she'd hoped— Well, it didn't matter what she'd hoped.

The fact was, she'd gotten used to Justin being around. But it was more than that, and she knew it. Something about the big man made her feel safe and protected and happy. They weren't a family, but they'd gotten into a groove that worked, and she'd come to rely on that comfort. Rely on *him*.

Maybe Jade's right with that protesting too much stuff I've got a major thing going for this cowboy. I was just trying to ignore it because I knew he'd leave one day.

And now it seemed that day had come.

Justin slept off and on, dozing in the room with the babies. It was weird how much he found himself enjoying taking care of them. As a man who'd never been interested in having children—not one bit—he was surprised by how Mackenzie's four little daughters tugged on his heartstrings.

He hated the idea of leaving them—all of them. And, somehow, he even hated the idea of Frog staying behind to take his place. Or any of the three men Ty was bringing on to replace him, for that matter.

The only reason he was leaving with Ty was because Ty had brought him here in the first place. He owed it to him out of a sense of brotherhood. Ty wouldn't ask him if he didn't need him. Mackenzie didn't really need him—not like Ty did.

He needed to talk to Ty a bit more, dig into the mission to settle the questions in his mind. But the thing that unsettled his mind the most was how much he hated the idea of three men he didn't know all that well roaming around the Hanging H and falling for Mackenzie and the girls.

Just as he was beginning to fall for them.

Whether he liked it or not, that was the truth. Justin closed his eyes as he rocked in the chair. The tiny night-light sent a soft glow over the room. An occasional baby snuffle or sigh reached him, the sound somehow comforting and not intimidating at all, not the way he'd thought it would be. During his wilder, crazier rodeo days, the idea of a family had been distinctly unappealing.

Mackenzie was recently divorced. No doubt the last thing she wanted was another man in her life. He couldn't blame her if that was the way she felt.

At dawn, when Betty Harper appeared in the nursery, Justin felt strangely rested. He smiled at Jade's mother. "Good morning."

"Go get some rest. I'll take over from here. Mackenzie said the babies didn't even move last night."

He felt like he hadn't, either. In fact, he couldn't remember the last time he'd felt so relaxed. "I thought I was awake all night. I didn't even realize Mackenzie came in the nursery."

Betty smiled. "I checked on you at five. Everybody

was sound asleep, which is a first for the girls. They probably feel comforted with a man's presence around. Babies do that sometimes. You have a nice deep voice with is probably soothing to them."

She disappeared from the room. Justin rose and stretched. Haven peered up at him from her blanket, and he had the uncanny notion that she was watching him. Did babies see anything at this tender age?

"Hello, little one," he said, approaching her crib. Gently he picked her up, held her close. "Good morning to you, too."

He kissed the top of her head, breathed in the sweet baby freshness of her skin, the scent of baby powder.

"Hi," Mackenzie said, her voice soft.

He turned and saw she was wide-awake and looking refreshed. "You're up bright and early."

"I got a lot more sleep than I have since before I became pregnant." She came to take Haven from him, and he smelled an entirely different smell: strawberry shampoo, delicate floral soap, sexy woman.

His heart did one of those funny flip-flops he'd gotten used to feeling around her.

"Thanks for watching them last night." She gazed up at him. "I think I slept so well because I knew you were standing guard."

Oh, boy. There went the heart. "It was no problem. Part of the job."

"Not part of the job I hired you to do." She looked at him funny.

He backed up a step when he realized he was staring at her pink, glossy lips. "It's the job Frog and Fellows are applying for."

"That's Ty's bright idea. And by now, you know Ty

can be a bit of a squirrel." She smiled. "Babysitting isn't part of your job description. But thank you."

Warmth expanded in his chest at her smile. He wondered if he'd ever met a woman he was so blindingly attracted to—and decided in a hurry that was a terrible thought to have about his boss. Definitely a dead end. There was no way on this planet he had any business being attracted to her.

"I'm going to get some coffee. You want a cup?"

"No, thank you. You go on."

He nodded and turned to leave.

Turned back around, met her gaze. Started to say that sitting up with her daughters hadn't been work; he hadn't done it because of Frog and Friends. He'd done it because he'd wanted to. Wanted to make her happy, help her out.

But it was a bad idea to make such a confession. No purpose to it at all, and he didn't do anything unless he knew the purpose.

Shutting his stupid yap tight before it could say weird, mushy things, he left.

Chapter 6

"Hello, handsome," Justin heard as he got out of his truck, which he'd parked right in front of Madame Matchmaker's small shop.

He turned, found Daisy Donovan just about too close for comfort, chest-high, tiny and dangerous. The brunette was dressed in a short denim skirt, brown cowboy boots and a white halter top. She smiled at him mischievously. All the sex appeal being aimed at him had warning bells ringing like mad inside his head.

"Hi, Daisy."

She wound an arm through his. "Where're you heading to?"

He wasn't about to tell her he'd been planning a visit to Madame Matchmaker. The kind of answers he was looking for required discretion. Daisy didn't look like she did discretion very well. "I was planning to grab lunch."

"Mind if I join you? I had some things I wanted to talk to you about."

He did mind—very much. Ty was hitting the road tomorrow and Justin was going with him, so he had a lot to get done. Lunch with Daisy wasn't on the to-do list.

"I'm leaving town tomorrow, so I'm grabbing takeout. Why don't you call the Hanging H and let Mackenzie know what you need, and maybe one of the new guys she's hired can help you out."

Daisy looked up at him, her dark eyes focused. "We need you here in Bridesmaids Creek."

He shook his head. If there was any reason he'd stay, it would be for Mackenzie. The reason he was leaving was Mackenzie—or, more to the point, the feelings he knew he was developing for his boss.

He extracted himself from Daisy's arm. "Bridesmaids Creek survived without me for many years."

He tipped his hat and pushed open the door of The Wedding Diner. It seemed as if every customer turned to stare at him. Conversation halted.

No, he wasn't imagining the stares. He nodded to the room at large and headed to the pink stand where Jane stared at him, too, her bright blue gaze curious.

Justin removed his hat. "If you have a booth open, ma'am, I'd appreciate it."

She nodded and took him to a white booth. He sat, noticing that everyone followed his progress. No one bothered to hide their curiosity. He hoped she'd bring him a cup of hot coffee sooner rather than later. His stomach rumbled. He could have eaten at the ranch—certainly he'd miss the good cooking there.

But today he really felt a need to put some space between him and the babies. And Mackenzie, most of all.

Jane gazed at him intently. "You're not a settling down kind of man."

"No, ma'am."

"But you're happy at the Hanging H."

The way she made statements instead of asking questions—like she already knew everything but was only giving him a chance to confirm her thoughts—forced his thoughts off the coffee he'd been hunting. "I've enjoyed my time out there."

"But you're not a family man."

He looked at her. "I wonder if I can get a cup of coffee, Jane."

She smiled. "You think I'm digging in your business."

"Yes, ma'am."

"That's what we do here. You'll get used to it. We're really pretty harmless here in Bridesmaids Creek." She cocked her head. "You don't need to worry about us matchmaking."

His brows rose. "I don't?"

"No. We're looking for family men in Bridesmaids Creek."

She strode off to get his coffee. Justin ran a finger around his collar.

A woman with pinkish hair piled high on her head slid into his booth. "Jane tell your fortune?"

He shook his head. "I don't think so."

"She just gave you the third degree." She nodded. "She'll tell your fortune to us later." She stuck a hand across the table for him to shake, which he did, slightly out of his element. "I'm Cosette Lafleur."

"Ah. Would you be Madame Matchmaker?" The French name and the pink-frosted hair seemed like a giveaway.

She looked at him closely. "*Absolument*. And you should have come to see me."

"But I'm not looking for a match."

"That's what we hear." She indicated the diner, whose patrons weren't even bothering to disguise their interest in Cosette's interview of him. "So you're leaving."

"Yes. Tomorrow." He looked at the grilled cheese sandwich and tomato soup a young, bouncy waitress with a nose stud put in front of him. "I didn't order this."

"It's what you get. Miss Jane says you're looking peaky and some protein and calcium will set you right." Cosette shrugged. "Nobody really orders. We all get what Jane thinks we need. It works for us. Most of us never get even a cold!"

Great. He had to pick the one place to get away from Mackenzie where he couldn't get away from talking about her and couldn't even order a nice, greasy burger.

"Go ahead. Take a bite. That cheese is County Line cheese, made off a local farm. You'll never taste better."

A grilled cheese sandwich was just bread and cheese. Nothing fancy. He took a bite, not expecting much. "That's good stuff," he said, surprised.

Cosette looked pleased. "So, back to you leaving. It's too bad you have to go, but Ty said he misjudged you."

"Misjudged me?"

"Ty thought you were probably a man looking for a change in your life. A family man in disguise."

That would be odd. He and Ty had never discussed it. "I'm pretty certain I've never misled anyone about the fact that I like life on the road."

"That's the problem, then, isn't it? Expectations?" She beamed. "Ty shouldn't have tried to put you in a position you wouldn't be comfortable with."

"Are you saying that Ty had me hired on at the Hanging H so I'd fall in love with Mackenzie?"

"Or at least the babies. It's very hard not to fall for those little angels." Cosette glanced up, her smile widening. "Hello, Mackenzie."

He started a little, surprised when Mackenzie slid in next to Cosette and hugged her.

"How are you feeling?" Mackenzie asked. "Your stomach virus has gone?"

"All gone. That soup you sent over for me did the trick. Thank you, dear friend."

Justin ate his sandwich, needing strength after everything he'd heard. Ty wouldn't have brought him to Bridesmaids Creek on a matchmaking mission. His buddy wouldn't have hung him out to dry like that.

But there was no denying that the "bait"—if Mackenzie had been Ty's bait—was worthy of any hook. If he were wired a little differently, if he could consider staying in one place with one woman, Mackenzie would be the one.

Whoa. That was a very strange thought.

She looked at him, her smile innocent and carefree, and he wondered why he hadn't seen it before. Apparently all of Bridesmaids Creek had seen it.

His buddy, best friend, old pal Ty had set him up.

It was a blind date without the date. Nothing more than the same service Madame Matchmaker might provide. And now Ty was pulling the plug, because Justin wasn't a settle-down kind of man, and Ty had found three better victims: Sam, Squint and Fish. No—Frog.

A jealous streak ran up his back.

Which was exactly why he had to leave tomorrow.

"It's such a shame Justin has to go," Cosette told

Mackenzie. "He was just telling me how much he was going to miss your little girls."

He hadn't said any such thing. Justin's mouth opened to deny the woman's claim; then he realized what a schmuck he'd sound like if he did. So he nodded and spooned his soup a little faster. Maybe if he kept his mouth busy, he'd keep his foot out of it.

Mackenzie looked at him, her expression polite. "Justin has been a big help at the ranch. And with the girls."

Justin swallowed uncomfortably. Why did he feel so guilty? Did Mackenzie know that her friend Ty had tried to set her up? There were few secrets in Bridesmaids Creek. She had to suspect.

Then again, she'd never given him half a signal that she was interested in him. Hadn't put up much of a fuss when Ty had mentioned they were leaving town, had seemed okay with the new hands.

Maybe he should probe that little situation a bit.

"The new guy should work out well at the Hanging H," Justin said a bit gruffly, not completely able to work out the jealous kink he got about Toad. Or whatever the man's name was.

"You mean *guys*," Mackenzie said. "Ty talked me into taking all three of the new hands on."

Good ol' Ty. If one bachelor didn't pan out, Ty had planned for backup. His friend was almost diabolical with his matchmaking.

"I hear through the BC grapevine," Cosette said, "that your sister is coming home tomorrow, Mackenzie."

Sister? He looked at Mackenzie, noticing instantly that she didn't smile, only nodded gravely.

"Yes. Suz will be home."

Good. Then Mackenzie would have more help, and he'd feel less like a heel for running out on her. Wasn't that what he was doing?

"What are you going to do?" Cosette asked in her sweet, lilting, French-accented voice.

Mackenzie shrugged. "It's her home, too. She can always come home to the Hanging H."

"You don't need a fifth child," Cosette said, and Mackenzie stirred the tea she'd poured a half a packet of sugar into and shrugged.

"Maybe she's changed," Mackenzie said.

"How old is your sister?" Justin asked, curious. The ladies' chatting had turned a bit ominous.

"Suz is twenty-three," Mackenzie said.

And Mackenzie was thirty. Not an uncommon age gap between siblings, but it didn't sound like they were entirely close.

Still, Mackenzie's family problems were none of his concern, and as Cosette had pointed out—much to his chagrin—he had no need to worry. He was being dragged off by Ty because he wasn't looking for a family. And family skeletons were one thing he made every effort to avoid.

Justin kept himself from helping put the babies to bed that night, though it was a ritual he enjoyed. He liked the smell of lavender-scented soap and the sweet sounds they made when Mackenzie slipped them into their cribs. They always looked so darling in their little nighties. Strangely enough, although most people wouldn't find four babies peaceful, that was exactly how he felt at night in the nursery.

Peaceful.

He loved watching Mackenzie do her mom thing, too. It was such a soothing sight as she lovingly slipped her daughters off to dreamland.

He was going to miss it. He'd been lucky that she'd allowed him to become part of the nightly ritual. Part of him wished he could stay at the Hanging H, because he sure did like it here.

On the other hand, now that he knew the price of staying, there was no reason to do so.

They left the nursery, the night-lights glowing softly in the wall sockets, the girls conked out from their busy day and all the good loving from their mother.

So he didn't say he would miss the girls—and Mackenzie—though he knew he would.

Mackenzie went into the kitchen, and he followed. Here was where he usually said good-night every night, another ritual, this one more professional. They put the babies to bed, they walked into the kitchen and he said *sayonara*.

"Thank you for everything," Mackenzie said. "You've been a big help. I'll admit that when Ty sent you here, I had my doubts." She pulled a cake dish toward her. "Betty left the coffee on and a pound cake she baked. You don't want to leave without tasting Betty's pound cake."

He found himself nodding before he even sat down, glad of the excuse to stay. "I'll take you up on that offer. Thanks."

She poured him a steaming mug of coffee he suddenly realized he didn't want. She cut him a fragrant slice of cake he suddenly didn't want, either.

And when Mackenzie passed him to rinse off the knife, he reached out and caught her hand. "I'm going to miss this."

Her face held surprise—then she smiled. "Thank you."

He noticed she didn't take her hand from his, so he did the only thing he could. He set her cake knife on the counter and pulled Mackenzie to him. She stared up at him with those beautiful brown eyes, and he kissed her lips, ever so lightly, just in case she didn't want to be kissed. There was still time to stop before it was a full-blown kiss. He'd know in a second if he'd gone someplace she didn't want him to go.

Mackenzie didn't move—she stayed still as the night, waiting—and Justin was never so glad of anything in his life. He pressed his lips against hers, letting himself sink into the sweetness. He heard rain begin spattering against the windows, but that was the outside world. In this warm, cake-scented kitchen, he held the softest woman in the country in his arms, and she was responding to him.

The back door blew open. Mackenzie and Justin jumped apart. He stared at the woman in the doorway. She was dripping from her head to her toes, her boots muddy, her jeans ragged and pocked with deliberate tears. She dropped a dirty duffel bag onto the floor. But it was her short pixie hair, blond with blue streaks, that stopped him, not to mention the cheek stud and the dark glaring eyes.

"Suz!" Mackenzie flew to hug her sister, enveloping her.

Suz stared at him over Mackenzie's shoulder. "Who's he?"

"This is Justin Morant." Mackenzie sounded uncomfortable. "He's the foreman. Until tomorrow, that is."

Suz didn't move to shake his hand. Didn't leave her sister's arms.

"What's he doing in the kitchen at this hour?" Suz demanded.

Damn good question. He grabbed his hat, went to the door. "I'll say goodbye tomorrow before I go, Mackenzie."

Suz glared, willing him gone. Mackenzie nodded. "Thank you."

Ouch. He nodded and headed out into the rain, leaving the cake and the coffee behind.

The kiss stayed with him.

Chapter 7

Justin came upon Frog, Squint and Sam spying on the house from the bunkhouse. "What the hell, fellows?" he demanded.

"Didn't you see her?" Frog asked. "That little bit of darling that roared up on the motorcycle?"

He hadn't seen a motorcycle, hadn't heard one, wouldn't have noticed one if it had run over his foot. All he'd been focused on was Mackenzie in his arms. He didn't think he'd ever forget that.

She was all woman, gentle and sweet-smelling. Curves. Heaven.

No wonder her sister was so protective of her. He would be, too.

"That *darling* is too much for any of you to handle." He hung his hat on the hook and went into the kitchen for a much-needed beer, eschewing the temptation to spy on the kitchen, which faced the bunkhouse.

"Who was she?" Frog asked.

"Little sister. Nothing for you to worry about." Justin flung himself onto the leather sofa.

"I'm not worried about her," Squint said. "If I can't have Mackenzie, I'll be happy to—"

"Whoa, whoa, whoa." Justin scowled at the three stooges he was stuck with for the moment. "No one said you were getting Mackenzie or Suz."

"Suz," Sam said dreamily. "I could have guessed she had a pretty name."

Justin mentally rolled his eyes. "Again, who said those women were available? You work for them. You can't hit on them."

They looked at him, grinning.

"If you had understood your assignment," Frog said, "you would have known that romancing is what we're all here for. We're all bachelors looking for a good wife and a home."

Justin blinked. "What assignment?"

"Didn't Ty tell you? In this town, the ladies are looking for a husband any way they can find one," Squint said. "And we are all preapproved to join the race to the altar."

"Where did you get a name like Squint?" Justin asked.

"Name's John Squint Mathison," the tall man said. Justin supposed he was a decent-looking fellow, the kind a lady might call a hunk. "I got *Squint* in the military."

"I don't like it," Justin said. "It sounds a bit shady."

"Au contraire," Sam said with a flourish. "If you'd been in the mountains of Afghanistan with us, you'd have wanted this one and his peashooter at your back. We called him Squint-Eye, Squint for short, for certain

reasons best not discussed. But you can trust it was a badge of honor."

"Yeah, well." He looked at the gentle giant next to him. "I guess I don't want to know what Frog is derived from," he said, feeling a little sour that these gentlemen would be staying and he'd be going. Gentlemen, indeed. More like woman-hunting, non-commitment-phobic, nice guys.

They shook their heads solemnly, and he sighed.

"What makes Ty so sure that Bridesmaids Creek is so ripe for marriage-hunting males?"

"Did you get a load of that beauty that pulled up on the motorcycle yesterday?" Sam's eyes went round.

"Daisy Donovan? Yes, I did." Justin shrugged.

"She's *fine*. And she invited us all to a special gathering." Frog looked pleased. "I'd marry her in a heartbeat."

From what he'd heard about Daisy, Justin didn't think that was necessarily a good idea. He sipped his beer, studied the eager bachelors in whose capable hands he was leaving Mackenzie.

"Don't worry," Squint said, as if reading his mind. "We'll take care of everything. We've figured out your routine."

They knew what he did outside the house. Inside the house with Mackenzie and the babies, they had no idea.

He'd like to keep it that way.

"I'm so glad you're home, Suz," Mackenzie told her sister when she wandered back into the kitchen, freshly showered and wearing comfortable pajamas. Mackenzie passed her sister the slice of pound cake she'd cut for Justin and made her a hot cup of tea. "How was Africa?"

Suz sat on a barstool and glared at her sister. "Africa was beautiful. I think we did a lot of good with the limited resources we had. We can talk about that later, after I've seen my nieces again. And after we talk about that cowboy you were in here sucking face with."

"I was not," Mackenzie said, placing the teacup in front of her sister and pushing the sugar bowl close, "sucking face with the cowboy."

Suz shook her head. "I do believe if I hadn't walked in, this kitchen would have seen some action."

Mackenzie looked at her little sister with a noncommittal shrug. "I doubt that."

"Do not fall into another man's arms just because what's-his-face went off with what's-her-face."

That familiar sting lodged deep inside her, yet stinging less than it once had. "I am not falling."

Pants on fire. It had been wonderful for the few seconds Justin had held her in his arms. The feeling had shocked her when he'd pulled her close against his broad chest, right up to his hard body. She'd watched him many a time from this kitchen window, admiring the muscles and the quiet, steady, strong way he went about his work. Being held by Justin had sent her heart rushing out of control.

"Oh, no," Suz said, staring at her sister. "I've seen that look on your face before."

"What look?"

"That about-to-fall look."

"I am not about to fall. In fact, Justin's leaving tomorrow. So falling is out of the question."

Suz shook her head, started in on the pound cake. "It's rebound. Surely you know that."

"So what?"

"I mean," Suz said, her mouth full, "if you were the type of woman who would just kiss and quit, that would be one thing. But you kiss and marry. And that's a problem."

Mackenzie laughed. "If you knew Justin, you wouldn't worry. He is so not the marrying kind. Everybody knows that."

"Everybody can't know that, because he was only here a short time." Suz was being practical. "You don't know for sure."

"Regardless, he's leaving tomorrow." She wasn't entirely happy about that, but Ty could be inscrutable about anything and everything. Certainly Justin hadn't argued about leaving.

So it was for the best.

"Anyway," Suz said, sipping her tea, "how are my angel cakes? I peeked in on them, and they were sleeping hard. Haven sucks her thumb, you know. It's cute."

"She doesn't do that when she's awake." Mackenzie smiled. "They're amazing. There's not a day I don't thank Heaven that I have them."

"Yeah, well," Suz said gruffly. "It was the least Knucklehead could do for you." She sniffed. "You look good."

Mackenzie smiled. "Do I?"

"Yeah. You gained a little weight. You look rested." Suz sniffed again. "In fact, you look beautiful."

Mackenzie stared at her normally unsentimental sister. "Why are you buttering me up?"

Suz laughed. "I'm not. I'm being my typical honest self. Some days it's brutal, and some days it's all good news. You really do look great. I'm sure I'm not the only one who's told you that recently."

"Believe it or not, the cowboy, as you call Justin, and I don't have some hot love affair going. Before today, we hadn't spoken more than twenty minutes at one time."

"I don't think talking's what's on his mind."

"He's been nothing but a gentleman. If you're done with your snack, I'm going to tuck you onto the sofa and turn on the TV. I may look great, but you look like the flight was long."

Her sister followed her from the kitchen. "It was long and hellish. I always say I'm quitting the Peace Corps. But then I don't. I can't. It's in my blood."

Mackenzie settled her sister in her old room, spreading a soft blue-and-white afghan over her that Betty had knitted. Suz had the reputation for being a wild child—she was tough and a little wild. But she had such a good heart. And she'd go places no one else would go, in the quest to do what few others wanted to do. Or could do. She gazed at her sister tenderly. "How long are you here?"

"Not long." Suz's eyes started to close. "Just until I determine that you're not suffering too much without me. And until I make sure you don't do something dumb, like fall for a cowboy with a restless leg."

Mackenzie brushed Suz's blue-streaked hair away from her forehead. "Restless side, darling. Restless leg is something entirely different."

"No, I'm pretty sure I'm worried about his restless leg." Suz's eyes drifted shut. "It's always so good to be home. This will always be our home, won't it?"

Mackenzie felt a pang of guilt. This was a discussion for another day. She patted Suz's hand, noted the cracked nails, the dry skin, the calluses. Suz was a warrior of a different kind, a misunderstood warrior, and Mackenzie would do anything to protect her.

But keeping the family home probably wasn't in the cards. "Rest now."

"I try," Suz said. "I try to rest, Mackenzie. But I always see them."

Mackenzie drew back a little. "Don't think about it. It's all over."

Suz nodded, and Mackenzie tucked the blanket close around her sister, cocooning her like she would one of her babies. Then she went into the kitchen and looked out toward the bunkhouse, staring into the darkness.

Suz was right about one thing—Justin had made it clear he was a footloose, rebellious kind of guy. There was no reason to fall for him. Suz walking in had probably stopped something that should never have been started.

But she was amazed by the feelings his kiss had awakened inside her, feelings she'd never had before. Suz was right. The kitchen table probably would have been used for something other than its intended purpose, because the last thing Mackenzie had wanted was for Justin to let her go.

And that's why it hurt so much that he was leaving.

Justin was awakened by the feel of something warm and curvy sliding into bed, curling right up against him. He blinked, realizing he wasn't dreaming.

But something was wrong. For one heavenly second he thought Mackenzie might have crawled into his bed.

The perfume wasn't right. The hands were too greedy. He caught the hands and sat up, switching on the lamp.

"Daisy! What the hell?"

She blinked and hopped out of his bed naked as the day she'd been born. He averted his gaze from the flash of skin as she scooped up her clothes and began dressing. "I thought—"

"You thought what?" He got up, pulled on his jeans, annoyed. There were three other occupants of the bunkhouse. Any one of them would probably have been happy to find Daisy in his bed.

He was not.

"Never mind." Daisy had pulled on some of her clothes but definitely couldn't be called "dressed."

Which of course was when the three stooges entered the room. Their eyes bugged from their sockets.

"This isn't what it looks like," Justin said, zipping his jeans. "She's lost."

The stooges looked concerned.

"Not that lost," Frog said.

"Damn, son," Squint said. "You're exactly what we heard about you."

"Which is what?" Justin demanded.

"Emotionally unavailable," Daisy said, slowly pulling the straps up on her dress. "A real renegade."

Justin hesitated, realizing Daisy was putting on something of an award-worthy act. "What the hell is going on here?"

"Nothing," Sam said, "except that you were in bed with Daisy."

"I was not in bed with Daisy!"

"Someone was in bed with Daisy, and it wasn't us," Frog said. "One of us, I should say," he said; then he was suddenly shoved aside.

Mackenzie stared at him. "What are you doing here, Daisy?"

"Nothing," Daisy said, her voice too sweet. Too silky, a bit catty.

Justin sighed. "Everybody out of my room. Now."

Mackenzie turned to leave, too. "Not you," he said, grabbing her hand and pulling her back into the room. He closed the door, took the lunch sack from her hand and set it on his dresser. "Were you bringing me a snack bag for the road?"

She glared at him. "Yes."

"Bet you'd like to take it back."

"Yes, I would!"

"Well, you can't." He pulled her into his arms, taking her lips with his, kissing her the way he'd wanted to kiss her earlier.

She put her hands on his chest, pushed him slightly away—though not too far. "Why would I want to kiss you after Daisy Donovan's been in your room?"

"Because you're in my room now."

"Which begs the question what was she doing in here?"

He smiled. "I think she'd lost her way."

"I very much doubt it."

"I'm pretty certain I wasn't the intended target. And you sound like you may have a jealous streak, boss lady."

"I'm not jealous in the least. I'm *concerned*."

Now she did try to tug away from him, though he didn't allow that. She didn't try hard enough for it to count—and he was pretty intrigued by this *concerned* side of her. "*I'm* concerned that you don't leave without what you came for," he said, slanting his lips over hers, drawing her in for a deep kiss. He loved holding her, that was for certain; she was soft and, at this moment, a trifle annoyed, which he was going to enjoy kissing right out of her.

Her lips were sweeter than he'd ever imagined. Every kiss, every stroke, was more amazing than before. Mackenzie let out what sounded like a tiny whimper, and he wasn't about to stop now. No longer stiff in his arms, she was pliable and leaning into him, her hands reaching up behind his neck, pulling him closer.

God, he didn't think he could leave this.

The thought brought him right down to earth. He really had no right to be doing this. Not to Mackenzie. If Daisy played fast and loose, Mackenzie was the kind of woman a man didn't play with at all. "Hey," he said, pulling back. He moved away, jerked his head toward the lunch sack. "Thanks for bringing my lunch. I really appreciate it."

She put her hands on her hips. "Chicken much?"

He was—he was a chicken with all the trimmings. "Maybe."

"At least you admit it."

"What else can I do?"

"Whatever you want to."

What he wanted to do was drag her into bed. Make love to her all night long. But what would that solve besides momentarily easing the overwhelming attraction he felt for her? It wasn't fair—he couldn't make love to Mackenzie and then hit the road. Not with those four little babies at the big house who needed a father, not a man who made love to their mother and then disappeared.

"You make things hard, Mackenzie."

She raised a brow. "If anyone's making anything hard for you, it's just you. I only brought you a lunch."

She had him there. He was all kinds of torn up, and he couldn't blame it on her. "I hate the thought of leaving you with the three amigos."

"Why? Ty trusts them."

Justin wasn't certain how much he trusted Ty. Heck, he didn't trust him at all. Ty was running a matchmaking game to get Mackenzie to the altar.

"Maybe I'll stay," he said, the words popping out of his mouth before he'd measured them.

She looked at him a long time. "Whether you stay or go is your decision," she said, disappearing from his room. He heard the front door close and took a deep breath.

I screwed that up every which way from Sunday. Holy cow.

Daisy climbing into his bed had started off a chain reaction. Mackenzie didn't trust him now; he could feel that. Already burned by one man, she had her guard up. It had taken him weeks to get past those shields, and now they were going to be stronger than ever.

He went to find his bunkhouse mates. Daisy was long gone, and Frog, Sam and Squint loafed on the leather sectional.

"Boss lady just blew out of here like a whirlwind," Squint observed. "Guess she didn't like what you were selling."

Ah. Ribbing from the dating-challenged. "If you have a point, make it, fellows."

"No point," Frog said quickly. "Except it seems to us your chips are down."

"And you see an opening?" He leaned against the wall, staring down at them. "Maybe. Maybe not."

Sam grinned at him. "The only maybe is maybe you shouldn't be leaving. Field's going to be wide-open."

"Thanks for the advice." Justin grabbed his lunch, headed to his truck.

The three boneheads followed him out.

"The only reason we're trying to help you is that Daisy says without you, this dump's going down," Squint said. "Kinda hate to see that happen to the little lady. She's got those four tiny whinies, you know."

Justin glanced toward the house. "Are you going to follow me out of town?"

Sam shoved his hands in his pockets. "No. We're going into town to meet Daisy. She wants to show us her place."

Justin turned. "So which one of you was Daisy coming to see this morning when she accidentally got in my bed?"

Frog shook his head. "That was no accident. She was trying to get you in trouble with Mackenzie."

"How do you know that?" It was a very strange thought.

"She left without getting into any of our beds, didn't she?" Squint asked. "Though believe me, we wouldn't have thrown her out of bed for eating crackers."

"I didn't throw her out of bed," Justin said. "I didn't *want* her in my bed." He frowned. "She wouldn't have had any idea that Mackenzie was coming to the bunkhouse to say goodbye. So how do you know it was a setup?"

"It's the way ladies work," Frog said. "At your age, you should know this."

"Daisy sure did disappear once she stirred up trouble," Squint said. "So if Trouble won't come to us, we're going to Trouble."

"But why?" Justin was confused. "Why would you want to bother with a wild woman like Daisy?"

"For many reasons." Sam thumped him jovially on the back. "We shouldn't have to draw you a picture, but one of those reasons involve the benefits you were going to receive this morning."

"Sex?" Justin frowned. "That seems cold-blooded, doesn't it?"

"The world runs on sex," Frog said expansively. "Do you know we get hit with like a bajillion sexual messages a day?"

"It's sort of like subliminal phone calls," Sam said. "Only you don't seem inclined to pick up the phone. So one of us will."

Justin shook his head. "I don't care." He got into his truck.

"Anyway," Squint said, "the real reason we're going to see Daisy is that we consider ourselves something like spies. Spies with muscles and highly desirable—"

"Brains," Frog interrupted. "This is brain warfare. We're not going to let Mackenzie and those little girls down."

Justin's gaze narrowed. "You just said your interest in Daisy is sex."

"All good spies do what they have to do," Squint said. "But the mission is to keep Daisy from sinking Mackenzie. But go on—run off if that's what you were born to do. Born to run and all that. We get it."

"Back up a second," Justin said. "You're going to try to seduce Daisy so she'll tell you what she and her father are up to in their plan to get Mackenzie to sell out? Because apparently this isn't the first rodeo with the Donovan crowd."

"Not seduce, exactly. More like romance," Sam said. "Sweet talk."

"There's just one problem with your plan. Daisy got into my bed. Not one of yours. What if she's not interested in the bait you're dangling?"

"Well, we figure absence makes the heart go wander. The three of us can convince her you were never here," Frog said.

"Sounds like a plan," Justin said, not wanting to hurt their feelings. "You do know that Mackenzie is planning to sell the Hanging H, don't you?"

"Yes, but Ty says she can't. He says we have to help her. Because Daisy's family will buy it and carve it up into tiny land parcels. And the Hanging H means jobs and commerce when Mackenzie starts the haunted house back up."

"But she doesn't want to," Justin said. "Mackenzie has four babies she's juggling. This plan of yours has so many holes in it that it could be your heads."

"Ty says Mackenzie just needs time. That she's all emotional right now, hormonal and stuff. Worried about the future. But he says that what's good for Bridesmaids Creek is Mackenzie, and what's good for Mackenzie is Bridesmaids Creek. So we're men on a mission, brother."

Justin considered their words, caught by their earnest worry about Mackenzie and her daughters.

"Gives you pause, doesn't it?" Squint asked.

Justin grunted.

"Don't bother him. He's beginning to see the light,"

Frog whispered. "It's like watching a fire slowly coming to life."

Justin ignored the ribbing. He had to admit the points were salient—*if* he trusted Ty's machinations, *if* he wanted to fall in with men with names like Squint, Frog and Toad—er, Sam. *If* he wanted to spend more time in a place with a crazy, totally female name like Bridesmaids Creek. That would be the address his mail was sent to from now on. Justin Morant, Bridesmaids Creek, Texas. Mr. Badass Bull Rider from Bridesmaids Creek.

"Shall we help you unpack that duffel from your truck for you?" Sam asked.

Justin thought about Mackenzie's sweet lips against his, responding ever so cautiously—and then more warmly as she opened up to him. It had been a helluva rush.

Ty wanted to drag him away from Mackenzie, open the playing field up to more serious contenders. But the little lady had an awful lot of serious warfare being waged against her.

He looked at his three new friends earnestly awaiting his answer.

"Do the right thing," Frog said softly.

What the hell. He got most of his correspondence by email or text anyway. Justin got out of the truck.

He realized Mackenzie and Suz were standing in the driveway not forty yards away. Suz's arms were crossed, her posture belligerent. He had some smoothing over to do with little sister.

But it was Mackenzie he was staying for—and that was something the man he'd been even a week ago wouldn't have ever considered.

Chapter 8

"I don't need four ranch hands," Mackenzie told Suz as she watched the men return to the bunkhouse. "Frankly, I'm not even sure I want one."

"Looks like you've got them. Maybe it's time to tell Ty his plan's not going to work." Suz sat down on a stool at the kitchen island and pondered a tat on her inner arm Mackenzie hadn't known she'd added to her collection, a tiny heart with the initials *HH* scrolled inside.

Hanging H.

"Would you please quit getting tattoos?" Mackenzie said. "When you get to be a hundred, you're going to be a wrinkled mass of ink."

Suz laughed. "Live for today, sister."

She didn't have that luxury. "Don't you ever want to settle down? Find the right guy?"

"Didn't work for you." Suz brightened. "Although

I can tell my nieces are going to be amazing women, with love and direction from their Aunt Suz."

Mackenzie sat across from her sister and reached out to take her hand. "When's your next assignment?"

"I've decided there isn't going to be one. Africa was my last stop." Suz sighed. "Even a rolling stone with a mission has to grow moss sometime."

Mackenzie looked at her sister, worried. "This isn't like you. You never wanted to settle down."

"Dearest sister. I didn't want to settle down before I did something with my life. Now I've done a little." She shrugged, and they both glanced up as the kitchen door opened a crack.

"Can I come in?" Justin asked.

Mackenzie's heart did a funny little skip. "Sure. Have a seat."

"I saw the kitchen light was still on. Figured that meant the coffeepot might still have a few grounds left in it."

"Not really," Suz said.

"Suz!" Mackenzie said.

"Oh, all right." She got up ungraciously to get Justin a mug. "It's not coffee. It's tea at this hour. Can you deal with that?"

Justin smiled. "Sure."

"You want the milk and the sugar and the full deal, or—"

"Just hot. Thanks." Justin sat across from Mackenzie. "I don't think you need four hands."

"I just said that to Suz."

Justin nodded. "The three eligible bachelors have appointed themselves your guardians, courtesy of Ty."

"Told you you're going to have to talk to him," Suz

said, setting the mug in front of Justin. "I'm going to bed, kids. Don't do anything I wouldn't do."

"Night, Suz." Mackenzie shook her head. "Wait—come back here!"

Suz turned in the doorway. "Yes, sister dear?"

"Finish the story about your life now that you're done with the Peace Corps."

"Oh. That's easy." Suz grinned. "I'm going to finish college. I only have two years left. Then I'm applying to medical school." She drifted out of the room, humming.

College. Medical school. Mackenzie ran through the amount of money she had left from their parents' estate.

"Problems?" Justin asked.

"No." She got up to cut them both a piece of pound cake and set one in front of him. "Why did you decide to stay? You didn't have to."

"Yeah, I kind of did. Those gentlemen Ty sent out here are bent on rescuing you."

Mackenzie was annoyed. "From what?"

"Life." He shrugged. "Yourself? Daisy? I don't know."

"You mean because I'm a single mother."

"Sure. Apparently Ty believes—"

"Ty needs to get bent." Mackenzie forked her cake. "I don't even know what that means, exactly, but I heard someone say it one day and it totally describes what Ty can do to himself."

He laughed. "Good cake."

She watched him happily munching away, not caring at all that his decision to stay had completely upended her world. He had no idea how crazy she was about him—or she'd bet he'd run like the wind. She glared at him. "So you're going to rescue me from the three stooges?"

"No." Justin shook his head. "My role is the innocent bystander."

"So what was Daisy doing in your bed?" She hated to ask but had to know.

"Probably what any red-blooded female would want to do."

She sniffed. "Not any red-blooded female."

"You win. I think she may have had the wrong room."

Mackenzie gave him a cool look. "Daisy never, ever gets the wrong room."

"Really?" He perked up. "Thanks for the ego boost."

Her cool expression went straight to hard stink-eye. "None intended. Just fact."

"Truthfully, it wasn't the most pleasant experience."

"I don't think I believe you," Mackenzie said sweetly.

He put a hand over hers, startling her. "Enough teasing. You know very well I have as much interest in Daisy as I do in wearing wet socks."

His hand was so warm over hers, so strong. She nodded. "I know. I'm sorry. I have no business saying anything—"

"Stop." He squeezed her fingers lightly. "This is your ranch."

"Still, your personal life is your business. If you're really staying, we should establish that up front. You don't worry about my three new hands, and I won't poke my nose into your business."

"Maybe I like your nose—" he lifted her hand to his mouth ever so slowly, kissed it "—in my business."

Her breath caught. His gaze held hers, mesmerizing yet somehow gentle.

She pulled her hand away. "Listen, Justin. You're going—now you're staying. I don't know what to think."

"I understand." He got up and put his dishes in the dishwasher after rinsing them.

Drat. He would be a dish rinser. She silently approved.

"I'm going to hit the hay. By now maybe the fellows are asleep."

She raised a brow. "I can't tell if you like them, or if you view them as carbuncles you have to deal with."

"You don't have the corner on a little healthy jealousy," he said, winking at her before closing the door behind him.

Stunned, she sat glued to her stool for a second, then shot to the window. Justin walked across to the bunkhouse, his big shoulders visible in the darkness.

Unless she was mistaken, that big man had come on to her in a big way. Almost like he'd decided to stay because of her. A feeling of warmth spread over her.

"You like him, don't you?"

Mackenzie squealed and whirled around. "You scared me!"

Suz got back on her stool, her spiky hair awry. "I couldn't sleep. Decided to come get another piece of this cake. Carbs will do something for me, if not make me sleep, then wake me up enough to start filling out some college apps. By the way, I checked on the munchkins. Sleeping like lambs." She cut the cake, glancing up at Mackenzie. "I don't even have to ask if you like Justin. I can tell you do."

Mackenzie returned to her stool. "He's a nice man.

Can we talk about college? Where are you planning on applying?"

"Everywhere and anywhere. I'll have to take the MCAT first, the medical school examination." Suz sighed as she ate her cake. "This, I missed."

"I have some money saved—"

"So do I. Thank you, sister dear. But you don't have to take care of me anymore. I'm a big girl, you know." She smiled at her sister. "I love you for it, though. You just don't always have to be mother hen."

"Mom and Dad left us money. They wanted you to have an education," Mackenzie said softly. "You've never touched your part."

"I don't need my part. I don't need much to live on." Suz looked around the kitchen. "If I never spent any of what you call my part, would we have enough to hang on to this place?"

"Suz—"

"Would we?"

Mackenzie looked at her sister. "I know what you're trying to do."

"You *think* you know what I'm trying to do."

"You're trying to figure out how the girls can grow up here and have the same wonderful childhoods we did." Mackenzie looked at her little sister. "We had good childhoods because Mom and Dad worked hard. It wasn't about the ranch so much as it was about our parents. They loved us. They took good care of us."

"It was partially the ranch," Suz said stubbornly. "And you're not respecting the Hanging H when you talk that way. Mom and Dad built this up from nothing. It's the heart and soul of who we are."

Suz gazed at her, unblinking. She never wore makeup.

There were tats and piercings and hair dye but never makeup. And somehow her eyes were still so very expressive.

"I know you're right," Mackenzie said, "and I love that you're trying to honor our parents' memory. But I think they'd want you to have your money for a rainy day. So you don't have to take loans for college or medical school. For whatever you may need. Remember how hard Mom and Dad worked to build the Hanging H? They wouldn't want you to struggle as hard as they did."

"Do I get any say in this? A vote?"

"Of course you do."

"Good. Because it didn't feel like it there for a minute." Suz ate some cake, waved her fork. "I've lived in Africa for a year. I just don't have needs like other people do. It's hard to think about material things when I understand what people live without. And what I developed a great appreciation for was home."

Mackenzie sighed. "I haven't even had a chance to see your Africa photos yet. Let's leave this for another day."

"It's not a decision that's going to wait long. You've got four hands signed on. And Jade told me that you were planning on selling out by Christmas."

"I was going to tell you—"

"I know. You were going to tell me when you quit mooning after the cowboy."

"I really was going to discuss it with you. I wouldn't make the decision without you. But I didn't know if you planned on coming home, Suz. Truthfully, I had no way of knowing if you would stay with the Peace Corps. Your letters sounded like you were so happy."

Suz waved a hand again. "This is why Daisy's buzzing around here, trying to steal your man. She knows you're weakening."

"I am not weakening!"

"It's clear I came home in the nick of time." Suz carried her plate to the dishwasher, then, without rinsing, just placed it inside. She turned to grin at Mackenzie. "I know. Your pet peeve." She pulled the plate back out and gave it a swift rinse before replacing it. "I don't want to sell the family home or the ranch. None of it. I'd rather see you married to one of the three new guys than—"

"Married!" Mackenzie shook her head. "You can forget that nonsense right now. I'm never going through that again."

"Speak in haste—"

"It's not haste. Marriage isn't for me." Not even to the hunky man who'd just kissed her hand. Luckily he was a rebel who had no interest in settling down.

"One of us is going to have to run Daisy off for good," Suz said darkly. "Remember when our folks passed, she was like a vampire, hanging around looking to suck the dollar bills out of this place."

"There are no dollar bills to suck. If we keep the ranch, we're going to have to think of a way to make it profitable. It's big enough that we could take in boarders," she said, looking around the kitchen.

"No!"

Mackenzie blinked. "All right. No boarders."

"It wouldn't be right. We have the babies to think of. I don't want anybody around them that we don't know."

"All right. Any other ideas?"

"I'll work for a couple of years, then apply to medical school."

"No!" Mackenzie said, protesting as forcefully as her sister had about boarders. "*That* is not an option."

"We'll think of something." Suz drummed her fingers. "I can be very creative."

"That worries me." Mackenzie could hear the wheels turning in her sister's head.

"Whatever we do, it has to be something that keeps Daisy from catwalking around here all the time, annoying the crap out of me."

"She really bugs you, doesn't she?"

"Yes." Suz got up to look out the kitchen window. "She's after Justin."

Mackenzie shook her head. "It's doesn't matter."

"It does. I can't bear to let her win." Suz giggled. "At anything. In fact, I like to see her lose."

"Suz!"

"She deserves it." Her sister laughed again. "You're too tenderhearted. Be tenderhearted about our home, okay?" She kissed Mackenzie on the cheek and opened the kitchen door.

"Where are you going?"

"To see the three musketeers. They might be up playing cards or something. They look like the types that would have something going on in the wee hours. 'Night, sis."

Suz drifted out the door. Mackenzie watched her from the kitchen window. Sure enough, the bunkhouse door opened and shut with alacrity, and more lights went on inside.

The new guys had no idea what they were in for.

Mackenzie turned out the kitchen lights and went to check on her babies. Like Suz had said, they were sleeping like lambs. She loved her daughters so much.

It felt as if her heart was tied to them in some way she couldn't have explained to anyone.

Maybe Suz was right. The Hanging H would be a wonderful place for the girls to grow up. Deep in her heart, she'd like them to have what she and her sister had as kids. Yet it cost money—a lot of money—to pay the bills at a ranch that wasn't bringing in income. She'd been dipping into her own inheritance to cover expenses.

The nursery smelled like baby powder and freshly laundered linen. She sat down in a rocker for a moment, enjoying the gentleness and peace in the room. In the soft glow from the night-light, Mackenzie thought life could probably never get better than this.

She thought about Justin kissing her and about Daisy leaving his bedroom. He just didn't strike her as a dishonest man. And Daisy could be such a finagler. Suz was right: Daisy had long had her eyes on the Hanging H acreage. Set on prime real estate, near to usable roads but back far enough from town to feel private, the ranch had intrinsic value for those who might dream of large homes designed in the new architecture. Not like their traditional home now, with its quaint rooms and hidden staircase and wide window views.

This was home, full of happy memories and the misty patina of childhood dreams. The four men she'd hired would help her get the place back in shape to put on the market—there was no other way she could see to secure the future for her daughters, for Suz and even for Bridesmaids Creek. Maybe someone with money would buy the place, bring it back to its former glory, where it could once again give back to the community she loved so much.

As for Justin, she was just too close to the past to count on a man Ty had brought here for the specific purpose of rescuing her. Ty thought she needed that, but she'd do just fine on her own.

"It's not going to work, fellows." Suz stared at the four men lounging around the room, settled in leather recliners and on the huge circular sectional that, despite its age, still looked in good condition. Someone had been smoking a cigar, but Suz supposed it was likely that worse had been smoked under this roof.

With the three new guys, anything could happen. They had a bit of a wild look to them, not too long out of the heat of a war zone. Justin was his cool-cucumber self. Suz eyed him, and he eyed her in return. She didn't know the man well enough to say, but she had the feeling that cowboy wasn't a smoker. "I get the plan. I even appreciate that you've taken the time to dream something up to try to help my sister."

This she directed at Squint, Frog and Sam, as she was pretty certain Justin hadn't had any part in the idea they'd sprung on her. "My sister isn't going to get married to one of you in order to have a father for her children. She has one of those, and he's a louse, and I can tell you that even though you're offering to sign away any financial or gainful rights to the ranch, Mackenzie will never stand at an altar again. At least not in the near future, and I believe she's putting the ranch on the market as soon as you get the place fixed up. She mentioned something about wanting to be out of here by Christmas."

Sam glanced at Justin. "Do you have anything to say, or are you just going to sit there like a bump on a log?"

Justin looked at his newfound companions but didn't say a word. Suz supposed the question didn't merit an answer, and, anyway, Justin wasn't the type of man who would be pushed into any harebrained schemes.

Marrying her sister off was certainly the most foolish scheme that had been floated. "Got any more practical ideas under those Stetsons?"

Justin laughed, which she thought might be rude. Was he even trying to help her sister? At least the new guys were focused on the problem, which was dire.

"Dig out your folks' business model and records from the days of the haunted house," Justin said, stunning her.

"Well, Mr. Helpful, that's not going to work, either. My sister thinks we're moving. Not opening a business."

"Tell her it's just for this last season. Sort of a goodbye to Bridesmaids Creek." Justin's gaze gleamed, his eyes intent, and she realized he'd been working on the problem all along, just waiting for the right time to spring it.

She frowned. "With you four as ringleaders?"

"Well, we all need jobs," Frog pointed out. "And we'd like to stay here."

"I don't get what's in it for you," Suz said.

"Money," Squint said. "And this place is nice. It's kind of storybook."

"And you have your eyes on Daisy Donovan." Suz noticed none of the three new guys seemed bothered by that pronouncement, but then Frog spoke up.

"Not me. Not my type," he said, his tone certain. "I go for the real wild girls."

Wilder than Daisy? Suz wrinkled her nose, suddenly

aware that Frog was looking at *her*. Intently. Like he had something on his mind.

He wasn't suggesting that she was wild? What would make him think that? "Er—"

"Look, Daisy's a nice woman, I'm sure," Justin said, "but you fellows best cast your nets elsewhere."

"Why?" Frog demanded, his face a bit crestfallen. "We're not horning in on you. You've got a thing for the boss lady, anyone with one eye can see that—"

Frog fell silent, dead silent, at Justin's raised brow. Suz stared at the big man, ready to hear the truth. "Well, Cowboy? Do you have a thing for my sister?"

Chapter 9

Justin found himself in the hot seat unexpectedly, and he knew it was best to get off in a hurry. "Don't listen to our friends. I've learned they talk a lot but say little of importance."

"Maybe we talk a lot but say a lot of importance that you don't want to admit," Frog said.

Suz was staring at him. "You're not denying it, Justin."

"I don't have to." He met the eyes of each of his new friends, daring them to say another thing. They all looked away from him after a moment—except Suz.

"O-*kay*," Suz said. "Anyway, what we need to do is figure out how to get my sister out of her pickle. Get *us* out of our pickle," she amended. "Any and all good ideas will be considered. For the sake of my nieces."

A sideways sensation hit Justin at the mention of those four tiny dolls. They deserved more than they were going to get out of life. He didn't need little sister to spell it out for him. Deadbeat Dad was long gone, and Mackenzie and her babies would be living off their wits. Suz was a different animal altogether, obviously a tough survivor. So was Mackenzie, but she had a soft edge to her. Soft, sexy, rounded edges.

"Aw, he's not going to step up to the plate," Frog said, staring at Justin derisively. "So here's my good idea. Marry me, Suz."

Suz blinked. Justin stayed out of this new twist. If Frog wanted to get tossed back into the pond on his head by Suz, that was no concern of his.

"Marry you?" Suz scoffed. "I said come up with a *good* idea."

Justin laughed. "She has you there."

Suz got up. "Marriage isn't the answer for anyone."

Justin crossed his legs. "You're too young to be so cynical."

"Not cynical. Practical," Suz replied.

He thought she was adorable in a little sister sort of way. "I agree marriage is a bad idea."

"Yeah," she said, looking at Frog. "Any woman who would marry a man named Frog needs to have her head examined."

Justin took pity on his new buddy. "Take it easy on the man. He's just trying to help."

"Yeah," Sam said. "Does anybody think that little Jade mama might be open to a date?"

Justin shook his head. "You have to ask to find out."

"Anyway," Squint said, "you're all too chicken. Let's head into town. Hunt up some trouble."

"We're trying to solve the Hanging H problem," Justin reminded the room at large.

"Yeah, but I want to find that ornery little brunette with the loud bike," Squint said. "I like my ladies loud and wild."

"If you go for Crazy Daisy," Suz said, "you deserve everything you get."

"Looking forward to that." Squint winked at them and went out the door. Sam looked disgusted, Frog surprised. Justin shook his head. "Let's table this meeting. We'll meet again when somebody has a real idea."

"I really think," Frog said, staring at Suz like he wanted to melt into her arms, "that you should let me take you into town for an ice-cream cone, Miss Suz."

"I've got ice cream in the freezer. Sorry, Frog." She drifted out the door, and Justin looked at his buddy with pity.

"Don't be discouraged. She's got a lot on her mind," Justin said.

"Pretty sure she shot me down," Frog said, his shoulders drooping.

"It'll work out, maybe," Justin said. "Good night, gentlemen." He headed off to his room, needing to disconnect from all the angst being shared. How to save the Hanging H—if Mackenzie even wanted it saved. He thought again about the murder near the Hanging H that had ruined the haunted house, wondered if that was the reason Mackenzie didn't want to open it again.

Maybe worrying about Mackenzie was a waste of time. Could be she didn't want him thinking about her situation. Maybe she'd shoot him down as hard as Suz had shot down Frog. Those Hawthorne girls seemed pretty independent. Wild child Suz with a guy named Frog? Not a chance.

For starters, Frog had to reveal his real name if he

was going to get the girl. But Justin figured advice to the lovelorn should stay in Madame Matchmaker's capable hands, because he had no desire to get involved in small-town love affairs and soap operas.

Me? I'm going to have to get the girl the old-fashioned way.

I'm going to win her.

Mackenzie wasn't looking for another man, as Suz had pointed out. In fact, it might be easier to be Frog with his insane crush on Suz.

He'd never let long odds stop him before.

"You've got the whole thing wrong," Mackenzie told Ty a week later when she ran into him at The Wedding Diner. "You sent four bachelors to my place on purpose."

Ty looked amused. "Would you rather I sent four happily married men?"

Mackenzie glanced around the diner, remembering her father bringing her there to have lunch and a piece of cake. They'd had those father–daughter luncheons many times over the years, as he'd also done with Suz, calling them his special times with his children. Maybe he'd done it to give her mother a break from the kids, she thought fondly. She would have understood that—right now Betty and Jade were watching the quadruplets. As much as she loved her children, a mini-break was nice, too. "You won't believe this, but the last thing I want in my life is a man. I just don't have room for one."

He winked. "There is always room for the right man."

"But I didn't elect you my matchmaker," Mackenzie protested, knowing by the gleam in his eye that her friend wasn't listening to her with any remorse. "When I want a matchmaker, I'll go to Madame Matchmaker."

"I'm not stealing any business from her." Ty grinned. "As far as I'm concerned, I owe you one from the first time."

"No one could have foretold how Tommy would feel about becoming a father to four children."

Ty's expression turned dark. "Look, Mackenzie, not to rub salt in the wound, but Tommy Fields never deserved you. He'd always considered himself a hot item with the ladies. I just believed him when he said he'd changed."

She shrugged. "I don't care anymore."

"I guess you do a little," he said softly, "or you wouldn't be so annoyed about the perfectly macho specimens I put out at your ranch."

She made a face. "So you admit you were being a Nosy Ned when you put that package together and sent it my way."

"They needed a job. You deserve better choices for a father for your daughters. How am I a bad guy?" He winked at her. "Look, you're young, Mackenzie."

"Thirty."

"Young. You're beautiful, smart and talented. You deserve a great guy."

She sniffed. "Why not you?" she demanded, just to wind him up. Ty would never settle down, never.

He looked aggrieved and reached to hold her hand in his. "Your hand is warm from your coffee cup."

She raised a brow.

"Friends don't let friends marry inappropriately. And I'm so inappropriate."

She laughed. "Yes, you are."

"I would marry you, you know, if I hadn't sent you

better options," he said, his tone convincing and yet the expression on his face somehow not.

"You're such a fibber. You'll never get married."

"Nope," he said happily, releasing her hand. "But I'd call it a day and go home happy if you'd get married again."

"You realize one of those men has a thing for Daisy—"

"That's a misfire," he said, frowning. "Squint needs to have his head examined. Think he left a critical part of his brain back in Afghanistan."

"And one might be developing a thing for Suz."

He pondered that news. "Not exactly a misfire, but not exactly encouraging, either."

"That's my sister," Mackenzie said. "Speak with respect."

"I'm just saying she's young—she's not pliable."

Mackenzie laughed. "You mean she wouldn't allow you to manipulate her. I'm completely on to you."

Justin walked into the diner. Everybody turned to look at him, and Mackenzie could easily see why he'd draw attention. He was so big and tall and he carried himself well, his aura strong and commanding. Her heart jumped a little.

If she was going to think about dating again, Justin would definitely be high on her list.

He'd be the only man she'd want on her list.

"Hi," Justin said, sliding into the booth next to her. "Who are we gossiping about today?"

He was muscular and warm beside her. Mackenzie told herself to ignore the sudden hormone surge. "I believe Ty was talking about you."

Justin eyed Ty. "Matchmaking again?"

Ty laughed. "You know me too well."

"Does Madame Matchmaker know you're horning in on her area of expertise?"

"She gave me her blessings." Ty winked at Mackenzie. "I have to go. Tell your sister no go on the new guys. Those are all for you."

Ty sauntered off, paid his tab and kissed Jane Chatham goodbye. Mackenzie wrinkled her nose. "He thinks so much of himself." She noticed Justin wasn't in a big hurry to shift to the other side of the booth.

After a moment he seemed to remember where he was and moved to the other side. She kind of wished he hadn't.

"Let me ask you something," Justin said. "Is there any circumstance under which you'd rethink bringing back your family's business?"

His question stunned her. "I haven't thought about it. All my time and energy is devoted to my daughters. In fact, I need to be getting back. It's about time for their lunch."

He caught her hand. "Give me five minutes. Then I'll head back and give you a hand."

"I didn't hire you to be a—"

"Hanny."

She sighed, put her shoulder bag back down in the seat. "That's such a stupid expression. Only Ty could have thought of it."

"I like the little ladies." He looked at her. "I have the strangest sensation you don't really want to move."

"Nobody ever wants to move. Sometimes you suck it up and know that life will be good anyway."

"Yeah." He rubbed her fingers, and tiny sparks tingled inside her. She realized the diner had gone totally silent, everyone focused on them.

Oh, boy. She discreetly pulled her fingers away, then hid them in her lap.

"Sorry," he said, glancing around. "I forgot we're in BC."

For a moment, she had, too. It had felt like they were in their own world.

Which was probably not a good thing.

The people in the diner—folks she'd known all her life—slowly turned back to their meals, but the buzz around them was low and excited. Definitely the gossip bandwagon was rolling merrily along now. "To answer your question honestly and fairly, I wish I could keep the ranch for the girls. But it's precisely because of the girls that I won't."

"I get it. I really do. I grew up in Whitefish, Montana. I'll never live there." He shrugged. "Life moves on."

"It's not just that," Mackenzie began, and the diner door opened again and Daisy walked in with Frog on her arm looking like the cat that ate the canary.

"That's not right," Mackenzie said, and Justin turned to see what was going on.

"No, it's not," he said.

Daisy and Frog slid into the booth.

"Hello, boss lady," Frog said. "Justin, thanks for the afternoon off. I'm putting it to good advantage." He beamed at Daisy, who gave him such a sexy look that Mackenzie thought the napkins at the table might combust.

But then Daisy's gaze slid to Justin, and Mackenzie knew it was all a show.

Jane Chatham came over. "What can I get everyone?"

"Spice cake and an iced tea for me," Daisy said. "I

want a piece with as much frosting as you can manage, Jane."

Frog looked besotted. "I'll have the same. Not so much frosting, though."

"I'll just stick with iced tea," Mackenzie said, wishing she could take off. She would go, except that Justin was looking at her with such an intense stare that her heart pounded. She wasn't about to leave him to Daisy's wiles.

That was a terrible thought she shouldn't even be thinking.

Didn't matter. "And a piece of spice cake," she added. *Might as well go the whole mile.*

"I figured you'd be watching your weight, Micki," Daisy said, bringing up an old nickname Mackenzie had always despised.

"I'll have some pecan pie," Justin said, cutting through the sudden tension at the table. "Hot coffee with that, if you don't mind, Jane."

"You should let me tell your fortune, Justin," Jane said, and Mackenzie looked at Justin to gauge his reaction.

Which was slightly amused.

"If it comes with the pie, I might take you up on it," Justin said, his tone easy.

It hit Mackenzie that Justin was trying to fit into the ways of BC, which probably weren't like any other town he'd lived in. Mackenzie hid a smile.

"Do let her, Justin," Daisy said. "You'll be surprised what Jane can tell you."

"I don't really believe in fortune-telling and horoscopes and hocus-pocus. No offense, Jane," Justin said.

Jane smiled. "None taken. How's the family in White-fish?"

He blinked. "They're fine, thank you."

"Knee hasn't been bothering you as much, has it?"

"No, ma'am, it hasn't."

Daisy giggled. Frog looked at her as if a goddess had landed in his sphere and he couldn't quite figure out how it had happened.

"Four drinks and desserts coming right up." Jane went off, her stride all-business, as it always was. Mackenzie looked at Justin.

"She doesn't really tell fortunes as much as she reads people," Mackenzie told him.

"She listens to gossip very well," Justin said. "But what the heck. I'll play."

"Gossip?" Daisy looked adorably confused; clearly she'd decided adorable was the key to Justin's heart. "What does gossip have to do with anything?"

"I told her husband down at the feed store today that my father was having a bit of trouble on the ranch in Whitefish," Justin said. His gaze hooked on Macken-zie's. "I also mentioned that my knee was doing a lot better."

Mackenzie shook her head. "When is Ty leaving, anyway?"

"You're not going with him, are you?" Daisy asked, her tone sweetly horrified. Designed to suck up to Jus-tin's ego.

"Staying right here." He leaned back in the booth, winking at Mackenzie. "Not going any place anytime soon."

Warmth ran all over Mackenzie. She didn't look away from Justin's gaze, even though it was hot, hot,

hot. No, she didn't look away, even though Daisy and Frog were kind of gawking at the two of them. Jane dropped off their desserts and drinks, just as they'd ordered, which seemed to surprise everyone at the table.

Then Justin shocked the entire diner by reaching over and placing his cowboy hat on top of Mackenzie's head.

"Little mama," he said, "you're the sexiest thing I've ever laid eyes on, and that's a fact."

And that was the moment Mackenzie felt herself falling.

It felt unexpectedly wonderful.

"No, Frog," Daisy said, glaring past him. He'd tried to plant a kiss on her and she was having none of that, as Justin could have foretold. In the shadows cast by the declining sun just dissipating around the barn, Justin shook his head. In a minute, he'd save Frog from himself—but not quite yet. It wouldn't hurt him to figure out that he wasn't quite the gift Daisy had led him to think he was. Oh, there'd be a little bit of ego bruising, but it wouldn't last long. Frog would snap back.

Frog tried again, a bit oblivious to the fact that he was out of Daisy's league. He'd really bought into Daisy's flirtation, which was dumb. Daisy flirted with every man.

Justin walked from the barn to the house on his way inside to find Mackenzie and the babies. "Frog, I need you to change out every single lightbulb in the spotlights and the lanterns on the corrals."

His demand seemed to jerk Frog out of his Daisy spell. "All right. Night, Daisy."

"Good night," Daisy said absently.

Frog ambled off, his shoulders slumping a bit. Mackenzie came outside, looking from Justin to Daisy. "What are you doing here, Daisy?"

"I heard a piece of gossip in town that you might be reopening the Haunted H, Mackenzie," Daisy said. "I was a little surprised when Jane Chatham told me, because I know how devastated you were when that man died out here. They never figured out what happened to him, did they?"

Mackenzie's face turned pale as the moon. Daisy looked pleased with herself.

"That was ten years ago, Daisy." She turned to Justin. "I got your text. You're welcome to dinner if you'd like." She closed the door, leaving Justin with Daisy outside.

"What was that all about?" Justin asked Daisy, knowing full well she had something up her tight sleeve.

"Well, if Mackenzie hadn't slammed the door in my face, I was going to tell her I'd be happy to help with the Haunted H. I'm good with kids," Daisy said, turning on the cute as hard as she could.

Daisy help Mackenzie? He doubted that. "I'm sure she got the message. Good night."

He went inside. Mackenzie sat at the kitchen table with the four babies in their carriers, gently wiping their faces. She didn't look at him.

"So," he said, going to pick up Haven—she'd already been given the cleaning treatment, so she smelled like sweet lavender. "You going to tell me what happened out here? Or are you going to let Daisy keep digging at you?"

Chapter 10

Mackenzie didn't say anything, and Justin thought he heard a sniffle, like maybe she was trying to hold back tears. He didn't know her well enough to say definitely, but Mackenzie didn't strike him as much of a crier.

Suz wandered into the room. "Here, give me Thing One," she said, trying to take Haven from him.

"Get your own Thing," he said, holding the baby against his chest so Suz couldn't get her.

Shrugging, Suz took Thing Number Two—Holly—out of her basket, kissed her and then caught a glimpse of Mackenzie's face. "Hey! Is he making you cry?" She glared at Justin. "You put Thing One back in her carrier and get out!"

"No!" Mackenzie shook her head. "I'm not crying, and nobody's putting any Things back!" She laughed, wiping her nose on a baby washcloth. "I wish you hadn't started calling the girls Things. It makes conversation really interesting."

"Yeah, well. I've been reading Dr. Seuss to the girls as part of their early reading program." She glared again at Justin. "You'd best watch yourself, Cowboy."

"Suz." Mackenzie took Heather out of her carrier and sat down to feed her. Justin couldn't bear it because that meant Hope was left with nobody to hold her, so he picked her up in his other arm. "Justin didn't do anything. I just let stupid old Daisy drag up ancient history. I shouldn't, but it happened."

"Is she still here? Because if she is, I'm going to kick her ass." Suz went to the window, but Justin had heard Daisy's motorcycle roar off a few minutes ago, saving her from the ass-kicking he had no doubt Suz could dish out. "Anyway, what's she hanging around here for?"

"She had a little outing with Frog." Mackenzie's gaze met Justin's. He got that jolt he always felt around Mackenzie and wished she'd let down her guard just an inch. An inch was all he'd need to get inside her heart.

"Daisy and Frog?" Suz came back to join them. Justin thought it was interesting that Suz looked surprised, and maybe not pleasantly. "Why would he want to take out the wicked witch of Bridesmaids Creek? Quite stupid, if you ask me. But that's a man for you." She drifted out of the room with Holly, cooing softly to her.

Mackenzie kissed the top of Heather's head. "Why was Frog hanging around with Daisy?"

"Because your sister turned him down flat as a very old pancake." Justin sighed, but the feeling of the two babies in his arms was at least comforting. "He had a momentary brain fart is the best way I can explain it."

"Frog seems to suffer from that."

"Yes, but don't tell Suz. Injured pride has been known to send a man into other arms."

Mackenzie didn't look convinced. "Weak argument."

"I'm just saying I think Daisy has strong allure. Frog's pride was dented. He folded when Daisy asked him to go running around today. But I suspect he'd rather Suz look on him with some fondness."

Mackenzie didn't say anything to that. She carried Heather from the room, and he followed. Together they placed the babies on a soft pallet in front of the fireplace, joining their sister Holly.

"You ever going to tell me about this information Daisy threw out that upset you so much?"

He sat on the sofa; she sat on the floor with her babies. He wished he dared pull out his phone and snap a photo of her. There was just nothing more beautiful than Mackenzie and those babies, a perfect four of a kind. A man could get real used to being around this little family.

"I don't like to talk about it. Suffice it to say someone died here. It made everything ugly. Before that happened, everyone looked at our children's haunted house as a wonderful, safe event. When the murderer was never found, it really hurt business. Mom and Dad held off as long as they could, and the town tried really hard to help. But the next year, attendance really dropped." She took a deep breath. "It's hard to erase such a stain, and my parents' health went down fast after that. First Dad went, and then Mom about five months later." She looked at Justin. "So, no, I'll never, ever reopen the haunted house."

"I don't blame you." He could make a little more sense of Ty's eagerness to help Mackenzie—although he was just as certain that Ty's idea of finding her a husband wasn't as brilliant as Ty thought it was. What he wanted to do more than anything was hold her in his arms, protect her from the sad memories he knew she could never forget. "How can I help you?"

"You can't." She looked at him. "But it means a lot that you want to, and I thank you for that."

He wanted to help her. Justin had never felt helpless before, but the fact was, he had nothing to offer Mackenzie. He could work at the ranch as long as she needed him, but so could the new guys. They were good men, hard workers. Eventually Mackenzie would sell the place—she'd said by Christmas.

There wasn't anything he could do for her.

She shocked him when she got up off the floor and sat next to him on the sofa, gazing into his eyes. "You don't have to rescue me. You don't have to take care of me. I know Ty sent you here on a mercy mission and I appreciate everything you've done. But I promise you, we'll be fine."

We'll be fine. Her and Suz and the angels. He glanced at the four babies on the floor, secure in their soft blankets, in the process of either practicing opening their eyelids or dozing off.

"I know you will." It was true. He wanted to kiss her in the worst way, feel her lips underneath his. Wanted to hold her in his arms. Didn't dare. Making more moves on the boss lady was no way to make her feel good about him staying around. And there was no way he wanted to leave. Mackenzie and her small, seemingly defenseless family had thoroughly stolen his heart.

A tap on the back door caught their attention, and Mackenzie went into the kitchen. Justin stared at the babies, thinking that whatever the ex hadn't seen in being a father to four daughters was completely obvious to him.

Frog, Sam and Squint walked in, following Mackenzie like puppies. "What's going on, fellows?" Justin asked.

"I—we have an idea," Sam said, and Justin thought, *Oh, no.*

"What's going on?" Suz asked, wandering in. "Sounds like Grand Central Station in here. I just started watching *Pride and Prejudice*, the 1940 version, and I can hear you over the Bennet sisters. Which is no easy feat."

She sat down cross-legged next to the blanket and picked up Holly, shooting an annoyed look Frog's way. Justin wondered if she even knew she'd done it.

"Sam has an idea," Justin said, his tone ironic. He arched a brow at Sam. "Go ahead. Share."

Mackenzie waved the men to some flowery chairs near the sofa, and they gawked at the babies.

"Four," Frog said. "I would never have believed all those babies could come out of such a little lady."

"Nice," Squint said. "Graceful even, Frog."

"Sorry." He honestly looked like he might be blushing. "I'm not always gifted with speech."

"No fooling." Suz looked pleased to get a dig in. Justin wondered if she felt more for Frog than she was letting on.

"What's your real name?" Justin demanded. "I can't go on calling you Frog. It's just all wrong," he said to the dark-haired big man.

Frog looked uncomfortable now that all the attention was squarely on him. "Francisco Rodriguez Olivier Grant. Mom was French, Dad was Spanish. They had some debate about how many relations in the family needed to be honored when I was born. Therefore, Frog. Deal with it."

Justin stared at him. "You're definitely not a Francisco."

His buddies laughed. "He's an F-R-O-G," Squint said.

"I think it's lovely," Mackenzie said quickly, and Justin gave her an appreciative look. He found himself feeling a little sorry for the big man.

"It's just a name," Suz said, and Frog perked up a bit. "They're all good names, too."

"My high school and college friends called me Rodriguez," Frog said. "It wasn't until the military that I became Frog."

Suz smiled at him. Practically batted her eyes.

"Now that we have that solved," Mackenzie said with a glance at Justin, "what idea do you want to share, Sam?"

He took a deep breath. "A cattle base, for one thing. You have enough land here to run about two dozen head. Could do milk goats, too. The whole organic thing has really taken off, and you have a great place here for opening your own organic kitchen and label."

Justin was stunned. "I didn't know you had it in you, Sam. I've misjudged you."

"Easy to do because I'm so quiet," he said, and they all hooted at him.

"Part two of the plan," Squint said, "is to consider storytelling tours. Like survival tours. People are interested in learning how to make their own cheese and raise their own organic food."

"And we'll all dress in costumes," Suz said. "I see where you're going with this."

They all looked at Mackenzie for her reaction. "I

don't know what to say," she said, and Justin could tell she was truly caught off guard. "It's actually a brilliant idea."

"It's in the early phase," Frog said. "We've been brainstorming. Once we develop a business plan, we'll bring it to you."

Suz went into the kitchen, then brought back a tray of cookies and a pitcher of milk. "All that brainstorming probably has you hungry," she said, setting the tray down on the coffee table.

Justin noticed she handed Frog a napkin, then flounced over to pick up Heather, who was starting to stir, as if she hadn't treated Frog just a little bit differently than the other men.

"I don't know what to think." Mackenzie went into the kitchen to get a bottle, brought it back and handed it to Suz. "Someone's tummy tanked out a little sooner than her sisters'."

"I know how she feels," Frog said earnestly. "I'm always hungry."

Justin looked at Mackenzie. "Any chance you could hang on to this place if a workable business model was drawn up? You're busy with the babies, but these three seem pretty eager to keep their bunks here."

"Yes, we are," Squint said. "I never imagined I'd like living in a small town, but I have to say after Afghanistan I have a whole new perspective on small-town friendly."

Justin leaned back in his chair, pondering Squint's words. He had to give the three amigos points for coming up with an idea—and maybe not even a half-bad idea—for trying to help Mackenzie and Suz out. He studied the sisters—polar opposites—and wondered how Mackenzie would feel if she knew he felt the same as the three amigos.

As if this had become sort of a home—and she was the person he wanted to come home to every night, forever.

Not long after the guys had shared their business idea, they left, and to Mackenzie's surprise her sister went with them. "You don't mind?" Suz had asked Mackenzie, and Justin said he'd stay and help put the babies to bed, so Suz had bolted out the door.

They were going into town to "hunt up trouble," as Sam said, and Suz had said trouble sounded good to her. Mackenzie wondered if Justin would have liked to go hunting trouble, too.

"You could have gone with them." Mackenzie closed the nursery door after making sure the baby monitor was on and the babies were totally settled.

Justin gave her a long look she couldn't quite read. "I could have. Didn't want to get in the way of Frog trying to figure out Suz."

She smiled as they walked back into the family room. "You really think she'll look at him twice after he was seen out with Daisy?"

"That did seem to tweak your sister a bit." He sat on the sofa, lounging, long and lean and sexy. "In fact, I'd bet that's why she so eagerly went with them tonight."

Mackenzie looked at the tray of cookies that had been polished off pretty well. "I'm going to get a cup of hot tea. Can I get you one?"

He followed her into the kitchen. "I'll take a glass of iced tea." He then proceeded to get it himself. Justin put the teakettle on to heat while she got down a tea-cup and saucer.

It struck her that she liked this, the sort of family feeling of togetherness that she felt with Justin.

"So what did you really think about the boys' idea?" he asked.

She put some loose-leaf tea into a tea ball and set it into her cup. "I'm going to think it over."

He turned her toward him. "I know you'd like to stay here, Mackenzie. When I look at this house, I think of you. It's like you're a part of it."

"Thank you." His hand lingered at her elbow for just a moment, a moment too short.

"Don't let Daisy drive you away," he said.

She hesitated. "Daisy has nothing to do with it."

"Felt like she struck a nerve today with that speech about the dead guy."

A chill ran over Mackenzie. "I don't like it, but it doesn't define whether I sell or not. It's just about finances."

"And leaving memories behind."

She studied him as he leaned against the counter, his boots crossed, his gaze on her. "Maybe. Sometimes."

He nodded. "I understand wanting a fresh start."

The kettle whistled and he reached behind her to turn it off, brushing her arm ever so slightly. He looked down at her and then lowered his mouth to hers.

Thankfully. Mackenzie didn't think she could have waited any longer to kiss Justin. He kissed her so sweetly, then turned more demanding as she melted into him. She heard a little moan, realized it was coming from her. Ran her hands around his back to hold him close—sank into his body as he devoured her mouth.

She'd never been kissed like this. *Don't stop—this time, don't stop*. She felt as though she was going to jump out of her skin if she didn't get closer to him.

Bed, she wanted to say, but her mouth wouldn't say the word. "Make love to me," she whispered, her mouth desperately getting out what she felt, and he scooped her into his arms to carry her down the hall.

He glanced at the old-fashioned four-poster bed dressed in sky blue and white. "Feminine. Just like you."

He placed her on the bed, making short work of her clothes. She just as quickly got rid of his, dying to get her hands on the muscles and tanned skin she'd watched working many times. His hands were work-rough but gentle on her, and she moaned again, pulling him into the bed with her. He stroked a strand of her hair from her face.

"You're beautiful," he told her, then kissed her, taking his time. Mackenzie closed her eyes, letting his lips work magic on her.

More magic as he held her in his arms and made long, gentle love to her. Mackenzie felt herself waking, coming to life, amazed by how much wonder a man could make her feel. Like a princess, kissed awake by a prince, Mackenzie wanted the magic to last forever.

Justin jerked awake at the sound of motorcycles roaring up the drive. Sudden baby tears and snuffles jerked him out of bed. He glanced at his watch—two o'clock in the morning. There shouldn't be motorcycles gunning outside at this hour.

"What's going on?" Mackenzie asked, sitting up, switching on a bedside lamp. "Oh, the babies are awake.

They don't usually get up this soon. All that noise must have woken them." She jumped out of bed and pulled on a robe, giving Justin a brief glimpse of bare skin he wished he could drag back to bed to kiss for a few more hours.

"I'll check out what's going on," he said. "You get the girls calmed down and I'll come help you."

"Thank you."

She dashed from the room. He'd sensed her hesitation, like she didn't want to accept that she needed his help.

He went to the kitchen door and hauled it open, prepared to give someone heck for being rodeo-loud when there were babies asleep—everyone in BC would know that it needed to be walking-on-eggshells quiet around here at this hour.

About six motorcycles wheeled around at the top of the drive—damn it, six—then drove past him, heading down the road, gunning like mad. One did a wheelie as it went by, and he recognized Daisy's long bronze hair and tight black gear.

He waited, but they didn't return. Damn them, they'd done a drive-by on purpose, either to wake the babies or to haze Mackenzie.

He went back inside, locking the door behind him. He headed straight to the nursery. Mackenzie had four unhappy little girls on her hands, and he couldn't blame them.

"Come here," he told Hope, picking her up. "Bottles or breast at this hour?"

"Bottles, I think. They're too upset from the noise." She rocked Haven, feeding her. "What was that?"

He turned on some soothing music on his phone,

Brahms's lullaby, as he popped a bottle into Hope's mouth, soothing the two remaining girls so they could relax long enough to wait their turns. "About six motorcycles."

"Daisy's gang."

"Gang?" He glanced at her. "A real gang?"

Mackenzie shrugged. "They've always hung out together. I don't know what they do exactly, but everyone calls them a gang."

Justin took that in. "She ever done a drive-by before?"

"Not like that."

He rocked Hope, who had begun to turn into a sleepy, content baby again. Mackenzie changed Haven, slipped her into bed and picked up Holly. One more to soothe. "I'll ask her not to do it again."

"I will. Thanks."

She met his gaze, her eyes determined. "You know, it's okay to accept help," Justin said.

"I appreciate your offer. But I know what Daisy wants, and I need to tell her she's not going to get it."

He could respect that. Still he wanted to protect Mackenzie and her babies all the more. "If you sell, won't she get this place eventually?"

"It's her father's conglomerate." Mackenzie stood, rubbing Heather's back with a hand to calm her. "Mr. Donovan is well-known to play dirty to get what he wants. He and his partners have made so much money chewing off the best parts of BC that they think they're invincible. I won't sell to them."

"Won't he just send in a dummy buyer?"

Mackenzie looked at him. "I'll figure it out."

He nodded. She would; she'd think of something.

"Then again," Mackenzie said, "I've been giving serious consideration to the suggestions you and the other guys have come up with."

"Yeah?"

She came to him, and, still holding the baby, leaned down and kissed him a sweet, hot one on the mouth. "Yeah. What do you think about that?"

He swallowed hard. Told himself it was time to face his future. Bad knee and all, he could handle this family. This amazing woman was basically saying she saw them as something of a partnership.

"I like it," he said, pulling her and the baby into his lap next to Hope. "I like it a lot."

Chapter 11

"This was just delivered to us by courier," Suz said the next morning, waving a large brown envelope at Mackenzie. "Or should I say served?"

A little ice slid down Mackenzie's back at the word *served*. "Who is it from?"

"A Dallas law office." Suz tore it open. "What do you know? It's a love letter from the Donovan Corporation, and your dear ex, Tommy. They have formed a dubious partnership to take over the ranch."

"How can they?" Mackenzie went to stare over her sister's shoulder.

"Because you were married to Tommy," Suz said, studying the papers. "Apparently, he feels entitled to half the ranch, which he wants to sell to the Donovan Corporation, Daisy's father, in essence."

"He never owned half the ranch," Mackenzie said.

"It wasn't in his name. And nothing came up about it in the divorce proceedings."

"Therein lies the rub." They sat down on the sofa together. Suz and Mackenzie glanced up when Justin walked in. "You're just in time," Suz said. "You might as well enjoy the next phase of the thrilling saga, Hanging H Tough, since this concerns your employment."

"It's nothing," Mackenzie said quickly.

"It's something," Suz shot back. "We're being sued by your pinheaded ex and Daisy's greedy father."

Justin sat down across from them. "Can I help in any way?"

"Well, I guess you could marry my sister," Suz said, still staring at the papers.

"Suz!" Mackenzie shook her head. "I don't think that will help. Please excuse my sister, Justin. Sometimes she has a mouth problem."

He grinned. "I'm okay with little sister."

"It says here," Suz said, "that we're behind on taxes. Is that true?"

Mackenzie's mind raced. "I don't think so, but I was in the last stages of my pregnancy at tax time, so there's a chance it slipped my mind." Horrified, she pulled out her laptop to check her records. "I guess I didn't pay them. But we're still in the grace window. I just have to pay interest on what I owed, which is a bummer but not the end of the world."

Suz looked up. "Which means Daddy Donovan has someone working in the records office if he knows we're behind by a couple of months. Dirtbag."

Mackenzie took the paperwork from her sister. "So I'll go down and pay them right now."

Suz hopped to her feet. "I'll go with you. In case there's any trouble."

"No. You stay here with the babies, if you don't mind." The last thing she needed was Suz raising hell in the tax office.

Justin stood. "I'll drive you."

She met his eyes, grateful for his calm, nonjudgmental strength. "Thank you."

"Please pop someone for me, Justin," Suz said, "if they give my sister any trouble. She's far too nice for her own good."

He laughed. "No popping will be necessary. Just a check will probably solve the whole matter."

"And then Daddy Donovan can shove this silly suit right up his—"

"Suz." Mackenzie grabbed her purse, making sure her checkbook was inside. "The babies will be up any second, but Jade and Betty are on the way. I'll be back in an hour."

"Take your time," Suz said cheerfully. "The girls and I will hold down the fort. When they wake up, we'll have a long chat about how they're not to ever fall for Daisy's—or anyone's—baloney. They have to be Hawthorne tough."

Justin walked Mackenzie to his truck and opened her door for her. "Your sister doesn't pull her punches."

"She never has. She's serious when she says she'd pop Robert Donovan a good one. And nothing good can come of spitting in your enemy's eye." She wasn't being entirely honest—she was so steamed with Tommy right now that were she to run across him, she certainly would pop him a good one. The man had no scruples.

The fact that he planned to rob his own daughters' of their birthright inflamed her.

"You're quiet. You sure you're all right?"

She tried to gather her temper into a neat, tidy ball. "I'm furious, to be honest."

"You're quiet about it. Suz is loud." He reached for her fingers, held them in his warm, comforting hand. "Maybe her idea is worth considering, Mackenzie."

"What id— Oh, no, Justin. Suz was teasing about us getting married. Actually, she was being annoying." Could this get any more embarrassing? She didn't think so. He clearly felt her circumstances were so dire that he had to sacrifice himself, which was noble, but he didn't know that she could survive the Donovans. "You working at the ranch is enough. Everything else you're doing is beyond the call of duty. Please don't let all the Bridesmaids Creek fun and games get to you."

He released her fingers after a moment. Didn't say anything. Mackenzie looked out the window, her hands tight on her purse, furious with Daisy and Tommy more than Mr. Donovan. Daisy and her gang riding through the ranch last night, deliberately trying to create a ruckus and wake the babies, had been the last straw.

She wasn't going to put up with being harassed out of the home that was her daughters' birthright—if they wanted it.

Of course they would—they'd love growing up at the Hanging H just as she and Suz had.

"The Donovans and Tommy Fields aren't getting my house," she said, and Justin laughed.

"That's my girl."

Mackenzie blinked. His girl? How did that work?

Wasn't he Mr. Never-Settle-Down? "I hope you know what you're letting yourself in for."

He wore a confident, amused smile just shaded by his cowboy hat, and Mackenzie slid her fingers back into his, just to let him know he'd best beat a hasty retreat now while he had a chance.

His fingers tightened on hers.

Suz saw Frog and Co. across the way, and since Jade and Betty were already in the house cooing at the babies, she struck out to chat up Frog. That man had the wrong idea if he thought he was going to bark up Daisy's tree. The long, tall, sturdy cowboy appealed to her, and, one day, she planned to steal a kiss from Rodriguez Grant. "Hi!" she yelled, waving at the men so they'd stop. They turned, and Frog headed her way—just as Daisy's motorcycle ripped up the drive. She pulled between them, parked her bike, got off and removed her helmet.

She was grinning at Frog with a sassy smile. "Hello, Francisco Rodriguez Olivier Grant," she said, and something inside Suz hit the boiling point. She leaped onto Daisy, pushing her down, and the two of them rolled over and over in the dirt.

"Chick fight!" Squint hollered.

"It's not a chick fight until they start pulling hair," Sam said, but Suz was too busy trying to grind Daisy and her dumb lawsuit into the ground to care. Suz was small, but she was tough—the Peace Corps had focused her—and there was no way Daisy was getting up until her hair was full of twigs and dust and her chamois skirt with the fringe was a darker shade.

She felt Frog pulling her off Daisy and she fought wildly to shake him off. "What are you doing?"

"Keeping you from going to jail, tiger." He set her on her feet behind him and let Squint help Daisy up, which Squint was only too glad to do by the mesmerized expression on his face.

"Ladies, ladies," Frog said.

"Oh, shut up!" Daisy said, abandoning all pretense of being a delicate flower. She glared at Suz. "What the hell was that for?"

Suz grinned at the mess she'd made of Daisy. "For waking the babies last night when you rode through here with your band of rowdies. Next time you pull that stunt, I'll pick you off with a well-placed BB—"

"Now, now," Frog said, covering her mouth with his hand and pulling her toward the house. "You have a nice day, Miss Daisy. Suz can't play anymore."

Suz ripped his hand off her mouth. "Have you lost your mind? That bimbo's suing my sister and me! The least I can do is make her think twice about what she's doing!"

Frog gazed at her admiringly as he dragged her into the house and into the kitchen. He retrieved a wet paper towel and proceeded to wash her face. She snatched the towel away from him. "Stop babying me."

He smiled. "I haven't babied you yet. You'll know when I do—and you'll like it."

She sighed. "You're so full of horse pucky. You had no right to stop me from doling out some just deserts on Daisy."

"I can't have you going to jail, cupcake. And that little lady is the type to press charges. You know what would happen if you went to jail?"

"I'd go to jail," Suz said, annoyed.

"And it would break my heart," Frog said.

She blinked. "Full of crap, Rodriguez."

He laughed. "You'll never know, love, unless you find out."

She had no intention of falling for his cowboy blather. "You can show yourself out."

"Yes, ma'am."

He did so, and Suz crept to the kitchen window to watch him walk away. The fellows were still standing around talking to Daisy, who was no doubt whining about the ever-so-tiny can of whup-ass Suz had uncorked on her.

Baby.

She was relieved to see Rodriguez walk a wide circle around Daisy and go into the bunkhouse.

"Smart man." *And a smart man is right up my alley.*

Justin was afraid Mackenzie was in over her head with the Donovan/ex-husband problem. Nothing good could come of the deck being stacked against her to that extent, and from the sound of things, there couldn't be a much worse posse to be after the Hanging H.

He waited while Mackenzie paid the tax bill, noting her relieved expression when she came out of the courthouse. "It's paid."

"Sorry you had to go through that." He helped her into the truck.

"It was embarrassing but nothing more." Mackenzie smiled at him. "Thanks for driving me."

He didn't say he wanted to be around in case there was a problem. His suspicion was that merely paying the tax bill wasn't going to be enough to stop Donovan and Tommy from teaming up to get Mackenzie and Suz's ranch. Back taxes had been the first look into how vulnerable the Hawthornes were. They'd find another crack to try to wedge open.

Very bad to have greedy takers in cahoots against you.

"You're going to need to consider legal counsel of your own," he said quietly, steering the truck toward the ranch.

"You think this won't be the end of the lawsuit?"

"I think that you're in a vulnerable spot and they're going to try to exploit that."

"Excuse me, but I don't feel particularly vulnerable."

He smiled. "That's good."

She sighed. "Oh, who am I kidding? You're right. The Donovans are known to be ruthless, and God knows Tommy is dumb enough to go along with anything if there's a buck involved."

He shook his head. "Wrapping up the estate for you and Suz would be a good idea. Do you have a will?"

"I'll call a lawyer. Get everything done." He felt her perk up beside him. "Monsieur Unmatchmaker will know who would be good in this situation."

He wished he felt comfortable about her asking legal advice from someone who billed himself as an unmatchmaker, but that was hardly his business. Mackenzie was vulnerable right now—any new mom would be, never mind a mom of quadruplets holding down a ranch basically on her own—but she also had a strong sense of independence. He was pretty certain she wouldn't appreciate him putting too much of his nose into her business until—if and when—she asked. She'd been recently burned by her divorce, and he didn't figure Mackenzie was all that interested in being overly advised by a man.

"Hey, what's Daisy doing here?" He pulled up the drive, surprised to see Daisy with Squint and Sam.

"Being her typical man-magnet self." Mackenzie hopped out of the truck. "Daisy, hit the road. Get off my property before I file a restraining order against you."

Justin switched off his truck right in the drive and strode after Mackenzie, whom he sensed was in no mood to be baited by Daisy. Mackenzie waved the brown envelope containing the lawsuit at Daisy.

"This isn't going to work," Mackenzie told Daisy. "I paid my tax bill. You're not going to get my ranch."

"You paid it?" Daisy looked at Justin. "Did he loan you money?"

Justin saw Mackenzie take a deep breath to contain her temper.

"Why would my employee need to loan me money, Daisy?" Mackenzie demanded.

"Everyone knows you're dead broke. Anyone would struggle with four kids. So it stands to reason—"

"Daisy, go away. Right now. I very seriously will file a complaint against you—what happened to your face?"

Justin had wondered the same thing.

"Your crazy sister happened to my face." Daisy looked to Squint and Sam for confirmation, and both men nodded.

"Suz?" Mackenzie headed toward the house.

"You put a muzzle on Suz, and I won't file charges for physical violence, whatever it's called," Daisy called after her. "I've got three witnesses."

Mackenzie turned around, marching right back to

the group. Justin steeled himself in case he was needed to protect Daisy.

"If you file anything against my sister," Mackenzie said, "you will wish you hadn't, Daisy."

"Why?" Daisy asked. "You have nothing. My father can buy and sell you all day long."

"And you think life is all about money?" Mackenzie asked.

Silently, Justin applauded this. "You'd best go, Daisy. The Hanging H is closed. You're trespassing."

Daisy glared at Justin. "I'll go, but this isn't the end of anything. Not by a long shot, Mackenzie."

Justin winced. Bad combination: Daddy's money and a spoiled brunette.

Daisy glared at all of them before she hopped on her motorcycle. "See you later, Squint, Sam."

He hauled ass after Mackenzie, who was long gone. Justin found her in the nursery, her hands on Suz's face, staring at the scratches on her sister's cheeks and arms.

"I just saw Daisy," Mackenzie said. "It looked like you won."

Suz looked pleased. "Never doubt it."

"Here's the thing," Justin said as Mackenzie hugged her sister. "I'll do the fighting from now on."

"You're a mom," Suz told Mackenzie before turning to Justin. "And you're not family. I'll do the fighting for the Hanging H."

"The next fight is going to be in a court of law." Mackenzie forced Suz to sit in a rocker. Smiling at her babies, she lifted Holly out of her crib when she started to stir. "Justin says we need to get some legal counsel, make certain everything is tied up tight."

"All of my portion can go to the girls," Suz said.

Mackenzie gasped. "Absolutely not!"

"It's not like I'm ever going to have kids." Suz glanced at Justin. "While the stork may not be finished visiting you."

Mackenzie blushed, which Justin thought was cute. She didn't look his way.

"Give me Holly," he said, reaching for the baby. "You girls have a lot to talk about. Holly and I will take a walk."

"There's no need." Mackenzie looked at him. "We're not talking anymore today. Suz needs to call up some friends and get out of the house for a change. Be a young person."

"I'll take care of your sister," Justin told Suz. "I agree with Mackenzie, though. I wouldn't make Daisy's life too miserable. We don't want her figuring out a way to have you arrested."

"The sheriff is a family friend," Suz said. "That's why the Donovans went straight to a lawsuit. They knew the sheriff's office would never bring any non-serious complaints to us. The town has been evenly split for a long time, with most folks siding with us instead of the Donovans. It chaps Daddy Donovan's big-bucks ass."

He looked at Mackenzie. She studied him for a minute, reached out to take Holly back. "You go, too."

Justin wasn't going anywhere. "I'd rather stay, if you don't mind."

Suz slipped out of the room. "I'm going into town," she called back down the hall.

"Suz is right," Mackenzie said. "You shouldn't try to fight our battles."

Justin shrugged. "I'm not fighting anything. But I'm here should you need anything."

"You've done enough." She kissed the top of Holly's

head, and Justin felt something tug at his heart. "We weren't looking for a knight in shining armor."

"Well, I'm no knight, and I wouldn't be caught dead in medieval armor." He glanced around the room at the babies suddenly stirring. Heather tried to roll over without much success—she was too young for that but she gave it her best shot, craning her neck around—Haven blew a bubble, then spit up, which Mackenzie was quick to wipe away, and Hope looked like she was about to let rip an ear-stunner. "You're sure you want me to go?"

"Yes." Mackenzie nodded, juggling burp cloths and babies. "We'll manage."

He had no doubt of that. Still, he cruised down the hall into the kitchen to give her privacy but to remain within earshot in case baby pandemonium hit a freakish level. But all sounded calm down the hall: infant wails were addressed, and he could hear Mackenzie singing and cooing to her babies.

Maybe she didn't need him. Actually, he knew she didn't, but he was hoping he fit somewhere in her life.

Mackenzie had a lot on her plate. Perhaps the best thing to do would be to give her some space. He understood needing space—if he didn't, he'd be in Whitefish right now, on his father's ranch, taking over the family business. There was no reason to do that, not with three other able-bodied brothers who were more interested in it than he was, even if the old man said Justin was his top choice to take over.

Sometimes space was necessary.

He left the house, closing the door quietly behind him.

Mackenzie was startled when the front doorbell rang, since everyone always used the back door and most people walked right in, anyway. So it couldn't be Jade or Betty, or even Daisy, who used the back door as if she were one of the close-knit circle that visited the Hanging H. Casting a quick eye over the babies to make certain they were all secure for the two minutes she'd need to be gone, Mackenzie picked up Hope and took her to the door with her.

"Who is it?"

"Robert Donovan."

"Lovely," she said to Hope. "Gird yourself for the first true annoyance in your young life." She pulled the door open. "I thought you do all your talking through a lawyer."

Robert Donovan cast a tall shadow, and he wasn't a particularly friendly-looking character, either. He had buzzed short hair—too impatient to be bothered with combing it, she supposed—and a self-righteous smirk.

"I should have called on you sooner," Robert said. "Instead of sending my request through my lawyer, for which I apologize and hope to make amends. May I come in?"

"Absolutely not."

"It's difficult to discuss what I have to say standing on the—"

"Mr. Donovan, I have four babies. I don't have time for this. Say what you came to say."

His smirk widened. Mackenzie stared at him, wondering if the man might be an idiot. She was two seconds from slamming the door when he sighed.

"I'm an old man, Mackenzie."

"That sounds like a personal problem to me."

He laughed. "Indeed. But old men like to build kingdoms."

"All well and good, but not my problem." She glanced over her shoulder, wondering if she'd heard something. One ear stayed cocked to listen for the babies. In her arms, Hope stayed very still, gazing out into the sunlight, which tall Mr. Donovan mostly obscured. "Can you get to your point?"

"I'll send all four of your daughters to private colleges or university, and pay twice the offer I made you on your property, if you agree to sell it to me by September."

"This September," Mackenzie said flatly. "Less than thirty days."

He nodded. "I'll buy all your equipment, horses and so on. And I'll buy whatever house in town you would like, in your name, if you're out before the end of September."

She'd been wanting to sell, hadn't she? Said she would? It was a generous offer, more generous than any she'd ever get for the Hanging H most likely. "What makes you think the Hanging H is for sale?"

"I heard in town you're not interested in reopening your family's business and that you've got your hands too full to run the place. Noticed you've hired on new hands." Robert shrugged. "Wanted to see if I could help you out. As you may know, I'm a generous man where Bridesmaids Creek is concerned. I try to be very civic-minded."

"If you're so generous, why didn't you make me this offer instead of roping my ex into a deal with you?"

Robert smiled. "Actually, Mr. Fields contacted me on the matter."

Mackenzie's body tightened to perfect stillness.

Hope bobbed a little in her arm. "It was Tommy's idea to file the lawsuit?"

The big man shrugged. "I generally prefer to work things out in person. Mr. Fields seemed to believe that as you'd parted on poor terms, as I believe he put it, the professionalism of legal papers would be a better instrument to conduct business."

That rat bastard. No scruples at all at trying to take his own daughters' inheritance.

"Mr. Donovan, the Hanging H isn't for sale. I'm not overwhelmed, contrary to what you might have heard." Mackenzie took a deep breath. "You're not the only one who likes to help out Bridesmaids Creek. My family spent many years building up this town, as you know, even though you only came here when Daisy was what? Two, three years old?"

Robert Donovan hated to be reminded that he wasn't born and bred BC, despised knowing that the town still considered him an outsider in spite of his money and the weight he liked to throw around.

"Daisy and Suz were in class together," Mackenzie said. "I remember it well when she came to the haunted house that year. She was afraid of the puppets, and one of the chickens pecked her finger and made her cry. City girls don't see that many chickens, of course, and she didn't know not to pull its feathers. But she's grown up a lot since then." Mackenzie kissed the top of Hope's head. "I do appreciate you stopping by and discussing your offer in person." She shook her head. "But if I were you, Mr. Donovan, I'd avoid doing business with Tommy Fields. No matter what he tells you, I'm difficult to deal with on any terms, whether legal instruments or face-to-face."

He looked frozen, not certain how to proceed.

She took another deep breath. "And the Haunted H will be open for business by October, so you're welcome to spread that news all over Bridesmaids Creek."

Mackenzie closed the door and walked into the kitchen, where she knew Justin would be sitting.

"I knew it was you I heard," she said. "Eavesdrop much?"

"I eavesdrop a lot, particularly when black Bentleys pull into your drive." Justin grinned. "Opening the Haunted H, huh?" He reached out to take Hope from her, snuggled her in his arms. "Your childhood just changed, sugar. You're going to grow up with a mother who runs a haunted house. How cool is that?"

Mackenzie shook her head and went to check on the other babies.

Cool? He had no idea.

Chapter 12

"I don't know what got into me, but I know it's the right thing to do, if all of you believe it's a good idea to bring the Haunted H back," Mackenzie told the people gathered in her kitchen. "I realized that this ranch isn't just mine—it's Bridesmaids Creek's, too. A lot of people have happy memories of this place, and I want my daughters to share those, as well as your children and grandchildren."

She pushed away the only bad memory she had of the Hanging H and looked at Frog, Sam, Squint, Suz, Jade, Betty and plenty of other townspeople who had showed up for the meeting.

"We'll all help," Jane Chatham said. "Let's open on a Sunday night, when our shops and diners are closed in town, so we can all be here. I, for one, look forward to celebrating the grand opening!"

"Good idea," Madame Matchmaker said. "Let's start small, get our feet wet. Not overpromise at first. It took your parents years to get the Haunted H built up to being the best children's harvest fun around."

"Agreed. Good idea." Mackenzie nodded. Suz grinned, delighted by Mackenzie's change of heart, and waved Haven's fist at her mother. Justin held Hope, Monsieur Matchmaker had Heather tucked into his arms and, for some reason Frog had ended up with Holly. Since Frog was wedged in as tight to Suz as he could get, maybe it wasn't all that surprising he'd ended up with a baby.

"What about the dead man?" Daisy's voice called from the back. "No report was ever filed on how he died. How do we know that doesn't happen again? It was a real black eye on Bridesmaids Creek, and we don't want another, bigger, black eye."

The room went deathly silent. A dark cloud seemed to rush past Mackenzie's eyes. "Why would anyone else die here?"

"We never knew what killed him. Could have been food poisoning. Could have been murder," Robert Donovan said.

Since she'd opened the meeting to anyone in BC who might be interested in learning more about the Haunted H reopening, Mackenzie wasn't all that shocked that the Donovans had showed up. Justin winked at her, fortifying her resolve.

"Food inspections are done routinely. It wasn't food poisoning."

"I'll say it wasn't!" Jane Chatham hopped to her feet. "Since my restaurant provides fifty percent of the food that comes to the haunted house, I sure hope you're not accusing me, Daisy Donovan!"

"Nor my cooking," Betty Harper said. "If Jane does half, I'm sure I contributed around twenty percent. Most of my ingredients are organic or grown by me and prepared by me." She stared around the room. "There's not a person in this room who has ever complained of food problems from my cooking!"

"Someone killed him," Robert said, throwing his weight around as usual. "And it didn't take too much digging to find out that the cause of death was undetermined on the death certificate."

"How would you know?" Sheriff Dennis McAdams said. "Death certificates can only be ordered by the family. Cause of death is private."

Robert sniffed. "Reporters dug that information up, Sheriff. Be fair. You've been covering for the Hawthornes long enough."

Mackenzie frowned. "Excuse me, no one covers for the Hawthornes. We pull our own around here."

"You're just mad," Suz piped up, "because we won't sell to you. Isn't that harassment or something, Sheriff?"

"There's probably a good case for it." Sheriff McAdams looked unimpressed by the Donovans' claim. "That man who died here was an out-of-towner, an unfortunate soul with no kin to claim him. The autopsy revealed nothing. Not sure what you're working at, Robert."

"Just saying that there was a stain on this place ever since that day, and everybody here knows it." Robert sat down, pleased with the trouble he'd caused.

"Anyway," Mackenzie said, refusing to let him get to her. "I want to open this to a vote. No one has to like the idea or participate. I'm doing this for my daughters, but if our town doesn't like the idea, if it no longer fits the needs of Bridesmaids Creek, I'm just as happy to be simply a mother and not the owner of an amusement park."

"All in?" Sheriff McAdams asked, and all hands went up but the Donovans' and their cronies'.

"Fine, fine. We're back in business, friends," Sheriff Dennis exclaimed.

Mackenzie met Justin's gaze, startled to see him smiling at her as he'd abstained from the vote. She'd expected that—he wasn't from here, and no matter what he said, he might not stay—but she felt his support, and it warmed her.

After the guests left, Justin waved and headed out the back door, as well. She hated to see him leave as she peeked out the window at him. Watched Daisy accost him, doing her best to crack his armor. Justin shook his head at her before he headed into the bunkhouse.

Daisy turned around, catching Mackenzie spying on her. Daisy glared and Mackenzie waved cheerfully, then went to check on her babies, still smiling.

Justin walked into the bunkhouse, his mind completely on the meeting that had just been conducted and the warmth he'd realized the town felt for Mackenzie and Suz. Favored daughters, for sure.

He'd never been a favored son, so seeing it in real life made him a little wistful for the family situation he didn't feel that he'd ever had—except for rodeo. Rodeo had been a different kind of family, but it had been all he'd had. It had sufficed.

Ty walked into the bunkhouse, slapped him on the back. "Mooning?"

"Have you ever known me to moon?" Justin demanded, returning the greeting. "Why are you here again?"

"BC is my home. You know that. I came to check on the boys." He glanced around. "Where is everyone?"

"Off working or finding trouble." Justin didn't really care. Sam, Squint and Frog had proved themselves able and hard workers. He didn't keep too close an eye on them.

"So you're happy with them."

He shrugged. "Sure. I don't think Mackenzie would have reopened the Haunted H without them being here."

Ty nodded. Grabbed himself a beer out of the fridge. "I've got a message to pass along from your family."

"Why?" Justin barely glanced his way. "Can't they call my cell?"

"It was just an offhand thing. I was out there doing some horse trading—"

"Stirring up trouble."

Ty shrugged. "I did need a new horse. And your father and brothers have the best around."

"I don't know anything about that."

"Yeah, you do. You can't go on being the rebel forever."

"Sure I can, if being a rebel means staying away from a place where you're not really wanted."

"Yeah, about that." Ty took a long drink of his beer. "Your dad's not doing too good. He didn't say it, but I think he wishes your mother would at least take a phone call from him."

"Can't help you much, old buddy."

"Justin, it's your dad. If you went home, you could set a lot right."

Justin fell into the nicely worn leather sofa, eyeing his friend. "Look, you brought me here. This was all your idea."

"Yeah, because Mackenzie needed help, and you needed a job. You were never going to rodeo again."

That stung more than it should have. "I'm twenty-seven. You don't know what might happen." He knew exactly what was going to happen. His knee injury was severe enough that surgery might fix it, but there'd be no guarantees of how stable it would be. He'd never rodeo again.

"But getting you on here wasn't a way to keep you away from your family. Now that you're not rodeoing anymore, they'd like to see you."

"You mean now that they've forgiven me for not staying to work the family business?" Justin shook his head. "I'm fine here." He wasn't about to leave Mackenzie and the babies just because his father had decided he finally wanted to acknowledge the prodigal son.

"You might think about it. No one is getting any younger, and you're not exactly barking up Mackenzie's tree. Believe me—I had high hopes on that," Ty said with a sigh. "But things would have happened between you by now if it was meant to be."

"Wait a minute." Justin glared at him. "You don't know that nothing's happened."

"Suz says it hasn't."

Great. Chatty little sis. "Let me worry about my personal life, okay? One thing has nothing to do with the other."

"Okay." Ty gave a melodramatic sigh. "Are you sure you're not bothered by the age thing?"

Justin blinked. "What age thing?"

"You know." Ty waved a hand in grandiose fashion. "You're twenty-seven. Mackenzie's thirty. She's already got four kids and you might want one yourself and she may have had enough of pregnancy."

"You're riding down a ridiculous road right now, bud."

"It all weighs on a man, I'm sure."

"I'm fine," Justin growled. "The reason nothing's happened is because the woman has plenty on her plate. Why do you think she's looking for a husband? To be honest, that seems like the last thing she wants."

"You have to change her mind."

"No, I don't," Justin said. "And you seriously need to butt out."

"All right," Ty said. "Don't say I never tried to help."

"There's help and then there's being freaking annoying."

Ty laughed. "So, Daisy and Frog, huh?"

"I doubt it very seriously. The lady in question is hot to trot for any man who may look her way. And if I didn't know better, I'd think Frog has eyes for Suz. But what do I know? I'm a cowboy, not Madame Matchmaker." He perked up. "I still think she'd be unhappy if she knew you were operating solo on this gig."

Ty laughed. "I have my marching orders from Madame Matchmaker—believe me."

Justin studied his friend. "Are you saying the two of you are working together?"

"You haven't been in BC long enough to know how things work, but this town is a team, old buddy. And once you're in the team's crosshairs, you're probably going down. Loner, rebel, family issues, financially independent, moody," Ty ticked off. "Then there's hardworking, determined, stubborn, good friend, loyal, daredevil. Catnip around here."

"BC's matchmaking is nothing more than coincidental. No more real than Jane Chatham's fortunetelling." Justin laughed. "Or that business about ladies swimming in Bridesmaids Creek and finding their soul mate."

"Okay, that one's a stretch. It's really just a charity function. But we like to see the gals in their bathing suits. And the week before it happens, we get everybody together to clean up the creek and we test the water. It serves many purposes, so don't critique our ways."

"I'm not." Justin held up a hand. "Just trying to figure out why BC runs so much on lucky charms and rabbits' feet."

"Don't knock it until you try it." Ty went to the door. "Be sure to call your father and brothers at some point They're ready to hear from you."

He wasn't ready to hear from them.

"Do you know Suz is out there sucking face with Frog?" Ty suddenly whispered.

"I don't care."

He slapped Ty on the back, a brotherly pat, hardly anything at all. Ty coughed and said something about friends shouldn't damage other friend's lungs. Shaking his head, Justin went outside, where he saw Mackenzie loading the van with her babies.

He strode to help her, lifting the carriers into the van, securing seat belts, tucking in blankets. Holly and Haven writhed around, not happy to be stuffed in a car seat and placed backward; Heather looked around at whatever she could focus on. Hope fell right asleep, unconcerned.

"An outing for the girls?" Justin asked.

"Yes. I've taken the idea under advisement that I need to secure my paperwork for my daughters' future." She looked at him. "Now that we've definitely decided to stay."

"I was glad to hear you say it in the meeting." Relieved had been more like it. He couldn't bear the thought of this little family heading off without him, because it was for sure that wherever they went, they wouldn't need a foreman.

Which meant he had some thinking to do. Justin looked at Mackenzie. Her eyes were on him, and all he could think of was how badly he wanted to kiss her.

So he did.

Gently, softly, he kissed Mackenzie's lips, kissing her again and again when he felt her lips moving against his, seeking the same response he was looking for.

Then, to his disappointment, Mackenzie turned away. "I have to go, Justin."

After getting in the car, she switched it on, looked at him one last time and drove away.

She was fighting it hard. That was clear.

But why?

Chapter 13

"We hear that handsome cowboy is living with you," Jane Chatham said after helping her settle the babies in The Wedding Diner. They sat in a quadruple row of darling, and Mackenzie couldn't believe they had a father who wanted to take everything away from them. "Of course, I told everyone that wasn't true," Jane continued.

Mackenzie stared at Jane, stunned. "Why would people think that?"

"Probably because he's a hunk with your name written all over him. Maybe they're hoping for a wedding in this town." Jane smiled. "Most likely, folks want you to be happy. Everyone knows Tommy's been giving you a rough road."

"How is my name written on Justin?"

"I think it's the way he watched your every move in

that meeting. He's the real reason you're reopening the place, isn't he?"

Mackenzie shook her head. "My decision is about my daughters. And Suz. I know Suz can take care of herself, but the Hanging H is still her home and she wanted to remain there. Just about the easiest way I know to do that is to do what I know best, running a circus."

Jane smiled. "We'll all help you."

"Thank you."

"But you have powerful enemies in this town," Jane said, her voice suddenly changing. Mackenzie had heard that tone before. An icy premonition tickled at her.

"Enemies who would rather see the Hanging H burn than come back to life," Jane said softly. Mackenzie gasped and grabbed Jane's wrist. Jane jumped, her eyes settling on Mackenzie.

"Gracious! I've left you sitting with no tea and no cake, Mackenzie." Jane hopped up from the booth. "I got so excited to see the babies I forgot about serving you. Please excuse me!"

She hurried off, not taking Mackenzie's order, because she wouldn't have, anyway. But she also didn't remember a word of her warning, because that was how Jane's visions worked. She literally didn't remember having visions sometimes.

But Mackenzie would never forget it. Jane's words slid through her memory like an icy wind. Her premonition was too terrible to contemplate. Surely Daisy and her gang of rowdies wouldn't burn down the Hanging H just to make sure it never came back to its former glory.

But even she knew anything was possible.

Jane set a piece of frosted strawberry cake and a glass of iced tea in front of her. Mackenzie knew she couldn't eat a bite. She sipped at the tea, trying to clear the fear from herself. The babies lay still for the moment in their carriers, and Jane bent down to coo over them.

"You young ladies have no idea how much fun you're going to have as you grow up. It's not many kids who get to grow up in a true haunted house!"

Jane must be wrong. The Donovans didn't want the Hanging H enough to get it by foul means.

She remembered Robert Donovan with his astounding offer to take care of the girls' education, to buy her a home, and she swallowed hard. Jane knew everything. She'd been born here, as her mother and her grandmother had. The names of the first settlers who established and named Bridesmaids Creek were on a stone in the courthouse, and one of those names was Eliza Chatham, Jane's great-great-great-grandmother. "Why do you think Robert Donovan wants the Hanging H so badly?"

"It's very valuable real estate due to its location," Jane said without hesitating. "He's planning big things for Bridesmaids Creek."

Mackenzie sat very still. "Some of which we've managed to thwart."

"Yes, but he's still bought up a lot of Bridesmaids Creek establishments and land just the same." Jane smiled when Holly grabbed on to her finger. "Your ranch just happens to be the crown jewel."

She blinked. "How?"

"Mineral rights, I'd say. You've heard about all the new shale drilling going on." Jane got up. "There's some theory that your land might hold some undiscovered secrets. You should consider making certain the mineral rights to your land are held by you and nothing that Tommy can lay claim to."

"Tommy!" Mackenzie shook her head. "We weren't married long enough for him to have a claim. The divorce is final. He can't sue me for anything." Her mind whirled. "What else should I know?"

"That your cowboy has dubbed himself something of your protector, and that's nothing to sneeze at," Jane said and went off to serve some customers.

Mackenzie looked at the strawberry cake. Beautiful and no doubt tasty as always, but Mackenzie couldn't eat it.

Justin considered himself her protector? She didn't need a protector.

Who was she kidding? She needed all the friends she could get. And a man who really seemed to want to help take care of her ranch—wasn't that almost a fairy tale come true?

Daisy was waiting for her on her porch when she got home. Mackenzie lifted the carriers from her van and set them on the ground, trying hard not to wish that Daisy would simply turn into a toad and hop away.

She came over to help her carry the babies inside instead.

"It wasn't my idea to go after your land when you fell behind on your taxes," Daisy said as she carted Haven inside.

Mackenzie wished she had four arms so she could carry all her babies at once. She really didn't want Daisy near them, though she supposed she was being terribly ungrateful. But Daisy never gave without taking, and what she took usually left you with a painful hole somewhere. "You don't have to help. Thanks."

"I want to. I wish I had a baby." Daisy went back for Heather and set her inside the den beside Haven as Mackenzie toted Hope and Holly. The babies set up a huge wail, Hope spit up and Mackenzie had a strong urge to create a little mayhem herself.

"Look." Mackenzie sighed and tended to Hope's dirty dress. "It doesn't matter about the lawsuit. I'm just back from my lawyer's office, and the ranch and all its holdings are airtight and in no danger, from your father or Tommy or you. So, if you don't mind, please go away. I have a million things to do, and sparring with you isn't going to be part of the game plan."

Daisy looked at her as she went to the front door. "You know, when we were growing up, I always wished I was you and Suz. You had everything. You still do."

Mackenzie frowned. "What are you talking about?"

"You had two parents who loved you. A haunted house that was all anybody in Bridesmaids Creek ever talked about." Daisy shook her head. "You and Suz were like princesses."

Mackenzie had certainly never felt like a princess, and she knew Suz would laugh out loud at such a notion. "Your father wouldn't try to buy this ranch just because you want it, would he?"

"Of course not." Daisy shrugged. "Dad doesn't discuss his business deals with me. But I think he'd heard through the grapevine that you wanted to sell. He was trying to help you out, like he would a charity or a struggling business."

Mackenzie's eyes went wide. Suz came speeding into

the den, Justin not far behind. He came to stand beside Mackenzie, his warmth comforting.

"It's true," Daisy said. "You Hawthorne girls always had everything."

She left with a lingering, almost inviting, glance at Justin. He looked down at Mackenzie, searching her eyes, gauging her mood.

"Okay, Miss Fussbucket," Suz said, bending down to pick up Holly and comfort her. "Gracious, ladies, the wicked witch is gone. You can all relax and stop crying. Uncle Justin can't stand to see a woman cry."

"That's right," he said softly. "You're not going to, are you?" he asked Mackenzie.

"Of course not." She went to wash Hope up, trying to settle her nerves. Darn Daisy, anyway—always looking for a way to get under someone's skin.

And yet something about her story had rung so true, so honest.

"So what was Daisy doing here?" Suz demanded when she returned with a fresh dress on Hope. "Doing what Daisy does best, showing that the apple really doesn't fall far from the old tree?"

"You need a Daisy alarm," Justin said, bringing baby bottles from the kitchen. "She sat on the porch for an hour waiting on you. I couldn't convince her that you'd gone to visit family in another state."

"Because we don't have family in another state," Suz said. "Nice try. Unlike Daisy, we've been in BC since we first saw daylight."

Mackenzie sat on the sofa and picked up a bottle to start feeding Hope. "I think that's part of Daisy's problem. She claims she was always jealous of us."

"The girl who has it all? I doubt it." Suz plunked

down with Heather and grabbed a bottle from Justin. "Don't let her work on you. You know that's what Daisy does best, gnaw away at something until it finally cracks."

Mackenzie smiled at Justin as he carried Holly to the window to check the front of the house. "We could turn the tables on her. Include her."

Suz's jaw dropped. "Include her in what?"

"The planning and setup for the haunted house. Put her in charge of a committee." Mackenzie caught Justin's expression and had a sudden flash memory of his kiss that morning. Jane's words about the handsome cowboy living with her made her look away.

What a silly rumor.

"Jane had a vision while I was at The Wedding Diner today," Mackenzie said, and Justin made what sounded like a scoffing noise.

"Oh?" Suz perked up. "I hope it was a juicy one!"

"You don't really believe in that nonsense," Justin said. "Isn't that just another way to sell Bridesmaids Creek's many tales of make-believe? Kind of like the small towns who rely on their ghost stories and sightings for tourist trade?"

Suz gasped. "Justin! Those are practically fighting words in BC! Our livelihood depends on our small-town charms!"

He looked at Mackenzie, who shrugged. "It was a real vision." There was no mistaking it when Jane went into a trance.

"So? So?" Suz prompted.

"She said the Hanging H is going to burn to the ground," Mackenzie said.

The babies all set up a tremendous wail, despite their bottles, almost like a sudden attack of four-way colic.

"Gosh!" Suz scrambled to grab Haven, who'd been so patient about waiting her turn. "You'd think they knew what we were talking about!"

Justin's mouth was set in a firm line the next time Mackenzie looked up. It had taken a full five minutes to calm the babies, but what Jane had seen still hung in the air, a specter that probably wasn't going to go away anytime soon.

"Look," Justin said slowly, "I'm no expert on BC. But I don't believe in spells or magic or visions. A bull rider might be superstitious, sure, but most of the time he's thinking about winning, not getting crushed under a bull. He can't afford to think about negative karma. I think it's best if you don't let word become deed, in Jane Chatham's case." He shrugged. "Not that my opinion counts for anything."

Suz's eyes were wide. "It is a terrible thought, Mackenzie."

She felt horrible that she'd brought it up. She'd just wanted so badly to get it off her mind, out of her head and into the daylight where it could be laughed away.

It just wasn't a laughing matter.

"It's okay," she said quickly, wanting to soothe the horrified look from Suz's eyes. "I shouldn't have told you."

"Of course you should have," Justin said, crossing back to the window. "Because you can't handle everything yourself. That's what friends are for, to share the load."

"That's right," Suz said. "We can't let Daisy and Jane and other people deter us from our goal, which is to bring the Hanging H back to all its wonderful splendor. I think Mom and Dad would be proud of us, don't you?"

Mackenzie looked at her little sister. In spite of her worldliness, Suz would always be her best friend and her connection to the family they'd once been. Suz was tough, but she could also be that child who tagged along after her big sister looking for reassurance. She remembered the scare when Suz had fallen from a tree, breaking her arm, and the late-night run to the emergency room in Austin when Suz had come down with meningitis. It had been so scary, such a frightening time. Mackenzie had been terrified she might lose her only sibling—the tiny baby her parents had brought home one day and allowed her to name. Betty Harper had come to babysit Mackenzie while her parents had taken Suz to the hospital, and Jade had comforted her, telling her she'd always be her friend.

Mackenzie caught Justin's gaze on her, and she needed desperately to change the subject. "Jane isn't all about visions. She also mentioned some folks in town seem to think you're living with me."

"Oh?" He raised a brow, seemed amused.

"I just mention it in case you're worried about your reputation."

He laughed. "A lot of BC gossip tends to be about this place, doesn't it?"

"It's not surprising when it's a onetime haunted house and one of the owners has four children all at once. Tends to make folks talk," Suz said practically.

He shook his head and turned away. Mackenzie caught him smiling, though. The only reason she'd brought the rumor up was to get his reaction and test that rebel reputation he held so dear.

"Guess I'd have to be pretty thin-skinned to worry about a rumor," Justin said.

"One never knows how a man feels about being the subject of such a rumor," Mackenzie said, knowing she sounded prim.

Suz laughed. "Men love it when ladies talk about them. Justin has all kinds of a reputation in town for being a major ladies' man."

Mackenzie stared at her sister. "How do you know that?"

"Because people don't just gossip about the Hanging H," Suz said. "They also gossip about newcomers. And the newcomers du jour are Justin and the three hunks we've hired on. Justin's right about this place being a gossip factory." Suz kissed the baby she held as she looked at Justin. "I've heard everything from you're married, to you didn't really leave the circuit because of your knee but because your heart was broken by a cheating fiancée, to—"

Suz's teasing words came to a stop. Justin's expression had turned grim. He put his baby gently onto the pallet, astonishing all of them, and walked out of the room. They heard the kitchen door close.

"Gosh! Was it something I said?" Suz asked.

Apparently so. But clearly Justin wasn't about to deny any of the rumors.

Chapter 14

Ty strolled into the kitchen the next day, pretty much grinning from ear to ear.

"Why are you so disgustingly happy?" Suz demanded.

"Life is good. Why shouldn't I smile?" Ty glanced at the four babies Suz and Mackenzie had put in the kitchen in a playpen while they did some baking. It was never too early to begin baking and freezing the treats the Haunted H was known for. "Anyway, I heard the big meeting is being held here today to discuss opening this joint back up."

"You missed it by a day," Mackenzie said, slightly miffed with Ty. The way Justin had lit out last night made it obvious that he wasn't the no-strings-attached bachelor Ty had portrayed him as—which was worrying, since Mackenzie recognized she'd begun falling for her foreman. "How does it feel to know that your usually sterling gossip line has failed you?"

Confusion crossed Ty's face. "The meeting was yesterday?"

"Yes, it was. And we are open for business," Suz said. "Do you want an assignment? We could put you in charge of the petting zoo. Maybe the carriage rides or the toss-the-water-balloon-at-the-clown game. That would be my choice for you."

Ty sank onto a barstool. "You can't reopen."

Mackenzie looked up from diapering Hope. "Why not? Everyone who was here for the meeting voted the idea in unanimously. They're looking forward to bringing tourists back here. Except for the Donovans, obviously. They were 'no' votes, but they don't count."

"I get it," Ty said. "But Justin's leaving."

"We don't need Justin," Suz said. "We can stand on our own two feet."

"What do you mean, Justin's leaving?" Mackenzie demanded, her heart skipping a beat.

"He called last night. Said he was ready to take me up on my offer. I'm here to pick him up. Didn't you know?" Ty asked, looking at her closely.

"Like any employee, Justin's free to give notice whenever it suits him," Mackenzie said, fibbing through her teeth so Ty wouldn't know how stunned she was. She felt Suz's stare on her.

Ty shifted uncomfortably. "He didn't sound too good when he called. He sounded like he had a lot on his mind, needed to unwind."

"Justin's personal affairs are his own business," Mackenzie said, dying a little inside.

"You're not as smooth as I thought you were," Suz told Ty, who looked a little disturbed by this news.

"If you'll both excuse me, and keep an eye on the babies," Mackenzie said, "I'm going to go hunt up my foreman. I'll let him know you're here."

She went out the door, heading across to the barns, anger carrying her boots across the dirt-and-stone path quickly. Justin was in the paddock behind the barn, working with a large chestnut. Mackenzie went up to him slowly so she wouldn't startle the horse.

"Ty's here."

"Great. Thanks." He patted the horse on the neck, praising it for its good work. "Listen, about yesterday, I want you to know that none of that gossip Suz was teasing me about is true."

He walked the horse to the barn, and Mackenzie followed. "Is that why you're leaving? Because of the gossip?"

Justin shook his head. "I'm not going anywhere."

Mackenzie stopped, eyeing him as he hosed the horse down. "Ty says you called him to say you're ready to hit the road again."

Justin nodded. "I'm ready to help him out. But I have no intention of leaving anytime soon." He glanced at her. "Did you think I was leaving? Is that why you came out here with a full head of steam? I could tell by the starch in your march that you were pissed about something. Had no idea it was me." He grinned. "On the other hand, I kind of like the idea that it would matter to you if I left."

"Of course it would matter. You're the foreman."

He nodded. "Okay."

She put her hands on her hips. "Were you testing me? My feelings?"

"No. I think I know what your feelings for me are."

He couldn't possibly know. She didn't even know herself, not anything she could admit out loud, to him or anyone else. "What do you think my feelings are?"

Justin shrugged. "You don't trust a relationship enough to allow yourself to fall into one right now. So just about anything I do, anything you feel for me, won't be enough to change your mind."

Mackenzie caught her breath. She'd expected anything but his stark assessment—which hit so close to the truth she didn't know what to say. She watched as he put the chestnut in its stall. "So you're leaving because of me?"

He came out, peering back in at the horse, who was now munching hay, then turned to face Mackenzie. "Not today, not for a while. But it's for the best."

She stared up at him. "I don't know what to say."

He touched her face, gently stroking a finger down her cheek. "There's nothing to say."

That was also uncomfortably true. Mackenzie nodded. She wished it were different, but he was right. She wasn't in a place right now to fall headlong in love. She couldn't allow herself to do it. There were the babies to consider—if she was going to get involved in a relationship, it would be with a man who would be a good father to her daughters—and there was the ranch to think about.

"It's all right," Justin said. "I understand more than you think I do. And if you want me to leave sooner, I can. No questions asked."

She shook her head. "Of course not. You're an important part of the ranch."

"I'm training my backup as fast as I can," he said, his tone a little teasing, but Mackenzie didn't smile.

"Frog, Sam and Squint are nice and they're hard workers." She looked into his eyes. "I'd like to keep you on as long as you're comfortable staying."

"I'll help out until October. That's when Ty's planning to hit the road looking for recruits."

Ty had done this—he'd brought a man here he knew she might find irresistible. When she didn't fall fast enough, he'd sent three more to sweeten the pot, which had only made Justin seem even more appealing by comparison.

She'd fallen for Justin, whether she wanted to admit it or not.

"Can I ask you a question?" Justin said.

"Sure." She gazed up at him, wondering if it would be any easier to say goodbye to him in a few weeks than it would be today.

It wouldn't.

"Did you believe any of that silly gossip Suz brought home? That bit about me being married or having a broken heart or something?"

She couldn't look away from the intensity in his eyes. "I didn't know."

"You don't trust me." He touched her cheek again. "I'm sorry that you don't."

It was true—she'd been upset because she'd been afraid something in the rumors meant that he wasn't the man he appeared to be. They'd never discussed personal issues—for all she knew, he'd had a love life he didn't want to discuss. The fear had worried her, slicing into her feelings for him.

She couldn't deny the gossip had hit her hard. Justin was right: she hadn't trusted him, hadn't trusted the lovemaking they'd shared.

After a long look into her eyes, Justin nodded, turned and walked out of the barn.

Mackenzie went back to the house, the babies and the baking, her heart splintered and ragged.

Squint, Frog and Sam were gathered around the babies on the floor, playing with them and gazing up at Suz, who was too busy rolling out dough to pay attention to their adoring looks.

Suz was totally oblivious to the heartsick look on Frog's—Suz called him Rodriguez only—face. She would never believe he cared about her after she'd seen him out with Daisy. Mackenzie grabbed the basket of cookie cutters and began pressing them into the dough.

"You're stabbing it," Suz complained, removing the heart-shaped cookie cutter from her sister's hand. "It requires a delicate touch, and that's something you don't have today. You can press cookies tomorrow when you're not taking your mood out on the poor dough. You do the sprinkles. And make them colorful and happy, not dark and moody."

"Moody?" Frog said. "You moody, Mackenzie? How can anyone be moody looking at these little princesses?" He cooed at the babies like a pro. Suz stared down at him, astonished.

"Get up, Rodriguez. You're making me nervous," Suz said. "You're sounding uncomfortably fatherly."

Mackenzie smiled until she saw Daisy roaring up the drive on her motorcycle. The men jumped to their feet like a food truck had arrived and hustled outside—except for Frog. He stared at Suz, one brow cocked. Mackenzie held her breath.

"Go on," Suz said. "I know it's killing you, Rodriguez."

"What's killing me?"

Suz put the cookie dough down. "Look. I know they say a girl has to kiss a lot of frogs to find her prince, but I'm not looking for a prince, so you might as well exercise those hunk skills elsewhere."

Frog looked to Mackenzie, who couldn't move, didn't know what to say. After a minute, he shrugged and went out the door.

"What did you do that for?" Mackenzie demanded.

"He was dying to go see Easy Rider," Suz said flippantly.

"I don't think so," Mackenzie said. "Pretty sure you sent him away. Why?"

"Why do you keep pushing Justin away?" Suz slung some cookies into the oven.

"I don't." Mackenzie flicked a few sprinkles onto the cookies and wished Suz hadn't brought that up. "It's none of my business what Justin does with his time off. You, on the other hand, are definitely being courted. I'm sure of it."

"Oh, Rodriguez is just a ladies' man," Suz began, but the back door flew open and Daisy marched in, waving a fistful of papers.

"These are the signatures of all the people here who don't want the haunted house reopening," Daisy announced. "There's over five hundred, and for a town of two thousand, that's a quarter of our population."

"How many fake signatures on that petition?" Suz asked sweetly, snatching the papers from Daisy's hand.

"All real and verifiable. Not everybody thinks that haunted house did great things for this town. Folks are concerned about the traffic, the parking problems, the trash violations, the pollution, the increase in theft as strangers are drawn here." She smiled triumphantly. "Some of us want our quiet little town to stay quiet."

Suz studied the papers. "The first five names on here are just your usual band of rowdies, Daisy. Carson Dare, Dig Bailey, Clint Shanahan, Red Holmes and Gabriel Conyers. Nothing new to see. We'd expect them to back you."

"Keep reading," Daisy said, her tone challenging.

Mackenzie took half the papers from her sister to cast an eye over the names. "Monsieur Unmatchmaker?"

Daisy nodded, delighted to let a little air out of Mackenzie's happy balloon.

"But Cosette is with us," Mackenzie said. "She was at the meeting yesterday and voted for it."

"As you know, those two commonly play on opposite sides. It's what makes their marriage tick." Daisy admired her nails and sat down on a barstool without asking if she was welcome, which she wasn't. That wouldn't matter to Daisy.

Mackenzie's heart sank as she read over the names, realizing the signatures were legit and recognizing some of the people she'd never imagined might not be supportive of the Haunted H reopening.

Justin walked into the kitchen, and it was as if someone threw a switch in the room and shined a light on Daisy. "Hello, Justin," she said, crossing her legs to show off smooth skin ending in a sexy pair of white cowboy boots that went perfectly with her carnation-pink sundress.

Justin nodded. "Daisy. Suz. Mackenzie, have you got a second?"

Mackenzie handed the papers back to Suz. "Sure." She followed him out. "What's going on?"

"I just got a call from my brother, Jack. He says my father's in the hospital with a little summer cold that seems to be settling in his lungs. They're worried enough to call me. Dad's always been strong as an ox, but apparently he's asking for me. This time I feel I need to go."

"I'm so sorry! We'll be fine here. Don't worry about a thing."

He gazed down at her, so strong and handsome her heart beat harder. The first thought that came to her mind was, *What if he never comes back?*

That was silly. Of course he would.

"Are you leaving today?"

He nodded. "I think it's best. The guys are going to take me to the airport."

He was leaving his truck here—a thought Mackenzie found a little comforting. "Can I do anything besides be selfishly hopeful that everything will be fine with your father and that you'll come back?"

He smiled. Touched her cheek. "I can't make any promises."

"I know." What was she, three years old? She felt needy for even having said it. Justin had mentioned that his father wanted him to take over the family business. If something happened to his father, Justin would have to do what he had to do. "Of course you can't. What time is your flight?"

"I need to leave now." He waved toward the window; she saw Rodriguez loading a duffel bag into his truck. "I was able to catch a flight this afternoon."

It was happening too fast. She tried to think past the sudden realization that the weeks Justin had been at the ranch might be over, felt selfish for even thinking it when he was worried about his father. "Safe travels. I'll be thinking about your father. And you."

Justin nodded. "Thanks."

He looked like he wanted to say something else, but he turned and walked out instead. Mackenzie stood still, waving as they pulled away, Rodriguez driving, Squint and Sam in the back of the cab.

Just like that, Justin was gone.

Mackenzie went back inside. All four babies were wailing up a storm, and the look on Daisy's face was priceless. Suz ignored the whole scene, blithely rolling dough.

"I guess I'll go," Daisy said.

"Now that the guys are gone," Suz observed icily.

"Now that I've explained the situation about how BC really feels about your haunted house," Daisy said. "Not that I enjoy being the bearer of bad news. Goodness, those babies are *loud!*"

She shot out the door. Suz dropped her rolling pin and rushed to the babies. "What good girls you are to chase off the wicked witch! Let Aunt Suz kiss you and hug you darling little things!" She scooped up Heather and Hope, and Mackenzie grabbed Haven and Holly.

"Suz," Mackenzie said, trying not to smile, "did you use my daughters as weapons against Daisy?"

"Darn right!" She kissed the babies' heads as she

grabbed bottles of formula she'd been warming in a bowl of hot water. "Are you nursing?"

"Slowly weaning. Four is just about too much for me, and they seem to appreciate the speed of the bottle."

"That's a Hawthorne for you, expediency over everything." Mackenzie and Suz each grabbed bottles, testing them to see if the chill was off. The babies writhed, wailing unhappily.

"I didn't let them howl long," Suz said. "Just long enough to knock the self-righteous smirk off ol' Daiz's face and send her skittering out of here like a roach."

Mackenzie giggled in spite of herself. "A little mean."

"And effective. So," Suz said. "Rodriguez texted me that he was taking Justin to the airport. What gives?"

"Family emergency." It would do no good to worry about Justin; he was a big boy. Still, that was small comfort. "His dad's fallen ill."

"He'll be back," Suz said confidently. They settled the babies into the carriers on top of the kitchen table, sitting them up, each feeding two babies at a time. "Do you realize you're going to have to buy four prom gowns at a time? Save for four college educations?"

"They'll have to work to go to college, of course. But I'll help them all I can." Mackenzie smiled at her daughters. "It's kind of fun to imagine the future."

"Do you see Justin in that future?"

Mackenzie glanced at her sister. "I'm sort of on a day-to-day schedule in my life right now."

"Daisy noticed Justin didn't kiss you goodbye. She was watching, spying like she was in the CIA or something. It was awesome when the babies let it rip because I knew Daisy couldn't stand not being the center of attention." Suz giggled. "I was hoping one of them would have a nice pooey diaper to add to the general ruckus, because I just know Daisy's perfect little nose would have wrinkled up like an accordion." She looked pleased with the image.

"What difference does it make to Daisy if Justin kissed me or not? Why would he have, anyway?" Mackenzie wasn't going to admit that she'd been disappointed he hadn't kissed her, too.

Suz shrugged. "Easy, young ladies. You don't have to suck down the whole bottle at once." She took a napkin and dabbed at their chins. "Kind of figures he might want a little sugar for the road."

Mackenzie had certainly hoped so, and the fact that Daisy had noticed Justin hadn't kissed her was annoying. "You have my permission to tell Daisy and everyone else in BC that the sugar will be waiting right here for Justin whenever he gets back."

"I'll do it," Suz said, with a mysterious little smile. "You can bet I will."

Chapter 15

When Justin returned to Bridesmaids Creek two weeks later, he was greeted like a long-lost hero, a virtual rock star in a small town of folks who suddenly knew all about him and his business. And seemed to think he was getting married.

Cosette—Madame Matchmaker—beamed at him, waving him over from her booth in The Wedding Diner. "Justin! You're back!"

He went to join her, and she practically pulled him into her booth. "My flight got in about two hours ago. I took a taxi out here, thought I might pick up some goodies from Jane." It had been his intention to eat a hot meal, then head to the Hawthorne spread. If he ate now, he wouldn't be tempted to grab something from Mackenzie's kitchen. All of this had seemed like a good idea until he'd been stopped on the sidewalk by so many people inquiring after his father and his family and wondering if he was back for good. And letting him know how very glad they were that he was back.

It was quite suspicious, but it wasn't until Daisy had sidled up to him and said, "So I hear you're practically ready to propose to Mackenzie," that he realized something had gone terribly wrong while he was gone.

"So," Cosette said, her eyes twinkling. Justin steeled himself, and, sure enough, she didn't sugarcoat it. "Word is you'll not be needing my services."

He sighed. Accepted the cup of coffee Jane Chatham brought him with a nod, wasn't shocked at all when she pushed Cosette over in the booth and plopped down beside her, her eyes eager.

"Did something happen while I was gone?" Justin asked. If anybody knew what was going on, it was probably these two. "There seems to be a consensus of opinion that I'm looking for a bride."

Cosette grinned. "We did hear something of the sort."

Jane nodded. "Yes, we did. What can I get you to eat, Justin? You've been gone so long that I'll be happy to whip you up anything you want. I just know you're ready for some pot roast and mashed potatoes!"

He was getting the full treatment if Jane wasn't just going to put whatever she had in the kitchen in front of him. "That sounds wonderful. Thank you."

She made no move to leave the booth. He sighed.

"I don't know what happened, but I'm not getting married. Nor do I think the lady in question has any interest, anyway." He looked at them curiously. "Mind if I ask what got everyone all stirred up? I've been asked by about ten people when the wedding is just in the five minutes I was on the pavement outside."

Cosette grinned. "Suz told us all about it. She said

Mackenzie can't wait for you to get home so she can give you lots of love and affection. That she misses you like a baby misses a tooth!"

Suz. It sort of made sense. "Suz is wrong. And I'm sure Mackenzie's going to give her what for when she hears what her sister's been sharing."

Jane and Cosette looked crushed. "You have no intentions at all?" Jane asked.

He wondered if he was still going to get the pot roast. Or anything at all to eat. "No intentions. I'm betting Mackenzie doesn't want me to have any intentions. Ladies, she's been pretty clear that ours is a professional relationship. I'm sure she's still not thrilled about her ex-husband and not ready to jump into another relationship." He wasn't any happier about it than they were, but he understood why Mackenzie wasn't looking for a new guy in her life.

Cosette and Jane looked so disturbed he knew he'd hit some kind of nerve.

"They weren't married very long," Jane said. "Tommy just did not turn out as expected."

"Yeah, we kind of misfired on that one." Cosette looked really down about it. "I look forward to the day we can erase that mistake from BC's books."

"Tommy was one of your deals? A Madame Matchmaker fix-up? Ty claimed he misfired."

Cosette and Jane's faces remained glum.

"Bridesmaids Creek is a family. One for all and all for one, or at least that's how most of us feel. Anyway," Cosette said, "never mind. Sorry for poking our noses where they weren't wanted, especially since we were really off-base. We don't usually embarrass ourselves this way."

Jane nodded. "We are the souls of discretion and genteel manners, usually. Sorry about that, Justin."

They vacated his booth like puffs of gentle wind. Justin sat alone with his coffee, which was getting cold, and his pride, which certainly was even colder and lonelier. Drumming his fingers on the tabletop, he wondered if the pot roast might ever arrive, figured it wouldn't. The ladies had clean forgotten about him now that he wasn't toting an engagement ring.

Which made him wonder if he should be.

Nah. Mackenzie didn't feel that way about him. She wasn't in love with him.

Was he in love with her?

Justin rubbed at the stubble that had grown during the past couple of weeks he'd been sitting by his father's side. He'd finally shaken off the pneumonia well enough to go home, got strong enough to tweak Justin about coming home to help with the ranch, run the family business. His brothers weren't really interested or suited. One was a fireman, another a big trader who at least kept the books but wasn't up for the running of a spread. Justin could appreciate that. A man either had the land in his soul or he didn't.

Justin did. But the land he felt strongly about was the land where Mackenzie and her babies were. Anywhere—it didn't matter. But he wanted to be with her, whether she ever felt anything for him or not.

He realized everyone in the diner was staring at him, curious, having already gotten the word from Jane and Cosette—however gossip was communicated here, either by osmosis or by superfast BC grapevine, he didn't know. Didn't matter. He could tell by the gawks and sympathetic—sometimes disappointed—faces that he wasn't the homecoming hero come to sweep their princess off her feet that they'd been hoping he was.

Still no pot roast, either, and he wasn't getting any. Justin stood, nodded to the diners who suddenly weren't staring, left a couple of dollars on the table for the cold coffee and headed to the Hanging H.

Mackenzie hung up the phone and whirled to face Suz. "Betty Harper just called! She said she heard a rumor in town that Justin's proposing to me when he gets into town, and that people seem to think the rumor started with you!"

Suz's hair stuck up a bit wildly as one of the babies pawed a tiny fist through it. "I didn't say anything about a proposal, exactly. I just told a few people that you were warm to Justin, warmer than you let on. And that you couldn't wait for him to come back."

"Suz!" Mackenzie was horrified. "Someone will tell Justin when he gets back—you know how BC is! In fact, someone will probably congratulate him on our upcoming wedding!" She gasped. "Or, worse, they might start planning it!"

"That's probably already happening," Suz said. "You know that BC believes in wedding preparedness. Keeps the threat of elopements at bay. We're nothing if not a man-friendly town, and weddings are celebrated like ancient Roman feasts."

"You just can't do that," Mackenzie said. "You can't stoke the gossip pot on purpose."

"But it's so much fun. And it was worth it to see the look on Daisy's face. Oh, if you could have only seen it, Mackenzie. It was like watching a cake fall." Suz giggled, not sorry at all. "I believe in stretching the truth when necessary."

Mackenzie looked down at Holly, who somehow

tugged a smile out of her no matter how upset she was with Suz at the moment. "It accomplished nothing. I'll be surprised if Justin even comes back to the Hanging H." She kissed her baby's head, then smiled at the other three. "I love these babies so much. It's hard to think about anything bad happening when I'm with them."

"What will you do, though, if Justin has to go back to Montana permanently?" Suz asked, her eyes round.

The sound of a motorcycle ripping up the drive stopped the practical answer Mackenzie had been about to make. The back door flew open.

"Ha! You think you're so smart," Daisy told the sisters. "You put out a rumor that Justin is taken, that he's even altar-bound. But funny thing," she said triumphantly. "He was in town today, and he specifically told Cosette and Jane that he has no intentions whatsoever of getting married. To you," she said to Mackenzie. She took a second to let that sink in. "Which means the field is wide, wide open, because if he's back, and you haven't even seen him yet, and the first place he went once he got back was into town, he's not too worried about returning to the Hanging H." She grinned. "Which also means that since he's been living here for a couple of months, and you've had him all to yourself, and apparently have made no impression whatsoever, you won't mind if I offer him a little bit of my own sugar," she said. She shot Suz's way, "I recall you saying something about your sister being all ready to sugar Justin up when he got back, but, obviously," she said, smiling at Mackenzie, "he's not too excited about *that* brand of sweet."

Suz looked like all the air had been taken out of her.

Mackenzie shrugged and handed Daisy Holly. "Burp her, Daisy."

She bent down and picked up Haven from the play-pen, cooing at her.

"Is that all you have to say?" Daisy demanded. "'Burp her, Daisy?'" she mimicked. She patted the baby on the back, making a sour face when Holly did indeed burp. "Peeuw. She smells like day-old bread." She handed the baby over to Suz.

Mackenzie laughed and handed her Haven. "Try this one. Maybe she smells different."

"I am not here to burp your babies," Daisy said. Haven burped like a sailor before Daisy even really got a pat going, spitting up a little on her shoulder. "Okay, I get it. You were just hoping one of them would do that. Very funny."

"Not really." Suz got up to take Haven, and Mackenzie handed Daisy a cloth so she could clean her dress. "We just press everyone into action who comes into our home. All hands on deck, as they say."

"No, thank you," Daisy said, when Mackenzie tried to hand her Hope.

"You'll like this one. She's friendlier than the other two," Mackenzie said, and, to her surprise, Daisy took the baby.

"She is soft," Daisy said reluctantly, patting her back. "But back to Justin—"

Justin knocked and walked in the back door. Mackenzie thought he'd never looked so handsome—a fact that wasn't missed by Daisy as she twirled close to him with Hope.

"Welcome back, Justin," Daisy exclaimed. "And this little dumpling says welcome back, too!"

Justin smiled and took Hope from her. His gaze

locked on Mackenzie, and she felt it right in her gut. Couldn't look away. Wished the two of them were alone in the kitchen so she could—

Then Daisy's words returned her to sanity. Clearly Mackenzie and Justin had been the subject of town gossip, and no doubt he felt awkward about it. "Hello, Justin," Mackenzie said. "It's good to see you."

"It's good to be back."

"Are you back for good?" Daisy asked, sidling nearer to him. "I sure hope so!"

"Depends on what the boss lady says." He flashed a smile at Mackenzie. Mackenzie smiled back, relaxing a little. Maybe Daisy was exaggerating. Maybe the gossip hadn't been on full boil in Bridesmaids Creek.

"You'll never believe what Daisy's father has talked me into," Justin said.

Mackenzie stiffened. "Robert Donovan?"

"Well, if it has anything to do with the Donovans, I'd recommend you steer clear," Suz said, sending a purposefully sweet smile Daisy's way.

"Hush, Suz, let Justin talk," Daisy said, and Mackenzie poured him a glass of iced tea and cut a slice of apple pie, which she put in front of him, taking Hope from him so he could eat. Their hands brushed as she took the baby, and, just for a second, it felt like he felt the same thing she did: a spark.

A very hot spark that was eager to flame to life.

"Robert Donovan says I need to do a run down Best Man's Fork for charity," Justin said. "That's some kind of race thing, right?"

Mackenzie stared at Justin, recognizing at once where this was going. "It's a race."

"Yeah." He nodded. "And the winner gets to donate

the prize to the charity of his choice. I thought that was a great idea."

Daisy grinned at Mackenzie, her eyes sly. "There's two prizes, you might say. We have a legend here in Bridesmaids Creek—"

"We have a few legends," Suz interrupted. "Most of them are really superstitions."

"Don't ruin it," Daisy said, wrapping an arm around Justin's. "Suz is a spoilsport. I'm so glad you took Dad up on his offer."

"You would be behind this," Mackenzie said.

"Hush, you," Daisy said. "Justin, did Dad tell you how the race works?"

"I and a bunch of other guys run down Best Man's Fork, which is some kind of magical road here." Justin sipped his tea, ate a bite of pie, then reached to take the baby back from Mackenzie. "It's winner take all, your father says. Donation of five thousand dollars to a charity and a secret prize of some sort."

"The 'some sort' is the kicker," Suz said. "If you pick the right side of the fork in Best Man's Fork, you win. You win because there's a woman waiting for you at the end—if you chose the right path—and you get the trophy, the prize and the woman. Supposedly, anyway."

Justin laughed. Met Mackenzie's eyes. "And if I don't pick the right side of the fork?"

"I'll be really sad," Daisy said. "I'm one of the women chosen this year to give the award. So I hope you run fast and pick the path where I am."

Justin looked at Mackenzie. "Are you handing out the trophies, too?"

She shook her head. "I had my turn. Tommy won that year."

"Jeez." Justin glanced at the other women. "You girls are serious about this superstition thing."

The baby in his arms got a fistful of Daisy's hair and gave it a good jerk. "Ow!" she exclaimed, moving away after disentangling the tiny fingers from her hair. "Like mother, like daughter."

Mackenzie didn't look away from Justin. Shrugging, he took another bite of pie. "I'm not much for superstitions, as I've said before. But I'm willing to play for charity. Frog's going to run, too."

"Rodriguez is running?" Suz's voice rose an octave. "He can't!"

"Why not?" Justin glanced at Mackenzie, his brows raised. "He said he was planning to donate his charity bucks to the pet shelter in town. Said they do good work."

Mackenzie took the baby from him again. "Suz wasn't asked to be a presenter, either."

"Because she's just back from Africa," Daisy said quickly. "She wasn't here when the names were chosen."

"And you want all the men to yourself," Mackenzie said. "Which is totally understandable."

"Yeah, how else are you going to get one unless you rig the game," Suz said. She sighed and got up from the table. "You've been a cheater ever since we were in school, Daisy. You haven't learned a thing." She wandered out, and Mackenzie had a funny notion her sister was going to find Frog. She put the baby in the playpen, not able to meet Justin's eyes anymore.

"I guess I'll go," Daisy said. "I'll stop by to check on you later, Mackenzie."

Mackenzie raised a brow at this sudden show of concern. Daisy smiled at Justin, rubbed his arm and floated out the door.

When she was gone, Mackenzie said, "How's your father?"

"Better. He's going to be fine."

She ate him up with her eyes, wishing she weren't annoyed like all heck that he'd gotten roped into the Best Man's Fork run. Maybe Justin was right: all superstitions were silly.

Bridesmaids Creek lived on its fairy tales and legends. It was a great part of what brought tourists to the town. "It's nice of you to participate in the charity run, but are you needed back home?" She was almost afraid to hear the answer. She steeled herself to hear that his family needed him to return to Montana for good.

"I'm back permanently. Or for as long as you need me here."

Forever. Was that an option? She didn't dare speak it out loud. Darn Daisy had shaken her confidence with her tale that Justin had supposedly said he wasn't looking for a relationship. "You have to watch out for our small-town functions. They're all designed to get men to our town to settle down." Mackenzie smiled at Justin. "BC is a very man-friendly town—I'm sure you've heard by now. We have the Best Man's Fork run, the Bridesmaids Creek swim, which is guaranteed to bring every hopeful bride a husband in a matter of months, and a few other traditions we cherish."

Justin got up and crossed to her. "I have a tradition I cherish."

Mackenzie stared up at him, aware that he was standing very close to her, in her space. Wished he was closer. Mouth-on-hers close. "Oh?"

"Yeah. And this is it."

Chapter 16

Suddenly Justin's mouth was on hers, kissing her, tasting her as if he'd missed her almost as much as she'd missed him, which wasn't possible. Mackenzie leaned into him, wrapping her hands in his jacket, wishing she could crawl into his arms and tell him how much she'd thought about him, but she let her lips do the talking as she kissed him back.

"You have no idea how badly I wanted to do that," Justin said, drawing back. "I thought Daisy and Suz would never leave so I could."

He smelled like wood and something spicy, felt hot in her hands. Mackenzie's heart raced, shocked by the adrenaline of his unexpected kiss. "Kiss me again. Don't stop."

He smiled. "I plan to kiss you much more, no worries about that. But right now, I come bearing gifts for the girls."

She let him go, though she didn't want to, watching as he went out to his truck, then came back inside with four small stuffed animals. A pink giraffe, a white bunny, a pink-and-white-striped bear and a soft, cream-colored dog, all terry cloth and perfectly sized for the playpen or the babies' cribs. Mackenzie watched Justin "give" each baby her new toy, which entailed placing it beside them in the playpen. She got a little misty—she refused to call it teary—felt herself fall a bit more in love.

"Thank you," Mackenzie said.

"For what?" He glanced up at her but didn't stop showing the babies their new toys. Young as they were, they definitely seemed to know that something new was being introduced into their lives.

"The gifts." She took a deep breath. "And for coming back." That was the greatest gift of all.

He shook his head and smiled. "There was no question I'd be back."

Her heart jumped—there was no other word for it. Everything he was saying was so completely the opposite of what she'd heard from Daisy, which was so like her to spread doom and gloom designed to make you doubt yourself.

But Justin was in her kitchen, cozying up to her babies—to say nothing of the amazing kiss he'd given her—and Mackenzie decided it was time to say exactly what was on her mind. Leave no stone unturned.

"I'm glad you're back. I was worried about your dad—"

"Nah. He's strong as an ox." Justin took a seat on a stool, shrugging. "Surprisingly, it was Dad who told me I should stay right here."

"Really?" She sat across from him, trying not to act like she was starved for another kiss, which she was.

"Yeah. Said I seemed happy. That my job agreed with me. Told him I had four little bosses and they kept me pretty busy."

Oh, God, that sounded good. Drew a smile from her. "The girls keep everyone busy."

"Daisy still causing trouble?"

So he'd noticed. "She goes from wanting to sue me to pretending to be my friend. When everything gets quiet with Daisy, I know a shoe is about to drop. It's all right. Daisy's got her group and her father, and the rest of us work around them."

"I heard about her petition."

"News does travel fast."

He nodded. "I've learned that about this town."

She felt a little warm, not quite a blush, but enough to wonder if he was teasing her about Suz's enthusiastic bragging about Justin and Mackenzie being a hot item. "Yes."

"I have an idea about Daisy."

"Don't worry about Daisy. She's always been this way." He had enough on his mind without having to worry about protecting her from a rival she completely understood.

"I'm not the slightest bit worried. So this fork-to-the-altar gig—"

"Best Man's Fork. It's a road that splits in two. You have to choose which path to take, sort of like Robert Frost's 'The Road Not Taken.'"

"And the gag is that a woman is waiting at the end of one lane, in this case Daisy."

She nodded. "This is what I hear."

"So you wait on the other lane. Make things interesting." He grinned. "Two rivals, two lanes, bachelors running wild for charity? That ought to liven things up for BC, right?"

Mackenzie smiled, aware that he was teasing. "That's the purpose of a manhunting scheme."

He winked at her, and Mackenzie couldn't help smiling back. He was just so darn sure of himself. "Who's in charge of this charity gig?"

"Cosette and Jane usually head it up."

"I'll tell them I want the rules changed to include you. School-yard rivals on the Fork." He got up to put his dishes in the sink. "Things will really get interesting if I should run down Daisy's side."

"Interesting, indeed."

"I have to go put up some feed I bought in town. I meant to get it before I left. Saw Ralph Chatham, by the way. Filled me in on the petition."

"I wasn't going to mention it. It's not important."

"It is if the Donovans are trying to drive a stake through your haunted house." He looked at her. "You wouldn't let them do that, would you?"

She shook her head.

"My guess is at least thirty percent of the nay votes on the petition were coerced."

The sting and hurt she'd felt at reading some of the names—her friends' names—on the petition began to melt away. "Why do you say that?"

"It was just something Mr. Chatham said. He'd received a visit from Donovan, as had Monsieur Matchmaker." Justin went to the door. "All of them received pressure from Donovan."

"Pressure?"

"You know Donovan owns a lot of this town. That's his deal, turn it into Donovan, Texas."

Mackenzie blinked. "How do you find all this out?"

"I talk to people." Justin grinned. "And I know that running a ranch like this isn't a game of bean bags. Small towns have their conspiracies and they pick sides. You have most on your side. Donovan has the money." Justin shrugged. "Money is a powerful tool."

"What a creep." She felt sorry for the people he'd leaned on, all in the name of taking over her ranch.

"Yeah, well, don't let him win. I've got my chips on you."

The back door opened, and Ty strode in.

"I thought I'd find you guys here," Ty said. "Heard you were back and—" He glanced down at the babies. "Is it my imagination or have they grown since I saw them last?"

"What's up, matchmaker?" Justin demanded.

"Matchmaker?" Ty looked confused until he saw Justin glance at Mackenzie. "Oh. I wasn't really playing matchmaker. Mackenzie needed help out here—you needed a job. I don't mess with Cosette's deal. That's bad juju."

"Sure," Justin said. "Why are you here?"

Ty glanced around the kitchen, and Mackenzie thought he looked a little wild-eyed, even for Ty. "I just heard in town that Cosette and her husband are getting a divorce!"

Mackenzie's jaw dropped. "That's not possible. You heard wrong. That's a mean rumor."

Ty sank onto a stool, dejected. "It's true. They're having financial problems. Donovan leaned on Philippe. Apparently Cosette didn't know that Philippe had gotten a lien on the store that he owns. It's bad, man." He looked at Justin desperately. "Without Madame Matchmaker and Monsieur Unmatchmaker, this town loses a lot of its magic. You may not believe in superstition, you can laugh all you like at our traditions and Jane's fortune-telling skills and Cosette's matchmaking games, but here we believe in stuff." His voice dropped, and Mackenzie could tell confident Ty was truly shaken. "This town runs on the power of positive thinking, man. You gotta do something!"

"I've got to do something?" Justin asked. "Like what?"

"I don't know. Help me think, for God's sake." Ty ran a hand through his short, bristly hair. "We have to put the magic back in BC or it's all over. No one comes to just another small town, a dot on the map, where there isn't any belief, wonder and magic."

Mackenzie patted Ty's shoulder, cut him a slice of pie and poured him some tea. "Poor Cosette. This is awful. For Philippe, too." She felt terrible.

"Hard times hit us all," Ty said, more low than she'd ever seen him.

"Are you sure they're filing?" Mackenzie asked, hoping this was just an overblown bit of gossip. Justin's gaze landed on her, and she saw that he looked as concerned as Ty.

"I got it from the courthouse. And then Jane Chatham. Not to mention Daisy." He practically growled the name. "Robert Donovan is going to buy up every inch of retail in our town. I hear he's planning on pressuring the planning and zoning committee to redraw the town square. And when that happens, we're lost. He'll open bars and

God knows what else. We'll be nothing but *commercial*," he said, alarmed.

"Take a deep breath. Eat your pie," Justin said. "Let us think."

"I feel awful for Cosette. And Philippe. It makes so much more sense that he signed Daisy's petition."

"And that's another thing." Ty waved his fork. "There's going to be no haunted house this year."

"What?" Mackenzie felt comforted when Justin put a hand over hers for a brief moment. "Why?"

"Apparently you have to have all kinds of new licenses for that. Everything you can imagine. Donovan's got this all figured out. He's prepared to tie up every single permit and license until the day the dinosaurs return. Lawyered up like mad."

Mackenzie shook her head. "He can't do that. One man can't ruin everyone's business."

"Donovan can. He just signed a major deal with a big chain of bars and liquor stores to bring their business here. You can bet there'll be strip clubs and—"

"Stop," Mackenzie said. "You're going to make yourself ill." She felt sick herself. "What can we do?"

"What can we do?" Ty asked rhetorically. "It's David against Goliath." He shook his head sadly. "When word gets out about all this, there really will be no magic left in Bridesmaids Creek, our little town that was built on fairy tales and wedding vows." He sighed deeply and hung his head. "It's going to take a miracle to keep our town from becoming a blot on the map instead of the shining star that it is."

Justin slid his arm around her shoulders and thumped Ty on the back in commiseration. Magic and wonder, belief and superstition wouldn't last long in a town that would be overrun by commercialism in the not too distant future. Mackenzie left Justin's side and went to pick up Hope, who'd begun thrashing and letting out little cries, no doubt disturbed by Uncle Ty's dire tone. Justin picked up Haven, and Ty sighed as he got up to retrieve Heather. "Sorry, baby doll—you drew short straw," he told Holly, but Justin reached in and scooped her up, too. Ty muttered, "Oh, so that's how it's done," and rain started to fall outside, first a slight pitter-patter, then a full-blown rainstorm. Mackenzie told herself that rain brought beneficial gifts.

The thought raised her spirits.

"I'm going to kill him," Ty muttered with dark determination. "Donovan must *die.*"

Chapter 17

"Whoa, buddy," Justin said. "It's not that bad. No one needs to die."

"I meant of natural causes," Ty said. "Soon."

"That's not the answer." Mackenzie looked at Justin, and he felt his heart pound. This was why he'd come back—Mackenzie and her daughters. "The answer is finding a way to beat the Donovans fair and square."

Spoken like the resilient fighter she was. Mackenzie had no idea what she was up against. But this was a woman who'd had four children with barely a complaint—he couldn't remember ever hearing her down and out about anything. She just kept rising to meet each challenge.

"Yeah, well, I came back here to win," Ty said. "I brought you here to help, not weenie out," he said to Justin. "You're a rebel, right? So get to rebelling here like you did on the rodeo circuit. By the way, how's the knee?"

Justin sank down on a stool. Mackenzie took the one next to him, cooing to the baby she held but still managing to press against his side, bulwarking him against Ty's idiocy.

It felt great.

"I saw the ortho guy while I was gone. The knee is good as new, for a twenty-seven-year-old rodeo rider, anyway."

"Well, I'd applaud and be happy that you can ride again, but you're not leaving here, and I'm not hitting the road to hunt up recruits. We're staying right here and helping Mackenzie and Suz beat the Donovans like a drum." Ty stabbed the counter with his finger, emphasizing his point.

"Ty, what exactly do you want Justin to do? How is he supposed to rebel? He's not from here," Mackenzie pointed out.

"Fair point. But sometimes an outsider's perspective is very helpful. Then again, Justin could become one of us," Ty said.

"And how would I do that?" Justin asked, instantly realizing he'd played right into Ty's harebrained game.

"Well, you'd marr—"

"No, he wouldn't." Mackenzie glared at Ty. "Look. I know about the matchmaking ad, Ty. And I know why you really sent Justin out here to help me. You claimed I needed help on the ranch, but you really wanted him to help me to the altar. Ty," she said, and Justin could practically feel her annoyance, "I've known you all my life, and I know your heart is in the right place, but please butt out."

Justin had gone still when he'd realized Ty's best suggestion was that he marry Mackenzie—but he was even more stunned that the idea didn't sound as ridiculous as it should. Shouldn't he be yelling at Ty, telling him marriage was the last thing he wanted?

Except it wasn't.

On the other hand, Mackenzie didn't sound all that warm to the idea—and who could blame her? Her ex had just tried to sue her for her ranch.

"Justin?" Ty said. "You've gotten awfully quiet over there."

Mackenzie didn't want to marry him. He could tell by the way she'd said it. Why did that feel like it cut him off somewhere around the knees?

Justin got up. "I'm fine," he said. He laid the babies gently back in the playpen, nodded to Mackenzie and Ty. "We'll get it figured out," he said. "I'll be back at work tomorrow," he told Mackenzie, and then he headed to the bunkhouse.

Justin regretted returning to the bunkhouse as soon as he opened the door. Frog, Sam and Squint were sitting around with several women, and one of those women was Suz, who sat in Squint's lap.

Which was all wrong on every level, because he knew darn well that if Suz had a thing going for anyone, it was the cowboy she called Rodriguez. He counted nine women and some men he didn't know. The fact that there were various stages of dress in the room indicated some kind of strip game was going on.

He reminded himself that Suz was very young—twenty-three—and she'd just gotten back from a Peace Corps tour in Africa, and he'd been a helluva lot wilder than she was when he was her age. "What the hell?" he demanded, his question directed to his three bunkmates.

"Join us," Sam said, and Justin shook his head.

"I don't think so." He looked at Suz. "What are you trying to do, kill these guys?"

She shrugged. "I didn't put this party together. I'm just livening it up."

At least she was fully dressed or he would have had to mess up his bunkmates big-time for stepping over the line with the boss's little sister. By the clearness of her eyes and the fact that her glass of wine had barely been touched, he figured Suz was a latecomer to the party. "All right, everybody out."

"Hey," Frog said, "we're developing our community relations."

"You dork." Justin jerked a thumb at the door. "Everybody out. If we want to get to know you, we'll do it with our clothes on."

The room vacated with no small amount of grumbling. When it was just his bunkmates and Suz left, Justin said, "We're going to plan how to help Mackenzie. You guys are not going to go rogue by making a play for the female population. And you are not going to encourage them in any of their hijinks," he said to Suz, "because your sister is up to her ass in alligators."

"Aye, aye, Cap'n sir," Suz shot back. "I was over here keeping these guys in line, by the way, not encouraging them."

She'd been keeping a careful eye on Rodriguez, if he had to bet. But whatever story she wanted to tell, Suz wasn't his problem. "Here's what I'm suggesting. This Best Man's Fork dog-and-pony show is something we need victims—I mean, participants—for. So you three are going to run with me." He waved at the three bunk-mates who had become his brotherhood, not unlike his rodeo brotherhood, except maybe a little less focused. A little less sane. He took a deep breath. "The four of us are going to do this."

Frog pulled his black T-shirt on. Justin figured he'd gotten there just in time, before more clothes were shed. Squint was only missing a belt, and Sam was missing his hat as he lounged in his chair like he'd been about to throw down a winning hand.

"You can't win," Sam said. "You have a gimp knee." He held up a hand as Justin was about to debate the point. "Speak whatever baloney you wish, and I heard all about you seeing your doc at home. Supposedly." Sam grimaced. "You didn't see a doctor because there wasn't time, and your knee isn't good enough for you to win. You know Daisy's going to put her band of rowdies up against you. You need us," he said, pointing to Frog and Squint, "to weight this in your favor."

Suz stared at him, her eyes huge. "Tag team? Relay? How are you going to do this if you can't run? The town blue hairs have their rules, and they're pretty tight."

Justin sat down and grabbed their cards to lay out a fork shape on the table. "Your sister will be here," he said, pointing to the ace of hearts.

"Daisy, you mean," Suz said.

"We're going to do this fun run a little differently. Mackenzie will be here, and Daisy will be here." He put the ace of clubs to indicate Daisy on the other fork. "The four of us will be here." He laid the four jacks at the beginning of the fork in the road.

Suz glanced at Rodriguez, clearly weighing whether

she wanted him running this race, where he might end up in Daisy's arms. Justin frowned.

"Explain this Best Man's Fork thing to me," he said. "I may not have the full significance."

"It's all about marriage," Suz said. "Every man who's made the run and chosen the proper path that leads to the woman has ended up married to her within thirty days."

"That's not possible," Justin said. The other three men stared at Suz, clearly calculating if making this run could be detrimental to their bachelorhood.

"It's a matter of town record. Go ask Jane Chatham for the book," Suz said. "She keeps a ledger of the date of each event in this town and what weddings may result from said event. She also keeps dates of divorces, in the back of the book, in order to discover if marriages stick or fail after BC's illustrious events."

"And?" Justin demanded, curious. Maybe he didn't want to get involved in something that had a high fail rate.

Suz smiled. "Scared?"

This woman very well could end up being his sister-in-law one day. Justin sighed, raising a hand at her teasing giggle. "Not scared. Looking to be informed. Information is power."

"Two percent."

Justin leaned back. "Two percent of these wedded couples didn't work out."

"Exactly. My sister. It is what it is." Suz shrugged. "They shouldn't have gotten married in the first place."

"Why?" Sam asked. "They had kids."

"Yeah, but Mackenzie was never in love with Tommy." She swept the fork of cards off the table, then shuffled the deck. "Tommy just wanted to marry the town's favorite daughter. Then he spooked because of the babies. No Best Man's Fork, no Bridesmaids Creek swim, can predict whether a man has a chicken side or not."

Justin frowned. Personally he thought the little girls were a huge bonus in his life. He loved those babies. When he'd been in Whitefish, he couldn't wait to get back to them and Mackenzie.

If this was the way things were done in Bridesmaids Creek, then he planned to win. "I don't have a chicken side."

"That I believe." Suz grinned at him. "It remains to be seen how fast you are. I can tell you right now that Daisy's going to be ticked when she finds out you've rigged the game with a fifty-fifty chance by putting Mackenzie in the other fork. Expect a formal protest. However, I'm willing to help you any way I can. Inside the rules, of course."

"Let me get this straight," Squint said. "I don't know why Daisy's using you for this event, because quite frankly, I'd be a more exciting candidate." He glared at Justin. "But if you're planning to secretly put Mackenzie on the other side of the game, I'd carry you on my back to get you over the finish line."

"I can run," Justin said. "Don't worry about me."

Sam looked at him doubtfully. "I guess we could make one of those chariot things. Like a litter or one of those Iditarod thingamabobs with the mush dogs." He grinned at Justin. "We'd drag you up to the finish line in record time."

"Or," Frog said with great bravado, "we'll run the

race to the finish line just to secure the win, then double back and get Justin."

Justin laughed. "Double back and get me?"

"We won't let you down, bud," Frog said earnestly. "We won't let anyone else get your girl."

"Get my girl?" Justin's brow wrinkled. "That's not what this is all about. I'm trying to support Mackenzie. And Suz and the Hanging H. Bridesmaids Creek, in general." He raised a brow at Suz's giggle. "I'm protecting her against the Donovans."

"And what if you win the race and Mackenzie is in the fork you choose? Are you prepared for what happens in thirty days or less?" She gave him a Suz smirk. "I should warn you that some of the participants just went ahead and eloped that very night, as soon as the race was completed."

"Whoa," Frog said. "Maybe I don't want to run. What if I win Mackenzie?"

"No, no, no," Justin said. "We're a team. My team. You guys are just backup. You're just—"

"We're the guarantee," Sam said. "We get it. We just want to make sure you're not going to make us do the deed, too."

"What if I—we, the three of us—" Frog pointed to his buddies "—what if we choose the wrong fork?" His brows rose. "Daisy's fork?"

"That's just not going to happen," Justin said. "I have a sixth sense about these things."

"No, you don't," Suz said. "Even I know you don't believe in those things. You've said so a hundred times. In fact, this whole race, the only reason you're participating in it is that you believe it's a bunch of hokum."

"True," Justin conceded.

"It's just a charity event in which you're determined to beat out the Donovans," Suz said. "Which is all very noble except that my sister's heart is at stake. What will happen if you pick Daisy's lane? Just because you don't believe in the legend doesn't mean everybody else in Bridesmaids Creek doesn't. Very strange things happen on that road, and there's a reason those superstitions have come to pass. You've heard the saying, where's there's smoke, there's fire?" She studied Justin. "For every action, there's a reaction. It would be a bad reaction if you end up as Daisy's trophy."

"Won't happen."

"Because you think it's dumb. Because you don't believe," Suz argued. "In that case, I'll just take my sister's place."

"Hey!" Frog exclaimed. "Suz on one side, Daisy on the other side? Perforce the road not taken?" He looked distinctly uncomfortable. "In that case, I'll kneecap Justin."

Justin sighed, ignoring Frog's outburst. "That would work, Suz. You're a Hawthorne. Technically, you're single, a never-married bachelorette. It would work." He shook his head. "Anyway, it's not that I don't believe. I'm a participant, a bystander, new to this town. I don't have to embrace everything. I just play along."

Mackenzie walked in, and just the sight of her made Justin smile. "What are you guys doing?" she asked.

"Justin's trying to weasel," Suz said. "Who's watching the babies?"

"Jade and her mom came over," Mackenzie said, glancing around. "If you're going to play cards, you're welcome to do it at the house." She looked at Justin, and it felt like someone hit him with a bag of rocks.

He was in love with this woman.

"Are you being a weasel about something?" Mackenzie asked.

"I don't think so," he said. "We're trying to figure out how to win this race and stay inside the rules."

"He's sandbagging the race by having these three doofs run with him," Suz explained. "That way, he's inoculated from the whole wedding-in-thirty-days issue of the run, but he gets to be the big hero, too."

Mackenzie met Justin's gaze. "The way the Best Man's Fork run works is that one man makes a run to find a woman with whom he's truly in love. If he picks the right path and she's waiting at the end of the race for him, they're meant to be together. If he picks the road with no woman at the end, he might as well just keep on running."

Justin laughed. "I like my way better. The purpose is to win this thing, right? I don't want to win Daisy. So you're going to be on the other side. These three guys are going to run with me."

"On account of Justin's wonky leg," Suz explained. "Here's the thing he's not saying about this whole deal. Justin doesn't believe in the legend, but he wants to give it a trial run, you might say. Just in case it's true. But no one will ever know who is meant to be with you—or Daisy—because there'll be four runners. So basically it's just a charity run on a pretty day."

Mackenzie smiled. "Sounds fair to me."

Justin perked up. "Really?"

"Yeah. Let's do it Justin's way. No matter what happens, we win." She glanced at Justin. "Although you realize you're taking a terrible chance, Justin. You could end up married in thirty days. To Daisy. Fifty-fifty chance."

"Nope." He shook his head. "That's the good part about these goofs running with me. The curse will land on one of them. Probably Sam."

"Hey!" Squint sat up. "Who said it would be a curse?"

"I'm going up to the house to talk to Jade," Sam said. "She hasn't been around in a while, and I think she might have a little thing for me and is trying not to show it."

He departed. Justin glanced at Suz and Mackenzie. "Does she have a thing for Sam?"

"I doubt it very seriously." Suz stretched. "None of the four of you are long-timers here. Big *S*'s on your foreheads that stand for short-timers." She got up and whacked Frog lightly on the arm. "I'm going to be at that race. And if you run down the road where Daisy is, you might as well just keep on running, Rodriguez. Because you won't like what you get from Crazy Daisy."

She went out the door.

"Wow," Frog said. "Your sister scares me a little. In a good way. Pretty sure I like it."

Justin had had enough. He took Mackenzie's arm and pulled her outside, walking her away from the house. "Since it's about time to milk the cows—"

"We don't have dairy cows."

"Since it's about time to get up and drink our morning coffee," Justin said, "can you spare five minutes before you have to get back to the babies?"

"Maybe. Why?" Mackenzie asked.

"Mainly I want to make out with you." He pulled her into his arms, kissing her long and slow and deep. Sighed when she wrapped her arms around him, inhaled the sweet perfume of her hair and the softness of her skin.

"Suz says you're trying to rig the game your way," Mackenzie said.

"She's right. Every game has a better way to win it, you know. I'm not going to let the Donovans win."

"What's it to you?"

"What's it to me? I think BC's starting to weave its spell around me, that's what. And I happen to know a beautiful woman I feel like slaying dragons for."

"Very romantic." She cuddled up to him. She felt like part of his own body, his own breath. Justin closed his eyes, felt her trace his lips with her fingertips.

"So, listen. How does this end, when I win?" Justin asked.

Mackenzie smiled. "When you win, the Donovans slink off to figure out their next move. It's the never-ending chess game."

"I mean me and you. I try not to make too many moves on you, because of a thousand different reasons, not the least of which is you're the boss lady and everything else, although I think I'm past that. But how does this end?"

"Everything else?" She studied him. "What does that mean?"

"You've got the ex-husband trying to sue you, et cetera, et cetera, and being a general pain in the ass." Justin didn't stop himself when his hands somehow wandered down to her waist. "I guess I've figured you might not be interested in a—"

She kissed him. "Win the race. Then we'll find out how this ends."

Chapter 18

The day of the race dawned clear and beautiful; the sun warming everything in its path with rich, soft rays. Justin felt good about today. Really good.

It was a town-saving kind of day.

His knee felt great. In fact, he felt like a warrior of old, like he could ride bulls until the moon came up again.

"Hey, stud," Daisy said, flouncing past him when he came out of the bunkhouse.

Trouble was up, and she was wearing a smile. "Hello, Daisy," he said cautiously. "Isn't there a rule about how the runner and the prospective bride shouldn't see each other the day of the race?"

She shrugged one dainty shoulder, tossed her bronze locks. "Rules were made to be broken, weren't they? And you're a rebel, right? That's what they say around the rodeo circuit, anyway." She went off, banged on the kitchen door and was allowed entrance. Justin hung back, deciding to delay his morning coffee and muffin with the babies—and of course their sweet mother.

Nothing good could come of seeing the woman he loved with the woman who intended to sabotage her on the big day.

Daisy had no idea they were intending to slip Mackenzie into the opposite fork. A decoy, as it were.

History was about to be made in BC.

Justin checked his watch. Two hours before he gathered up his team, put on his running shoes and got ready to prove everybody in Bridesmaids Creek wrong.

There was no such thing as a charmed and lucky road.

No such thing as a creek with mystic powers.

All there was was hard work. Determination. And a desire to win.

That was how you made magic.

"Good morning, Mackenzie," Daisy said with a smile that somehow grated on Mackenzie's nerves right off the bat. "How are the babies?"

"The girls are fine. They're just down for a nap." Mackenzie glanced at the baby monitor to make sure she'd switched it on. The girls had gotten into a routine that was almost regular, no easy feat with four of them. Somehow they seemed to have an intuition about each other. When one was upset, they all got upset. Happiness seemed to settle over them as a general mood, as well.

They'd come a long way.

"So today's the big race." Daisy looked at her. "It's like being crowned the king and queen of homecoming, only this is for real."

Mackenzie looked at her. "Whatever." She went to wash up the baby bottles in the sink.

Daisy cocked her head. "You seem very unconcerned about Justin running the Best Man's Fork. I'm the prize, you know."

"Daisy, there isn't a magic spell on earth strong enough to get Justin anywhere near an altar that you're standing at."

Daisy laughed. "You're sure?"

"Positive." She checked the pound cake and the level on the tea, her mind on what she needed to leave behind for Jade and Betty's comfort. "Justin sees this as a charity function. The legend eludes him."

"That's because he's not from here. He doesn't understand how this town works."

"He's got a pretty fair idea." And he'd returned. Mackenzie smiled.

"You seem awfully confident."

"Look." Mackenzie turned to face Daisy just as Justin came in the back door. "Let me spell this out for you. You and your father and your gang can do anything you want to do to me, but you can't take the thing from me that I love most. You can't take my children, and you can't change who I am. You can talk about the man who died at our haunted house—"

"Was murdered," Daisy inserted.

"Never proven," Mackenzie snapped. "You can spread all the gossip and lies you want, and I'm still going to wake up every day being the same old Mackenzie Hawthorne my parents raised me to be. Which is more than you can take, because that's exactly what you're missing. Your spirit is damaged."

"Excuse me," Justin said. "I was going to grab a

piece of that pound cake and maybe some coffee." He looked at Daisy. "Shame you picked me to be your runner. I'm really slow. Did anybody tell you they used to call me Turtle in high school?"

"What I heard," Daisy said, "is that you once ran a mile in under four minutes just to prove you could."

Mackenzie smiled at Justin. "I'll cut you some cake and get you some coffee. 'Bye, Daisy."

"I didn't come by just to talk," Daisy said. "I came by to let you know that there's going to be a tea after the race at The Wedding Diner. Held in our honor by Madame Matchmaker and Monsieur Unmatchmaker."

"I thought they were getting divorced," Mackenzie said.

"They are," Daisy said.

"Because your father ruined their marriage, the way the Donovans ruin everything."

"How is it our fault if Monsieur Unmatchmaker couldn't manage his finances?" Daisy asked. "Dad didn't have to loan him money."

"I'm sure he didn't." Mackenzie placed the cake and coffee in front of Justin.

To her absolute shock, he swept her into his lap, kissing her thoroughly.

"Wow," Mackenzie murmured.

"Um," Daisy said, "what the hell is that?"

"Collecting my prize early," Justin said.

Daisy's jaw dropped. "Are you two…an item?"

Mackenzie looked at Justin.

"Are we an item?" he asked.

"Do you want to be an item?" Mackenzie asked.

"Hey," Daisy said. "I want a different runner! You're out," she told Justin. "I'm going down right now to tell

Jane Chatham and Cosette that I'm choosing a new guy to run the race."

She went out the door in a huff.

"Uh-oh. Look what you did," Mackenzie said.

"Couldn't help it." He kissed her again, this time longer.

"Guess you don't have to run today," Mackenzie said.

"Guess I don't."

"Which means I don't have to be waiting in the Fork to sabotage Daisy."

"It was such a great plan," Justin said. His hands stole up to her waist so he could tuck her closer against him.

"It was a great plan. But now that neither of us have to be at the race, we have time to do something else." Mackenzie touched his cheek, nibbled his lip, tried not to inhale him.

"Did you have something in mind?"

"I most certainly do."

"I was hoping you'd say that," Justin said.

Making love to Mackenzie was better than running a charity race for sure. It was sweet kisses and soft skin and gentle heat that grew into a fire he had no desire to control. Justin stared up at the ceiling while Mackenzie slept beside him, feeling satisfied for maybe the first time in his life.

All the old feelings of rebellion were gone. And they'd started to be erased in this house, with this woman, with her children.

Felt like the family he'd always wanted.

Not that he didn't love his family, but a man wanted his own—and this was the one he hoped to put down roots with.

If Mackenzie would have him.

She got up to dress, and he let his eyes roam wildly, drinking in every bit of smooth naked skin he could. Wondered if he could drag her back into bed before the babies awakened.

He heard a baby cry and banging at the back door at the same time. Time to get up.

"I'll get the baby," he said.

"Thanks." She kissed him and hurried down the hall.

There were excited voices coming from the kitchen. "Sounds like something fun is happening down there," he told the babies, who were gazing around, riled by Hope's crying, wondering if they should join the chorus. He picked Hope up, calmed her and then heard footsteps flying down the hall.

Mackenzie burst into the nursery. "Suz is in town and she's going to hobble Daisy for life because Daisy chose Frog—Rodriguez—to run in your place. Suz told Jade that Daisy will never walk in high heels again when she gets through with her."

Justin shook his head and resumed changing Hope's diaper. "Young lady, you have a firebrand of an aunt."

"I have to go into town." Mackenzie hurried off.

"Which means I need to go into town to keep your mother out of trouble. Would you girls like to go into town?"

"This is all my fault," he heard Mackenzie mutter.

"Your fault how?"

"Because I kissed you in front of Daisy. She decided to cut her losses."

"Hey!" Justin laughed. "I resent that. I kissed you."

"And I liked it," Mackenzie called from the other room. "But now my sister is going to turn Daisy into a pretzel."

He didn't doubt that at all. "But Frog and Suz don't have anything going on, do they?"

"No, but that won't stop Suz and Daisy. Daisy thought she was going to be homecoming queen, but Suz won. It's bad blood."

"Let's pack the girls up and let them watch their first Bridesmaids Creek brawl. Think we could make a legend about that?"

Mackenzie hurried into the nursery.

"I'll watch them," Jade called. "By the way, I can hear every word over the baby monitor. I feel a bit like a creeper. And I like the idea of a Bridesmaids Creek brawl."

"I don't want my little sister fighting over a man." Mackenzie looked at Justin. "I've got to stop her."

"That I agree with," Jade called. "People will just say that bad things happen at the Hawthorne place."

Mackenzie gasped. "She's right."

There was a lot at stake, even if he couldn't grasp the whole concept of the underlying currents. "Do we even know if Frog agreed to take my place?"

"He did," Jade said, coming into the room. "I hope you guys are decent. I didn't want to keep listening over the monitor. Feels so third wheel."

Mackenzie hugged her. "You're never third wheel. You're family."

"Go. Just hurry." Jade waved them on. "Your sister's been spring-loaded ever since Daisy started flirting with Frog. It's really weird, because I never saw Suz get giddy over a guy."

"That's true. This is serious." Mackenzie hugged Jade and grabbed Justin's hand. "You're sure you don't mind going with me?"

"Mind?" Justin smiled, feeling like a king with Mackenzie's hand in his. "I wouldn't miss it for the world."

* * *

Justin realized how serious Bridesmaids Creek was about their social events when he saw that at least half the town had shown up at Best Man's Fork, expecting a race of some type.

What they got instead was an all-out vigorous debate between Suz and Daisy, with Rodriguez clearly the focal point of the discussion. Somehow that got other ladies and gentlemen involved, and the next thing he knew, even Cosette and Philippe were standing on opposite sides of the road that branched off into the fork where the victims—or bachelors, depending on how one looked at it—went off on the adventure of a lifetime.

"The Road Not Taken," by Robert Frost. Deep stuff this town lived by.

And it got a little deeper when Suz jumped on Daisy and dragged her by her long dark hair to the ground.

"Oh, no!" Before he could stop her, Mackenzie jumped into the fray, and then it was on. He looked at Frog, whose boots seemed glued to the ground. A hundred people either yelled insults or rolled in the dirt, engaged in some kind of combat. The sheriff and his men watched from the sidelines, and Robert Donovan complained loudly to the sheriff about his daughter's handling at Suz's hands, despite the fact that Mackenzie was working as hard as she could to drag her off.

"Are you going to do something?" Justin asked Frog.

Rodriguez shrugged. "Personally, girl-on-girl conflict is something a man probably wants to avoid. It's a no-win situation, or haven't you heard?"

"That's nice." Justin waded in, separated Suz and Daisy. "What the hell is wrong with you two?"

"I've wanted to tear you up for years," Suz said. "You just remember that, Daisy Donovan."

Daisy flounced off, straight to Frog.

Like a frog wanting out of a skillet, Frog took off. Squint and Sam looked at Justin.

"Are you going to help me separate the rest of these people?" Justin demanded.

"Not our battle," Squint said.

"Seems to be some kind of bad feelings in the general population around here," Sam said.

It wasn't his battle. Why did he feel so responsible?

Because he hadn't wanted to run. Hadn't believed in what the town believed in, what mattered to them—the legend that really covered up the last bits of hope they had that their town was going to survive.

It was falling apart.

Mackenzie ran to Suz. "Are you all right?"

Of course she was all right. Daisy was tough, but Suz was tougher. Daisy was sporting a fat lip and a scratch across a cheek, from what he could see at a distance, while Suz looked ready to go another round.

"I'm fine," Suz snapped. "It's just time someone taught Daisy Donovan a lesson, and her father, too."

That was all true. Even someone who was new to town could tell that the Donovans made consistent trouble for everyone. Even the haunted house might not ever rise from the ashes of the past.

Justin looked at the people scrabbling and arguing with each other all along the road—neighbors and friends who loved each other, when the Donovans weren't yanking everybody's chain and stealing their dreams—and took a deep breath.

"I'll run!" he yelled.

Chapter 19

Mackenzie gasped at Justin's pronouncement. Everyone within earshot quit arguing and battling, which made the rest of the people take a break to find out what was happening.

"You can't run," Mackenzie said. "You have a bad knee."

"It's fine."

No way was she allowing this to happen. If he thought for one second he was going to run with Daisy standing at the other end of Best Man's Fork, she was going to go all Suz on him. Well, not physically, of course, but definitely she was going to give him a piece of her mind.

"Not to me, it's not fine," Mackenzie said, glaring at him.

Now that someone else's annoyance was front and center, everybody grouped around to hear every word.

"I'll do the run," Justin said, holding her gaze with his, "if Mackenzie's at the end of the race."

Jane Chatham came to the front of the group, clearly in her official position as marshal and rules enforcer. "Typically it's a bachelorette who—"

"Mackenzie's single," Justin said.

"No, Justin," Mackenzie said. "If you pick the wrong road—"

"I know, I know, keep running because the charm's broken, and we won't get married in thirty days, and I might as well be cast out of society because I'll never marry." He grinned. "Did I sum it up?"

"Well, you're pretty close," Mackenzie said, "because I don't want to lose you this soon."

He grinned. "I have a feeling it'll be fine."

"It's supposed to be my run," Daisy complained loudly. "I ask for the right to put in a champion."

"A champion?" Cosette wrinkled her nose, checked the papers Jane held. "Is that in the rules?"

"I choose Carson Dare, Dig Bailey, Clint Shanahan, Red Holmes and Gabriel Conyers to run as my champions, as I'm obviously being thrown over here," Daisy announced loudly, and the entire crowd gasped.

Mackenzie glanced over at the five men in black jackets, boots and blue jeans. Of course the purpose of Daisy's plan was to keep Justin from winning. Any of those men could outrun Justin, even if he claimed his leg was whole now. "You just can't stand for anyone to be happy, can you, Daisy Donovan?"

"I'm very happy." Daisy smiled at her. "And since it's a charity race, I'll donate five thousand dollars to the charity of the winner's choice."

"Even the haunted house fund?" Justin demanded.

The crowd went totally silent.

"Sure. I don't care. One good cause is the same as

another," Daisy said. "There won't ever be a haunted house, but I understand the Hawthorne ranch is underwater these days."

Mackenzie shook her head. "Actually, we're in a good place. Thanks."

"We'll see." She glanced at Suz. "Neither one of you makes any money. It can't go on forever."

Those were words straight from Robert Donovan's mouth. Justin smiled. "So, are we doing this thing or not?"

"Justin," Mackenzie said, "I really wish you wouldn't do this."

"You just go pick your side of the road." Justin winked at her. "I'll be right there."

"I don't get to pick," Mackenzie said a little desperately. "The sheriff takes the lady in his truck to the finish line. She draws a straw to determine which side she takes."

"It's okay." He kissed her. "I'll find you."

"I wish you wouldn't do this." What terrified her most was what Daisy's band of jacket-wearing rowdies would do once they got past the view of the people. The forks wound through forest and brush-lined trails. It was a five-mile run, with no shortcuts. The sheriff and Cosette and Jane had driven it several times to check the distance and condition of the road. "I don't like it."

Sam, Squint and Frog stepped up to the line. "We'll run with him," Sam said.

"We're a team," Frog said.

"Like to keep things even," Squint said, glaring at Daisy's gang.

"There's five of them and four of you," Suz said. "Are you just itching to get a beatdown?"

Frog grinned. "We kind of thought the fight was weighted toward our side."

"Very funny," Dig Bailey said.

"All right, then," Cosette said. "The rules have been agreed upon—the game begins. Everyone who wants to be at the finish line will pay the race fund five dollars, no charge for anyone under twelve years of age! Monsieur Unmatchmaker, will you please fire the starting gun?"

Philippe grinned at his wife. "I'm honored. Let's get ready to run!" he yelled, excited to be chosen.

"When's the last time one of these races was held?" Justin asked Mackenzie.

"When my ex ran it," Mackenzie said. "Although he didn't really run it so much as walk it. And he didn't get to the right lane."

"He quit," Suz interjected. "He had a blister on his heel. It wasn't a race so much as a walk."

Justin looked at Mackenzie. "So history is indeed being made today."

She grinned at him. "Actually, history is being made because there's never been a race like this one. The rules are completely changed."

"You just remember that there's never been a race like this one," Justin said, kissing her.

"How are you going to run in boots?"

He smiled. "You just get in the sheriff's truck. The people want a battle, and a battle they're going to get."

Justin wasn't stupid. He'd known when he and Mackenzie headed down here that there was going to be a race, and no man attended a race without a decent pair of running shoes. He'd tossed those in his truck, and he'd also tossed in a T-shirt.

"That's what you're running in?" Squint demanded, eyeing his jeans as the intrepid three pulled on extreme running gear. Their truck was parked beside his, providing perfect cover for their costume change.

"Yeah. I'm fine," Justin said.

Frog eyed him doubtfully. Reached over and lightly pounded his leg, scoffing in disgust. "You're still wearing that leg brace. Your leg isn't any better at all!"

"My leg is better," Justin said. "The doc said my knee would take a couple more weeks to fully heal the tear."

"That's just great," Sam said. "You can't run wearing a leg brace."

"I can run."

"Sure, Peg Leg." Frog's tone was total disgust. "You realize that if you take that brace off, your leg is frozen for a few days. You have to do therapy and crap to get the tendons and muscles and stuff back to normal. So you can't take that brace off because it won't do any good."

"I wasn't planning on taking it off," Justin said.

"Great," Squint said. "We're backing up Hopalong Cassidy. For five miles through forest and bush."

"Here's the deal," Frog said. "We've got your back. We're a team. So you run like hell and never look back, no matter what you hear behind you."

"What are you going to do?" Justin asked. They looked like they were getting ready for some kind of reconnaissance mission, all in black and camo. This was clearly just another mission to them.

"Just planning on keeping things honest," Sam said.

"We're quite familiar with the way nonbeneficial things can happen in competitive times."

"Remember," Squint said. "No looking back. Very critical to your success. You've heard about Lot's wife and the saltshaker?"

Justin forbore a sigh and eyed his stalwart companions. "I really appreciate you guys stepping up on my behalf."

"Nah," Frog said. "It's not about you. It's about the boss lady."

Justin smiled. "Yes, it is."

Mackenzie was nervous as she rode with the sheriff. Not nervous. Apprehensive.

Maybe Justin was right—maybe this whole legend thing was dumb.

Except it wasn't. Cosette, Jane and Jane's husband had been busy taking money for tickets. Most of the town had turned out, since this wasn't an event that happened often and no one wanted to be left out. It was good for the town, it was good for the people and hopefully it would be good for her and her family.

The amazing thing was that Justin had been game to do it.

"I think you like that cowboy," Sheriff Dennis said.

"I wouldn't do this if I didn't." Maybe that's why she was apprehensive—it really, really mattered to her which lane Justin chose.

"I guess we should have all known from how the race went down with Tommy that he was a mistake," Dennis said.

"It's hard for me to regret anything because of my daughters."

Sheriff Dennis smiled. "I'd feel the same way. By the way, I heard through the proverbial grapevine that Tommy was dumped. His little girlfriend went off to greener pastures."

Mackenzie shook her head. "Somehow it doesn't matter anymore."

"True love," Sheriff Dennis said happily, parking the truck near the end of the thick woods where the paths converged again. "You know, whoever dreamed this race up was a genius. We should hold one every six months just on principle."

"You know very well who thought it up," Mackenzie said. "Cosette, Philippe, Jane, her husband and you."

Sheriff Dennis laughed. "You have to build a town from something. This was as good as anything. And we started this thirty years ago. How would you know?"

"Because I remember my parents talking about it," Mackenzie said softly. "They always said they were going to try it out one day."

Sheriff Dennis patted her hand. "They'll be tickled that their daughter is getting to do it right this time." He pulled out two straws, then hid them in his beefy palms. "Pick. You either want the right side or the left side of the road. East or west, there can only be one." He extended his hands to Mackenzie. "Choose wisely, Mackenzie. I've always thought of you as a daughter. This time I want you to be happy."

Her hand hovered over his. "What made you dream up the idea of Best Man's Fork?"

"There's a best man at every wedding, isn't there?" He looked at her, his eyes twinkling. "The spotlight can't always be on the bride and groom. Guys want to get married more than you ladies think we do. And we want a big deal made of it, too!"

Mackenzie smiled. "That one." She tapped his left hand, and he opened it.

She stared at the straw in his hand. If she hadn't known better, she would have thought it sparkled. Twinkled.

"I'll be leaving you right here," Sheriff Dennis said. "Good luck, Mackenzie."

She got out. "Thanks."

"You know the drill. That right there is your path. In a few minutes, there'll be all kinds of people swarming the finish line, anxious to see if Justin chooses the right road. Have you got faith in your cowboy?"

She closed the truck door and waved goodbye. Set out for the lane she'd chosen. There was no need to answer Sheriff Dennis's rhetorical question; they both knew she did or she wouldn't be waiting here for him.

Sheriff Dennis drove away. Mackenzie pulled out her cell phone and called Jade.

"Hello?"

"How are the girls?"

"They're darling! Mom and I are having a blast. Where are you?"

"At the finish line."

"Already?" Jade gasped. "It's going to go very different this time, you know. This time it's going to be—"

"Oof," Mackenzie said as something knocked her to the ground. Her phone flew, shattering when it hit a rock.

"Daisy Donovan! What was that for?" Mackenzie sat up and glared at Daisy, who looked proud of her handiwork. "Do not make me kick your butt today!"

She jumped to her feet.

"I'm not missing out on my chance," Daisy said. "You've already had your turn. Now move."

"Move?" Mackenzie frowned. "I'm not going anywhere."

"Yes, you are. Either you get in that other lane, or I'm going to make you wish you had!"

Mackenzie raised a brow. "What are you doing?"

"I'm going to be right here when Justin arrives." Daisy pointed to the other lane. "Go."

"Why don't you go to that side?"

"Because I know this whole gig is a bunch of hooey. Either the sheriff told you which side to choose or you just called your position in to someone."

"I was checking on the babies," Mackenzie said, disgusted.

"And giving her a coded location so that she could call one of the three dunces to clue Justin in on which road to take." Daisy pointed again. "Go, or you'll regret making me lose my temper."

"Daisy, you're never going to learn. Has your scheming ever gotten you anything you wanted?"

"We'll know soon enough."

"Justin isn't going to marry you."

"He may not marry you, either. But at least I'll have the charmed legend on my side."

Mackenzie sighed. "You realize that's about as good as believing in Santa Claus."

"Which I do. He was a saint, thanks. You know, that's part of your problem, Mackenzie Hawthorne— you're not a romantic."

"And you are?" Mackenzie could feel her brows elevate involuntarily. "Daisy, this is dumb. If you want this lane so badly, you can have it."

"Good. Because I really didn't want to have to knock you out and hide you in the bushes."

There was no point in arguing with Daisy. She'd always wanted what everyone else had; nothing was going to change now. She was Suz's age, still young, but as tough as Suz could be, Daisy could be tougher. It was as if she missed a key part of her soul that most humans had that made them compassionate.

"I thought you had a thing for Frog," Mackenzie said.

"Just flirting, nothing serious," Daisy said. "Move along."

"Just flirting?" Poor Frog might have actually thought Daisy cared about him. "What about Squint? Are you just flirting with him, too?"

Something strange came over Daisy's face. "Don't talk to me about Squint. He thinks he's special."

"So he turned you down?"

"He did not turn me down." Daisy's gaze slid away. "He said he isn't available for anything resembling dating, a relationship or even friendship."

"Ouch." Mackenzie hadn't meant to say it, and once the word was out of her mouth, Daisy glowered at her.

"Get over there, and when Justin sweeps me off my feet, you accept your just deserts. You've had this coming to you for a long time." Daisy stalked around a rock, dusted it off and sat down. "Dad's going to make marrying me very lucrative for Justin."

"You live in a dream world where Daddy's money gets you what you want."

"And you live in a dream world where Daddy's money didn't. Get lost."

Mackenzie went to the other lane, a good thousand yards away, and decided she liked the way the sun dappled the trees and the light breeze touched the lane. There was a tall tree made for climbing, with a slab someone had hammered in it for a seat that rose just above the canopy. There also was a tree swing and a bench, so Mackenzie took the bench and made herself comfortable.

"What the hell are you doing?" Suz demanded, hidden by a clump of leafy bushes.

"I might ask you the same!"

"Don't look like you're talking to me," Suz instructed. "It would be frowned upon by the town busybodies. And Daisy is an epic tattletale." She looked at her sister with exasperation. "I heard the whole verbal squall. Why did you let Daisy push you around?"

"Because I don't care." Mackenzie scooted closer to the end of the bench so she could see Suz better. "She can do what she likes. It won't change my destiny."

"Well, that's serene of you. It was all I could do not to jump out of the bushes and perform major facial rearrangement on her. And your phone is totaled."

"I'll replace it. And I can handle Daisy. You've got to quit worrying. Back to why you're hanging out in the hedge?"

"Keeping Daisy kosher. I knew she'd pull something. I've known her ever since she came to BC, and she's always been a brat." Suz grinned. "Just happens to be I'm a bigger brat."

Suz was no brat. She was an angel with a good heart. "You're my darling sister, and I love you."

"Well, I wasn't going to let my big sister sit here on the biggest day of her life by herself," Suz said impishly. "I've got a good mind to go over there and do something to Daisy."

They both hesitated as the roar of vehicles heading up the road came to them.

"It's on," Suz said. "You've had your last five minutes to reflect on life as a single woman."

Mackenzie smiled. "It may not happen that way."

"Of course it will. Don't be silly. Daisy wouldn't have been so desperate to fight you for it if the legend hadn't come true every single time. Now you just sit there and think blissful thoughts. Your happy ending is on the way. By the way, this race is going to be a long one. You might want to get a nap in so you're fresh for your prince."

"Okay, I'll bite. What have you been up to?"

"Not me." Suz's face was the picture of innocence. "A little birdie told me Justin's knee is still in a soft cast. So he won't be tearing up the finish line to get to you." She grinned. "But he will."

"What are you talking about?" Mackenzie was alarmed. She hadn't seen anything on his leg. Not even when they'd made love.

"Just telling you what the birdies tell me." Suz grinned. "I think it's sweet."

She fell in love with Justin that much more, helplessly, happily in love. "Where are you going?" Mackenzie peered over the leaves that folded over where her sister's face had been.

Silence.

"Suz?"

But Suz was gone. Mackenzie smiled, thinking about how much she loved her sister. Nobody had helped her through her divorce and the ensuing bad times more than Suz.

She glanced over at Daisy to see what she was doing. No shock, she was combing her hair, primping in a mirror. Her long brown locks shone in the sun, her shapely, tanned legs daintily stretched in front of her in a skirt short enough to cause male heart failure.

While I'm wearing capri jeans, a sleeveless blouse and flat tennies, my hair in a ponytail.

It didn't matter. She'd held Justin in her arms. Even though he hadn't said the words, she knew he loved her.

She certainly was in love with him.

Mackenzie heard a squeal and commotion, and she glanced at Daisy again. Suz leaped on Daisy with a burlap bag, stuffing her in it before Ty carted her, struggling, to his truck bed and put her in it as if she were nothing more than a hay bale. He waved at Mackenzie; then he and Suz hopped in the truck and drove away.

Maybe it was cheating. Technically it was breaking the rules. Certainly she'd raised her sister to be more genteel and ladylike than to pin someone down and stuff them into a sack.

One day she'd return the favor for Suz. The very thought made her smile, and now that she was alone at the finish line of Best Man's Fork, Mackenzie suddenly felt very, very happy. In love.

As if this was the moment she'd been waiting for all her life.

Chapter 20

"Ready, set, go!" Cosette yelled and Philippe fired the starting gun, which brought a cheer from the crowd anxious to see Justin start the race.

He waved at everyone and took off at what he hoped was an impressive pace. His buddies had disappeared.

Which was fine with him. "I've got this," he muttered and headed to the fork. He didn't even hesitate; he already knew which way he was going.

He chose the left side of the fork, and a cheer went up from the crowd who'd gathered at the starting line. Justin couldn't say that this was something he'd ever imagined he'd be doing, but he was having a ton of fun. He felt like a warrior of some kind, a troubadour of old, going off to win his lady.

Which no doubt was exactly how Bridesmaids Creek intended a man to feel. Part of the fairy-tale charm and all that. Kind of silly, but if this was the way things were done here, he'd play along.

At the one-mile marker, the race monitor waved at him, offered him a water bottle, which Justin accepted, heading off without resting, determined to make a good showing.

At the one-and-a-half-mile marker—so designated by a giant heart-shaped sign posted on a tree—Justin was joined by the five doorknobs.

Daisy's gang set a pace behind him without saying a word. "More the merrier," he muttered and kept going.

They surrounded him at the two-mile marker, not touching him, but pacing along, in back and in front of him.

Annoying but not important. He had a job to do.

"Nice day, huh, fellows?" he said, just to be friendly, and then he ignored them as he tried to dismiss the fact that his knee was beginning to protest the treatment it was receiving.

Daisy's gang changed position, two on either side and one in the back. What the hell, maybe they figured they no longer needed a leader. He knew exactly where he was going, after all.

At the two-and-a-half-mile marker—another big heart-shaped sign—a commotion broke out behind him. Justin kept moving, not looking back, but his companions on either side of him did, and suddenly all hell broke loose.

Then silence.

"Don't look back, remember," he muttered and kept on going.

He ran alone after that, his thoughts busy with Mackenzie and the babies and how great it was going to feel when she told him yes. What man didn't think of the woman he loved telling him she wanted to be his wife?

He stopped dead in his tracks.

He'd *never* thought of it. Yet suddenly he couldn't *stop* thinking about it.

"Holy cow, there *is* something in the air around here." He glanced around, studying the thick foliage on either side of him. His shoes were dusty from the dirt road and his leg ached—he was far from his rodeo shape. The air was completely silent but for the occasional birdcall—mockingbird, for sure—and the sun beat down on him.

Some sixth sense or maybe even some of Bridesmaids Creek's enchantment pushed him into the woods. He crunched through tall grass and ground cover, beat back branches that rarely had experienced human contact until he got to the other road.

This was right. It was a rebel move, but he was playing a game with folks who were known to make the rules to suit themselves.

At the end of this road would be the woman of his dreams. That was how the legend went.

He ran like he'd never run before.

Justin nearly had heart failure when he saw the final race monitor a hundred yards from the finish line, because Mackenzie wasn't there. His spirits sank. He looked wildly past the monitor, barely heard the greeting offered to him and crossed the tape at the finish line, bent over to gasp for air.

He could not believe he'd picked the wrong road. He hung his head. What the hell—it was a dumb charity race. He'd made the town some money, felt like he was a newfound son they were trying to weave into the fabric of their town.

It would all work out. He'd still ask Mackenzie to marry him, and hopefully she would say yes.

She might be a little tangled up because of that business with her ex being a loser at the race and the legend not working out too well for her that first time, but he could get her past that. Somehow.

He'd just have to convince her how much he wanted to be with her and the girls, forever.

"Hi," he heard at his elbow, and Justin stood straight up. Stared into his gorgeous lady's eyes, felt the mysterious wonder of Bridesmaids Creek fill him, changing him forever.

"Mackenzie!" He swept her into his arms. "Will you marry me?"

She laughed, and it sounded like pure joy to him. "Yes! Yes, of course. I would love to be your wife."

"I'm sorry." Justin took a deep breath. "I meant to ask you more romantically with flowers, a ring, maybe some hot sex to convince you I'm the only man for you."

"That was all pretty romantic." She kissed him, and it *was* the happiest moment of his life. Justin held Mackenzie in his arms, hardly believing how perfect his world had suddenly become.

"You were supposed to be at the finish line, weren't you? I thought I'd taken the wrong road." He ate her up with his eyes, wondering if he could get her to a wedding ceremony fast enough to suit him.

"I had to get the girls." She smiled up at him, and he saw Jade and Betty with the stroller of babies waiting under a shady tree. "The babies wanted to see you win."

"I'm a dad," he said. "I'm going to be a father to four

beautiful little girls! I'm going to have four beautiful daughters and a gorgeous wife!" He laughed, hugging Mackenzie to him, his whole world opening up in a new way he'd waited his entire life to feel. Justin held Mackenzie, basking in the cheers from the townspeople who realized they were about to get their fondest wish, a wedding to attend.

"I love you, Mackenzie Hawthorne. The best thing that ever happened to me was the day Ty sent me to your ranch. I'm the luckiest man in the world."

Mackenzie laughed. "I love you, too," she said, "welcome home."

Justin grinned, reveling in the most magical, heavenly moment of his life. How had this happened to him? How had he gotten the woman of his dreams, and the family he'd always hoped he'd one day have? He looked at the smiling faces of the people around them, felt their joy as they shared this amazing moment with them. It didn't matter how the fairy tale had happened. All that mattered was Mackenzie and the daughters he loved with all his heart.

He was home at last.

Epilogue

"So what about the haunted house?" Ty asked Justin on a day that was so beautiful Justin didn't think he'd ever known a better one. Of course most of the beauty that was in his life now was thanks to Mackenzie and her babies. He grumbled, slightly nervous as Ty situated his jacket and tie, having never been a groom before, only the man running in the Best Man's Fork race just last week.

It had been worth everything he had to see the smile on Mackenzie's face when he'd chosen the right path.

He allowed Ty to stuff a pocket square in his jacket, a useless detail he felt was unnecessary for the casual wedding he and Mackenzie wanted, but Ty was a stickler for details. "Mackenzie says the haunted house is part of Bridesmaids Creek. Now that there's some confusion about whether folks really want it reopened or not—"

"Hogwash," Ty said. "That was just stuff Daisy stirred up."

True, but Justin had done his part, which was rescuing fair maidens, all five of them. Actually, they'd rescued him. Now he was going to enjoy life in their world. "Mackenzie says it's a battle she's going to let Suz handle at this point. She says if anyone can corral Daisy, it's Suz." Mackenzie had also said that her time would now be completely taken up by making love to him, and haunted houses would have to take a backseat to that.

Which made him very, very happy.

"I don't like it," Ty grumbled. "No one else has any good ideas on how to save BC. That was my best one."

"It's fine, old buddy. You did your part. You can relax now." He slapped Ty on the back. "I want to thank you for telling me about Mackenzie's fake dating ad, by the way. Madame Matchmaker better watch out for you, obviously."

Ty laughed, pleased with himself. "It wasn't fake. I just never let it go live. And that's the last thing you're dragging out of me. I can't give up all my trade secrets."

They went downstairs and made a path to the altar. Justin was amazed by how many people had arrived to see their wedding, but then he realized he shouldn't be—this was BC. Everybody was always going to be in everybody's business—which was something that no longer worried him.

"Now I just need my bride," Justin said, and on cue the three-piece orchestra of two violins and a harp began playing and the guests swiveled their heads to look for the bride.

Suz came down the aisle first, sassy in a short pink dress, unable to resist squashing Ty on the toe with her high heel before she took her place at the altar.

"What was that for?" Ty asked Justin.

"I think you're in the doghouse for not fixing her up,

too." But Justin couldn't worry about his buddy right now, because Mackenzie came around the corner, escorted by Sheriff Dennis, and Justin's heart felt like it was going to explode with joy. The babies were wheeled in a white carriage hung with pretty pink-and-white bows to the edge of the altar so they could have a front-row seat, and a happy sigh went up from the guests.

Mackenzie stood beside him, a short veil gracing her midlength faint pink wedding gown, her smile all for him.

"You're beautiful," he said. "The happiest moment in my life was watching you and the babies come down that aisle." He took her hand and kissed it, and the guests sighed again. "I love you so much."

"I love you," Mackenzie said. "I do, and my girls do, too. We all do."

"Yeah," Suz whispered. "Welcome to our family."

Okay, so maybe most sisters-in-law wouldn't butt in, but it was Suz, and, frankly, he was delighted to hear that she thought he was a good thing for her sister. Mackenzie laughed and he smiled; the babies laid almost perfectly still in their pram, fussed over by Cosette and Jane, and Justin's life became a rodeo of a different kind. Bigger, better, happier.

Which was a completely happy ending for a rebel cowboy.

And if he thought he heard Ty mutter, "One down, three to go," he paid no attention to his buddy at all.

It was a most enchanted day in Bridesmaids Creek.

* * * * *

Since 2002, *USA TODAY* bestselling author **Judy Duarte** has written over forty books for Harlequin Special Edition, earned two RITA® Award nominations, won two MAGGIE® Awards and received a National Readers' Choice Award. When she's not cooped up in her writing cave, she enjoys traveling with her husband and spending quality time with her grandchildren. You can learn more about Judy and her books on her website, judyduarte.com, or at Facebook.com/judyduartenovelist.

Books by Judy Duarte

Harlequin Special Edition

Rocking Chair Rodeo

Roping in the Cowgirl

**The Fortunes of Texas:
All Fortune's Children**

Wed by Fortune

Brighton Valley Cowboys

*The Cowboy's Double Trouble
Having the Cowboy's Baby
The Boss, the Bride
& the Baby*

Return to Brighton Valley

*The Soldier's Holiday
Homecoming
The Bachelor's Brighton
Valley Bride
The Daddy Secret*

**The Fortunes of Texas:
Cowboy Country**

A Royal Fortune

**The Fortunes of Texas:
Welcome to
Horseback Hollow**

A House Full of Fortunes!

Brighton Valley Babies

*The Cowboy's Family Plan
The Rancher's Hired Fiancée
A Baby Under the Tree*

Visit the Author Profile page at Harlequin.com for more titles.

THE COWBOY'S
FAMILY PLAN

JUDY DUARTE

To Bob and Betty Astleford, whose family plan included me. Thank you for all your love and support through the years. I love you!

Chapter 1

As Alex Connor reached the door of the community education room at the Brighton Valley Wellness Center, a shudder of apprehension shot through him, and he froze momentarily.

Once he stepped inside, he was going to feel as out of place as a circus clown on a wild bronc, but he wasn't going to wallow in it. He owed it to Mary, his late wife, to learn all he could about surrogacy. So he shook off his uneasiness, swallowed his pride and entered the classroom, his limp a bit more pronounced than it had been when he woke up this morning.

The room wasn't full, although there were plenty of people already seated, most of them couples, whose expressions ran the gamut from hopeful to uneasy to I'd-rather-be-anywhere-but-here-tonight. And Alex knew how every one of them felt, especially the ones who looked as if it wouldn't take much for them to bolt.

A few of those in attendance were women on their own, with no husband or partner in sight. Alex did his best not to look at them, not to think about Mary, who'd had to research in vitro fertilization on her own four years ago.

Now here he was, learning what he should have learned with her back then.

Alex wasn't the only man in the room this evening, but he was the only one who'd arrived by himself. Shaking off his uneasiness, he chose a seat in the front row and placed his Stetson on the empty chair next to him. Then he waited for the class to begin.

It had been nearly three years since he'd lost Mary, along with the baby she carried. And now that he'd dealt with the grief, he was determined to do everything he could to make sure his and Mary's remaining two babies, just frozen embryos now, had a chance to live. Unfortunately, Mary had been the one who'd had any real understanding of the whole in vitro process. She'd merely showed him the papers he needed to sign and told him how much to pay, where to be and what to do. So he found himself at a bit of a loss now—and a bit guilty at not being more involved during the whole clinical part of the process.

He would have made an appointment to talk to Dr. Avery, Mary's obstetrician, if the guy hadn't retired a while back and sold his practice to a Dr. Ramirez.

Alex had planned to talk to the new doctor, but as luck would have it, the guy was giving a series of three lectures on fertility options on Tuesday nights.

Luck, huh? Alex might have been fortunate to chance upon that flyer, but his reason for being at the wellness center in the first place had been the result of a preventable accident and an order for physical therapy.

Nearly six months ago, he'd walked behind his prize stallion, Blazing Thunder, and gotten kicked, which had been a dumb move on his part. As a result, he'd suffered a broken kneecap, which had sidelined him for months. He'd needed orthopedic surgery, and after the bones had healed, he'd been sent to physical therapy.

Last week, while working with Maria, his therapist at the wellness center, he'd spotted that poster. Because one of the topics dealt with finding and hiring a surrogate, he'd signed up to take the classes, which were being taught by none other than Dr. Ramirez.

So call it luck or fate or chance, here he was.

He'd planned to sit through this first lecture, then afterward, catch the doctor alone and pick his brain.

Mary had thought the world of Dr. Avery. Alex just hoped that Dr. Ramirez, whoever he was, would be just as competent.

So what was keeping him?

Alex glanced at his wristwatch, noting it was almost seven. The doctor ought to be here by now.

Moments later, he heard the sound of the door swinging open at the back of the room.

Footsteps clicked upon the tile floor, drawing closer.

Alex turned and glanced to the right, just as an attractive brunette wearing a white lab coat over a green dress strode toward the lectern.

Alex wasn't sure why he'd assumed that the obstetrician would be a man. It's not as though he had any qualms about a female physician; it's just that this one appeared to be too...young...too petite...too attractive.

But she certainly had an air of confidence about her.

He slowly turned to the front and waited for her to step behind the podium.

As she did so, she offered the audience a pretty yet professional smile and said, "Good evening, everyone. I'm Dr. Ramirez."

Her voice held a slight Spanish accent, although just barely, and he listened as she began covering the basic causes of infertility. Alex wasn't all that interested in that particular topic, though. And as he tried to focus on what she had to say, he couldn't seem to think about anything other than the fact that none of his doctors had ever looked like her. And was he ever grateful for that.

If the lovely Dr. Ramirez would have walked into an exam room while he'd been seated on the table, she would have had to treat him for an excessive heart rate and high blood pressure.

For that reason, he'd better rein in his thoughts and listen to what she was saying.

While he did his best to concentrate on her words, he was struck by her mannerisms: the way she cocked her head slightly to the side, the way she gripped the side of the lectern and leaned forward to make a point, the way she lifted her left hand—which wasn't wearing a ring.

Several times during the talk, he could have sworn he'd caught her looking right at him, her cheeks slightly flushed. And when she turned away to scan the audience, she cleared her throat and took a moment to skim over her notes.

Maybe public speaking made her nervous.

Or maybe she found a lone male sitting in the front row to be a little unnerving.

On the other hand, it might have been something about Alex that had caught her eye.

Nah, it couldn't be that. He'd probably just imagined her interest in him. Sleeping solo in a king-size bed for the past three years did crazy things to a man, he supposed, made him think that it was time to start looking for another woman to share his life once again.

And right now, that's the last thing Alex needed to think about. He had a surrogate to hire. Then, God willing, both remaining embryos would be implanted and he'd have two babies to raise.

As the audience broke into applause, Alex clapped, too, realizing the lecture was over and that he'd missed almost everything Dr. Ramirez said.

When she asked if there were any questions, he kept his arms crossed over his chest and let the others raise their hands instead. He had plenty of questions, of course, but most of them had to do with surrogacy, which she was supposed to discuss during the last class.

Finally, his classmates began to file out of the room, providing him with the opportunity he'd wanted—to quiz the doctor in private.

So he remained in his seat, while she gathered her notes and folded them back in the file on the podium. Then he rose and made his way to her, his Stetson in hand.

When she noticed his approach, her movements froze and her lips parted.

Her brown eyes, which were almost hazel, widened. Her thick dark lashes, natural and unenhanced by mascara, fluttered once, twice. Then she licked her bottom lip and cleared her throat.

Clearly he'd caught her off guard, so he offered her a friendly grin and said, "I wondered if I could have a few minutes of your time."

Selena Ramirez hadn't expected the handsome cowboy who'd been sitting in the front row to come up to her after her class. In fact, his presence had caused her to lose her train of thought several times during the lecture.

Who was he?

What was he doing here?

Where was his wife or partner?

And why was he coming to speak to her now?

He must have read the questions in her eyes because he added, "I'd like to pick your brain, if I may."

Goodness, right now, he could "pick" just about anything he wanted. But she shook off the inappropriate thoughts. She'd certainly provided time for questions and answers, but maybe he was too embarrassed or shy to speak in front of people. So she asked, "What did you want to know, Mr.…."

"Connor. Alex. My late wife was a patient of Dr. Avery."

Selena wasn't sure what had stunned her the most, the fact that he was a widower or that he'd come to the lecture on infertility by himself.

"I'm not sure I understand," she said.

"I'd like to ask you a couple of questions that I didn't want to bring up in front of everyone else."

She could understand that, but she wasn't able to talk to him here and now. "There's a board meeting scheduled at eight, so we'll need to clear the room."

Disappointment swept across his brow, revealing an intensity she hadn't expected, an emotion she couldn't quite peg.

She glanced at her watch, a silver bangle style, then

looked up at him and smiled. "But I have a little time. We can talk out in the lobby."

"Why don't we go to the cafeteria?" he asked. "I'll buy you a cup of coffee, latte or whatever."

The suggestion took her by surprise. And so did the boyish grin that set off an impish glimmer in his blue eyes.

"Please?" he asked.

She was certainly tempted. She also had a few questions she'd like to ask him. From the first moment she'd scanned the audience and spotted him sitting front and center, his hat lying on the chair next to him, she'd wondered about him. So what would it hurt to spend a few minutes with him in the cafeteria?

"All right. Coffee actually sounds good."

His smile broadened, lighting up those eyes like a Texas summer sky and knocking her completely off stride.

How was that possible? She'd never been into cowboys. Not that there was anything wrong with them. It's just that she'd always dated professional men.

Dated? Now that was a joke. When was the last time she'd had a date? Not since settling in Brighton Valley, that was for sure.

She noticed that he seemed to favor his left leg.

A new injury? she wondered. Or an old one?

Either way, she found herself heading to the cafeteria with a man who wanted to "pick her brain."

The cafeteria in the wellness center was actually a small counter area just off the lobby called The Health Nut, where they sold coffee and tea, as well as various waters, energy drinks, fruit juices and smoothies. They also provided nutritious snacks for people on the run.

While Dr. Ramirez carried her cup of coffee to one of several tables set out for those people who had more time on their hands, Alex paid with a twenty, then joined her.

"Thanks for giving me a few minutes of your time," he said as he took a seat next to hers.

"No problem."

"You're probably wondering why I signed up for your class," Alex said, his hands braced around the disposable cup.

"When I first spotted you sitting alone in the front row, I thought you might be a reporter," she said.

"I'm afraid not. I actually came to learn more about the topic you'll address during week three."

"Surrogacy?"

He nodded, then lifted his cup and took a sip. "My late wife and I had planned to have children through in vitro fertilization. We'd gotten through the fertilization process. And after the first attempt at implantation failed, we finally managed to get pregnant, but…" He paused for a moment, then glanced down at the coffee in his cup, while he relived the phone call he'd received from the sheriff's office, telling him that Mary had been involved in a car accident, that she was being rushed to the Brighton Valley Medical Center E.R., that she… might not make it.

"But…?" the doctor prodded.

Alex sucked it up, the memory, the grief, the guilt, the promise he was determined to keep. "My wife died when she was twenty weeks pregnant."

"I'm sorry." The softness in the doctor's voice, the

light cadence of her accent, provided an unexpected balm to feelings that were still raw at times.

It seemed surreal now, like a bad dream. But he gave a half shrug, as if that was all there was to it, when, in truth, it was all too complicated to explain.

"So how can I help?" she asked, the sincerity in her tone, the sympathy in her eyes making him wonder if she just might hold the key to everything.

So he took a deep breath, then slowly let it out. "I still have two embryos left, and I want to hire a surrogate to carry them. But I need to learn more about the process—the pitfalls, that sort of thing. I'll be looking for someone healthy and of sound mind. I also want to feel completely assured that whoever I choose won't have a change of heart after the implantation. You know what I mean?"

"Absolutely. Your concerns are all valid, and you're wise to learn all you can before making any decisions."

"So how do I go about finding the right surrogate?"

"What you're actually looking for is a gestational carrier because you don't need a woman to donate any of her eggs. Of course, with only two remaining embryos, you'll have only one shot at implanting them."

"If it doesn't work, I'll deal with it." He wasn't interested in going through the whole process again, unless he needed to down the line. But then again, the first go-round had been way too clinical for him to ever want to go through it again.

The doctor nodded, as if she understood.

"So where do I start?" he asked.

"You can, of course, try to find someone on your own. Oftentimes a friend or a family member will help. But there are also several reputable agencies, most of which are based in Houston, that can help you. I'd planned to give a list of them to the class during the third week, but if you'll be here next Tuesday, I can give you one then."

"That would be great." He tossed her a warm, appreciative grin, glad he'd come tonight, glad he'd asked her to have coffee with him. "I'll definitely be back next week and would like that list, so thank you."

"I'm sure you've invested a lot in the process already, but you're looking at another big investment."

Alex knew that, but he could afford it. And even if he couldn't, he hadn't touched any of the insurance money he'd received after Mary's death yet.

Still, he wanted to be sure he'd been given the right scoop. "I've heard it can cost up to a hundred grand, plus medical expenses."

"That sounds about right, although it varies with each agency. And with each carrier. Those with a proven track record will cost more." Dr. Ramirez lifted her cup and took a drink.

It was weird, Alex thought. Here he was, sitting across from a beautiful woman, having coffee as if they were friends, yet he didn't even know her first name.

He wouldn't ask—at least, not now.

"You must have loved your wife a lot," she said. "The whole surrogacy/implantation process can be daunting at times, especially when someone has to go through it alone."

To be honest, Alex hadn't been very receptive to the idea when Mary had first mentioned in vitro. He'd thought it sounded too cold, too unnatural. But rather than admit to Dr. Ramirez that he'd been less than enthusiastic at the start of the whole process, he said,

"Mary was a good wife and would have made a great mother."

A shadow of emotion crossed the doctor's face—sympathy, Alex supposed—but she didn't comment. And he was glad that she hadn't.

What was there to say? Mary would've been a wonderful mother, and Alex was sorry she'd never had the chance. All she'd ever wanted in life was to have kids and create a happy home. So when she'd learned that she wasn't able to get pregnant, she'd been devastated by the news. But she'd rallied by researching all the options available to her, and before long, she'd become obsessed with having a baby—*their* baby.

Alex had wanted to start a family, too, and had suggested they consider adoption. But Mary had refused to even think about it until they'd exhausted all their chances of having their own biological child.

He'd finally agreed, and after the second implantation had been successful, resulting in a positive pregnancy test, he'd been as excited as Mary to think that they'd finally have a little one around the house. A baby. Imagine that.

But they hadn't even had time to think about decorating and stocking a nursery when Mary had the accident.

The afternoon Alex had received the call from the sheriff's office, telling him that his wife had been critically injured and wasn't expected to live, he'd raced to the Brighton Valley Medical Center E.R., just in time to have a few last words with her. Important words.

She'd known that the baby she carried at the time wouldn't make it. But Alex still had the other embryos. And Mary had begged him to make sure they had a chance to live.

"How did your wife die?" Dr. Ramirez asked, drawing him from his somber musing.

"In a car accident."

"I'm sorry," she said again.

"Yeah." Alex cleared his throat. "Me, too."

He'd grieved Mary's death, of course, but he blamed himself for it, too. She'd asked him to pick up a list of groceries while he'd been in town, but he'd gotten so caught up talking to a couple of friends at the feed store that the errand she'd asked him to run had completely slipped his mind, and he'd gone home before a predicted summer rain hit.

Now I'll just have to go get them myself, Mary had told him.

And Alex had let her go out to her car that rainy day—a decision he'd felt sorry about the moment he'd realized how dark and ugly the sky had turned, a regret he'd have until his own dying day.

Why hadn't he made a note for himself? Why hadn't he picked up the items she'd needed before stopping to talk to Dan Walker and Ray Mendez?

Now Mary was gone, leaving him with the last two embryos to think about, to protect and nurture.

No, he told himself. *Not* embryos. *Babies. His and Mary's babies.*

But he didn't want to open old wounds any more than he already had this evening. So after he finished off the last of his coffee, he said, "Thank you for talking to me, Doctor."

"Please," she said. "Call me Selena."

Selena. It was a pretty name, and one that fit her, if you left "Doctor" out of the equation.

"All right, Selena." Her name rolled right off the tip

of his tongue as if it was the easiest word in the world to say. And as he came to that realization, a smile formed from somewhere deep inside of him.

Were they becoming friends? If so, he was okay with it.

Was she?

Selena wasn't sure why she'd suggested that Mr. Connor—or rather, Alex—call her by her first name. Maybe it was because they'd somehow bonded over the time it took to drink a cup of coffee.

Or maybe they were kindred spirits because his plight was similar to her own. He couldn't have his wife's babies without the help of someone willing to carry them. And Selena couldn't have a child unless a birth mother was willing to give up a baby she couldn't keep or didn't want to raise.

Eighteen months ago, following a routine exam, Selena had learned that she'd never be able to get pregnant or carry a baby to term. The news had been heartbreaking for a woman who'd always dreamed of being a mother.

She'd hoped that with time, she would adjust to the reality and deal with it, but knowing that she'd never be able to experience the miracle of conception or go through the birth process had really begun to niggle at her lately.

Okay, she admitted. It was way more than a niggle. She'd been so dismayed, so crushed by the situation that doing her job had become more and more difficult with each passing day. Every time she thought of the miracle of conception, heard the cries of a newborn or spotted the happy tears of a new mommy holding her baby for the very first time, her disappointment grew.

At one time, she'd thought she had the perfect career. She loved delivering babies. But ever since the surgery and learning that she'd never be able to experience the miracle of childbirth herself, she'd found it getting tougher to go to the office each day.

But she shook off the melancholic thought, picked up her empty, heat-resistant paper cup and got to her feet. "Thanks for the coffee."

"You're more than welcome." Alex pushed back his seat and stood. "Thank you for agreeing to teach the class. You're providing a great service to people who are struggling with fertility issues."

She probably ought to respond and say something about being happy to offer those couples various options, but the truth was, she'd been seriously considering a career change of some kind and had almost refused to give the lecture series at all.

"Can I walk you to your car?" he asked.

For a moment, she wondered if his interest in her had been more romantic in nature than merely polite and appreciative, but she dismissed that thought as quickly as it had come to her. Alex Connor had loved his wife so much that he was determined to bring their children into the world and raise them without her.

She glanced at the handsome cowboy beside her, deciding that his offer had been a gallant gesture. "Thanks, but I'm parked in a safe place."

"All right." He lobbed another smile her way, sending her heart on a scavenger hunt for miracles that didn't exist.

"Good night, Selena."

She clung to the sound of her name on his lips, to the sincerity in those green eyes. But she cleared her voice and took a step back. "Good night, Alex."

"I'll see you next week."

Yes, she supposed he would. As she turned and strode toward the exit, she couldn't help thinking that Alex Connor was an attractive and appealing man. But she'd never dated the cowboy types—and didn't plan to in the future.

Yet even more than that, he was still devoted to his late-wife's memory. So Selena would do her best to shake any inappropriate thoughts about him.

She knew how it felt to fall for a man who'd never gotten over his first true love. And she knew just how painful a broken heart could be.

As a result, she'd vowed never to play second fiddle again.

Still, as she stepped into the parking lot, she couldn't help being a little envious of the late Mary Connor.

Chapter 2

Late Thursday afternoon, when her last patient had left and she'd closed up the office, Selena had driven to the new Brighton Valley Wellness Center.

A few days after it had opened for business, Selena had taken a tour with several of her colleagues. She'd been amazed at all the facility had to offer the community, including a rehab unit, a state-of-the-art gym, physical trainers on hand to answer questions or provide private lessons, an indoor pool, a variety of classes. But more than that, it also catered to the disabled and elderly because of its close connection to the medical center.

In fact, Selena had been so impressed with the center that she'd signed up before leaving that day, telling herself it wasn't just about becoming more physically fit. After all, she watched her diet and jogged daily. But joining the BVWC would also fit nicely into her get-out-into-the-real-world-and-start-living-again campaign.

Now all she had to do was find the time to work out, because she usually kept busy with her ever-growing practice. However, on the days she had another doctor covering for her, she slipped on a pair of shorts, a T-shirt and a pair of sneakers, just as she'd done today.

Now here she was, jogging on the treadmill and working up a sweat. With each stride she made, she pondered her options and considered the other medical specialties that had always interested her. The problem was, without going back to school and racking up more student loans, she'd have to settle on general or family medicine.

But not in Brighton Valley. In spite of the respect she'd earned in the medical community, she was giving some serious thought to selling her practice and moving back to Houston, where she'd change her specialty to one that didn't revolve around pregnancy and newborns.

That was her secret, though. That and the fact that there were way too many nights she'd found her small condominium overlooking the playground at the city park to be painfully quiet, nights when she'd cry herself to sleep.

She'd loved that complex and the two-bedroom condo. But after learning she'd never get pregnant, she'd listed it for sale. And just six months ago, after selling her first home to a couple of newlyweds, she'd moved to a quiet, older neighborhood in town.

When her time on the treadmill came to an end and she began the cool-down process, she scanned the gym and spotted a man who looked a lot like Alex Connor. In fact, it *was* Alex, only minus his Stetson and boots. Today he wore a Texas Aggies T-shirt and a pair of sweatpants, rather than the cowboy garb he'd had on Tuesday night.

He was talking to one of the female fitness instructors—a tall, lean blonde with a healthy glow.

What was he doing here? Not that it mattered, she supposed. It's just that she'd been a little surprised when he hadn't blinked about the cost of hiring a gestational carrier to bear his children.

At the time, she'd suspected that he might own a ranch. But why was he working out at a gym in town? Wouldn't he get enough exercise from riding and roping and doing whatever else was required of him?

So who was Alex Connor?

Ever since she'd shared a cup of coffee with him, she'd found herself thinking about him, wondering about him. She'd chalked it up to her interest in the relationship he must have had with his late wife, but the man himself intrigued her.

She shut off the treadmill, then stepped onto the floor, her knees a little wobbly from the exertion. Then she started for the women's locker room, where she would shower and change into her street clothes.

Before she could get ten steps—or tear her gaze from Alex and the female trainer—he glanced across the room and noticed her. He waved, then moments later, he left the blonde's side and made his way to Selena.

"Hey, fancy meeting you here," he said.

She could say the same thing. Instead, she smiled. "It's my day off, and I thought I'd get a little exercise in."

"Do you like it here?" he asked.

"Yes, I do. It's a great facility." Her curiosity mounted until she asked, "Are you thinking about joining?"

"I would if I lived in town."

Where *did* he live? And why was he here?

She couldn't very well come out and pummel him with all of her questions, so she tossed out an easy one, hoping to get a little more information.

"So why are you dressed as if you're thinking about joining?" she asked, prodding him again.

"I'm here for a couple of other reasons, one of which is business."

At that, she couldn't help but cock a brow. And he chuckled.

"Jim Ragsdale, who's on the wellness center board of directors, wanted to meet with me today. They're interested in providing hippotherapy for adults and children with physical and emotional difficulties, and he wanted to run a couple of ideas past me."

She didn't know all that much about the program that used horseback riding as therapy for the disabled, other than those who'd taken part often showed improved balance, coordination, speech and mobility.

"It's interesting that they're thinking of adding that to their wellness program," she said.

He nodded. "I was intrigued when Jim first mentioned it, too, so I agreed to meet with him while I was in town today."

"Why the gym clothes?" she finally asked, unable to avoid a more direct approach.

"Yeah, well…" He sighed and gave a little shrug. "I messed up my knee a while back, and my orthopedic surgeon sent me to physical therapy, which I get here."

"How did you get hurt?" she asked.

"I…uh… Well, it was pretty stupid."

"Most accidents are."

Alex chuffed. "I thought I was immune to that sort of thing, but that's what I get for taking shortcuts and not keeping my mind on my work."

He still hadn't told her what he'd done, but she refrained from pushing any further. After all, his injury really wasn't any of her business.

"So what are you doing now?" he asked.

"I'm going to head home and get a bite to eat."

"Oh, yeah? Me, too. Why don't you let me buy you dinner? There's a little café a couple of blocks from here."

She wondered if he had more questions this time around—or if he just wanted to spend some quiet time with her. As appealing as the latter seemed to be, she shook off the feminine thoughts. "You don't need to buy my dinner."

"All right. Then we'll ask for separate checks."

As she pondered the invitation, shaking off the urge to agree too quickly, he added, "You probably spend way too much time around the hospital and this place anyway."

He was right. And she had made up her mind to spend a little more time getting out into the world… So she said, "Sounds good to me. Do you mind if I take a quick shower and put on my street clothes? I won't take long."

"I'll wait for you in the lobby area."

"All right."

True to her word, she returned within ten minutes. "Sorry I took so long."

"You didn't." He got to his feet, and they made their way to the entrance. He opened the door and waited for her to exit first.

How about that? The handsome cowboy was well-mannered as well. She'd have to make a note of that.

Oh, for Pete's sake. Alex Connor wasn't the kind of man she'd ever allow herself to crush on—and for several reasons, the biggest of which was the fact that he still seemed to be in love with his late-wife.

In college, Selena had fallen for a graduate student in the biotech program. They'd had something special, or so Selena had thought. She'd even started daydreaming about June weddings.

Then, when he went home for Christmas break, he met up with his first love, and their high school romance had blossomed again.

Selena, of course, had been heartbroken and had vowed never to get involved with a man who still pined over a lost lover—and that would certainly include late wives.

Of course, sharing a cup of coffee and killing an hour or so before bedtime wasn't even close to having a date or "getting involved."

"It's a nice evening for walking," Alex said, as they made their way across the parking lot and to the street.

Selena looked up at a nearly full moon and an array of bright, twinkling stars. "You're right."

When was the last time she'd taken time to gaze at the evening sky, let alone noticed the natural beauty in nature?

She couldn't remember. She'd been so caught up in her practice that she'd spent her days and nights either holed up at the medical center or at home. But she was trying to change that—first with the membership at the wellness center and maybe even with her agreement to walk to the coffee shop this evening with Alex Connor.

As they stepped onto the sidewalk and turned to the right on a side street that ran along the busier county road, she realized that Alex walked with a limp.

"Maybe we should have driven," she said.

"It's only a couple of blocks."

They continued in silence until Alex asked, "What made you want to be a doctor?"

"I don't know. I've always had an interest in medicine. And science and math were my favorite subjects when I was in high school, so it seemed like a natural career choice to make."

Her efforts had also pleased her parents, something that was important to a girl who was the middle child in a family with seven siblings. And those same efforts had proven to be invaluable because she'd been offered a full-ride scholarship at almost every college to which she'd applied.

"Why did you choose obstetrics?" Alex asked.

Because she'd loved babies ever since the time her mother had first laid her newborn brother in her chubby little arms. But because she'd always thought her reason for choosing obstetrics wasn't all that impressive, she gave him her standard response when people asked the same question. "I found the birth process fascinating."

At least she'd found it fascinating when she'd envisioned experiencing it herself once or twice.

But enough about her. The conversation and the questions were getting way too personal for comfort, and she was ready for a change in subject.

She was tempted to start by turning his original question right back on him and ask, *What made you want to be a cowboy?*

But maybe she'd been wrong about him. Maybe there was more to Alex than a Stetson and boots.

The Aggie T-shirt he was wearing suggested he might have attended college. And he hadn't blinked about the cost of having a woman carry those embryos for him.

Maybe she'd been right. Maybe he was a rancher. After all, he'd mentioned that he lived outside of town.

Either way, if Jim Ragsdale had approached him about the hippotherapy program, his background with horses had to be pretty impressive. So he was more than the average cowboy.

Before she could ask what line of work he was in, he pointed to the red-and-white-striped awning over the entrance of the coffee shop he'd been talking about. "There it is. Katie's Country Café."

Even though the diner was located within sight of those who traveled along the nearby county road, it didn't appear to be too busy this evening.

As they neared the entry, a pregnant brunette who'd parked her weathered sedan in one of several spaces in front opened the rear passenger door and removed a preschool-age girl from her car seat. Then she waited for an older boy to climb from the car.

The mother and children walked into the diner, just in front of Selena and Alex. The boy, who was about seven or eight, spotted the refrigerator display case that held a variety of pies and cakes.

"Look," the boy said to his sister as he pointed to the goodies. "Maybe we can have dessert, Kimmie."

"Grandma will have cookies for us when we get to her house," the pregnant woman said. "So we'll just grab a quick bite to eat here."

As they all waited to be seated, a waitress serving slices of chocolate cake to an elderly couple in one of the booths in back said, "Y'all can choose any table you like."

The mother reached for her daughter's hand, then gasped and looked down at her feet, where her amniotic fluid had formed a puddle. "Uh-oh."

The little girl pointed to the wet spot and asked, "Mommy, did you potty in your pants?"

"No, sweetie. I…" The woman, her cheeks flushed, her eyes wide, glanced at Selena, her embarrassment and apprehension obvious. "My water broke."

It certainly had. And she just stood there, clearly perplexed.

"Can I call someone for you?" Selena asked, thinking the woman's husband ought to be notified.

"My mother, but that's not going to do me much good now."

"Why not?"

"Because she doesn't drive at night. The kids and I were on our way to pick her up and take her back home with us so she could help out when the baby came, but…"

"But what?" Selena prodded.

The woman paled and bit down on her bottom lip. "This wasn't supposed to happen. I'm not due for another five or six weeks."

Selena turned to Alex, who'd taken a step back and was watching the drama unfold with an expression that said he was out of his league when it came to this sort of thing.

About that time, the waitress made her way to the

front of the diner with a mop. "Here, sweetie. I'll get this cleaned up for you."

The pregnant woman blew out a ragged sigh. "I don't know what to do."

"Who's your doctor?" Selena asked, reaching into her purse to pull out her cell phone.

"Martin Staley, but he's not from around here. He's in Houston. And my mom…" The woman reached for her lower belly and groaned as another pain gripped her.

Apparently, her contractions weren't going to waste any time in starting up. She was clearly going into labor—and before term.

As the pain subsided, Selena studied the woman. If the boy and girl with her were her natural-born children, she'd given birth before. So if that was the case, her labor could go more quickly than that of a first-time mother.

"Oh, no," the woman said, raking a hand through her head. "What do I do? Who do I call?"

Selena placed a hand on her back, trying to relieve her fear. "I'm a doctor, so you're not alone. How long was your last labor?"

"Two and a half hours. It went so fast, I almost didn't make it to the hospital in time. In fact, that's why Dr. Staley told me to stick close to home when I got within a month of my due date. But…" She glanced at Selena. "I thought I still had plenty of time. And because my husband left me, I'm going to need help when the baby comes. That's why I decided to get my mother tonight and take her home with us."

"Where does she live?"

"In Oakville, which is more than two hours away. I should have kept driving, but the kids were hungry. So when I saw the restaurant sign, I decided to stop and get them something to eat."

"It's a good thing you stopped when you did," Selena said. "Otherwise you would have been on the road when this happened. And Brighton Valley has a medical center a couple of miles from here."

The woman groaned and reached for her belly again. "Here comes another one. Why are they starting out so close together?"

Because this baby might come faster than her other two, which meant they couldn't very well stand here and time her contractions. Besides, there were also a lot of complications that could arise during a preterm labor and delivery, so it was best if she got medical attention as soon as possible.

Selena turned to Alex. "I'm going to have to drive her to the hospital. Would you mind coming to get me in a little while?"

Although he still appeared to be a bit stunned by all of this, he straightened and said, "No, not at all. And because the kids are hungry, why don't I order them something to go? I can bring it with me when I come to pick you up."

"That's a great idea. Thanks, Alex."

The woman reached for her purse, which had a safety pin holding one of the straps to the bag. "Here, let me get you some money."

"Don't worry about it," Alex said. "I'll get it. You'd better get to the hospital."

"If you'll give me your keys," Selena told the woman, "I'll take you and the kids there in your car. It's only a five- or ten-minute drive."

"I hate to put you out."

"It's either that or we call an ambulance," Selena told her.

The woman reached into her purse and handed over her keys. Then she told the kids to get back in the car.

"But we're hungry," the little girl said.

"This nice man is going to bring dinner to us." The woman stroked her belly, resigned to the inevitable.

"Don't worry," Alex said. "I'll be right behind you guys."

Selena sure hoped so. One of the obstetrical residents would be the one to deliver the woman's baby. So there was no reason for her to hang out once they arrived.

But then again, someone was going to have to watch the children and figure out a way to get them to Grandma's house. And she wasn't sure if Alex would be up for a task like that.

Once they were in the car and on the road, they exchanged names. "I'm Shannon Bedford, and these are my kids, Tommy and Kimberly."

"I'm Selena Ramirez. I'm going to need your mother's name and number."

"Speaking of my mom, I'd better call her. Then I'll give you her contact information."

Eight minutes and three painful contractions later, Selena drove the old Ford sedan up to the E.R. entrance and honked her horn to let the staff know she was going to need some help. Within seconds, an orderly had come out to assess the situation.

"This is Shannon Bedford," Selena told the man. "She's going to need a ride up to Obstetrics."

"Is she your patient, Dr. Ramirez?" the orderly asked.

"No, her doctor is in Houston. But she'll need to be admitted. Her water broke, and she's in active labor."

He nodded, then headed back inside for a wheelchair.

Selena placed her hand on Shannon's shoulder and gave it a comforting squeeze. "Brighton Valley Medical Center has a top-notch obstetrics ward. You'll be in great hands, so relax."

When the orderly returned with the wheelchair, Shannon took a seat as another pain gripped her.

They'd explained to the children what was happening while they'd been in the car, but little Kimberly was still worried. "Where's he going to take my mommy?"

"Upstairs to have the new baby," Selena said. "But don't worry, honey. I'll stay with you and Tommy until the baby is born. And then I'll make sure you get to your grandma's house."

Selena and the children followed Shannon through the E.R., into an elevator and on to the O.B. floor. They stopped when they reached the waiting room.

"I'm sure my friend Alex will be arriving with your dinner soon," Selena said.

They'd no more than settled into chairs near the television when Alex—thank goodness for reinforcements!—popped his head into the room. "I hope you guys like grilled cheese sandwiches and chicken tenders."

"We do," Tommy said, getting up from his chair. "Thanks."

"I also brought milk to drink and cookies for dessert," Alex added, as he placed the bags on a nearby coffee table.

Selena couldn't help but grin. The cowboy was proving to be both thoughtful and generous.

After setting out the food and watching the children take seats on the floor around the coffee table, Alex nodded for Selena to step off to the side. As she did so, he lowered his voice. "How's their mother doing?"

"She's already been admitted and is being examined now."

"Is everything going to be okay?"

"I called her doctor in Houston and let him know what was happening. He said the baby was breech at her last appointment. Unless it's turned, the delivery will be more complicated. She's also nearly six weeks early, but Dr. Chin, the resident in charge, is competent. So I'm sure everything will be okay."

"What about the kids?" he asked. "What are you going to do with them?"

"I'll wait here until Shannon is out of delivery. Then I'll drive them to Oakville to stay with their grandmother."

"Are you taking her car?"

"No, it was making some weird noises on the way here, so I'd rather take my own. I'll have to transfer the car seat, though." The minutes the words were out of her mouth, she realized she'd have to ask Alex to give her a ride back to the wellness center.

"Okay," he said. "I'll just hang out here until you're ready to go back."

"You don't have to do that."

"I know." His gaze locked on hers, and for a moment, she felt as though they were a team.

Selena couldn't remember the last time she'd felt like she had someone on her side—a friend, a lover…

Oh, for Pete's sake. They might be developing a friendship, but they'd never become lovers.

Before she could tear her gaze from his and get her

mind back on track, Ella Wilkins poked her head into the doorway. "Dr. Ramirez?"

Selena's gaze moved from the handsome cowboy who was proving to have a protective streak to the obstetrics nurse who'd just arrived. "Yes, Ella?"

"Dr. Chin has decided on a C-section and wanted to know if you'd assist."

Selena stiffened. "Of course. I'll be right there."

"He's also put out a call for Dr. Parnell," Ella added.

Roger Parnell was a neonatologist, who'd be in charge of the baby when it was born. It was standard procedure in a C-section, but had something unexpected happened?

Why was Darren Chin asking her to assist?

Selena turned to Alex, who was no longer smiling.

"What can I do to help?" he asked.

"Watch the kids. I'll be back as soon as I can."

She just hoped she wouldn't have to bear bad news to Shannon's children when she returned.

Chapter 3

Alex didn't have any idea what was going on beyond the double doors that led to the obstetrics unit, but he was glad Selena was in there with the kids' mother.

He'd always been uneasy in hospital settings, and even more so after Mary's accident. In fact, when he'd entered the main lobby of the medical center tonight, carrying the takeout food, his gut had clenched and his steps had slowed. The memory of that rainy afternoon he'd rushed to the E.R. to be with his dying wife had slammed into him, knocking him off stride.

He'd shaken it off the best he could, telling himself he had a job to do, kids to feed. So he'd bypassed the hospital volunteers who guarded the lobby entrance and went right for the elevator. All the while, his heart had pounded like a son of a gun, but he'd pressed on.

Selena had told him she'd be in the waiting room

just outside the maternity ward. And that's right where he'd found her.

Once he'd entered the small room and seen Selena and the children seated together and watching some animal show on television, his pulse rate had slowed to a normal pace and the painful memory had faded away.

Selena had looked up and blessed him with a smile that had gone a long way in chasing off the bad memories and promising to create a new one. But before either of them could speak or move, a nurse in scrubs entered the room.

As soon as Alex heard her say "C-section" and watched Selena's expression turn somber, all those dark memories he'd held at bay came flooding back.

Most people came to hospitals to get well, to heal. But some, like Mary, weren't that lucky. And Alex couldn't seem to shake the feeling that things weren't going as expected in delivery.

Thank God Selena was in there now.

It was weird, though. He had no personal knowledge of Selena's medical skill, yet just knowing she was with the pregnant mother provided him with an inexplicable sense of relief. For some reason, he was convinced the mother and her newborn were in good hands.

When it came time for his babies to be born, he hoped the doctor delivering them was a lot like Selena.

Alex glanced at the clock on the wall. How long did this sort of thing take? When would Selena come back?

He wasn't sure how he'd gotten involved in all of this in the first place. He'd just been at the wrong place at the wrong time, he supposed.

Either way, he'd do his part by looking after the pregnant woman's children. Only trouble was, he didn't have a clue what to do with them, other than to feed them and let them watch television. So he'd just have to wing it.

At least they seemed to be good kids—quiet, obedient. But what did he know? They were probably scared, just like he was.

For a guy who was determined to be a father, he sure didn't know much about raising children. Was he going to have to take some parenting classes, too?

Probably, although he had no idea where something like that would be offered. He'd have to ask Selena about it.

Again he looked at the clock. What was keeping her?

"Hey, look, Kimmie." The boy pointed to the television screen, where a commercial for kitty litter filled the screen. "Doesn't that cat look a lot like Whiskers?"

The girl looked up and nodded. "Only Whiskers has more white on his paws."

Alex made his way to the oak coffee table, where he'd spread out the grilled cheese sandwich and the chicken fingers he'd purchased at the café. He spotted the bag that still held the coffee he'd brought back for him and Selena to drink.

Would she still want it? It would probably be cold by the time she returned.

He'd sure feel a lot better if she were here with him now. He reached into the sack, removed one of the heat-resistant cups and took a seat near the children.

So far, so good, he thought. But they'd be finished eating soon. Then what was he going to do with them?

God only knew. In the meantime he tried to focus on the television screen, rather than the slow-moving clock on the wall.

Hopefully, Selena would be back before word got out that he was completely out of his element when it came to dealing with kids.

At 9:47 that evening, Michael Allan Bedford entered the world, red-faced and squalling. Even at four pounds two ounces, the little guy seemed to be a fighter, which was a good sign that he'd have little trouble while in the new neonatal intensive care unit.

Selena had assisted the delivery which had been fairly uneventful, then she'd followed Shannon's gurney into the recovery room, where she took note of the grandmother's name, address and phone number.

"As soon as you're taken to your room, you can give your mom a call," she told Shannon. "But in the meantime, I'll let her know that everything is okay—and that I'll be taking the kids to her within the next hour or so."

"I don't know how to thank you for all you've done for me, for all you're doing." Shannon's eyes filled with tears.

"I'm glad I was there when you needed me," Selena said.

"Me, too. You've been a real godsend, Dr. Ramirez."

Selena had just done what most women or doctors would have done in her place. But she thanked Shannon just the same and said, "I'll stop by to check on you tomorrow."

Then she went to find Alex and the kids.

When she reached the doorway to the waiting room, she spotted little Kimberly stretched out on the small love seat in the corner, sound asleep. Tommy and Alex were sitting on the floor in front of the coffee table, a coloring book and crayons spread out before them.

So Alex truly *was* daddy material. A smile stretched

across her face, and she remained in the doorway for a moment longer, taking it all in.

As if sensing her presence, Alex glanced up. His gaze immediately sought hers, seeking an answer to the question he hadn't needed to ask.

She nodded and offered him a weary smile, letting him know that the mother and baby were both doing fine.

"Hey, Tommy," Selena said, as she made her way into the room. "Your mom wanted me to tell you that your baby brother has been born."

"Cool." The boy scrambled to his feet and hurried to Selena. "Can I see them?"

"Not yet. Your mom will be in recovery for another hour or so, and the doctors are still examining the baby. But he looks good. They both do."

If all went well, the pediatrician might even release little Michael within the next week, although the jury was still out on that.

She wondered if it would be difficult for Shannon to leave her newborn in the hospital of a strange town and go to her mother's house, which was more than an hour away. Probably. Most new mothers wanted to keep their babies close. But there wasn't anything Selena could do about that. Right now, she had a promise to keep—to see that the children were delivered to their grandmother.

"I'm going to need that ride back to my car at the wellness center," Selena told Alex. "I have to drive the kids to Oakville."

"Do you have an address?" he asked.

"Yes, I do."

"Good. We can take my car. I'll drop you off at the wellness center when we get back."

"You want to go with me?"

He flashed a smile at her that lit up every raw spot in her heart, exposing every pain and disappointment she'd ever had—at least, in her own mind.

Torn between the wisdom of traveling with him and the desire to have him come along for the ride, she asked, "Are you sure? You didn't sign on for all of this."

"Neither did you. Besides, it's getting late. There's no reason for you to go all that way alone." His gaze sought hers, creating a connection she could almost feel, she could almost…trust.

She pondered his offer, but only for a moment. Why insist that she could handle the drive on her own when she had someone willing to go with her? And not just anyone, but a handsome cowboy who threatened to turn her heart every which way but loose.

"Okay," she said. "I'll take you up on that."

"Good."

Was it? She certainly hoped so.

"Tommy," Alex said, "if you'll put those crayons and coloring books back where we found them, I'll pick up your sister and carry her to my truck."

"Will we all fit?" Selena asked.

"It's a dual-wheel Dodge with a king cab. So we'll be fine, although we'll need to transfer that car seat."

As Alex tenderly scooped a sleeping Kimberly up in his arms, triggering visions of home and heart and family, he said, "Let's not keep Grandma waiting."

For the briefest of moments, Selena wondered what it would be like to have a family, but she brushed off the thought as quickly as it had sparked.

The cowboy had a family plan already in place, and it didn't include her.

* * *

In spite of the late hour and a minimal amount of cars on the road, the drive to Oakville took nearly two hours, so Alex and Selena would be pulling an all-nighter before getting back to Brighton Valley. But Alex didn't mind. He liked having the pretty doctor ride shotgun with him, sharing her company as well as a smile or two.

On the way to Oakville they hadn't done much talking. When they did speak, they kept their voices down so they wouldn't risk waking the children who slept in the backseat.

Once they'd reached the small tract home on Blue Ridge Court, Ruth Morgan had welcomed them inside and showed them to the spare bedroom, where the coverlets on two twin beds had already been turned down, awaiting her grandchildren.

After Alex had carried the kids from the car and they'd been tucked in, Ruth had thanked them again for making sure her daughter got to the hospital and for bringing the kids all the way to Oakville.

"I would have jumped in the car and met you in Brighton Valley," she said, "but I'm having some vision problems, and the doctor won't allow me to drive at night."

"I'm glad we were there when Shannon needed us," Selena said. "Maybe after you talk to her in the morning, the two of you can figure out a way to pick up her car. She'll also need a ride home from the hospital in a couple of days. In fact, because she had surgery, she won't be allowed to drive either—at least for a few weeks."

"I'll call my church first thing in the morning," Ruth said. "I'm sure I'll find someone who can help out."

Alex was glad to know the woman had options. And because it appeared their job was through, he said, "We'd better hit the road."

"All right," Ruth said. "But wait here for a moment. I fixed you a snack to take with you—oatmeal cookies. And I prepared a thermos of coffee. It'll help keep you awake on the way home."

She'd been right. The caffeine and sweets had helped. So had a late-night radio station that played classic country music.

By the time Alex spotted a sign that claimed Brighton Valley was twenty miles away, the sun had begun to rise, painting streaks of orange and purple in the east Texas sky.

"Do you have to work today?" Selena asked.

"There's always work to be done on a ranch, but I might find time for a nap. We'll see." Alex shot a glance across the seat at his lovely passenger. "How about you?"

"I have patients coming in from nine to five, so a nap's out of the question. But at least I'm not on call today. One of my associates is going to have hospital duty, so I can turn in early this evening and catch up on my sleep."

It was becoming clear to Alex that Selena was a good doctor—and that she had a great bedside manner.

For a moment, his sleep-deprived mind veered far away from hospital beds and gowns and medicinal smells. Instead, he wondered just what kind of bedside attention a man like him might get from a woman like her, what kind of silky sleepwear she might choose, what kind of tempting perfume. But he shook off the inappropriate thoughts and scolded himself for getting so far off base.

"Mary used to think the world of Dr. Avery," Alex said. "So I was a little disappointed to learn that he'd retired. I didn't know him very well, but I'd hoped his replacement was just as good."

Selena turned to him, her expression suggesting that she was waiting for his assessment of her.

He tossed her a smile. "I was impressed with you tonight, Selena. You're going to make a fine replacement for Doc Avery."

A slow smile stretched across her face, lighting her eyes. "Thank you."

He returned his gaze to the road, although he wished he could keep his mind on track just as easily. But it was hard to do when he couldn't help thinking that Selena was an amazing woman. She'd stepped right in to help a laboring woman who wasn't her patient, when she could have called in paramedics. Then she'd stuck around after the surgery and had lost a night's sleep to see that Tommy and Kimmie were delivered safely to their grandmother's house.

As something warm and tingly spread through the cab of his truck, he reached for a safe topic to tackle. One that wouldn't have him tripping all over himself to sing her praises.

"Where did you go to college?" he asked.

"Baylor University. How about you?" She pointed at the shirt he wore. "Is it safe to assume you're a Texas A&M alum?"

"Yes, I am."

"So the cowboy hat, jeans and boots you were wearing last Tuesday night was just a prop?" she asked.

"Not at all. I'm a cowboy through and through."

"Oh, yeah?"

His dad, if he'd still been alive, would have had the same reaction. But then again, his uncle had been more an of influence on Alex.

"So you grew up on a ranch?" she asked.

"Actually, I spent the first ten years of my life in Dallas. I never even rode a horse until after I moved to Brighton Valley."

"How did you end up there?"

"When my dad died unexpectedly of a heart attack, my mom sold the house in the city and moved in with her brother. She'd been raised in the country and wanted me to have the same experience."

"So the city kid morphed into a rancher?"

"That's pretty much how it happened. It didn't take long either. My mother always said I'd been born with a cowboy's heart. And she's probably right. I can't imagine what my life would have been like had I remained in Dallas. It seems as if I was meant to be a rancher."

In fact, he hadn't even wanted to leave the Rocking B to attend college, but the details of his father's trust had not only provided for an education, but had pretty much locked him into one, whether he wanted one or not. So while his dad—if he'd still been alive—might have insisted he attend law school or get an MBA, Alex had chosen to go to Texas A&M, where he got a degree in animal science, something practical he could use back on his uncle's ranch.

They continued to drive in silence, and he wondered if they were both thinking the same thing. How had such a chance meeting turned into…well, whatever this was? A friendship, he supposed.

But just being with Selena this evening made him realize that he'd been living on the periphery of life ever since Mary's death. And that maybe it was time to cross over to the real world again.

When they reached the turnoff to the wellness center, the sun had begun its slow rise. Alex followed the driveway into the parking lot, where Selena's white Lexus was the only one left.

He pulled into the space next to hers, then shut off the ignition. It wasn't necessary, he supposed, but he got out of the car anyway. He told himself it was to make sure that she got into her vehicle okay, that it started right up. That she wasn't stranded in a parking lot while he was driving off to his ranch.

Who was he kidding? He wasn't quite ready to say goodbye. At least, not from inside his truck.

"I see you're chivalrous, too," she said.

"Too?" Had she been keeping a list of his qualities?

She flushed, then glanced down. "I'm sorry. Just a little slip of the tongue."

He knew she was talking about her choice of words, yet the thought of tongues slipping set his imagination soaring.

There he went again, veering dangerously off course.

"I guess the lack of sleep makes you say and think all kinds of things," he said.

"You've got that right." She reached into her purse, then pulled out a set of keys. "Oops. These are Shannon's. I should have left them with Ruth."

"Since her car is still parked in front of the hospital, we probably ought to give them to Shane Hollister," Alex said.

"The sheriff?"

"Wouldn't you hate to see Shannon get a parking ticket?"

Selena nodded. "Poor thing. She's really got her hands full. That's the last thing in the world she needs right now."

Alex didn't respond.

He didn't move either. He just stood there, watching as Selena fumbled around in her purse again.

After a moment, she broke into a beautiful smile and removed her hand, dangling another set of keys. "Good news. I found mine."

For the life of him, he couldn't manage to agree. That it was good that she'd found her keys. That it was time to say goodbye.

How could he? He wasn't quite ready to see her drive away and end a most unusual—and surreal—day.

So how in blazes did he go about prolonging it when they were both tired, when they both needed to go home and get ready to face a new day?

In spite of his better judgment, in spite of the fact that sleep deprivation led to accidents, he placed his hand on her cheek. "It was an interesting evening—and so much better than watching TV. I'm glad I spent it with you."

Then he did something he'd probably live to regret—or, after getting some shuteye, he'd *wake* to regret.

He lowered his mouth, intending to brush a kiss on her cheek, yet finding her lips instead.

The last thing in the world Selena had expected from Alex had been a goodnight kiss, but she'd been too surprised by the move to stop it.

As his mouth met hers and she caught his musky scent, she held not only her breath, but every thought and whisper and dream she'd ever had.

Who was this man?

And what was he doing to her?

As the kiss deepened, as their lips parted and tongues touched, she thought she might swoon. So she gripped the fabric of his T-shirt and held on for dear life.

The kiss was amazing. What began soft and sweet evolved into the kind that could make a woman lose her head. Her mind spun out of control as she tried to make sense of it all—the allure of his kiss and the effect it had on her—but it was over before she knew it, leaving her stunned and speechless.

And yearning for more.

Alex straightened and blessed her with a boyish grin. "I meant to aim for your cheek."

"You missed."

"Yeah." His grin deepened to a full-on smile. "Sorry about that."

Was he? Because she darn sure wasn't.

And shouldn't she be?

"Drive carefully," he said.

Yeah. Right. Her cue to leave and to segue from the awkward to the familiar. She needed to get into her car and drive away. Yet something held her here. Lack of sleep, she suspected. And maybe the easy camaraderie they'd shared on the trip back from Oakville. Yet there was something else going on, too.

Selena hadn't been that unbalanced by a kiss in a long, long time—if ever. But she did her best to steady herself, to get back on track and pretend that they'd reached that level of friendship where an affectionate parting was the norm.

Eager to escape the confusion, she reached for the door handle, using the keyless entry, and slid behind the wheel. "Thanks for riding with me and helping with the kids."

"My pleasure."

"Have a good day," she said as she reached to pull her door shut.

"You, too."

She didn't know about that. Her day was already off to a surreal start. How was she going to keep her mind on her work and on her patients when she'd be reliving that kiss for the rest of her waking hours?

Then there'd be those bedtime hours, when it was sure to come back and haunt her dreams.

After shutting the car door, she pressed the button to start the engine. Then she slowly backed out of the parking space, trying to put a little distance between her and the man who'd set her off course.

Once she reached the exit and prepared to pull out on to the street, she glanced in the rearview mirror and spotted Alex still standing by his truck.

But she feared that neither of them was in the same place they'd been before they'd started out last night.

That unexpected kiss had linked them in a way she hadn't anticipated and set off a slew of romantic thoughts and yearnings, which was too bad.

The last thing in the world she needed to do was to imagine herself playing house with a handsome cowboy who was still in love with his late wife.

Chapter 4

After leaving the wellness center, Selena arrived at her new two-bedroom digs on Hawthorne Lane, one of the older neighborhoods in Brighton Valley. She checked her voice mail, took a quick shower and dressed for the day. While tempted to grab something she could eat on the run, she took time for a good breakfast—a veggie omelet, a fruit cup and a blueberry muffin—to fuel her body and keep her going until noon.

It was almost seven-thirty when she made the fifteen-minute drive to the medical center, which was just a few blocks down the street from her office.

Because she still had an hour before her first patient would arrive, she decided to swing by the hospital so she could check on Shannon and her baby.

Her first stop was at the neonatal intensive care unit, where little Michael slept in a heated isolette. He wasn't the tiniest baby in the NICU, but at just over four pounds, he was still smaller than a full-term newborn.

Last night, while Shannon had been in labor, his heart rate had dropped, indicating he was in distress, so Dr. Chin had decided upon an immediate C-section. His initial Apgar score had been a little low, but Roger Parnell, the neonatologist at the delivery, hadn't been too concerned. And thank goodness Michael's subsequent scores had improved.

His color looked good today, Selena decided, as she studied the sleeping newborn. Her medical assessment soon took a maternal shift, and she found herself taking note of his little fingers and toes. He was a beautiful baby, with dark tufts of hair.... And look at that sweet little grimace on his face.

"Good morning, Dr. Ramirez."

Tearing her gaze from the newborn, Selena turned to Margie Kaufman, the charge nurse, and offered her a smile. "Good morning, Margie. I stopped by to check on Baby Bedford before visiting his mother. How's he doing?"

"So far, so good. He doesn't seem to have any major issues, although we're watching him closely. We'll probably bring his mom in to visit later this morning."

"I'll let her know. I'm sure she's eager to see him." Still, Selena made no immediate move to leave. Instead, she continued to watch little Michael and to imagine having a baby like him someday. But longing for something that wasn't meant to be wasn't doing her any good, so she forced herself to leave the NICU and head for the maternity floor. When she reached the nurses' station, she learned that Shannon Bedford was in room 407.

Moments later, she found her sitting up in bed, her breakfast tray in front of her.

"Good morning," Selena said. "How are you feeling?"

"Sore, but I guess that's to be expected."

"I'm afraid so. Dr. Chin should have ordered pain meds for you."

"He did. I had a shot a few minutes ago. Well, an injection into my IV. I hate it, though, because it makes me feel loopy and weird." Shannon pushed her half-eaten tray aside. "How are the kids?"

"They're fine."

"Did you have any trouble finding my mother's house?"

"No, not at all. The drive was easy. Alex, my... friend, went with me to Oakville."

"I don't know how to thank you. Would you please let Alex know how grateful I am? He's a darn good friend in my book."

Selena suspected that Shannon was right, although she was still trying to wrap her mind around the whole "friend" idea.

Somehow, as the evening wore on, they'd become more than acquaintances, that's for sure. And that goodnight kiss had her wondering if they'd become even more than friends, at least in his eyes. But rather than ponder that possibility, she decided to chalk the whole thing up to exhaustion and relief that the ordeal was over.

"Where did you meet him?" Shannon asked.

The question struck Selena as being unusual, but the events that had unfolded last night had all been a little dreamlike. And she found herself saying, "At the wellness center down the street. He took a class I offered."

No need to mention anything about the topic of the class. Or the fact that Alex was determined to find a woman to carry his and his late wife's unborn children. But maybe Selena would be wise to make a note of that, to keep in mind that Alex and his wife must have had a good and loving marriage.

Would Selena ever find a man who cared that deeply for her, even if she died?

"Are you dating him?" Shannon asked. "Not that it's any of my business, of course. It's just that... Well, I don't know why I even asked. I'm sorry. I've always been a little too nosy for my own good. And a little impulsive." She blew out a ragged breath and clucked her tongue. "Just look where that impulsiveness landed me."

Now it was Selena's turn to be nosy. "I'm not sure I'm following you."

"I met this guy—Joey Delgado—in a bar one night. I'm a little embarrassed to admit this but I went home with him. We dated a week or so, then called it quits. He was about five years younger than I was. And I had kids. I should have known something solid wouldn't have worked out."

Selena met her first love, a graduate student, in college. And that hadn't worked out so well either. Sometimes the whole dating thing was a complete crapshoot, if you asked her.

"Do you plan to tell him about the baby?" Selena asked.

"I don't know."

Silence stretched between them for a moment. Then Selena said, "I stopped by the NICU earlier."

"How's the baby doing?" Shannon asked.

The fact that she'd asked about Michael as a second thought struck Selena as a little unusual. Most mothers in her situation would have been more…

No, it was wrong to make those kinds of assumptions. After all, Shannon probably had a lot of other things on her mind, like two children who'd been transported by strangers to stay with her mother, bills to pay, a new day care dilemma and probably a lot more than that. Besides, she'd just been given an injection for pain, which she claimed made her feel "loopy."

"I thought being a single mom with two kids was tough," Shannon added. "But now look at me. I'm still single and have three."

Selena wondered if Shannon would consider adoption as a solution to her problems. At that rogue thought, a seed of hope surged through her, but she didn't dare let it take root and blossom.

After all, when someone finally wheeled Shannon to the NICU to see that precious little boy for the very first time, she was going to bond with him. And where would that leave Selena and her dream of instant motherhood?

Disappointed yet again.

So she put it all behind her—Shannon and her newborn, Alex and the unexpected kiss—then went back to the office to focus on her practice and her patients.

And it worked beautifully—until Tuesday night, when Selena arrived to teach the second class.

Once again, she found Alex sitting front and center, his Stetson resting on the chair next to him.

She hadn't seen him for five days, since the night Shannon's baby was born. Of course, there'd been a good reason for that. She'd avoided going to the wellness center, hoping she wouldn't run across him there. Instead, she'd exercised at home and jogged in the neighborhood.

But now here she was, trying to focus on her notes and her presentation, which was even more difficult to do this evening than it had been last week before they'd spent time together.

And before he'd kissed her.

She tried her best to pretend it had never happened and that he wasn't back in full force—a cowboy to be reckoned with. So while she did cast an occasional glance his way during her lecture, she kept her focus on the others in the room, on their questions.

And just like he'd done last week, he'd waited until the room had begun to clear before walking up to the podium.

"Hey," he said, flashing a heart-thumping grin her way. "Did you catch up on your sleep the other day?"

"Eventually." She returned his smile with one of her own. "How about you?"

"I didn't get a nap like I'd planned, so I made it an early night." As she gathered her notes, she paused, her lips parting. "Oh, I nearly forgot. I brought that list of agencies for you." She reached for a sheet of paper at the back of her stack and handed it to him.

"Thank you." He glanced at it for a moment, then rolled it up and placed it in his hip pocket.

She supposed he had no place else to put it, but he seemed to discard it without much fanfare. Was that a sign that his plan to have his wife's children was fading?

As she closed her file of notes, she caught a hint of his musky scent and, when added to the rather intoxicating sound of a slight southern drawl, the whole effect was entirely too sexy to ignore.

"Have you eaten dinner yet?" he asked.

Her movements froze. Was he asking her out?

Oh, for Pete's sake. Joining him for a bite to eat wouldn't be a date. If he'd had a romantic interest in her, he would have said or done something on the night they'd driven the kids to Oakville.

Okay, so he'd kissed her at sunrise, which had been surprisingly sweet and romantic. But that could have been his way to end their unexpected nocturnal adventure. Right?

So she said, "No, I haven't eaten yet. But I have some leftover chicken vegetable soup I'm going to warm up when I get home."

As he took a step closer, that arousing cowboy scent, all musky and manly, played havoc with her senses, making her wonder just what he was really thinking.

"Why don't you save that for lunch tomorrow," he said. "I'd like to take you to Emilio's tonight. I've been craving some Italian food, and that's the best place in town to get it."

His suggestion was tempting—and for a lot more reasons than an empty stomach. Yet instead of coming up with a polite way to decline, she said, "Okay. Why not?"

"Good. I hate eating alone."

All right, then. He'd only suggested they dine together as a friendly offer. She was relieved to know she'd been right about his motive.

Yet being right was a little unsettling, too—and maybe even disappointing. So why was that?

Probably because if things were different, if they'd

met elsewhere, if he wasn't determined to see his late-wife live on by having the family they'd once planned...

Enough of that. The compulsion to analyze everything was going to drive her crazy, so she slipped her notes into her purse, determined to let it all go. But when she glanced up and spotted a glimmer in his eyes, her heart skittered to a stop, and she found herself trying to read into his expression, his smile.

Maybe going out to dinner with him wasn't such a good idea, after all.

Still, she followed the handsome and mesmerizing cowboy out of the wellness center and to his truck.

As she walked beside him, she couldn't help noting that he seemed to have lost his limp in favor of a sexy swagger. A girl could really lose her head around a man like him. She just hoped that wouldn't be her fate.

Alex had no idea why he'd suggested they eat at Emilio's, one of the newest restaurants in town—and one of the more romantic. He'd told Selena that he liked Italian food, which was true. But there'd been better, more casual places he could have suggested, like Pistol Pete's Pizzeria and Mama Mia's Italian Kitchen, both of which were located in nearby Wexler and not that far away.

Instead, here they were, sitting across from each other at a white linen-draped table for two, which had been adorned with a candle and a single red rose in a bud vase. As they sipped glasses of Chianti, a crooner in the adjacent lounge sang "That's *Amore*."

A dinner didn't get much more romantic than that, Alex supposed. Not that he minded. He was a bit too dazzled by the lovely woman sitting across from him.

Selena Ramirez might be a respected doctor, but right now, with the candlelight providing a warm and cozy glow, the wine offering just enough of a buzz to lower one's guard, she was everything a man might want in a woman: petite and shapely, with soulful brown eyes the color of fine Tennessee bourbon and lush dark hair that cascaded over her shoulders.

Of course, he'd best keep reminding himself that she was merely a dinner companion and not a date. But the longer they sat here, the more difficult it was to keep things casual between them.

Just moments ago, the waiter had taken their dinner order, leaving them to chat. Alex had done his best not to ask everything there was to know about her, thinking it would be pushy and out of line if he did. But that didn't quash his mounting curiosity.

Who was Selena Ramirez—the woman, not just the doctor?

"This bread is delicious," she said. "I could make a meal of it. In fact, I probably shouldn't have ordered pasta. The salad would have been plenty."

"You can always take the leftovers home."

"That's true. I can eat it for lunch tomorrow, along with the chicken soup."

As she reached for her wineglass, he wondered what she thought about the setting he'd chosen. Did she suspect that he had ulterior motives by bringing her here?

Heck, he was wondering the same thing. Why *had* he chosen this place? And when had the desire to "pick her brain" about surrogacy issues morphed into a longing to know her better on a personal level?

On top of that, there was another question that concerned him even more. Why did the idea of kissing her again keep cropping up? Was there something going on in his subconscious that only his libido was privy to?

That might be the case, because for some darn reason, he wanted a chance to show her that he had a lot more up his sleeve than sweet goodnight kisses.

But getting involved with Selena—or any woman at this point in his life—would only complicate his plan to give those embryos a chance at life.

"I have a question for you," Selena said. "Why did Jim Ragsdale want to talk to you about his plans to use hippotherapy at the wellness center?"

"Because I know a lot about horses and can train them for him."

She leaned forward, her expressive gaze zeroing in on him. "So you raise horses on your ranch?"

He wondered what she found so intriguing—the fact that he owned a ranch in the first place or that he didn't raise cattle like most ranchers in these parts.

"Are you interested in hippotherapy?" he asked. "Or do you just like horses?"

"Both. I find the whole idea of using a horse's movements as therapy interesting. And I've always loved horses. As a girl, I dreamed of having one of my own, but we lived in a small house with very little yard. And even if we'd had a bigger place, my folks had a hard enough time feeding seven kids."

"Seven?" Alex, who'd been an only child, could hardly imagine what it would've been like to grow up in a family that large. "Where did you fit into the lineup?"

"I was the fourth child and the second daughter."

"Sounds to me as if it was pretty easy to get lost in the crowd."

She laughed. "That just about sums it up. Our family was loud and boisterous, and someone was always trying to be top dog."

"So there was some sibling rivalry going on."

"Some, but not as much as you'd think. We might have each gone out of our way to make our own mark, but we loved each other. And we've always been supportive."

"You undoubtedly studied hard, excelled in school and became a doctor. Your parents must be proud of you."

"They're proud of *all* of us. My sister Lucia is an award-winning graphic artist, and Diego graduated from West Point and is a lieutenant in the army." Selena sat back and smiled. "Let's see, there's a high school guidance counselor, a third-grade teacher, and Carlitos, the youngest, is a starting running back at Oklahoma State. Even Maria, who disliked sitting in a classroom and refused to consider college, is doing great. She married her high school sweetheart right after graduation. And now she's the best wife and mother in all of Tomball, Texas."

Alex chuckled, along with Selena, until her laughter stilled, her smile faded and her brow furrowed.

"What's the matter?" he asked.

She looked up as though surprised by his question, then shook off whatever had stolen the light from her eyes. "Nothing's wrong. I was just…thinking about something."

"What's that?"

She paused for a moment, as if she might share it with him, then she shrugged. "It was just a random thought."

He had an urge to coax it out of her, but let it go. "So you all succeeded one way or another."

"Yes, and we have our parents to thank for that. They encouraged us to try our best. And even when one of us struggled or failed, we never doubted their love or support for a minute."

"And no one rebelled?" Alex found that odd, especially with seven kids in the family.

"Not really. Our neighborhood was a bit rough, so we all had to deal with the occasional gang- and drug-related issues. Carlitos, my little brother, gave them a few sleepless nights, but the older boys took him aside and let him know there'd be hell to pay if he gave my folks any trouble. And apparently, they made their point. He's doing really well now—in the classroom and on the football field."

For a moment, Alex thought about the babies he planned to raise, the kids who would depend on him for love and support. Would he prove to be the kind of father that Selena had? Would his children grow up to be happy and successful?

He certainly hoped so.

"I know I'm repeating myself," Alex said, "but your parents must be incredibly proud."

"Actually, we're just as proud of them as they are of us. They were both Mexican immigrants who didn't have a high school diploma. Instead, they had to work during their teen years to help support their families. But they were smart enough to know an education was the key to their kids' success."

It was probably safe to assume that her parents had some kind of blue-collar or service jobs, and while it really didn't matter, he couldn't quell his curiosity. "What did they do for a living?"

"My dad was a janitor at the elementary school near our house. And my mom cleaned houses. They were determined to cash in on the American dream and eventually bought a small, modest tract home in a better neighborhood."

The waiter returned with their meals at that point, and for a few minutes they ate in relative silence.

Then Alex's thoughts drifted back to her love of horses as a young girl and her wish to have one of her own. "So when was the last time you rode a horse?"

Selena looked up from her pasta primavera and smiled. "Not since high school. When I was a freshman, one of my girlfriends would invite me over for the weekend. Sometimes we'd go for a ride—when she wasn't competing in gymkhana."

Alex was familiar with the equestrian event she was talking about, which included barrel and flag racing, as well as other competitions that required teamwork between the horse and rider.

"She was really good," Selena added, "and I enjoyed watching her."

"It's too bad you didn't have a horse of your own."

"I would have been happy to have a dog, but that was out of the question, too." Selena glanced down at the table, those lush dark lashes drawing his attention, even without the use of mascara.

For a moment, he forgot that she was a doctor with a busy practice, that she probably was on call most weekends and that it was unlikely that the two of them would ever become more than friends.

"You ought to come out to my ranch someday," he said. "I'd let you ride one of my horses."

She looked up, emotion filling her eyes, making them glimmer in the candlelight. "Are you kidding?"

When she looked at him like that—with wonder splashed across her pretty face, the hope, the awe...

Hell, he'd never joke with her about anything that was special or important to her. "When is your next day off?"

"Sunday."

"Do you have plans?"

"Only to do laundry, pick up groceries for the week and maybe go to the wellness center and work out."

"Why don't you drive out to my place instead?" He watched her vacillate between an OMG-type response and a thanks-but-I'd-better-pass.

What was holding her back?

"I haven't been on a horse in ages," she finally said. "I probably wouldn't remember what to do."

"I've heard it's like riding a bicycle."

She laughed. "I haven't done that in a long time either—unless, of course, you count the stationary bike at the wellness center. I'd probably fall off a two-wheeler."

Right now, he was struggling to keep his own balance. Just the thought of showing Selena around—maybe saddling Sugar Foot, one of the gentler old mares—and taking her on a tour of the ranch had slapped a big old grin on his face. "I'm sure you'll do fine."

When she didn't challenge him, he figured she was leaning toward a yes. He sure hoped that was the case.

"Why don't you come out around nine or ten?" he suggested.

"Are you sure about that?"

"Absolutely. It'll be fun to take a pleasure ride for a change."

While they continued to eat their meals, he gave her directions to his ranch, as well as his cell phone number in case she got lost—or needed to make a change of plans.

He sure hoped nothing came up because he was looking forward to having her on his home turf.

After the waiter brought the bill and Alex paid with a credit card, he took Selena back to the wellness center, where she'd left her car. And once again, in spite of his plan to take things slow and not complicate his family plan, he got out of his truck and walked with her to her vehicle, telling himself he was just being polite.

But the fact was, he wanted to kiss her good-night again. And the silvery moon overhead wasn't making it any easier to walk away without doing what seemed to be natural at the end of a romantic evening.

Trouble was, a sweet, goodnight kiss might be considered appropriate, but that wasn't the kind he was tempted to give her.

So now what?

He thought it over for as long as he dared to.

Aw, what the hell...

Chapter 5

Selena had sensed that a kiss was coming the moment Alex had climbed out of his car. She'd felt it in the soft glimmer of moonlight, heard it in the crunch of his boots on the dusty pavement. And she'd seen it sparkle in his eyes—even before he reached for her waist, drew her close and placed his mouth on hers.

She could have taken a step back to let him know she wasn't interested—and she probably should have. Yet she didn't do one darn thing to avoid it. Instead, she leaned into him and slipped her arms around him as well.

Their first kiss had been sweet, tentative. But there was something bolder about this one, something decisive.

As their lips parted, as their tongues touched, Selena's common sense slipped by the wayside, and she kissed him right back—just as bold, just as decisive.

Within a heartbeat, the kiss deepened. Their breaths mingled, their tongues mated.

Had any man ever tasted so good, smelled so musky, felt so right in her arms?

As her pulse rate soared, her imagination took flight. Did she dare tiptoe around romance again?

Of course, wasn't she doing that now? Stepping out on a romantic limb, testing, pretending, wondering...

She had no idea what was really going on between her and Alex. And God only knew what tomorrow might hold, but there was no disputing the fact that something other than friendship was brewing between them.

And while she might go home tonight and regret that she'd let things come to this, she was determined to enjoy every sweet moment, every heated sensation now.

When Alex slowly drew back, allowing them both to come up for air, he placed his hand on her cheek and grinned. But Selena didn't dare return his smile. Instead, she stood there awestruck.

Who would have ever guessed that the handsome cowboy who'd sat in the front row of her lecture could kiss like that?

But as she took a deep, fortifying breath, reality chased away her romantic musing. She took a step back, desperate to regain her footing.

"I'll see you Sunday morning at nine," he said, as if that's all there was to it. But things had taken a complicated turn, and there was so much more to consider.

"I don't have boots," she said, scurrying for some kind of excuse, some way to backpedal.

"Sneakers are fine. Don't worry about it."

But she *was* worried. And not just about what to

wear or staying balanced in the saddle. She was worried about letting Alex think there was something between them, some kind of future.

Now wait a minute. It's not as if they'd actually gone out on a real date. Or if he'd asked her to do anything other than drive out to his ranch and go horseback riding.

Sure, the kiss had thrown her for a loop. And so had the romantic dinner. But that didn't mean she couldn't take things one day at a time.

"If something comes up," she said, "I'll give you a call." Then she climbed in her car and closed the door. Once she'd backed out of the parking lot and drove to the exit, she glanced in her rearview mirror, taking in the sight of the alluring man standing near his truck, the rancher who'd invited her to go riding with him on Sunday.

She probably ought to call him after she got home and tell him that something unexpected had come up, that she'd been called in to cover for a colleague, that she had to...wash her hair.

But she had a feeling she wouldn't do that.

For some reason, she wanted to see his ranch on Sunday, to go for a ride. And she wanted to spend more time with him, even if she feared it might be the riskiest thing she'd ever done.

The memory of Selena's kiss followed Alex all the way back to his ranch. But then again, why wouldn't it? The beautiful doctor had set off an unexpected flurry of testosterone that had damn near turned him inside out.

He'd never expected things to escalate between them like that, and he had to admit that he was glad it had.

For the first time in two years—or maybe much longer than that—he'd felt alive again.

After parking his truck near the barn, he headed for the sprawling ranch house and let himself inside, where a lazy fire burned in the stone hearth of the wood-paneled living room, with its colorful southwestern paintings and decor.

"Lydia?" he called, as he hung his hat on the hook by the door. "I'm home."

Moments later, his housekeeper swept into the room wearing a smile of relief. "Oh, good. I was getting worried about you."

"I'm sorry. Something unexpected came up."

"At the fertility lecture?"

"Afterward." Alex wouldn't mention anything about Selena just yet, so that would require some stretching of the truth. "I ran into a friend at the wellness center, and we had dinner together. So that 'quick bite' I'd said I would get in town took a lot longer than I'd expected."

"I'm glad to hear you finally took some time for yourself. You don't get out as much as you should." She glanced at the mantel, at the framed photograph that had been taken on Alex and Mary's wedding day, then looked away as if realizing she'd been caught.

Alex had been tempted to remove that picture on several occasions because it always seemed to dampen his mood. But the babies would need to know who their mother was, so keeping her image close would be a good way to do that.

"I can warm up that leftover pot roast," Lydia said. "That is, if you're still hungry."

"Thanks, but I had lasagna this evening, so I'm stuffed." He crossed the hardwood floor to the center of the room and took a seat on the beige leather sofa Mary had purchased just months before she died. It suited the rest of the decor, but he'd always preferred the comfy overstuffed sofa that had been there for years.

"How about some coffee?" Lydia asked. "It's fresh. And I made brownies earlier this afternoon."

Lydia hadn't always doted on him before—not that she'd ever been less than professional. But she was a widow herself, so she understood the pain and grief of losing a spouse unexpectedly.

After the accident, Lydia had become more nurturing than she'd been when Mary had first hired her. And then last spring, after her youngest daughter got married and moved to Austin, she'd really taken Alex under her wing.

But he really didn't mind. It had been a long time since he'd known a mother's love. His mom had died when he was thirteen, so he appreciated Lydia's maternal side. In fact, she'd become more than a household employee. She'd turned into a friend—and the only real family Alex had left.

"All right," he said, "I'll take you up on the coffee and brownies. Thanks."

Her grin brightened, and then she bustled off to the kitchen. When she returned, she carried a tray with two steaming mugs and a platter of the chocolate treats and set it on the glass-top coffee table.

"So how was the lecture?" she asked.

"It was somewhat helpful."

Lydia knew all about Alex's plan to hire a gestational carrier and to raise the children on his own. In fact, he suspected she was nearly as eager as he was to have little ones in the house. He was even considering the idea of hiring a new cook and housekeeper because

Lydia would be the one watching over the babies while he worked on the ranch.

"I expect to learn more next Tuesday," he added.

Of course, Selena had given him a list of agencies that might help him find someone to carry the babies. To be honest, it had nearly slipped his mind. He hadn't thought much about Mary or their future children today, even during the lecture. He'd been too caught up in watching the lovely doctor at the lectern—and then later, in the candlelight.

He wondered what Lydia would think of Selena when they met on Sunday. Not that it mattered, he supposed, but his housekeeper had gotten pretty protective over the past few months. Still, he imagined she'd be just as taken by the lovely doctor as he'd been.

Taken?

He blew out a ragged sigh, then reached for one of the mugs from the tray on the coffee table. He'd made a promise to his late wife that he intended to keep. But it wasn't just the promise prodding him to move forward. Having those children was something he needed to do. Somewhere down the road, Mary's obsession had become his own. And he wanted those babies—whether they were girls or boys, red-haired like she was, or blond like him.

God willing, he'd keep his vow to Mary, the death-bed promise he'd made to do all in his power to give their children a chance to live.

Alex had no idea what the future held for him and Selena, although he really liked the direction things were headed. For the first time in what seemed like forever, he found himself smiling for no reason at all.

Okay, so there actually was a reason—the memory

of Selena sitting across a table from him, flashing him a pretty, dimpled smile.

He could imagine them dating and growing closer—both physically and emotionally.

Of course, he didn't know how she felt about dating a man who planned to hire a gestational carrier or what she thought about being involved with the pregnancy as well as the birth. Because if he went that route, he couldn't think of a better doctor to use.

But what about him? Did he even want to think about a romantic relationship at a time like this?

He hadn't even considered it until he'd met Selena, until he'd kissed her and held her in his arms.

It might be all right, though. Maybe even better than all right—just as long as she understood his desire to raise his and Mary's babies. If she did, then maybe they could give the whole relationship thing a whirl.

And if she couldn't?

Then all bets were off.

Alex hadn't taken time to call any of the agencies on the list Selena had given him Tuesday. However, on Saturday night, after dinner, he'd checked out each one on the internet. In fact, one in particular caught his eye.

Family Solutions was located in Wexler, so it was close. And if he was going to hire a gestational carrier, he liked the idea of knowing she lived nearby. He also liked the things he read on the website. In fact, he'd been so impressed that he'd sent an email asking for more information and had filled out a short questionnaire. At the end, it asked, Who can we thank for the referral, and Alex typed in: Dr. Selena Ramirez.

With that out of the way, he'd gone to sleep, eager

to wake the next morning, when Selena would arrive at the ranch.

The day dawned bright, and he found himself looking forward to a long, leisurely ride with the lovely doctor.

He'd just poured his second cup of coffee and sat down to look over the Sports page in the Sunday paper when she arrived. The moment he'd heard her car drive up, he got up from the kitchen table, went to the sink, where he poured out his cup. Then he went to greet her.

As he swung open the door, he found her standing on the porch, a shy smile on her pretty face. Her hair had been pulled back and woven in a single braid that hung down her back, her makeup applied lightly, her lipstick a pretty and kissable shade of pink.

He made a quick scan over the length of her, wishing he could allow his gaze to linger. In spite of claiming that she didn't have any boots, she'd obviously found a pair. She also wore jeans that hugged her hips and a lightweight knit top that caressed her curves.

He was going to have a tough time keeping his thoughts on horses, leisurely rides and the countryside.

"Do you think I'll need a jacket?" she asked.

"That's up to you. It's going to warm up soon."

Heck, it was warming up already. Somehow, overnight, Selena had morphed from a lovely, soft-spoken doctor to a sexy cowgirl. And he had no idea how that had happened.

It didn't matter, he supposed. Just as long as she was here.

"Would you like some breakfast?" he asked. "Or maybe a cup of coffee?"

"No, thanks. I've already eaten."

"Good. Then I'll take you out to meet Sugar Foot, a mare I think you'll like."

But before taking a step outside, a voice sounded from behind him. "Don't forget your lunch, Mr. Connor."

Alex turned to see Lydia standing in the wings, no doubt waiting for an introduction. Why had she referred to him as mister? They'd been on a first-name basis ever since she'd come to work for him and Mary.

"Lydia," he said, moving aside so his housekeeper could greet his guest, "this is Selena...or rather, Dr. Ramirez."

Selena offered Lydia a warm smile and extended her arm in greeting. "Let's not be formal. Please call me Selena."

Lydia took the pretty doctor's hand and gave it a gentle shake, gracefully moving from loyal employee to family friend. "It's nice to meet you."

Before either woman could turn a casual introduction into a longer chat, Alex said, "I'll take Selena with me so she can meet her horse. Before we ride out, we'll stop by the kitchen and pick up our lunch."

Then he stepped onto the porch, joining Selena and starting toward the barn, where he'd stabled the two horses he'd planned for them to ride.

"Thanks again for inviting me out to the ranch," she said.

"I'm glad you came. To be honest, you're doing me a favor. I haven't taken the time to ride just for the fun of it in a long time. And it looks like today will be the perfect day for it." He wasn't just talking about the mild temperature or the warmth of the sun either.

As they crossed the yard toward the barn, Gus Barrows, one of the ranch hands, came ambling toward them. He was leading a bay gelding with one hand and had a red bandana tied around the other.

"What did you do to yourself?" Alex asked.

The gruff fifty-something cowboy let out a huff, then slowly shook his head. "I cut my dad-burn hand on a piece of twisted metal on one of the corral gates. I thought I'd better come in and put a real bandage on it before going back to work."

"Do you mind if I take a look at that?" Selena asked.

"It ain't nothing." Still, Gus lifted his hand and unwrapped the cloth from his palm, where a cut ran jagged and deep.

As Selena looked at his injury, her pretty face scrunched in concern. "That cut is severe. You might have damaged a tendon. And even if you didn't, it's not going to heal without stitches."

"Aw, it ain't so bad." Gus slowly drew his hand back.

"When was your last tetanus shot?" she asked.

"I don't know. When I was a kid, I suppose."

Selena glanced at Alex, her expression filled with unspoken words, each one coaxing him to put his foot down and insist that Gus seek medical attention.

"I'll ask Lydia to drive you to the urgent care," Alex said.

"That ain't necessary, boss. If you want me to have it checked out, I can drive my…" Gus glanced at the house, and his expression softened. "Well, maybe it would be best if Lydia took me. That is, if you don't think she'd mind."

Alex had noticed a starry-eyed look in Gus's eyes once or twice when the housekeeper had been in sight.

Maybe Gus would appreciate a little feminine TLC for a change.

"I'm sure you can drive yourself into town," Alex said, "but I'd feel better if someone took you. And the only one available today, since it's Sunday, is Lydia."

"If you think she wouldn't mind…"

"I'm sure she'd be happy to." Besides, it would give her someone else to fuss over for a change.

"Okay, then," Gus said. "Maybe I ought to go and… you know, wash up."

A grin tugged at Alex's lips. "Sure. You do that. And I'll tell Lydia you'll be waiting by her car."

As the rough and tough old cowboy headed for the bunkhouse, leaving Alex and Selena standing in the middle of the yard, Alex nodded toward the house. "If you'll give me a moment, I'll let Lydia know what's going on."

"No problem."

Moments later, while Lydia went hunting for her purse and the keys to her car, Alex returned to Selena. While he'd been in the house, she'd wandered over to the corral nearest the barn, where Lady Gwen grazed with her foal.

"I'm sorry to keep you waiting."

Selena turned to him, her eyes wide and sparkling. "I didn't mind."

He didn't suppose she did. She might have grown up and gone to medical school, but she still loved horses. And the sparkle in her eye was doing something to him, especially because her visit to his ranch had put it there. Or was something else happening?

They stood like that for a moment, gazes locked, attraction flaring—at least on his part. And while he was tempted to ease forward, to cross some platonic line that remained between them in spite of two kisses that had been a little more than friendly, he couldn't let things get out of hand yet. So he shook it off and said, "Come on, let's go saddle our horses."

Once inside the barn, he led her to the stall of his favorite broodmare, a roan filly that was gentle enough for an inexperienced rider. "This little gal is Sugar Foot."

Selena reached out and stroked the horse's nose. "Hi, there, Sugar. It's nice to meet you."

The mare gave a little whinny, and Selena broke into a beautiful smile that stirred up something warm in Alex's heart.

He watched the woman and the mare for a moment, then leaned against the rails of the stall. "So what do you think? She's a good horse—and gentle. I can find one with more spunk, if you'd rather."

"Oh, no. I like Sugar Foot. I think we'll get along just fine." As she smiled, her eyes lit up, making her look younger than she probably was—early to mid-thirties.

He could imagine her as a teenager again, eagerly preparing to mount her friend's horse, dreaming it was her own. And he was glad he'd been able to offer her something special, an afternoon she was sure to enjoy.

He was glad for himself, too. This was the first time he'd met a woman who'd taken his mind off his loss. He actually enjoyed the time he'd spent with Selena. Maybe that meant his heart was on the mend.

And that the shadow of guilt that had dogged him these past two years would finally lift.

"Okay," he said, "let's get her saddled for you."

Ten minutes later, he'd saddled both Sugar Foot and a roan gelding he'd just acquired, along with several others, at auction last week. Because he'd wanted to try him out, he figured today was as good a day as any.

"What's his name?" Selena asked, as she stroked the roan's neck.

"I don't remember. Bailey something or other." Alex stole a glance at Selena, saw her brow furrowed as she processed his response. For some reason, even though his spread numbered in the hundreds and he couldn't remember each horse by name, he didn't like knowing that she was bothered by it.

"He's registered with the American Quarter Horse Association," he explained, "so he has an official name. But we've been calling him Bailey for short." At least, that would be his nickname now.

Her expression lifted at that, apparently pleased that the new horse wasn't merely one of hundreds when that actually was the case.

After leading the horses out of the barn, they stopped near the service porch, which was at the back of the house, just off the kitchen.

"Wait here," Alex said, leaving Selena to hold both sets of reins. Then he went inside, just long enough to pick up the knapsack Lydia had packed with their lunch, as well as a small checkered tablecloth on which they could set out their picnic.

When he returned, he helped Selena mount, giving her a foot up. She might be dressed like a cowgirl, yet her scent—something soft and floral—whispered "Lady" through and through.

As she climbed into her saddle, her denim-clad derriere rising to his eye level, he tried to ignore the growing attraction to the lovely doctor to no avail.

Once she was mounted, he climbed onto his own

horse, sitting a bit taller in the saddle than he had in recent months, or maybe even in recent years. And as they headed out, his heart soared at the thought of leaving it all behind—the house, the chores, the daily grind.

But more than that, he seemed to have finally—or at least, temporarily—shaken that dark shadow of grief and guilt that plagued him more often than not.

As the sun stretched high over the cloud-speckled Texas sky, Alex and Selena continued a leisurely ride, following the creek that ran through his property to a small lake surrounded by cottonwood trees, where they slowed to a stop.

"This is where I learned to fish and to swim," Alex told her.

"I can't imagine what it would have been like to grow up on a ranch like this. It would have been a dream come true for me." Having been raised in a small desert town in New Mexico, where trees and streams and swimming holes didn't even exist, other than in travel magazines or books in the library, Selena relished the sight of the lush green pastures and the horses grazing with their foals, as well as the scent of fertile ground that mingled with the hint of autumn.

"Then I'm glad I was able to share this with you."

She stole a glance at Alex, saw him leaning forward in the saddle, his hands resting on the pommel. The man had an amazing profile and an even more remarkable build—lean, strong and as sexy as they came.

His black Stetson shielded his eyes from the sun, but not from her. As their gazes met and locked, something sparked between them—something more powerful than she'd expected, more alluring.

"Come on," Alex said, breaking eye contact and drawing her from her musing. "I'm sure you're getting hungry. I certainly am. And I know the perfect place to eat."

She'd had a light breakfast this morning because she'd been plagued by nerves. But they'd dissipated the moment she and Alex had struck out on their ride, so she was more than ready for a lunch break. "All right. That sounds like a good idea."

They continued on for another twenty minutes or so, following a trail that led up a mountain—or maybe it was more of a hillside.

"We call this summit Ol' Piney," he said.

We? Had he brought his wife here?

Well, of course, he had. Why wouldn't he have done that? It was beautiful.

"My uncle was the first to bring me out here, and that's what he called it."

Selena studied the pine trees that lined the trail, reminding her of a view one might see on a postcard.

"Let's eat here," he said, as he swung off his horse. "It has a great view of the valley."

Again, she thought of his late wife because she couldn't imagine him and his uncle having picnics together. She wasn't sure what bothered her about the idea. After all, the poor woman was dead and gone.

But the fact that Alex had cared so deeply for her, that he planned to utilize the embryos they'd created together and raise them himself, left her uneasy and even a bit sad. The woman who was destined to become Alex's second wife would have to compete with Mary Connor's memory, and Selena wasn't up for the task.

Besides, she really wasn't interested in dating Alex.

Not really. They'd merely struck up a friendship—at least, so far.

"Can I help you down?" Alex asked, as he approached her horse.

She figured she could make it on her own, but for some silly reason, she liked the idea of letting the handsome cowboy help her dismount. "All right."

As she held the reins and gripped the pommel, she pulled her foot from the stirrup and swung her leg over the saddle.

Alex reached for her. As his hands wrapped around her waist, setting off tremors of heat to her core, her breath caught.

The moment her feet touched the ground, her legs wobbled. She wasn't sure if her unsteadiness was due to her reaction to his touch and his rugged cowboy scent, both of which sent her senses reeling, or whether it was from being in the saddle so long. Either way, the combination was doing a real number on her.

He continued to hold her steady, which was a good thing, because she'd hate to collapse on the ground in a heap. As she slowly turned to face him, his hands remained loosely at her waist, setting off a flutter in her heart.

As their gazes met and held, her pulse spiked, and for a moment, she thought he was going to kiss her.

Yes, she thought. Her heart hammered in anticipation, and her breathing nearly stopped. Yet instead of slipping his arms around her, drawing her close and placing his lips on hers, he slowly eased back.

Why hadn't he taken the opportunity while he'd had it?

And why did she find his reluctance so disheartening?

"Come here," he said, dropping the reins and heading toward a large rock. "I want to show you something."

What could he possibly think she'd find more interesting than a kiss? And why had he released the gelding's reins? Wasn't he worried it would run off?

"What about the horses?" she asked.

"Let them graze."

As Selena released the reins, allowing Sugar Foot to lower her head and nibble on the grass, she followed Alex to the rock where he stood.

He pointed to the valley below, where a small town lay nestled against the trees. Thanks to the arrival of autumn, the leaves were a kaleidoscope of fall shades—rust, red, yellow and the occasional green.

"It's Brighton Valley," she said, scanning the small buildings and houses and noting the steeple of the community church. "It looks different from up here, doesn't it?"

He pointed to the east. "That's Main Street and the old part of town."

She nodded, spotting the cars parked along the storefronts.

"Now look to the west, just beyond the medical center. On a clear day, you can even see Wexler."

"It's an amazing view from up here. It looks like something you'd find on a postcard."

"I thought you'd like it."

She studied the quaint and colorful scene a moment longer, then turned to him and smiled. "Thank you."

"For what? Bringing you to Ol' Piney?"

"For everything—the ride, the tour of your ranch, the lovely view…"

"I'm glad you're having fun."

It was more than fun. She'd been waiting for this day since the moment he'd invited her to come out to the ranch, yet it was more than the outdoors and horseback riding she'd been dreaming about. But she didn't dare let on about that.

"Are you ready to eat?" he asked.

"Sure."

Yet he didn't make a move to get their lunch out of the knapsack. Instead, he remained in front of her, face-to-face. An arm's distance apart.

His gaze held an intensity that set her heart on edge again. And she sensed another kiss coming her way. But this time, she didn't want to risk the chance of him drawing away, like he did just moments ago. So she did something she might regret later.

She reached up, slipped her arms around his neck and drew his mouth to hers.

Chapter 6

Alex hadn't expected Selena to make the first move, but he was glad that she had. He'd been dying to wrap his arms around her all day, and it was nice to know that he wasn't the only one caught up in a growing sexual attraction and succumbing to temptation.

As their mouths met, her lips parted, inviting him to be an active participant. And that's just what he did. He kissed her as if there were no tomorrow, as if there were every reason in the world for them to be lovers— and nothing waiting in the wings to hold them back.

And maybe there wasn't. She'd known what he planned to do. And she'd still instigated the kiss.

Didn't that mean she'd be on the same page with him when it came to hiring a woman to carry the embryos to term?

Of course the answer to that question, as well as his baby plan, quickly dissipated in the heat of the moment.

As Selena leaned into him, pressing her breasts against his chest, their bodies melded together as if they were meant for each other. And right now, Alex didn't have any reason to doubt that they hadn't been.

While they continued to kiss, he ran his hands along her back, exploring the slope of her hips, caressing each feminine curve. As he relished the feel of her in his arms, he savored her taste and her soft floral scent until his hormones spun out of control.

What he wouldn't give to have her back at the ranch house with him at this very minute, with music playing in the background, a fire in the hearth, candles lit, the coverlet pulled back on the bed in readiness.

But he wasn't at home. They were several miles away, in an outdoor world of their own making.

So what was he supposed to do here and now? Stretch that tablecloth across the ground for them to use in lieu of a king-size bed?

While tempted to do just that, he slowly drew back, breaking the kiss and allowing them both to come up for air. Still, his heart was pounding like a son of a gun, and his blood continued to rush through his veins.

She looked up at him with an expression that asked, *Where do we go from here?*

He'd be damned if he knew, especially when he had no idea how she'd feel about raising another woman's babies. And that's something Selena would have to consider doing if they took the whole idea of a relationship any further than this.

But it was too soon to discuss a complex future between them like that, especially because he would begin to earnestly search for a gestational carrier soon.

Or would Selena be willing to carry the babies for him?

It was a lot to ask a woman, especially one who hadn't had any children of her own yet.

For a moment, he envisioned having a baby the old-fashioned way—by making love with Selena and then watching her belly grow with a child they'd created. The thought, while warm and tender, wasn't one he could consider. Not when he still had those embryos waiting to be born.

Besides, it was far too early at this stage of their budding relationship to even broach a subject like that, so he decided to focus on something else, something other than a burning sexual desire that could very easily lead to broken promises and shattered dreams.

"Are you ready for lunch?" he asked, deciding to make light of it for now.

She blinked, then blinked a second time as if she was having trouble distancing her physical hunger from a sexual one. And he couldn't blame her one bit for that. Hell, that's exactly what was going on with him. He was drowning in a flood of testosterone, grasping for straws that made sense, desperate with longing…

And hungry for a hell of a lot more than the sandwiches Lydia had made them.

But there was no way he could let Selena know all that.

How could he when he didn't know if his attraction to her was only a passing fancy? So he strode toward Bailey, reached for the knapsack he'd secured to the saddle and untied it. "I'll water the horses if you'd like to set out the food."

As he handed the canvas sack to her, he noted bewilderment splashed across her face.

"Would you rather I did it?" he asked. "I'll just be a minute or two."

She blinked again, clearly reeling from the kiss—or maybe from his reluctance to talk about it.

"No," she said softly, taking the knapsack from him. "I'll do it."

"There's a tablecloth inside," he said, as he returned to the horses.

She glanced at the bag that had been packed with their lunch, and when she broke eye contact with him, he collected the reins and started toward the creek with both horses.

Had he defused the situation? Or merely made things worse by leaving her confused and maybe a bit angry?

He was tempted to steal a glance over his shoulder, but he continued toward the stream instead.

Rather than spread the tablecloth on the ground and set out their lunches as Alex had asked her to do, Selena remained rooted to the spot where she stood, gaping at the man who'd just kissed her senseless, then shrugged it all off as if it were nothing and walked away.

How could he kiss her like that, turning her inside out, then pretend as if it had never happened, as if they didn't have to broach the subject of relationships, dating or even making love?

Her first thought was that it was just a matter of hormones and biology at work. After all, his wife had been gone for two years—unless he'd dated in the past, which she doubted. She had a feeling he might still be married in his heart, so he probably hadn't had sex in a long time.

Yet she couldn't ignore what had just happened between them. So she brought it out in the open. "What was that all about, Alex?"

His steps slowed to a stop and he turned to her. "What do you mean? The *kiss?*"

"For starters, yes."

A slow grin stretched across his face. "You made the first move this time. Maybe I should be the one asking the questions."

"You didn't fight it."

His grin deepened, and his eyes gleamed. "Only a fool would have done that, Selena."

She opened her mouth to object, then set the knapsack on the ground and crossed her arms instead. "Well, thanks for giving it the old college try."

"Wait a second. Are you upset?"

Of course she was upset. And embarrassed, too.

"Why?" he asked. "I thought you enjoyed it."

"I did. And unless you're a big fat liar, you did, too."

"Oh, there's no doubt about that."

"Then why did you just walk away as if it never happened?"

He stood there for a moment, holding the reins of the horses, then dropped his head. When he looked up, he said, "I'm sorry. I should have addressed it, I guess, but I wasn't sure what to say. A part of me wanted to ask if you'd ever made love outdoors."

She hadn't. And with that kiss still fresh in her mind, she thought the whole idea sounded...intriguing. And far more tempting than she could have imagined. But she had to get something other than the vision of their bare bodies out in the open.

"What's going on between us?" she asked, determined to learn what he thought, what he might feel.

"I'm not sure." His smile faded, and his expression grew serious. "There's definitely a strong sexual attraction between us. And some genuine feelings. But to be honest, I'm not sure what to do about it at this stage of the game."

She arched a brow.

"Well, let me rephrase that. I know *exactly* what to do about it, but I'm not sure if that would be wise."

Her arms loosened and slowly uncrossed. "I'm reluctant to get involved with you, too. But what's holding you back?"

He paused for the longest time, as if he wasn't sure if he wanted to reveal his concerns or not. Then he said, "I'd like nothing more than to date you and to see where things go. But I have some things I need to do. And I'm not sure…"

"If I'd fit into those plans?"

Again he pondered his answer for a beat. "No, it's not that. You'd fit in nicely. But I'm not sure how you'd feel about dating a single father, which is what I plan to be within the next year if things work out."

The embryos. His plan to have his late wife's children.

Selena might be dealing with a growing attraction to Alex, but part of that was curiosity and maybe even envy. What she wouldn't give to find a man who'd love her in the way Alex had obviously loved his wife.

And look what she'd just done. She'd stepped out on a limb and kissed him.

But how could she not? He was far more tempting than he ought to be. If things were different, she could easily fall for a man like Alex, but that would lock her into a second-place role she couldn't and wouldn't accept.

So she unfolded her arms and reached for the knapsack on the ground. "You're right. It's a complex situation. And we really need to take things slowly." That is, if they took things anywhere at all.

"I'm glad you understand."

Sadly, she did. "You have a family waiting to be born."

"Are you okay with that?" he asked.

To be honest? "I'm not sure."

The whole idea of dating a single dad was one thing. She would actually end up having children and a family that way. But in this case, she'd be playing second fiddle to his wife's memory and to the children they'd planned to raise together before that tragic accident left Alex heartbroken and alone. So it wasn't the same thing at all.

"Let's just take things one day at a time," she said. "Is that all right with you?"

Alex's smile sent Selena's heart hurtling through her chest as though it might disintegrate upon landing. "Okay, that's fair enough."

Then he turned and walked the horses to the creek.

But it wasn't okay. And it wasn't the least bit fair. The last thing in the world Selena needed to do was to fall for a man whose heart would always belong to someone else.

The picnic they shared—Dagwood sandwiches, oranges and homemade chocolate chip cookies—was tasty. And while they'd kept the mealtime conversation light, the memory of that arousing kiss remained on Selena's mind for the rest of the afternoon.

Was Alex thinking about it, too?

She couldn't see how he wouldn't be, even though he appeared to have shut it out of his mind as if it had never happened. She probably ought to consider skirting emotional issues to be a fault of his, yet there was something about Alex she found appealing. And she couldn't help forgiving him for that weakness.

Would she ever meet another man like him someday? She certainly hoped so. She'd have to make it a point to get out in the real world more often so she would have more opportunities for romance.

Of course, she'd certainly gotten out of the office and away from the medical center today. Riding with Alex, seeing his beautiful ranch and breathing in the fresh air had been invigorating—and just what she'd needed. There was something to the old "all work and no play" adage.

She'd probably be sore tomorrow from her time spent in the saddle, but she didn't care. The day had been amazing so far, and she was sorry to see the sun descending in the west Texas sky.

When they returned to the ranch and rode into the yard, a young cowboy wearing a black felt hat, a red plaid shirt and jeans met them and approached Alex. "Hey, boss. If you're done with those horses, I can take them for you."

"What are you doing here?" Alex asked, as he dismounted. "This is your day off, Troy."

"Yeah, I know, but Lydia called and asked me to cover for Gus. She took him to the urgent care in town, only they sent him to the hospital. I guess he did a real number on his hand. He's having surgery this afternoon."

Selena had suspected the ranch hand's cut had reached the tendons, so she was glad the housekeeper had taken him to have it checked.

"Lydia's still at the hospital," Troy added. "She plans to stay there until Gus gets out of recovery."

"I really appreciate your coming out here on such short notice," Alex told the cowboy. "I'm sorry if it interfered with any plans you might have had."

"I was just going to shoot a little pool down at the Stagecoach Inn, but it's not a problem. Gus would have done the same for me." Troy glanced at Selena, then back at Alex. "So what do you say, boss? Do you want me to cool down those horses for you?"

"Sure, that would be great." Alex handed over his reins, then he made his way to Sugar Foot's side and reached up to help Selena down.

She was glad they had an audience. It might make being in Alex's arms a little less awkward, a little less tempting. So she carefully removed her foot from the stirrup, then lifted her leg over the saddle.

Alex reached for her, setting off a shiver of arousal through her bloodstream. So much for avoiding any awkward feelings and urges.

"Why don't you come inside for a while?" Alex asked. "Lydia probably has some iced tea or lemonade made. I can even open a beer or a bottle of wine, if you'd like."

She pondered the wisdom of accepting his invitation, but only for a moment, because it seemed that he wasn't ready to say goodbye. And for some fool reason, neither was she.

"Actually," she said, brushing her hands against her denim-clad hips, "something thirst-quenching sounds great."

"You got it. Come on in."

Selena followed Alex to the back door of the house,

entering through the service porch, where they both washed up at the utility sink. Then he led her to a tidy kitchen, which had been painted a rusted red color.

It was a nice room, she decided, functional and newly remodeled, with gray faux-marble countertops, a fairly new stainless steel stove and oven, as well as a built-in refrigerator.

Someone had gone all out on decorating the room that was central to any house. Had it been Lydia, the housekeeper?

Or had Alex's late wife been the one to create an efficient place to cook and to eat?

"Why don't you have a seat?" Alex indicated a round oak table that Selena suspected was an antique—the only thing in the room that wasn't modern and new. "I'll get our drinks."

As Selena pulled out one of the chairs, she noted the scarred wood tabletop as well as a vase that bore a bouquet of multicolored roses.

"We're in luck," Alex said. "There's sun tea on the counter as well as fresh lemonade in the fridge. Which would you prefer?"

"Lemonade," she said.

As she watched him take a pitcher from the refrigerator, glasses from the cupboard and ice cubes from the freezer, she realized she'd have to use the bathroom sooner or later, especially if she had anything to drink. So she asked him where she could find the nearest one.

"Just go through the doorway into the living room. You'll see a hallway near the fireplace. The guest bathroom is the first door on the right."

She thanked him, then followed his directions, pausing long enough to study the cozy living area, with its beige-colored walls, dark wood beams and a stone fireplace. Like the kitchen, the decor in this room also bore the markings of a woman's hand—like the red knit throw that draped over the back and the armrest of a beige leather sofa, the floral watercolor artwork, the crystal figurines on the mantel.

Unable to help herself, Selena wandered to the fireplace, where several framed pictures were displayed. She would have checked them all out, but one in particular drew her complete attention—a wedding photo of Alex and his late wife.

Mary Connor was a pretty bride, a wholesome redhead with a scatter of freckles across her nose and a starry-eyed smile. Alex, stunningly handsome in a tuxedo and a black bow tie, appeared to be just as happy.

A pang of sadness pierced Selena's heart. Alex had lost the woman he'd vowed to love for as long as they both would live. And the fact that he kept that photo in such a prominent position on the mantel was proof that he'd never forgotten her, even two years after her unexpected death.

Was he destined to love her even beyond that?

Selena couldn't help but think that he was, and at that realization, apprehension flared and she was forced to face the inevitable. If Alex ever married again, his new wife would always have to compete with the woman he'd lost.

Selena continued to study the picture longer than she should have, imagining the beautiful children the couple would have produced—the children he would actually have if he went through with his plan to hire a woman to carry those embryos to term.

And why shouldn't he? They were his future sons or daughters, conceived with eggs of the woman he loved.

Realizing that she'd lingered too long and afraid that Alex would wonder what was keeping her, she replaced the frame on the mantel, then hurried to the bathroom to do what she'd set out to do. All the while, she continued to think about Alex, about the heated kiss they'd shared while out on their ride. The kiss he'd tried to ignore.

He'd admitted to being aroused by it—and tempted to suggest that they make love.

The tone of his voice, his expression, insisted that he'd been telling the truth. So why did he just walk away as if it had never happened?

She'd asked him flat out, then held her breath, awaiting his answer. But his response had surprised her. He'd told her that he hadn't known what to say.

But why was that?

In spite of her disbelief and skepticism at the time, she'd told herself that he'd been so swept away by his desire for more than a kiss that he'd been speechless. But now she realized it was probably more than that. Maybe he'd felt guilty for kissing her—and even more so by his physical response to it and his desire for a sexual release.

Of course, he'd mentioned that a part of him had wanted to ask if she'd ever made love outdoors.

She hadn't, of course, done anything that bold before. But his question and her answer had only masked what he hadn't come out and said.

If a part of him had wondered about sex, what had the rest of him been thinking?

Rather than try to second guess his reservations, Selena turned on the water in the bathroom sink and

reached for the soap, hoping to rid herself of the per-
plexing thoughts as easily as she washed any lingering
trail dust from her hands.

One thing was for certain, though. A relationship
with Alex wasn't in the cards for her. She'd already suffered a major breakup while in college, when her first
love had gone home to visit during Christmas break,
only to fall in love with his high school sweetheart all
over again.

Why in the world would she want to set herself up
for another failed romance?

She dried her hands on one of the fluffy blue towels
hanging on the rack, then headed back to the kitchen
where she'd left Alex and the lemonade.

She'd no more than reached the living room when she
spotted Alex greeting his housekeeper at the front door.

"How's Gus doing?" Alex asked her.

"He came through the surgery just fine and is in the
recovery room now. So I headed home. I promised to
come back and check on him tonight."

"It's a good thing Selena was here," Alex said, as he
stepped aside to let Lydia in the house. "If she hadn't
seen how serious that injury was, Gus probably wouldn't
have let a doctor check it out."

Lydia, an attractive woman in her late forties to early
fifties, slowly shook her head and clicked her tongue.
"Can you believe it? That man complained about going
to the E.R. all the way to Brighton Valley. He insisted
that he didn't need any help, that he'd had worse injuries before."

"Gus has always been a tough old bird," Alex said.

"Tell me about it." Lydia placed her black handbag
on the table by the door. "When the doctor in the emer-

gency room told him he was going to need surgery, he argued with her for a while, telling her it would be just fine. But when she explained that he stood to lose the use of his hand, if not lose it altogether, he finally agreed. But he insisted that they do it as an outpatient procedure."

"What did the doctor say to that?"

"She referred him to a surgeon, who said he would have considered it, but Gus's blood pressure was high when we arrived. They ended up doing the surgery anyway, but they wanted to keep him overnight for observation."

"I'm glad they're being cautious." Alex closed the door, then joined Lydia in the living area. "Gus never mentioned anything about having high blood pressure to me."

"I'm sure he never even knew it. He told me that he hadn't seen a doctor since he'd been in the army back in the late seventies."

"Who did the surgery?" Selena asked, as she entered the living room and joined Alex and his housekeeper.

"Dr. Goldman," Lydia said. "Do you know him?"

"He's done some amazing work with hand injuries, so I'm glad Betsy was able to call him in."

"Betsy?" Lydia asked.

"Oh, I'm sorry. The only female doctor working in the E.R. at the medical center is Betsy Nielson-Alvarez."

"Yes, that's her. She was awesome. If I'm ever in need of an E.R. doctor, I hope she's on call. She was good with Gus, even though he was a lousy patient." Lydia plopped down on one of the overstuffed chairs in the living room. "I swear, Alex, I've never seen a more bullheaded man in my life. He probably drove his first wife crazy."

"He's never been married," Alex said.

"Well, that's too bad. A good woman might have put a smile on his face."

Alex laughed. "Maybe it's not too late for that."

Lydia studied her boss for a moment, their gazes speaking through the silence. Then she said, "I'm not so sure he'd be interested."

"You never know unless you try."

Lydia crossed her arms, and furrowed her brow, clearly pondering Alex's suggestion. Moments later, she looked up and grinned. "Maybe you're right. I think I'll pack up some of those chocolate chip cookies I made yesterday and take them to him when I go back to the hospital this evening."

As Lydia got to her feet and headed to the kitchen, Selena took the opportunity to escape the temptation to pursue what would only end up being a star-crossed relationship with Alex.

"I'm going to have to go," she said, as she crossed the hardwood floor to where Alex stood.

Selena's sudden announcement threw Alex for a moment, and he turned to her, stunned. "What about that lemonade?"

"I'm afraid I'll have to take a rain check. I just remembered a meeting I'd scheduled with a colleague. If I leave now, I'll make it just in time."

As Selena started for the front door, Alex followed her. "I'll walk you to the car."

She glanced over her shoulder. "You don't need to."

"I know, but I want to." And he did. He'd found himself increasingly drawn to the lovely obstetrician. She was bright and funny, compassionate and sweet.

And on top of that, the kisses they'd shared, especially the one up on Ol' Piney, had nearly knocked him to his knees. Of course, it also had him running a bit scared because getting involved with Selena might complicate the future he'd planned.

Okay, so he and Selena really hadn't gotten "involved" quite yet. But all afternoon he'd found himself comparing Selena to Mary, which wasn't fair to either of them.

Now, as he followed Selena out the front door and onto the veranda, he watched her pat the small bulge in the front pocket of her jeans, assuming it had been made by her car keys since she didn't have a purse with her.

"Thanks so much for inviting me out to the ranch today," she said as she made her way toward the barn where she'd parked her Lexus. "I really enjoyed that ride. It was a real treat for a wannabe cowgirl."

"I'm glad," he said, walking along with her. "I enjoyed it, too. I'd forgotten how nice it is to go on a ride just for the fun of it. You'll have to come out again—soon."

"Thank you." She smiled, yet her eyes had lost the spark they'd had earlier.

Had something happened between the time she'd agreed to have a glass of lemonade and Lydia's arrival? It sure seemed that way.

Or maybe she'd been telling the truth when she said that she'd just remembered an appointment she had. Maybe the talk about Gus and the surgery and the E.R. doctor had been a reminder of her meeting.

Yeah, that had to be it. He shook off his apprehension as they approached her vehicle.

"I wasn't kidding when I told you that you're always welcome here," he said, trying to stretch things out.

"I really appreciate that, Alex. You have a beautiful ranch. It's a great place to ride. And I really like Sugar Foot. She's the kind of horse I would have wanted when I was a girl." Selena reached for the door handle on the driver's side and opened it.

He probably ought to just step back and let her go because they were both tiptoeing around the idea of a relationship—and for good reason. Yet his hormones seemed to have a mind of their own.

Instead of stepping back, he eased forward and placed a hand along her jaw. Then he brushed a good-bye kiss across her lips.

It was a gentle movement, a friendly way to end the day. And while he was sorely tempted to kiss her sense-less, he managed to hold himself in check.

"Drive carefully," he said.

"I will."

She hesitated for a moment, and his resolve to keep things simple, platonic and safe withered in the after-noon breeze.

As her fading floral scent snaked round him, bind-ing him to her somehow, his thumb brushed against her cheek.

Her eyes widened, and her lips parted, letting him know they were both fighting the same temptation. So he threw caution to the wind and kissed her the way he'd been dying to do since lunchtime.

Chapter 7

As Alex leaned in to kiss Selena a second time, she should have stopped him, yet for some reason, against her better judgment, she wrapped her arms around him and kissed him right back.

How could she do anything else? After all, Alex had been right when he'd said only a fool would have fought their sexual attraction.

And while that might be true, Selena couldn't risk becoming a fool when it came to getting emotionally involved with a handsome rancher who hadn't gotten over his late wife—and probably never would.

Sure, biology and hormones might play in Selena's favor. Alex would eventually lower his guard and have sex again, either with her or with someone else. And she suspected that it would happen sooner rather than later. But that didn't mean the woman who finally made love with him would win his undying devotion.

Sadly, it appeared that his first wife already had a lock on that.

So Selena placed her hands on his chest and gently pressed against him while drawing her lips from his.

It was the best thing to do, she told herself. Hadn't she already decided to end their harmless flirtation— or whatever it was—before it was too late to walk away without risking her heart?

Yet as they drew apart, she yearned for more of his taste, his touch, his scent.

Did he realize that ending things—and not just the kiss—was a real struggle for her?

Probably not, because a boyish grin tugged at his lips, and a glimmer lit his eyes.

"Kissing you is becoming a habit," he said.

A bad one, she feared. But why make a remark like that now? She'd already decided that she wasn't up for any heavy discussions, especially when she was determined to leave the ranch as quickly as possible.

But to clear up any false assumptions he might have made about what that goodnight kiss meant, she would have to lay it on the line.

"We talked about this earlier," she said. "Your future is going to be complicated enough without having to deal with a new relationship."

He seemed to ponder her comment for the longest time. With each second that passed, something in her chest gripped and tightened, squeezing the breath right out of her.

Why didn't he argue with her and tell her that she was wrong?

He couldn't, of course, because they both knew the truth.

"About those embryos," he said, getting right to the heart of the matter.

When he didn't immediately finish what he'd started to say, she was tempted to prompt him by asking, *What about the embryos?*

Instead, she held her tongue and waited for him to find the words he appeared to be tossing around in his mind.

Finally, he said, "It's not something I have to do right away."

It *wasn't?*

"I'm not in any real hurry," he added.

The tightness in her chest eased, making it easier to breathe, to think, to speak.

"Your plan sounded pretty solid—and imminent—to me," she said.

"Actually, I'm thinking about postponing things for a while."

That was a good sign, wasn't it? Maybe he wasn't so gung ho on having his and Mary's babies, after all.

Not that Selena would have any objections to his using those embryos if his motive for doing so was right. She completely understood his wanting to have them because they were a part of him. It was only natural that he would. But if he planned to have them as a way to keep a part of Mary alive, then Selena couldn't get involved with him. It would be too risky.

However, it now sounded as if he wasn't so all-fired determined to hire a gestational carrier.

Did that mean his heart was finally on the mend?

And if so, had Selena been instrumental in the healing process?

Alex took her hand and gave it a gentle squeeze.

"Would you feel better about going out with me if my plan to have those babies was further down the road?"

Yes, but she didn't want to admit it. Not when there was an even bigger question looming before them.

"Would *you* feel better?" she asked.

"Probably."

They stood there for a moment, so much hanging in the balance. More than he probably realized.

"Before you go," he said, "I have a question I'd like to ask you."

She braced herself for that heavy conversation she hadn't been ready for just moments ago, fearing an emotional gunshot to the heart.

"All right," she said. *Shoot*.

"There's a line dancing contest down at the Stagecoach Inn next Friday night. I think it would be a lot of fun to watch. Would you like to go with me?"

Was he asking her on a date? It certainly seemed that way. Moments ago, she would have turned him down flat. But now?

"Do you have to work?" he asked.

"On Friday? Yes, at the office. But I'm not on call, if that's what you mean." Still, she didn't come out and agree to go, even though she was sorely tempted.

When was the last time she'd kicked up her heels or did something just for the fun of it?

Not often enough.

"Have you ever been to a honky-tonk?" he asked.

She chuckled at the thought, releasing the last bit of tension that had built up in her chest. "I can't say that I have."

"Then you're in for a real treat."

She didn't know about that. She'd never been a big

fan of country music, but by the crooked grin splashed across Alex's face, she got the feeling that she'd been missing out on a little known secret.

"I'll tell you what," she said. "I'll think about it."

"Fair enough."

They continued to stand there, as if waiting for something else to happen, something elusive. An opportunity Selena might never have again.

"You'd better get out of here," he said, taking a step back.

He must have read the surprise on her face because he smiled and added, "You're going to be late to that meeting, remember?"

"Oh. Yes. You're right. I can't forget that."

Still, she waited a beat before slipping behind the wheel and closing the driver's door. Then she started the engine, continuing the pretense that she had to rush off to a meeting she'd never scheduled.

And wondering just what the heck one wore to a honky-tonk.

Alex hadn't talked to Selena in more than forty-eight hours, not since they'd ridden horses up to Ol' Piney. But he hadn't seen any reason to. He knew she'd be at the wellness center on Tuesday night. They'd have plenty of time to talk afterward.

When she'd left his house Sunday afternoon, he'd gone out on a limb and mentioned the embryos, telling her he would postpone hiring a gestational carrier for a while. Because she'd agreed that the future was complicated, he'd begun to think that the whole baby plan might be holding her back.

And, apparently, it had been.

Of course, he hadn't changed his mind about having those children. He was determined to go forward with the plan. He owed it to Mary—and to himself.

But if he was interested in dating Selena—and he definitely was—they'd need to spend more time together to see if they were actually as suited as they seemed to be. If they were, and if things became serious enough to consider a long-term relationship, they could discuss the whole idea of his raising the babies or the two of them raising them together.

At that point, if Selena wasn't on board with his plan for the near future, then he'd know that they weren't meant for each other.

But why end their friendship—or whatever it was destined to become—before it even had a chance to get off the ground?

For that reason, as he drove to the wellness center Tuesday evening, he was determined to date Selena. After class, he would ask her out to dinner again, just as he'd done last time. He'd level with her about how that kiss had affected him—and what he'd like to do about it.

He'd already asked her to go to the line dancing contest at the Stagecoach Inn on Friday, although she hadn't agreed yet. But he'd do his best to talk her into it.

Once he arrived at the wellness center, he parked his truck, entered the building and made his way to the community classroom.

Just as he'd done both Tuesdays before, he took a seat in the front row and waited for Selena to arrive.

He'd had a devil of a time trying not to peer over his shoulder to look at the door each time it opened. But that didn't stop him from glancing at his wristwatch every now and then.

She was a few minutes late tonight.

When she finally made her way to the front, her high heels clicking on the linoleum, Alex sat up straight and offered her an it's-good-to-see-you smile, which she returned before placing her file upon the podium.

She wore a white lab coat over a black dress tonight, and she'd applied a fresh coat of lipstick. A classy lady, inside and out.

"Good evening," she said, glancing out at the others in the classroom. "I'm sorry I'm late. Let's get started."

As she began to speak about the difference between surrogates and gestational carriers, her focus was clearly on her class and the lecture she'd prepared. But Alex was too caught up in the lovely instructor to process what she was saying.

The spark of attraction that struck hard each time she was with him darn near blazed right now, making it impossible to take note of anything other than how beautiful she was, how bright, how…

How weird was that? This was the one lecture he'd been waiting to hear. But he'd be damned if he could wrap his mind around any of it.

He'd missed her more than he'd expected to. And just being in the same room with her again had his pulse and his hormones doing all kinds of wacky things.

Still, he managed to pull a few sentences out of the air and made a mental note or two. As he'd expected, there were things he needed to watch out for in choosing a gestational carrier as well as other considerations he hadn't realized.

While Selena continued to talk about surrogacy, Alex studied the list of agencies she'd given the class, the handout she'd given him last week. He'd stuck it in his rear pocket, and they hadn't mentioned it since.

He'd never put much stock in Freudian theory, but he couldn't help wondering if they both wanted to avoid talking about his quest to have those babies.

Was that because he'd been right? That Selena wasn't interested in dating a man with kids?

Or was it merely his fear that his baby plan had her dragging her feet about getting involved with him, when the kids had nothing at all to do with it?

Either way, he supposed it didn't matter. He'd give their relationship a chance to blossom, then he'd move ahead on his game plan. After all, what would it hurt to postpone things for a couple of months—six at the most?

When the class finally ended and everyone's questions had been answered or at least addressed, several women and one couple went up to the podium to speak to Selena privately. Most of them thanked the doctor for her time and expertise, but a few wanted to share their personal struggles.

Alex remained in his seat until everyone finally filed out of the classroom, then he walked up to the podium.

"How about dinner?" he asked. "I've got a hankering for tacos, and I have a feeling you haven't had a chance to eat yet."

"I had a late lunch, so I'm really not very hungry."

"Then have a salad or a cup of soup, something light. Please? I'd really like you to come with me tonight."

"Why?"

"Because we need to talk."

Selena reached for the file that held her notes and handouts. "About what?"

"All the things we should have discussed while we were at Ol' Piney."

Her gaze sought his, her eyes narrowing as if trying to read something in his words or his expression. But he couldn't blame her for that. He'd been keeping his thoughts and feelings to himself for most of his life. Or maybe all of it. He'd learned to clam up early on, when his father had clamped down on him at the dinner table, saying that children were to be seen and not heard. Even after he'd gone to live with his maternal uncle, a man who believed certain things—like feelings and other weaknesses a man might have—ought to be kept close to the vest, the lessons had continued.

Mary used to complain about that, although she'd gotten pretty good at getting him to speak up sometimes—and second guessing him when he didn't.

Selena tucked a strand of hair behind her ear. "I thought we *did* talk about…*things*."

Not without her forcing the issue. And if truth be told, Alex had held back a lot. But marriage to Mary had kind of softened him a bit, and he'd learned to be more up front with a woman he loved.

Not that he loved Selena at this point, but who knew what could develop if they spent more time together?

"You were right to get angry with me," he said. "When I went to water the horses."

Her head cocked slightly to the side, her hair cascading down her shoulder.

"I really dropped the ball," he added. "That kiss was out of this world, and I should have told you so. At the time, discussing something as complex as a relationship seemed too soon and I just… Well, I guess you could say I balked."

"Why the change of heart?" she asked.

He shrugged, holding back the truth. Okay, so some old habits were hard to break. But he wasn't ready to lose out on an opportunity to date Selena and see what became of it. Neither did he want to risk laying all that on the line and having her throw it back at him. So he offered her another reason on the list, which was just as honest but a bit lower in terms of importance. "I've enjoyed our time together."

Her once-guarded expression relaxed, and a hint of a smile tugged at her lips. "I've liked it, too."

"Good. Then let's go to Anita's tonight."

She pondered it for a beat before saying, "All right. You drive a hard bargain." Then she tossed a smile his way before taking her file of notes and placing it in her handbag.

Alex still planned to hire a gestational carrier, of course, but why scare Selena off with his family plan before they'd had a chance to decide if they were willing to be a couple?

Once he knew that she was in it for the long run, he'd add two newborn babies to the mix.

In the meantime, while they were dating, he would do a little more research on those agencies that were on the list she'd given him. He could also look over the information that Family Solutions was sending to him.

But Selena didn't need to know about any of that just yet.

Anita's was located in one of several two-story houses on Third Avenue, just three blocks from the quaint shops that lined both sides of Main Street.

At one time, the redbrick building had been the home

of Edmond Calhoun, Brighton Valley's first mayor. Back in the 1990s, the Calhoun family had sold the property to Dale "Sully" Sullivan, who'd converted it to a bakery and sweet shop. But about ten years ago, the baker retired and moved out of state. So Sully put the house back on the market.

Shirley Salas and her husband purchased the building next and turned it into a restaurant. Because most of Shirley's recipes had been handed down to her from her husband's mother, she'd named the eatery Anita's, after her mother-in-law.

It hadn't taken long for word to travel, and Anita's soon became a favorite of the locals.

Not only was the setting homey, with its antique furnishings and colorful southwest artwork, but also the food was to die for. In fact, some of the dishes were almost as good as the meals Selena used to have when she visited her *abuelita,* who'd been, at least in Selena's opinion, the absolute best Mexican cook in the world.

Because Anita's was located just down the street from Selena's house, she and Alex decided to take both vehicles and meet outside the restaurant.

Finding a parking space wasn't always easy in this part of town, especially during the lunch or dinner hours, so Selena left her car in her own driveway and went inside the house, where she left her lab coat. She also took a few extra minutes to apply a fresh coat of lipstick and to run a brush through her hair. Then she walked several tree-lined blocks to meet Alex.

Just as she'd suspected, he had arrived first and was now waiting for her.

He stood near the steps that led to the entrance, a grin splashed across his gorgeous face. Even without boots and a hat, the man had a boatload of cowboy charm that Selena found amazing—and more than a little appealing.

"Have you eaten here before?" she asked as she joined him on the sidewalk.

"Every chance I get. How about you?"

"Not nearly as often as I'd like to."

"Then I'm glad I chose the right place." He placed his hand on her back and walked with her up the steps. After opening the door, he followed her inside the restaurant.

A silver-haired hostess wearing a turquoise peasant-style blouse and a black skirt greeted them with a friendly smile. "Good evening. Welcome to Anita's."

"Two for dinner," Alex told her.

The woman gathered up the menus, then stepped away from her station. "Please come this way."

They crossed the ceramic tile floor to the carpeted stairway. As the hostess led them up to the second floor, the lights overhead flickered off and on.

"Goodness," she said, slowing to a stop. "I'm not sure what's going on with that. It's happened a couple of times this evening."

When the flickering stopped, she continued to lead them to a room that had once been the Calhouns' library.

Selena scanned the wall-to-wall shelves laden with books, giving it a unique setting.

"It's been a slow night," the hostess said. "So you'll have the room almost to yourselves."

The only other diners in the room, an elderly couple seated near a cozy brick fireplace, were drinking coffee and having flan for dessert. So they'd probably be leaving soon.

Indicating a white-linen-draped table for two near a window that looked out on the street, the hostess asked, "How's this?"

"It's fine," Alex said, pulling out a chair for Selena. "Thank you."

They'd no more than settled into their seats when the busboy brought them water with lemon, a basket of warm chips and a bowl of salsa.

"Your waiter will be right with you," the young man said, before leaving them to study their menus.

Selena really hadn't needed to look over the offerings. She'd decided on a bowl of albondigas when Alex had mentioned it earlier this evening. The traditional Mexican meatball soup had always been a family favorite.

After the waiter, a heavyset man in his mid- to late-fifties, took their orders, they munched on chips and salsa while making small talk.

Alex asked her about college, about her decision to go to medical school.

"I wanted to be a doctor for as long as I can remember," Selena said. "So going to med school was a given."

In spite of her efforts to put Max Culver, her college sweetheart, out of her mind, Alex's question about school triggered the memory she'd tried hard to forget.

While in her second year of school, she'd actually considered marrying Max. In fact, she'd even thought about changing her major to something that wouldn't require as much education or as many student loans to secure a degree. But then Max had thrown a wrench into those plans, which ended up being a good thing, she supposed.

Once she'd licked her wounds and shaken off her disappointment, she'd focused on her studies, graduating with honors.

"How did you end up in Brighton Valley?" Alex asked.

"I did my residency at the medical center here, then went to work with Dr. Avery for a while. When I learned he was retiring, I took over his practice."

Before Alex could quiz her anymore, the waiter brought their food—the taco combination plate for him and a bowl of soup for her.

They'd only begun to eat when the lights flickered again.

"There must be a short in the wiring," Alex said as he scanned the room.

Selena glanced out the window, spotting the streetlight that shone steadily, suggesting the problem was limited to the restaurant. When she returned her gaze to Alex, the electricity went out.

"Well, thanks to the fire in the hearth," Selena added, "we're not completely in the dark."

"I guess we can consider this an unexpected adventure."

And a rather romantic one at that.

Yet before she could savor the aura and the handsome man sitting across from her, Selena's cell rang. If she weren't a doctor, she might have ignored it, but the tone told her it was the hospital calling.

"Excuse me, Alex." She reached into her purse and pulled out the phone. When the line connected, she answered, "Dr. Ramirez."

"Selena, it's Darren Chin. I just admitted Bella Hastings, one of your patients. Since you have a note in your chart to be notified if she went into labor, I thought I'd better give you a call."

Bella had miscarried three times in the past and had finally made it to the seventh month. Selena cared about all her patients, but Bella was special.

"Thanks, Darren. Tell her I'll be right there." Selena ended the call, then looked across the table at Alex. "I'm sorry. I need to go to the hospital."

"I didn't realize you were on call tonight."

"I'm not. It's just that… Well, I have a high-risk patient who's gone into premature labor. She and her husband have struggled with infertility for years, and she's gone through a lot of heartbreak. So I'd like to be there."

"I understand."

Before Selena could respond, the waiter approached their table holding a flashlight. "I'm sorry, folks. The electricity is out, and the kitchen has shut down for the night. So we have to close for safety purposes."

"No problem," Alex said. "If you'll get our bill, we'll be on our way."

"Actually, our cash register isn't operating, so your meals are on the house tonight."

Selena scooted her chair away from the table and stood, waiting for Alex to do the same. Then she grabbed her purse.

The waiter shone his light, leading the way to the stairs.

When they reached the door and stepped outside, the streetlight illuminated their steps as they made their way to the sidewalk.

"Does this happen to you very often?" Alex asked.

"What do you mean? Power outages, or hospital calls?"

"Both, I suppose. We've been to restaurants on three occasions, and you've had to help a woman in premature labor the first time and now you're rushing to the hospital to see about another. That's two out of three. And then, back at the ranch, there was Gus."

She found herself smiling at his assumption. "No, I'm afraid that's a little unusual. Why?"

"I just figured it might be par for the course when a man dates a doctor."

Is that what they were doing? *Dating?*

She supposed they were.

Her heart twisted at the thought of the risk she was taking by getting involved with a man who might never forget his late wife. But something told her there was a better question she ought to be asking herself.

Did she dare not to?

Chapter 8

Outside Anita's, Alex stood with Selena under the golden glow of the streetlight, reluctant to say goodnight, yet knowing she needed to hurry.

"Thank you for dinner," she said.

He chuckled. "It was on the house, remember?"

She smiled. "Still, you invited me."

"Then you're welcome."

Alex placed his hand on Selena's shoulder. "Come on, I'll give you a ride."

"Thank you," Selena said. "I'll take you up on the offer."

Overhead, the evening sky was filled with bright, twinkling stars, and the autumn air was crisp. It would have been a nice night to walk Selena home, rather than drive her.

He would have been tempted to slip his hand in hers, to let her know how proud he was of her, how glad he was to be her...

To be her what? Her friend? That didn't quite cut it. But then again, "girlfriend" sounded juvenile.

Lover came to mind. And if he'd actually had the opportunity to walk her home, to wait for an invitation to come inside...

Instead, he opened the passenger door and waited for her to climb into his truck. Then he slid behind the wheel and backed out of the parking space.

"Where to?" he asked.

"Five blocks north, then take a right on Hawthorne."

When they reached the intersection she'd mentioned, he headed right on Hawthorne, a tree-lined street with homes that had been built in the late 1940s and early 1950s. The neighborhood appeared to be quiet, and the kind Norman Rockwell might have used as a model for some of his artwork.

"This is it." Selena pointed to a pale yellow house with brick trim and a dark green door. "It's not much, but it's where I call home."

Alex wasn't sure why she downplayed the place. It certainly looked appealing to him, with its manicured lawn and all the lush plants and flowers that lined the path to the stoop. Two ceramic pots of red geraniums flanked the front door, which sported a floral wreath.

He pulled along the curb and shut off the ignition. Before he could slide out of the driver's side, go around to her side and open the door for her, she let herself out.

"So what time will you pick me up Friday evening?" she asked as though it was all decided.

He couldn't stop a smile from stealing across his face. The last they'd left it, she was going to think about going with him to the Stagecoach Inn.

Apparently she'd decided to go. And he was grateful for that. It was nice to know they were both feeling a natural pull toward romance.

"The line-dancing competition starts at eight," he said. "Is seven o'clock too early for me to pick you up?"

"No, that's fine."

He waited a beat, then did what he'd been dying to do all evening. He kissed her good-night.

As he'd come to expect, her taste was just as unique as her scent, and so was the way she melded into his arms. A man could get used to kissing her senseless. And as much as Alex was tempted to kiss that soft spot behind her ear, to trail kisses along her throat, to let the hormones and pheromones take over as they moved on to the next step toward intimacy, he released her instead, knowing she had to go.

"Good night," he said. "Sleep tight."

"You, too."

He offered her a parting smile, then turned and headed back to his truck.

If he'd ever had any qualms about dating Selena, their arousing kisses had taken care of that. They'd also left him planning to give her a good-morning kiss in the very near future.

True to his word, Alex arrived at Selena's house a few minutes before seven on Friday night. When the doorbell rang, she'd just come out of the bedroom, where she'd been double checking her appearance. After all, she didn't wear snug-fitting jeans very often, so she couldn't help taking another gander in the full-length mirror to study the way the denim hugged her hips.

She looked all right, she supposed. But instead of seeing the familiar professional woman who usually peered back at her, her image reflected a small-town Texas gal who reminded her of the teenager she'd once been.

Of course, tonight she filled out her cotton T-shirt and jeans in a way she'd never been able to do back then.

Okay, enough of that. Shaking off any lingering insecurity, she hurried to answer the door, where she found Alex standing on the stoop.

He wore the cowboy garb she'd seen him in the first night she'd met him—boots, jeans and a Western shirt, as well as a heart-thumping grin that set her heart on edge.

As he scanned the length of her, the boyish glimmer in his eyes morphed into a full-blown, dazzling smile.

She ran her hands along her hips, dreading the way those old insecurities crept back after she'd done her best to shake them off just moments ago. But she'd never been to a honky-tonk before, so she hoped she'd chosen the right thing to wear.

"You look great," Alex said, as if he'd been reading her mind or sensing her uncertainty. "Every cowboy in the place will be doing double takes at you all night long. I'm going to have to stick close to you so some other guy doesn't try to horn in on my position."

She almost told him that he didn't have a worry in the world, which was the truth. But she wasn't ready to make a revelation like that yet. So she tossed him a playful grin instead. "I doubt that'll be the case, but if so, you're the only cowboy I'm going home with."

Going home with? The moment the words rolled off her tongue, her cheeks warmed at the unintended sexual innuendo.

If Alex thought anything of it, he didn't say anything,

thank goodness. So rather than dwell on the slip of the tongue or draw attention to it, she reached for her purse, which she'd left by the front door.

"You know," Alex said, as he stepped aside to let her out of the house, "I probably should have asked you if we could go earlier than this."

"Why is that?"

"Because the Stagecoach Inn is a popular place, especially with the TGIF crowd, and it's probably going to be tough to find a parking space."

"Then why don't you leave your car here? It isn't all that far. I don't mind walking. Besides, the weather's been especially nice today."

"All right. That sounds good to me."

After Selena locked the front door, they started down the sidewalk together.

It was still light out, but the setting sun had already begun to paint the western horizon in amazing shades of pink, lavender and gray.

She wondered what the sky would look like hours from now, when their date was over. There would be a full moon, she suspected, and a scatter of bright stars. It would probably make a lovely ending to their date, a romantic sight on their way home.

Without conscious thought, her slip of the tongue came back to mind. *You're the only cowboy I'll be going home with.*

That was true. And the thought of inviting him into the house was far more appealing than it should be.

Or was there a good reason inviting him in—to the house or her bed—was so appealing?

Why fight something that was merely a natural progression to romance? After all, if their goodnight kisses were any indication of how good sex would be, making love was sure to be magical.

Maybe she ought to see how tonight went, then decide what to do.

When they reached the end of Hawthorne Lane, they turned on to Third Avenue. Other than the sound of their boots tapping on the sidewalk, they remained silent.

Finally, Selena asked, "Do you like country music?"

"I practically grew up on it," he said. "I like the beat, the words, the stories the lyrics tell. How about you?"

"I've never been a big fan. I've always preferred jazz or soft rock."

"You may change your mind after tonight."

Something told her tonight was going to change a lot of things.

Ten minutes later, they arrived at the Stagecoach Inn, which sat along the county road. Just as Alex had predicted, the parking lot was busting out at the seams.

"You were right," she said. "The place is really hopping. Is it always like this on a Friday night?"

"It's usually busy every weekend, but the line dancing competition is a special event."

As they crossed the graveled parking lot to the entrance, their boots crunched on the dirt.

Selena was looking forward to her first peek inside a real honky-tonk. She'd passed the Stagecoach Inn many times and had always been curious about the cowboy bar as well as its patrons. So once they entered, she found herself studying the interior, the scuffed and scarred hardwood floor, the antique red-and-chrome jukebox, the Old West-style bar that stretched the length of the building.

"Come on," Alex said. "I see a table. We'd better snag it before someone else does."

They made their way to the back of the room, not far from an orange neon sign pointing the way to the restrooms, and took a seat near a couple of cowboys who'd been drinking all afternoon, if the empty beer bottles on the table were a clue. They weren't dressed as nicely as Alex, but not many men stood out in a crowd like he did.

A couple of minutes after Alex and Selena had claimed their seat, a blonde, harried waitress stopped by and asked, "Can I get y'all a drink?"

Selena was just about to ask for a glass of red wine, when the waitress noticed Alex and recognition splashed across her face. "Well, I'll be darned. Look what the cat finally dragged in. It's been a long time, Alex."

"It sure has."

The bleached blonde studied him a couple of beats longer than usual. All the while, Alex seemed to be doing the same thing to her.

Had Selena been wrong when she'd assumed he hadn't gotten involved with another woman, that he hadn't had sex since his wife died?

Her stomach clenched at the thought, and she couldn't help wondering what kind of connection the two of them had.

"It's good to see you out and about," the waitress told him.

"Thanks, Trina. I figured it was time. How've you been?"

"All right." The waitress he knew by name turned to Selena, but instead of asking for her drink order, she studied her for a moment. Assessing her, it seemed.

Why was that? Jealousy? Or just run-of-the-mill curiosity?

"Selena," Alex said, "this is Trina Shepherd. She's an old friend."

Oh, yeah? How old? Where had they met?

The fact that having answers to her growing number of questions mattered more than she'd like it to was a little unsettling, but she shook it off and extended her hand for the customary greeting. "It's nice to meet you."

"Trina," Alex said, "This is Dr. Selena Ramirez. She's an obstetrician in town."

"Oh, really?" Trina tucked a stringy strand of hair behind her ear. "Are you the same Dr. Ramirez who took over Dr. Avery's practice?"

"Yes, I am."

The woman brightened, shedding a couple of unearned years from her face. "I've been meaning to make an appointment to see you. Dr. Avery was my obstetrician, and it seems I'll need one again."

She was pregnant?

The cocktail waitress sighed, then glanced at Alex and clicked her tongue. "I swear, my mother was right. I never learn from my mistakes."

Selena, who would love to have an unexpected pregnancy, couldn't help a momentary twinge of envy. But she shrugged it off as quickly as it came. It wouldn't do to dwell on her misfortune, especially when she had a practice full of expectant mothers.

"How far along are you?" Selena asked.

"Eight weeks and six days, to be exact." Trina blew out a sigh. "I won't need an ultrasound to figure that out."

Still, the sooner Trina saw a doctor, the better. She needed an exam as well as some prenatal vitamins. Pregnancy was going to take a lot out of her, and she already appeared to be tired, and maybe even undernourished.

"If you call in on Monday," Selena said, "ask for Maryanne, who sets my appointments. Tell her we met this weekend, and that I said I'd squeeze you in—even if it's during the lunch hour."

"Thanks. That's really nice of you. As soon as I get the kids off to school, I'll make that call." Trina glanced down at her notepad, then at Alex. "So what would y'all like to drink?"

Selena asked for a glass of merlot, and Alex ordered a Corona with lime.

"You got it." Trina scratched out their requests on the pad, then headed to the bar.

When she was out of hearing range, Alex said, "Thanks for offering to squeeze her in as a favor. Trina doesn't get many breaks."

It didn't seem like it. Selena leaned forward and lowered her voice. "Something tells me she's not happy about being pregnant."

"I'm sure she isn't. She already has her hands full raising two kids without any help from her ex-husband—financial or otherwise."

Apparently, she'd gotten involved with men who were neither supportive nor loyal. But then again, some women made the mistake of falling for a man who would never return the love she deserved.

Selena certainly had, so she was in no position to pass judgment. But that didn't quell her curiosity. "So where did you meet Trina?"

"She was a friend of Mary's."

At the mention of Alex's late wife's name, Selena's stomach clenched again. But he didn't seem to give it more than a passing thought, which she hoped was a good sign that he was moving on, that his love for his late wife would soon be a memory.

At a table next to theirs, a man who'd been drinking something amber-colored, like whiskey or scotch, threw back his head and laughed. Then he got to his feet, taking his glass with him.

"Tell Trina to bring us another round," he told his friend. "I'm going to make a pit stop, then I'll give Darla a call and ask her to come on down here and get us. We're going to need a ride home."

Still chuckling, the happy drunk started toward the bathroom. When he passed by Alex's chair, he swayed on his feet. In an effort to regain his balance, he flung out both arms. As he tried to prevent a tumble, the drink slipped out of his hands, splattering on Selena's shoulder before hitting the floor and shattering.

"Oh, damn," the drunk said to Selena. "I'm sorry, ma'am. I... Aw, hell. Would you look what I did?"

A bit annoyed, Selena studied her wet T-shirt, wondering if the brown liquid would leave a stain. "Maybe I'd better go to the ladies' room and wash this out." Then she got to her feet.

"I'm sorry," Alex said.

Selena gave a little shrug. "You didn't spill the drink on me."

No, he didn't, but he'd brought her to a honky-tonk, where this sort of thing could happen. And a beautiful, classy and professional woman like her might not appreciate close encounters with inebriated cowboys.

"I'm really sorry about spilling my drink," the sloppy but remorseful drunk said to Alex. "I'd be happy to buy your lady a new shirt if that stain don't come out."

Alex might have made an issue about the spill if the

guy had been a jerk about it. As it was, he shrugged. "Those things happen." He just wished it wouldn't have happened to Selena.

About that time, Trina arrived with a plastic tub and a damp rag.

The cowboy went down on one knee, prepared to help her clean up the mess on the floor.

"Daryl," Trina said to the drunk, "please get out of the way and let me clean up that spill and the broken glass before someone slips or gets cut."

"Sorry about that, Trina." The man got to his feet and took a step back. "I didn't mean to cause all this trouble."

"I know you didn't." Trina set the tub on the floor, then began picking up the biggest glass shards. "But the last thing I need is for a customer to get hurt. Bob's on his way with a mop to help me. You go on back to your friend."

When Daryl took off toward the restrooms, Alex said, "You shouldn't be doing that in your condition."

She glanced up. "Doing what?"

"Picking up broken glass and mopping spills."

Trina chuffed. "This is all in a day's work, whether I'm at home or here. Don't worry about me."

Alex did worry. Trina hadn't just been a friend of Mary's; she'd been his friend, too. After Mary's accident, he'd spent a couple of evenings at the Stagecoach Inn, trying to drown his grief and guilt. And Trina had made sure that he'd gotten home safely both times. She'd also reminded him that Mary wouldn't have wanted him to go off the deep end like that, and she'd been right.

When a man with a mop approached Trina, he asked, "What have we got here?"

"Just another day in cowboy paradise," Trina said, as she got to her feet. "I've already picked up the biggest pieces of glass."

"All righty. I'll take it from here."

"Thanks, Bob." Trina turned to Alex. "I'm sorry for the disturbance."

"No problem. Things happen."

"Yeah, they do." Trina glanced at the chair Selena had just vacated. "She's a pretty lady, and obviously smart and successful. Are you two dating?"

Mary and Trina had been friends as teenagers, so it felt a little weird to be out with another woman, even if it had been two years since Mary's death. But the question called for an answer, even if he wasn't quite sure he could say they were actually "dating."

"This is our first official date," Alex admitted. "But after tonight, she might realize she doesn't like my idea of a fun evening."

"I suppose you'll find out if she's a good sport or not when she returns from the restroom."

That was probably true.

"Either way," Trina added, "it's nice to know you're finally getting out and living again. Mary wouldn't have wanted you to hole up at home."

Alex hadn't been in town all that much, but that didn't mean he'd been hiding out and avoiding people. He'd just found that hard work and staying busy had helped. And there was always plenty to do on a ranch.

"So how's it really going?" Alex asked her, trying to steer the conversation off him and Mary.

Trina shrugged. "Same old, same old."

He was sorry to hear that. Life hadn't been easy for her, and not all of her trouble had been of her own making.

She was only thirty-six, although she appeared to be a lot older. At one time, a lot of men would have found her pretty. But that was before she'd made a few bad choices.

And before life had kicked her while she'd been down. Now she was pregnant again, which was too bad. The last Alex had heard, she'd finally gotten a divorce from an abusive husband she'd held on to for too damn long.

"It seems that I can't pick a nice guy if my life depended upon it," she said. "So I'm going to swear off romance once and for all. It's pretty clear that I'm not good at weeding out the jerks from the keepers."

Before Alex could respond, Selena returned, sporting a big wet spot that had soaked through one sleeve and the shoulder of her T-shirt.

But at least she wasn't frowning. Did that mean she actually was a good sport?

Somewhere in the midst of all the background noise and the hoots of laughter, the old red-and-chrome jukebox jumped to life, thanks to someone's desire to hear a little music before the band had set up for the evening's competition. Over the din, Alex heard Patsy Cline singing "Crazy," one of her biggest hits.

Call him crazy, but he was going to take a gamble on Selena being a good sport—and more. So he pushed back his chair and stood, then he reached out his hand to her. "Come on. I really like this song. Let's dance."

The suggestion seemed to take her aback for a moment, and she glanced at her wet T-shirt. He thought she was going to decline. Instead, she smiled and let him draw her to her feet.

Alex led Selena through the throng of Friday night revelers to a dance floor, where a few other couples had already gathered.

Then he opened his arms, and she slipped into his embrace. As they slowly moved to the music, he savored the floral scent of her shampoo, the silky strands of her hair.

It had been a long time since he'd enjoyed holding a woman close—and it had been forever since he'd held one quite like Selena. Without a conscious thought, he drew her close and placed his cheek against hers.

As Patsy sang about a love gone wrong, Alex couldn't help thinking about one that was going right. And he found himself lost in the music, completely under the spell of the woman in his arms.

It was magic, all right. Even with the other couples beside them.

He'd never really liked getting out on the dance floor and preferred to watch this sort of thing as a bystander. In fact, that's why the line dancing competition had interested him.

But that no longer seemed to be true, at least not when he held Selena. Not when he wanted to nuzzle her neck, to kiss her senseless, to take her to bed.

As they swayed to the music, it was easy to pretend that they were an actual couple and not just skating around a relationship.

And maybe they weren't skating. Maybe they both knew where they'd wind up this evening.

He certainly did.

Chapter 9

Spending Friday evening at the Stagecoach Inn had been more fun than Selena had imagined, and she was glad that she'd gone.

The whole honky-tonk experience had been a blast, but more than that, being with Alex had made it a night to remember. And it wasn't over yet. Not while they were taking a slow, leisurely walk home under a scattering of bright stars and a nearly full moon.

"You were right," Selena said, as their arms brushed against each other. "I enjoyed the dance competition, but what I found even more interesting was watching all the people who'd come to hang out at the Stagecoach."

"The cowboy crowd can be pretty entertaining," he said.

"That's for sure." She'd also liked slow dancing with Alex, his arms wrapped around her, his cheek pressed against hers, his woodsy cologne snaking around her senses, holding her captive.

"I'm glad you had a good time. When that cowboy spilled his drink on you, I thought you were history."

A smile teased her lips. "I couldn't get angry at a guy who fell all over himself trying to apologize and to clean up his mess. Besides, he was respectful. He was also responsible. When it happened, he'd been on his way to call his girlfriend to pick him up, rather than drive himself home."

"She was a pretty good sport about it," Alex said.

Selena had thought the same thing when she'd first seen the woman who'd come to take him home within ten minutes of his call. She'd crossed her arms and appeared to be scolding him, but there'd been affection in her eyes.

He'd called her his darlin' Darla, and in a way, their relationship had seemed…sweet. And loving.

Strangely enough, it was easy to be a bit envious of them and what they'd apparently found together. She wondered if Alex had noticed it, too.

"I could be wrong," Selena said, "but they seemed to have a good relationship."

"That's possible, but she might have given him hell when she got him home."

"I don't think so."

Alex didn't respond, and they continued to walk in silence, their steps echoing in the night.

They'd be home soon—in just a few short blocks.

Would he try to kiss her again? She certainly hoped he would. If he didn't, she might have to take the bull by the horns and be bolder than she'd ever been before, at least in a budding romance.

Their arms brushed again, and this time Alex reached for her hand, curling his fingers around hers, warming her from head to toe with a single touch.

Yes, he was going to kiss her goodnight. She was sure of it. But did she want him to stop at that?

As they turned down Hawthorne Lane toward her house, she imagined them a couple, with no concerns in the world. But she had plenty to worry about. What if she did the unthinkable? What if she fell head over heels in love with a man whose heart would always belong to another woman?

She knew firsthand how badly a situation like that would turn out. But the possibility of heartbreak in the future didn't seem to matter right now.

In spite of the need to protect herself from being hurt, she couldn't let Alex walk away tonight without giving him a chance to prove her wrong. So she lowered her guard and chose to ignore her apprehension.

By the time they reached her house, her heartbeat was soaring in anticipation. Just how far would they go tonight?

As far as he was willing, she decided.

He walked her to the front door, then waited for her to reach into her purse for her key.

"Would you like to come in?" she asked. "I can make some coffee or tea for us. I also have wine…."

"You decide. I'll have whatever you're having."

"Okay. Then I'll open a bottle of merlot."

"Good choice."

His words were compliant and polite, yet his tone was suggestive—and full of promise. Did he know what she was thinking? What she was hoping? Maybe even planning?

Oh, for Pete's sake. She wasn't even sure what she had in mind, just that she wasn't ready for the night to end.

"Do you want some help with the wine?" he asked.

"No, I've got it. I'll be back in a flash." She offered him a parting smile, then left him in the living room while she went in search of the bottle of merlot she'd been storing since she'd received it in a gift exchange during last year's hospital Christmas party.

As she reached the doorway, she had to force herself not to glance over her shoulder and take one more gander at the handsome cowboy she'd love to…love.

And maybe even seduce.

Alex stood in Selena's living room and watched her walk away. He'd planned to kiss her good-night on the stoop, but he'd been hoping for a lot more than that. So her invitation to come inside, to have a glass of wine, suggested that she'd been thinking the same thing.

As he waited for her to return, he scanned the cozy room, checking out the colorful artwork on the walls as well as the overstuffed green sofa and chairs. On a table near a built-in bookshelf, he spotted a Bose stereo.

Should he turn on some music? Would she think he was being presumptuous if he did?

Aw, what the heck. Why not? The anticipation in the silence was almost deafening. So he crossed the room to the stereo, which had a stack of CDs nearby.

It didn't take long to find something soft and mellow, something to set a romantic mood.

As the melody filled the room, he lowered the volume. Then he took a seat on the sofa, just as Selena entered carrying a tray with two glasses and an uncorked bottle of red wine.

"Service with a smile," he said.

"And a little background music. That's a nice touch." Her eyes, the color of rich Tennessee bourbon in the lamplight, brightened, kicking his pulse rate up a notch.

After she set the tray on the coffee table, she sat on the center cushion, just an arm's distance from him.

Yes, he decided, they were clearly on the same page.

He reached for the bottle of merlot and poured them each a half serving, then handed one of the goblets to her.

"Thank you."

"My pleasure."

He lifted his wine to her in a toast. As she clicked her glass against his, the crystal resonated crisp and clear.

"To...friendship," he said. "And whatever that might bring."

She smiled, giving him reason to believe that she'd heard the subtext behind his words.

As much as he'd like to take things slow and easy, his feelings for Selena had gone beyond friendship. And he wanted to have a sexual relationship with her—perhaps even one that was lasting.

Of course, his future would one day include his babies, so there was still that hurdle to cross. But they had plenty of time to discuss kids, family and anything else that the coming months might bring their way.

As he savored a taste of the merlot, he pondered the decision he'd just made, the strength of his feelings for her, the possibilities that laced the pheromone-charged air. It had been a long time since he'd had to take the romantic lead, but it seemed natural to do so now.

In the background, a Michael Bublé CD played softly. Rather than risk an awkward attempt at conversation, Alex set his glass on the table in front of them and reached for her hand. "Dance with me, Selena."

Her intoxicating gaze locked on his, as she let him draw her to her feet.

He led her around the coffee table and to an empty space in the center of the room. When he opened his arms, she stepped into his embrace.

As they moved to the music, he held her close, their bodies pressed together. What he wouldn't give to have this night last forever, but the song ended long before he was ready to release her and return to the sofa for more small talk.

Instead, he wanted to kiss her senseless. And that's just what he set out to do.

While his arms remained around her, he drew back long enough to see the unspoken emotion in her eyes, to watch her lips part, to hear her breath catch.

That was all he needed. He lowered his head and placed his mouth on hers. As their tongues met and mated, his blood pumped strong and steady. His hands slid along her back, stroking, caressing, exploring each womanly curve.

Finally, when they came up for air, he asked the question that had been burning inside him for days. "What are we going to do about this?"

"I'm not sure. I can tell you what I'd like to do." The glimmer in her eyes convinced him they had the same idea.

"I hope you don't plan to send me home," he said, his own eyes glimmering, no doubt.

"No, I don't want to do that. Not yet." She took his hand. This time she did the leading—to her bedroom.

He was glad he'd thought to bring a condom with him, even though he hadn't been sure if they'd have need of one.

If he hadn't been so caught up in the heat of the moment, in the desire to make love with her all night long, he might have told her they were in luck. But then again, maybe she was prepared, too.

Once in the bedroom, Selena made her way to the bed, then turned to face him.

Damn, she was beautiful. And tonight, she was all his.

He took her in his arms again and kissed her, long and deep. As he explored the curve of her back and the slope of her hips, a surge of desire shot through him, reminding him just how long it had been since he'd had sex. And if truth be told, it had been months before Mary's death.

She'd been so afraid of losing the babies that she hadn't wanted to make love once the implantation had taken place.

And he'd been okay with that. He'd understood the maternal hormones that had been at work. But right now, his male hormones had built to the bursting point.

If the kisses he'd shared with Selena meant anything at all, making love with her was going to be amazing— the kind of thing dreams were made of.

When the heated kiss demanded they move on to something more intimate, Alex drew his lips from hers, only to find Selena's gaze riveted on him. Rather than speak, she began to peel off her T-shirt, revealing a white lace bra, an expanse of skin...

He watched as she slid the fabric over her shoulders and removed her arms from the sleeves. She dropped her top to the floor, then unbuttoned her jeans and peeled them over her hips.

Before he knew it, she was standing before him wearing only her pretty, delicate undergarments.

"You're even more beautiful than I'd imagined, Selena."

Her cheeks flushed at the compliment, yet she still didn't respond. Instead, she reached for his shirt and tugged it out of the waistband of his jeans. Then she helped him remove it altogether.

When he stood before her, his chest bare, she skimmed her fingers over his skin. One of her nails sketched over his nipple. His gut clenched in reaction to the arousing touch, and he sucked in a breath.

Unable to hold off any longer, he lifted her in his arms and placed her on top of the bed. Then he reached into his front pocket and removed the condom he'd placed there earlier.

"You don't need that," she said.

He was glad to hear it, because he preferred not to use protection if he didn't need to.

"I'm not going to get pregnant," she added.

She seemed so certain that he assumed she was on the pill. Either way, she was a doctor; she obviously knew best.

"If you haven't been with anyone since…" She paused, her eyes searching his, clearly asking if he'd been with any other women after Mary had died.

He hadn't. No one had interested him until he'd met Selena. And because he and Mary had been tested for everything imaginable during the in vitro process…

Alex dropped the packet on to the floor. "We don't have anything else to worry about. We're safe all the way around."

After removing his jeans and boxers, he joined her on the bed and continued right where he'd left off, kissing, stroking, exploring...

When they were both overcome with need, he entered her. Her body responded to his, giving and taking, until they both reached a peak. As she cried out with her release, he let go with his at the same time, shuddering at the sheer pleasure of being one with the woman he...

Loved?

He didn't know about that, but it sure seemed like a possibility—and an amazing one at that. He could certainly get used to sleeping in Selena's bed, wrapped in her arms for the rest of his life.

As the last wave of their climax ebbed, he rolled to the side, taking Selena with him. He didn't have to ask if it had been good for her. He'd heard her passionate whispers, seen the pleasure in her eyes. Still, it had been more than sex to him. And he hoped it had been more than that to her, too.

As Selena lay stretched out on the bed, facing Alex, his arms around her, the sheets tangled, the sweet scent of their lovemaking fresh, she savored the amazing afterglow, unable to believe how good they'd been together.

In spite of her earlier apprehension, she couldn't help thinking that she'd finally met the one man she'd been waiting for all her life, a man who could give her everything she'd ever wanted—true love and a family, whether they adopted a baby or chose to use the embryos he'd created with Mary.

Of course, Selena would have to be convinced that she wasn't just a convenient replacement for the woman who'd died.

She had no way of knowing that, of course—unless she laid her heart on the line and allowed a relationship between them to develop. But she couldn't tell him what she was feeling.

Not yet.

She'd just experienced the night to end all nights, and while she longed to hear him say he felt the same way about her, she still feared that he wouldn't.

That he couldn't.

He pressed a kiss on her brow, then ran his hand along the curve of her hip and back up again. "It's only going to get better."

Her heart soared. So he wasn't content with just one night together either. He, too, knew that they'd found something special in each other's arms—a blood-stirring attraction, an awesome sexual connection and maybe even…love.

She placed her hand on his face, trailing her fingers on his cheek. "I can't imagine anything being better than that."

He smiled. "Neither can I."

She read sincerity in his expression, truth in his eyes. He either hadn't made any comparisons between her and his late wife, or if he had, Selena had come out on top.

"Do you have to go back to the ranch tonight?" she asked.

"Do you want me to?"

"No, I'd like you to stay for breakfast."

A grin slid across his handsome face. "I was hoping you'd say that."

He kissed her then, and she found herself wanting to make love with him all over again. But it was more than a physical response to sexual stimulation going on. Her feelings were involved.

She nearly told him that she was falling in love with him, when in truth, she feared that she'd already toppled head over heels. And while she believed all the signs, sensing that he was falling for her, too, she just wasn't ready to admit it to him—or even to herself.

It's too bad they didn't have the entire weekend to explore their new feelings. She was on call tomorrow morning at eight, so in a few short hours she'd have to drive to the medical center and relieve the colleague who'd been covering for her.

But that was okay. Maybe after another bout of lovemaking tonight, she'd find the courage to tell Alex how she was feeling about him.

Somewhere around two o'clock, Selena had gotten out of bed and set the alarm so she wouldn't oversleep and run late for her shift. But she hadn't needed to do that.

Alex apparently had a built-in biological clock that woke him each day at the crack of dawn. So just like Sleeping Beauty of fairy-tale fame, Selena found herself awakened by a kiss.

"Good morning," Alex said as he sat on the side of the mattress.

Her lips slipped into a sated smile, even before her eyes opened.

"Coffee's ready," he added. "And breakfast will be on the table soon."

Selena glanced at the clock on the nightstand and realized the alarm was set to go off within the next ten minutes. "I didn't mean for you to do the cooking. I was going to do that."

"Maybe next time. I knew you had to work, and because I was the one who kept you up half the night, it only seemed fair to let you sleep as long as possible."

"That's amazing," she said, stretching and biting back a yawn.

He smiled, his eyes as bright as the morning sun. Then he brushed a kiss on her brow. "You probably ought to hold the compliments until after you've eaten."

"Okay, I'll do that." She returned his smile. "Do I have time to take a shower?"

"You bet."

Ten minutes later, Selena was dressed for the day and seated at the breakfast nook with Alex, tasting a fluffy batch of scrambled eggs and ham.

"This is wonderful," she said.

"You're just hungry."

"That's true. But my taste buds are still picky. Who taught you how to cook?"

"My housekeeper."

"Lydia?"

"No, the one we had when I was a kid living in Dallas." He took a sip of coffee.

"She taught you well," Selena said.

"That she did. She was a nice lady, and we were pretty close. My mom and dad traveled on business more times than I could count, so I spent a lot of time with her."

How sad. If Selena was ever blessed with children, she'd covet the time she had with them. Of course, as a doctor with a busy practice, she might have to leave them with a sitter more than she'd like.

Maybe Alex's parents had had careers, too.

His father certainly had. Would he have spent more quality time with his son if he'd known his days were numbered?

The question gave her something to consider.

"It must have been tough to lose your dad when you were so young," she said.

"Yes, it was. But my uncle was good to me. He was strict, though, and didn't put up with any nonsense. But he wasn't as stern and demanding as my father had been." Alex dug his fork into the eggs and took a bite, as if the childhood memories no longer mattered.

Still, Selena hurt for the lonely little boy he'd once been. "Did your mom spend more time with you after you moved to the ranch?"

"Yes, but by that time, I preferred to spend time with my uncle and the ranch hands."

As she reached for her coffee cup, Alex glanced up from his plate and blessed her with an unaffected grin. "Actually, you would have liked my uncle."

"I wish I could have met him."

"He was one of a kind, a real cowboy with a dry wit." Alex sat back in his seat and slowly shook his head. "One day, a stray dog showed up on the ranch, and I was determined to adopt him. My uncle agreed as long as I promised to keep him out of trouble. I figured it would be easy, but later that afternoon, one of the chickens got out of the coop, and the dog, Bear, took off after it. By the time I caught up with them, Bear had cornered the thing and chewed off its tail feathers.

"My uncle heard the commotion, came out of the barn and gave me heck."

"What did you do?"

"I stuck up for the dog, of course, saying it wasn't his fault. If the chicken had been in the coop where it belonged, it wouldn't have happened." Alex chuckled at the memory. "My uncle said, 'That chicken lives on the ranch, and that dog doesn't.' Then he shook his finger at me and said, 'Boy, if you don't get that mutt under control, he's going to be history.'"

"Did you get to keep the dog?"

"Yep, I sure did. Good ol' Bear was the proverbial boy's best friend."

"Whatever happened to the chicken?"

"That's the funny part, at least looking back on it. I told my uncle that I thought those tail feathers would probably grow back. And he said, 'They'd better. If I have to call the vet out here to see about that chicken, you're going to have to work a month of Sundays to pay the bill.'"

"Did he call the vet?"

Alex laughed. "He was just pulling my leg. If the dog had really hurt the bird, he wouldn't have bothered calling the vet. We would have had fried chicken that night for dinner."

She smiled, finding the story heartwarming. Still, she was sorry that Alex's early years had been sad and lonely, but it was nice to know that it had eventually worked out for him, that he'd found happiness on the ranch.

And with Mary.

Her heart twisted at the thought, but she did her best to shrug it off, to hold firm to the belief that he'd set memories of his late wife aside, that he was ready to embrace a new and maybe even better relationship with Selena.

"I hope I can be a loving and understanding father," he said.

"I'm sure you will be." She glanced at the clock on the stove, making sure she wasn't running late and re-alizing she'd have to go soon.

They finished breakfast in silence, and she wished that she had the guts to bring up the future, to ask when they'd see each other again.

Was he wondering the same thing? Was he consid-ering the logistics of having a lover who lived in town, while his ranch was at least fifteen miles away?

And what about the hours she kept, the nights she stayed at the hospital when one of her patients was in labor?

She supposed they'd find a way to make it work.

After finishing off the rest of her scrambled eggs, she lifted her cup and took a sip. Then she glanced across the table at Alex, whose brow was furrowed as though deep in thought.

"What's the matter?" she asked.

"Nothing, really. I was just thinking about some-thing."

It appeared to be serious enough to force a smile from his face. "What's that?"

He set his cup down, then looked up and caught her gaze. "You know about my plans to hire a gestational carrier in the near future."

She nearly choked on the mouthful of coffee she'd

just swallowed. The *near* future? What had happened to putting it on hold for a while?

"I was just wondering if—" he paused for a beat "—maybe you'd be interested in the job."

Her?

"You'd be my first choice," he added with a smile.

His eyes glimmered, but she didn't find anything amusing about it. After all, she couldn't even carry her own child, let alone carry one for someone else.

And even if she could, did she want to be the means to an end? The uterus he needed to nurture Mary's babies until term?

The reality, the truth, the crushing disappointment balled up in her throat as her eyes welled.

"What's the matter?" he asked.

Her heart twisted, and she blinked back the tears. "I'm sorry, Alex. I can't do that."

He reached across the table and placed his hand on top of hers. "I'm the one who should be sorry, Selena. I was way out of line to even bring something like that up—especially now. Please forget I said anything."

She'd never be able to forget that he still intended to have Mary's babies. Or that he thought Selena would agree to be a fill-in wife and mother.

But rather than let him know how badly she was hurt, she forced a wobbly smile. "It's already forgotten."

He paused a beat, watching her as if trying to read her expression, which she fought to keep hidden until she was ready to explain why his comment was so unsettling.

"Are you crying?" he asked.

"No," she lied. "I just have something in my eye."

She blinked again, then used her fingers to rub away an imaginary lash or piece of lint.

After a quick glance at the clock on the oven, she got to her feet. "Oh, shoot. I can't believe this. I completely forgot I have an early appointment this morning. I need to go or I'll be late."

"Is there anything I can do to help you get out of here any sooner?" he asked.

"I wish there were." She left the kitchen in search of her purse—and a quiet place to wipe the telltale tears from her eyes.

Rather than slip into her bedroom, where the reminder of their lovemaking was too fresh, she hurried to the bathroom. There she tried to control her sadness until she could leave the house.

After she'd splashed cold water onto her face, she went to find her purse in the living room, where Alex was waiting.

"I'll do the dishes and lock up your house," he said.

"Thanks. I'd appreciate that."

He followed her out to the car, where he bent to kiss her goodbye. She ought to object, to refuse his embrace, but she wasn't ready to explain why their all-too-brief affair was over. So she kissed him back as if nothing were wrong, when her whole world had imploded.

One of these days they'd have to talk about it, but not now. Not while the pain was so fresh, so intense. And not until she figured out a way to explain that it wasn't because of the babies. She didn't blame him one bit for wanting them. And if it weren't for his love of Mary, she might actually be thrilled to have the chance to mother them.

"Are you sure that comment I made about the… gestational carrier didn't upset you?"

"What comment?"

He seemed relieved. And so was she. This wasn't the time to talk about her objections, her pain, her disappointment.

She didn't trust her voice or her heart to provide more than a few words as an answer.

As she climbed behind the wheel, Alex said, "Drive carefully."

"I will." She shut the door and started the engine.

As she backed out of the driveway, he waved. Just as if nothing was wrong, she lifted her hand and fluttered her fingers.

Once on the road, she headed for the office, where she would face her patients and continue the charade, pretending that her heart wasn't breaking.

She wished she could say that the farther she drove away from Alex, the better she felt. But that wasn't the case. The ache in her chest intensified, and the tears she'd been holding back slid down her cheeks, one right after another.

Alex might have meant that kiss to be a way to end their night together, but it had actually been an end to whatever brief relationship they might have had.

Still, as sad as it was, as much as it hurt, Selena refused to be second place in Alex's life, to merely walk in the shadow of the woman he'd never forget.

Chapter 10

Several days had passed since Alex and Selena had made love, and he had yet to talk to her.

Not that he hadn't tried. He'd called her on several occasions, only to leave a message on her answering machine or with her receptionist. He'd even given his name and number to her after-hours service.

At first, he figured she was either on call or at the hospital, delivering a baby. But it didn't take a membership in Mensa to come to the conclusion that she was avoiding him.

He'd be darned if he knew why. Time and again, he went over the conversation that had unfolded at her house that morning after they'd slept together, trying to figure out what went wrong and when.

That night they'd spent in her bed had been amazing. They'd even cuddled together until dawn. Things really hadn't gone south until he'd tossed out that tongue-in-cheek comment about her being his gestational carrier.

He hadn't meant anything by it. He'd just thrown it out there as a way to gauge her thoughts and feelings about his baby plan. And to broach the possibility of her actually carrying his future children for him. She'd be invested in the pregnancy, in the children. But that had been too wild of an idea to ponder for more reasons than one.

Before they'd even slept together, he'd sensed she was apprehensive about his becoming a single father. And now it appeared that he'd been right.

She probably wanted to conceive a baby the old-fashioned way—her own flesh and blood, and not another woman's child.

If so, Alex could understand that. But he'd promised his dying wife he'd bring those embryos into the world one way or another. And that's exactly what he planned to do.

Had Selena really forgotten an early appointment at the office? Or had the mention of babies and a gestational carrier sent her running?

He supposed he'd never know for sure unless he got a chance to talk to her. He glanced at the telephone, wondering if he ought to give it one more try. Trouble was, he didn't want her to think he was that desperate to talk to her. After all, the phone line went both ways.

His first thought was to say, "The hell with it." If she wasn't interested in him, if she didn't want a romantic relationship, then so be it.

But he was falling in love with her—if he hadn't done so already. And her not returning his calls was a complication he hadn't anticipated.

Again he reached for the receiver, tempted to pick it up one more time, only to cross his arms instead. He'd never had to chase after a woman in his life, and he'd be damned if he'd start doing it now.

He glanced at the clock on the mantel. It was getting late. The last time he'd called her at the house he'd left a voice mail. It seemed pointless to leave another one when she was clearly avoiding him. Maybe he ought to just turn in for the night. He could read for a while or catch the tail end of a movie.

As he got to his feet, the telephone rang and he nearly jumped. A glance at the caller ID told him the Brighton Valley Medical Center was on the line.

Okay, maybe Selena hadn't been at home today. Maybe she hadn't received all of his messages. Or if she had, she'd probably been extremely busy.

Or had she gotten sick or injured? He'd never even considered the possibility that she truly hadn't been able to call.

While tempted to snatch up the receiver in record time, he didn't want to appear too eager, too concerned, too ruffled. So he waited to pick up until the third ring.

"Hello."

"Alex?" The sound of his name rolling off her tongue set his heart on edge.

He wanted to blurt out, *What in the hell's going on? Why haven't you returned my calls? I know you're busy, but...* Instead, he maintained his composure and said, "Hey. How's it going?"

"All right. How are you?"

Angry. Confused. Hurt. But he kept that to himself and said, "Fine."

"It's been crazy busy around here."

Had it really?

"I can only imagine," he said.

"One of the other obstetricians in town had a heart attack Sunday morning, so I've been covering for him."

A sense of relief washed through him. Okay, so there was a good reason after all. Still, it was hard to believe that she hadn't been able to find two minutes to pick up a telephone or to reach for her cell.

"I'm sorry for not returning your call earlier," she added.

So she *had* gotten at least one of the messages he'd left. He steeled himself for an explanation, which he wasn't sure he'd buy, even if she offered it.

"There's really no excuse," she said.

He'd been right. She *had* been cooling her heels. The fact that she hadn't had the guts to be honest rubbed against the grain, and he couldn't help addressing the issue.

"I didn't expect a commitment, Selena. But after Friday night…" He paused, as the memory of their lovemaking unfurled in his mind. "Well, it seemed as though you shut me out before we had a chance to decide where we wanted to go from there, if anywhere."

Silence filled the line.

Finally she said, "You're right, Alex. I took the coward's way out. I care about you—a *lot*. And it's possible that whatever I'm feeling for you could turn into love. But I'm reluctant to get involved with anyone right now."

So she *was* giving him the brush-off. His first instinct was to pretend that it was no big deal, that it was actually a relief to him that they both felt the same way.

But disappointment wadded up in his throat, making

it too difficult to speak at all, let alone to lie or feign indifference.

"Friday night was great," she added. "In fact, it was all I'd imagined it would be and more. But I have no business getting romantically involved with anyone right now. My focus is on my patients and my practice. So I wanted to... Well, I thought it was best that we lay that out on the table."

Oh, yeah? Then he was going to take a gamble and lay it *all* out there.

"It's not your practice that's bothering you, Selena. It's the fact that I plan to find someone to carry those embryos."

Again, her only response was dead silence, which spoke volumes.

"I admire your baby plan," she finally said. "I really do. I think it's awesome that you loved your wife so much, that you're so determined to have the children you were meant to have with her. But that's not something I want to be a part of."

There it was. The truth. As much as it hurt, he was glad she'd admitted it.

"Fair enough," he said. "If there's one thing I value in a relationship, it's honesty." *Even if it hurt like hell.* "So thank you for that."

Then he told her goodbye and ended the call. After all, there'd been nothing more to say.

Alex had not only promised Mary he'd find a way to have those babies, but he wanted them, too. He couldn't very well hold on to those frozen embryos forever. What was he supposed to do, offer them to someone else?

Or worse yet, destroy them?

His stomach knotted at the thought.

No, those kids—if they were destined to live—were his flesh and blood, his sons or daughters. And he'd do whatever he could to make sure they got the best possible chance to thrive—until birth and beyond.

And if that meant losing Selena for good, then so be it.

He just hadn't realized how badly it would hurt to let her go.

Alex waited three weeks for Selena to have a change of heart, for her to call or to stop by the ranch and say she'd changed her mind. But when that didn't happen, he followed through with his plan to hire a gestational carrier.

The agreement had been drawn up by Family Solutions. And the procedure was going to be costly—$80,000 plus medical expenses. But Alex had a good feeling about the agency as well as the woman he'd hired.

Kristy O'Malley was happily married with two healthy children of her own. Three years ago, she'd been a surrogate for an infertile couple in Wexler, so she knew what it was like to carry a child for someone else and to give it up.

All in all, Alex was pleased with his choice and with the entire process so far.

When he and Mary had gone through the in vitro process, it had been a nightmare—at least as far as Alex had been concerned.

First of all, before he and Mary had realized that she was unable to conceive without medical intervention, they'd gone through the whole clinical kit and caboodle, including morning temperatures and ovulation charts. Sex lost a bit of the magic when it had to be scheduled.

Then, after they'd found out their only option for conception was in a laboratory, the word *clinical* took on a whole new meaning. They'd removed nature from the equation, letting science take its place.

The months leading up to the first implantation had been enough to make a man think he might give up sex forever.

Well, not forever. But when push had come to shove, Alex would have preferred to have adopted a baby than to have gone through all that.

The counselor at Family Solutions had promised him that the worst was over, as far as his part of it was concerned. And she'd been right.

He wasn't sure what Kristy had gone through, preparing for the implantation, but he'd only had to wait to hear that it had all gone according to plan.

And it had. According to David Samuels, the doctor at Family Solutions, as well as Kristy, the implantation had been a piece of cake. And when Dr. Samuels called with the good news—Kristy was pregnant with both babies—Alex was thrilled.

Okay, so he was a little insecure, too. But he planned to read books—a lot of them. And he'd ask questions, too. He'd… Well, he'd do whatever it took to be the best expectant father, as well as the best all-round daddy in the whole world.

He just wished Selena had been willing to be a part of it all. Not a day went by—not to mention a night— that he didn't think about her, dream about her. But she'd made her decision, and he had to abide by it.

For the first few weeks, Dr. Samuels had monitored the pregnancy. Once everything appeared to be on

track, he asked if either Kristy or Alex had a prefer-
ence of obstetricians or hospitals for the delivery.

While Alex probably should have left that decision
to Kristy, he was the one who'd be footing the bill. So
he'd said, "How about Selena Ramirez at the Brighton
Valley Medical Center?"

"That's fine with me," Dr. Samuels said. "The decision is up to you—and to Kristy, I suppose."

After the call ended, Alex had run the idea past
Kristy, and she was okay with it.

"No problem," she'd said. "I delivered at BVMC
three years ago so I'm cool with that."

With that out of the way, Alex called Selena's office
and spoke to the receptionist.

"I'm calling for Kristy O'Malley," he said. "I'd like
to make an appointment for her to see Dr. Ramirez.
She's six weeks pregnant with twins."

"How do you know she's expecting twins?" the receptionist asked.

"She just had an ultrasound at Family Solutions."

"Oh, I see."

When the woman asked about Kristy's insurance,
Alex told her he was the father, and that he'd be paying cash—up front, if necessary. The babies, of course,
would be covered under his health plan.

"We have an opening next Thursday at three," the
receptionist said. "Will that be okay?"

It would have to be. He wanted Kristy to be under
an obstetrician's care as soon as possible. But in this
case, he was also eager to see Selena again, even if it
was on a strictly professional basis.

Should he give Selena a heads-up before the appointment? Or should he just show up with Kristy in tow?

"You know," he said to the receptionist, "on second thought, I probably ought to make an appointment for a consultation with Dr. Ramirez first."

"All right. Why don't you take that three o'clock on Thursday for the consultation. I can schedule Ms. O'Malley the following Monday at ten."

"That's great."

Alex just hoped it would be okay with Selena. But he couldn't think of another doctor he'd rather have deliver his babies.

On Thursday afternoon, a few minutes after three, Selena studied the chart her nurse had placed in the rack on the door, playing catch-up with the patient who was waiting in the exam room.

She'd met Trina Shepherd when she'd been at the Stagecoach Inn with Alex, and the pregnant waitress was now entering her seventh month. Both expectant mom and baby had been doing well.

The baby's father, who Trina hadn't thought she could rely upon, was back in the picture. At least, he had been at her last visit.

Selena gave a little knock before entering the exam room.

Trina, who'd been sitting on the table, broke into a happy grin. "Hi, Doctor."

The expectant mother was clearly a lot happier than she'd been on the night Selena had first met her at the Stagecoach Inn.

"How about that," Selena said, as she set the chart down on the counter. "You've certainly developed a healthy pregnant glow over the past few months."

Trina laughed. "Well, I'm not surprised." She held

up her left hand, where she sported a diamond on her finger. "Mark asked me to marry him, and I said yes."

"That's wonderful. I assume you're happy about it."

"I'm thrilled. And he's so good with the kids. I worried that he wouldn't be because he's never had any of his own. But I guess my old fears and baggage got in the way, and I didn't give him a chance to prove he was a completely different man from my two ex-husbands. I think I found a keeper this time."

Selena was glad to hear it. She didn't often get attached to patients, but there was something about Trina that tugged at her heart.

"So how about you?" Trina asked. "Are you and Alex still seeing each other?"

The question came out of the blue and struck fast and hard. Yet she found herself answering truthfully. "No, we're not."

"Too bad. He's a great guy." Trina gave a little shrug. "Just saying, that's all."

Selena wasn't about to discuss Alex or her decision with anyone, although Trina was right. Alex was one of the good guys, the white hats. And if there'd been reason to believe that Selena had a chance of being his one and only, she might still be seeing him.

After going over Trina's chart and determining that everything looked good, Selena measured the growth of her uterus and listened to the baby's heartbeat.

"Everything is coming along just fine," Selena said.

"Will I be having another ultrasound?"

"Actually, I'd planned to schedule one at your next appointment."

"That's great. Can I bring Mark in with me? He's

never had a baby before, and… Well, I think he'd like seeing his son."

"Absolutely. I think it's great when fathers are involved with a pregnancy and delivery."

Moments later, after Selena told Trina to come back in three weeks, she moved down to exam room number two. As she picked up the chart on the door, she had no reason to believe that this afternoon would be any different from the rest.

And no idea that Alex Connor, who was already very involved in his children's pregnancy and delivery, was her three o'clock appointment.

After entering Selena's office and signing in with the receptionist, Alex took a seat in the busy waiting room.

It felt a little weird being the only man seated in an obstetrician's office. Well, that wasn't exactly true. He was the only man without a woman seated beside him.

But he'd better get used to being here. He planned to take an active role throughout Kristy's pregnancy as well as the delivery. So he shook off the uneasiness, reached for a copy of *Parents* magazine and listened for someone to call his name.

As he scanned the colorful pages aimed at the moms and dads with kids of various ages, he glossed over the articles, unable to focus on anything other than seeing Selena again.

She'd made it clear that her patients and her practice came first, above romance and a relationship. And he understood that. He just wondered how she'd feel when he asked her to be Kristy's doctor. He suspected that she'd be okay with it. Why wouldn't she?

But now that he was here, now that his heart rate

had escalated and his blood was strumming through his veins in anticipation of seeing her again, he wondered if he'd made a mistake in calling her office for an appointment.

Could he keep emotions from getting in the way? He supposed he'd have to, or he'd need to choose another obstetrician, and he didn't want to do that. His babies deserved the best, and as far as Alex was concerned, Selena Ramirez was at the top of her field.

A door opened, and a middle-aged nurse wearing pink scrubs peered into the waiting room. "Kristy O'Malley?"

Apparently, the woman who'd made the appointments had gotten mixed up about who was coming when, but that was okay. He would just have to straighten it all out once he was behind closed doors. So he set down the magazine, stood and headed for the doorway.

"I'm Alex Connor," he told the nurse. "And I'm here for a consultation with Dr. Ramirez. Kristy's appointment is Monday at ten."

The nurse, with her graying hair pulled back in a twist, her brow furrowed and lips pursed into a frown, reminded Alex of one of his least favorite college professors, the one who'd given him a D minus in English Composition. She glanced at the chart in her hand, obviously double checking the name on the paperwork.

"Kristy is the gestational carrier of my twins," Alex added, his voice lowered. "I'll be paying the medical bills, so I wanted a chance to speak to Dr. Ramirez before Kristy came in Monday."

"Oh, I see. Maryanne must have flip-flopped the names, but that's not a problem. We'll have everything squared away before Monday rolls around." The nurse looked up and smiled at Alex, no longer resembling the stern English prof. "Right this way."

Alex followed her past a scale and several exam rooms until they reached a small office with pale blue walls, a shelf of books and a view of the greenbelt below.

"Here we are," the nurse said. "Dr. Ramirez has her consults in her office, rather than in one of the exam rooms."

He was glad of that. He'd hate to have his first appointment with Selena be in small, sterile quarters, with him sitting on a paper-covered table and her on a stool.

The nurse indicated a cherrywood desk, with two chairs in front of it. "If you'll have a seat, I'll let Dr. Ramirez know you're here."

"Marge?" Someone called to the nurse. "You've got a phone call on line three."

"I'll be right there," Marge said to the woman who'd called her name. Then, as the woman approached, she handed over the file she held. "Maryanne, would you please give this to Dr. Ramirez and let her know the next appointment is a consult in her office?"

"Of course."

Marge turned back to Alex. "The doctor shouldn't be long. Why don't you make yourself comfortable?"

"Thanks."

As Marge left the room, Alex pulled out one of the chairs and took a seat. Then he scanned the small office, looking for photographs or personal items that would remind him of Selena.

Other than a bouquet of flowers near the window and an interesting watercolor behind her desk, it seemed liked a pretty generic office. That was a bit surprising because Selena was anything but generic.

He wondered what she would say when she heard he was here, rather than Kristy.

Either way, it really didn't matter now. He'd come too far to backpedal or to choose another obstetrician at this point—unless Selena wasn't interested in even becoming professionally involved with him.

But then again, why would she feel that way? She was a doctor. She'd learned to distance herself from her patients.

Hell, she'd even distanced herself from him, and he'd been her lover. Albeit for one night.

One amazing night.

His heart ached at the memory. Had he made a huge mistake in coming here?

Using Selena had seemed so logical. But how would it feel to be so close to her again, to have her treat him as a patient, instead of as the friend he'd thought he was, the lover he'd once been?

Right now, it wasn't looking good.

He glanced at his wristwatch, wondering how long he'd have to wait. But before he could ponder a guess, the door swung open, and Selena stepped inside, wearing a pink blouse and black slacks, with a white lab coat rounding out the ensemble.

At the sight of her in the flesh, his heart skipped a couple of beats, reminding him of how much he'd missed her.

Her lips parted and her eyes widened. Apparently, no one had told her about the mix-up, because she seemed to be doing her own assessment of him.

"Alex." His name rolled off her tongue softly, yet weighed down by emotion. "What are you doing here?"

Before he could find the words to tell her he'd gone ahead with his plan, she said, "I thought this appointment was with someone else."

"Kristy O'Malley?" he asked.

She glanced down at the name on the file, then nodded.

"I hired her to carry the embryos for me. And I wanted you to monitor the pregnancy and deliver the babies. That is, if you're willing to do that."

She seemed to struggle with an answer.

"I made this appointment to see you first, to ask if you'd mind." He studied Selena as if she held the whole world in her hands.

And in a way, she did.

Selena couldn't seem to make a move one way or another, into the office or back into the hall. Just seeing Alex again set her heart skidding through her chest. And not just because his visit had been a complete surprise.

"I'm sorry," she said. "I didn't have any idea you were coming in today. And… Well, it's good to see you."

Or was it?

Not a day went by that she didn't think about him. And not a night went by when he wasn't in her dreams.

"I'm sorry." Alex got to his feet and faced her, his hat in hand. "I didn't try to spring a surprise. They probably have me on the list for Monday at ten. But that's when Kristy is supposed to come in. I wanted to talk to you first."

Someone in the office had clearly screwed up, but she couldn't very well stand here, gawking at the handsome cowboy. So she pointed at the chair he'd been sitting in. "Why don't you take your seat? Let's start over."

As she made her way behind her desk, she still wasn't sure what to say. Certainly not the words that begged to be said, like, *I missed you. It's good to see you again. So very good.*

Instead, she cleared her throat and offered him a professional smile. "Congratulations, Alex. I know how badly you wanted those babies."

He smiled, as he waited for her to sit, then followed suit. "Thanks, Selena. I was very lucky. Both embryos implanted, so Kristy, the woman I hired, is expecting twins."

"I'm happy for you." And she was. Babies were a blessing, no matter how they were conceived. Besides, in spite of her decision to steer clear of him—romantically speaking—she wanted the best for him, for the family he was creating.

"So what do you say?" he asked. "Will you be Kristy's doctor? I wouldn't want her to use anyone else."

Selena was both touched and flattered. But could she get that involved with Alex?

How was she supposed to keep a professional air about her when she was attracted to the father-to-be? And not just attracted to him, they'd once been lovers. In fact, she'd fallen head over heels for him, which only made it worse.

So getting involved with him and his baby plan just wasn't right. Couldn't he understand that?

The way he was looking at her, leaning forward, gaze

filled with hope, suggested he didn't have a clue what she was thinking or feeling.

"Under the circumstances," she began, "I'm not sure if it's a good idea."

"What circumstances?"

The fact that he could be the love of her life—if she knew that he felt that way for her. But that place in his heart would always belong to Mary.

Still, there were other circumstances that might make things difficult, awkward. So she leaned forward and lowered her voice. "Because we were lovers."

"How does that change the fact that you're one of the best doctors around, and that I want my kids to have the best?"

If truth be told?

She didn't have a clue.

Having those babies had been Alex's dream, and even though she'd been the one to end their relationship, it didn't mean that she didn't want him to be happy, that she didn't want the best for him.

So in spite of her reservations, she found herself saying, "Okay, Alex. I'll be Kristy's doctor."

He broke into a grin that sent her heart careening through her chest. "Thanks, Selena. I really appreciate this."

She knew he did. She'd just have to hope and pray that she hadn't made the biggest mistake of her life.

Chapter 11

When Monday rolled around, Selena didn't need to check the daily appointment list to know who'd be coming in this morning. Once she'd had the consultation with Alex and had agreed to be his gestational carrier's obstetrician, she'd been counting down the days until Kristy O'Malley's visit.

Sure, she was looking forward to meeting the woman. But more than that, she knew, without a doubt, that Alex would be attending that first appointment. The babies were too important to him. So there was no way he'd stay on the ranch and let nature take its course—at least, not after the babies had been successfully implanted.

By ten o'clock, Selena had already seen three patients and returned calls from two more.

So far, it was just a typical day at Brighton Valley OB-GYN.

But next up, in exam room three, Kristy O'Malley and Alex Connor waited for their first obstetrics appointment.

Selena paused at the closed door, going over the new chart, which held very little information yet, other than the vitals Marge had taken when she'd shown them to their room. However, it wasn't Kristy's blood pressure or heart rate she was concerned about, it was her own.

Right now, as she prepared to enter the room and see Alex again, as she readied herself to meet the woman who was pregnant with his twins, her pulse pounded in her ears. She would soon become fully engaged, fully committed to the pregnancy and to the health of the babies—Mary's babies.

But she couldn't stand here, bogged down by apprehension and a swarm of butterflies in her tummy. She was going to have to put on her big-girl/doctor panties and become the professional she knew she could be. So she rapped lightly on the door, then let herself into the small exam room.

Sure enough, a woman with strawberry-blond hair sat on the exam table. She appeared to be in her early to mid-thirties and of average height and weight. But it wasn't so much the new patient who'd commanded her attention. It was the handsome blond-haired cowboy who sat next to her, his hat resting under his chair.

Her heart rate spiked, and the blasted butterflies went ballistic. How could he do that to her with a simple smile, a soul-stirring gaze?

Selena tore her attention from Alex, turned to Kristy and extended her hand. "I'm Dr. Ramirez."

"It's nice to meet you," the pregnant woman said. "Alex has been singing your praises."

Medically speaking, no doubt. Too bad he hadn't been singing more personal praises. But Selena couldn't allow herself to waste time on what-ifs.

"Alex mentioned that the implantation was done at Family Solutions," she said to Kristy. "How long ago was that?"

"It'll be seven weeks on Thursday," Kristy said. "I had a vaginal ultrasound a couple of weeks ago, and they saw both heartbeats."

After asking the standard questions, she quizzed Kristy about how she was feeling.

"Tired and a little nauseous, but nothing out of the ordinary."

Selena was glad to know Kristy had gone through several successful pregnancies already.

"Dr. Samuels said my due date is August twenty-eighth," Kristy added, "but he also said the babies would probably come early."

"He's right," Selena said. "Multiple births don't always go to term."

After giving Kristy a sample of prenatal vitamins to take and some healthy eating handouts, Selena added, "I'll order your medical records from Family Solutions as well as from the last obstetrician you used, if you don't mind."

"Not at all. My doctor was Bradley Leighton at Parkview OB-GYN in Wexler."

Selena made a note of it in the chart, then turned to Alex. "I'd like to give Kristy an internal exam on this first visit. So I'm going to ask you to step out of the room for a few minutes. When I'm done, I'll also do an ultrasound, which I'm sure you'd like to see."

"No problem." Alex got to his feet, then walked out of the room.

When the pelvic exam was over, Selena opened the door and asked Marge to wheel in the portable equipment. Then she called Alex back into the room.

Moments later, with Kristy lying on the table, her still-flat belly exposed and covered in gel, Selena ran the transducer probe over the uterus and watched the screen.

"There's the first baby," she said, as she located Twin A. "See the heartbeat?"

Alex eased closer. "That's amazing."

Yes, it was. And Selena never tired of looking at the miracle of new life. But even more than that, standing next to Alex, close enough to breathe in his scent, to see the wonder in his eyes, made her happy she'd agreed to be a part of this.

Her only regret was not being the woman on the table, studying the grainy, black-and-white images of the two tiny babies growing in her womb.

What Selena wouldn't do to be able to provide the gift of life to herself as well as to Alex. As it was, she'd have to be content taking on a medical role.

Returning to the work at hand, she moved on to Twin B, whose heartbeat was strong and steady. "Here's the second one."

She waited for Alex to study the screen, then removed the transducer probe. After wiping the bulk of the gel from Kristy's lower belly with a tissue, she took a step back from the table, distancing herself and doing her best to remember her place.

Alex, who'd been standing by the pregnant woman's side, reached out and placed his hand on Kristy's shoulder. "Thanks for giving me the opportunity to be a father."

A twinge of envy reared its head, snaking around Selena's heart until it ached. But she had to face the facts.

Even the hired gestational carrier, a mother of two children herself, was able to provide Alex with something Selena would never be able to give him.

Alex nearly danced his way out of Selena's office that morning. He'd already seen the proof of Kristy's pregnancy during the first ultrasound at Family Solutions, although he'd pretty much had to take Dr. Samuels's word for it. But this morning he'd actually seen the two hearts beating.

Medical science was amazing, and Alex had been moved beyond measure. As he'd studied that screen, he'd tried to wrap his mind around the fact that he was going to be a father—to twins.

He had no idea whether they'd be boys or girls or one of each, but it really didn't matter. What did matter was that he was going to have a family again, that there'd be a reason to celebrate holidays.

After Kristy made her next doctor's appointment, Alex walked her to the parking lot, where they'd each left their cars. He wasn't quite sure what to say to her, other than to thank her one more time, which wasn't necessary.

"Do you have time for a cup of coffee?" he asked.

"No, I have a parent-teacher conference at the kids' school. So I'll have to take a rain check."

While she got into her sedan, he climbed into his pickup. But instead of heading home, he would spend the day in town. So he drove to Babies and More in nearby Wexler. There he ordered another crib and dresser, just like the set he already had at home. The set Mary had chosen and had planned to use for their daughter, if mother and child had lived.

For a moment, he ached for what could have been. Yet he knew Mary would have given her blessing for him to move on. Why else would she have made him promise to give the embryos life? She would want them to live that life to the fullest—to play Little League, to have a puppy, to join the Girl Scouts and take piano lessons.

Once Alex paid for his purchase and scheduled the delivery, he ran some other errands, including a stop at the feed store, where he placed an order for grain. While there, he called Shane Hollister, the Brighton Valley sheriff, and asked if he had time for lunch.

"As long as we can make it after one o'clock," Shane said, "lunch sounds good to me."

Waiting an hour or so wasn't a problem for a man dragging his feet about leaving town. So Alex agreed, then met Shane at Caroline's Diner a few minutes after one.

It was nice to catch up with the Brighton Valley sheriff, who'd had a baby girl a year ago last December.

"How are Jillian and little Mary Rose doing?" Alex asked as he picked up a French fry and dipped it into the dab of ketchup he'd squeezed onto his plate.

"They're doing great. It seems that Mary Rose was taking a few wobbly steps one day, then running the next. She sure keeps her mom and me on our toes."

Kids certainly grew up fast. Alex remembered when Mary Rose was just a newborn. The Hollisters had thrown a party at their new house just last December, when the baby had been only a few weeks old.

"I have some news of my own," Alex told his friend.

Shane reached for his glass of iced tea. "What's that?"

"Remember my plan to use those embryos?"

"You went through with it?" Shane set down his glass without taking a drink. "You hired a surrogate?"

Alex didn't see any point in explaining the difference between a gestational carrier and a surrogate to Shane. So he merely nodded and said, "The implantation was a success. If all goes well, I'll be the father of twins next summer."

"That's amazing."

Yeah, it was pretty miraculous. Even though he'd promised Mary he would do his best to see those embryos born, he hadn't been sure of the chances. And now, almost three years after Mary's death...

It was a shame she'd never have the chance to hold them, to mother them. But he'd have to be both mom and dad to them.

"Did you ever see an ultrasound of Mary Rose?" Alex asked Shane.

"Yes, I did. And it was awesome. I mean, I knew she was in there, but to actually see her hands and feet, her fingers and toes..." Shane slowly shook his head, a goofy grin splayed across his face. "It was priceless."

"Yeah, well, there wasn't much for me to see today— other than two tiny hearts beating. But I'm looking forward to watching them grow."

"Congratulations, Alex. I know how much this means to you."

"Thanks." It would have meant even more to have Selena's support, to have her understand why he had to do what he did, but Shane didn't need to know any of that.

The two friends went back to eating, and when they'd finished, Shane tried to grab the bill.

"Oh, no, you don't," Alex said. "It's my turn to pay. You got it last time."

After settling up at the front register, Shane and Alex walked out to the curb on Main Street.

"Are you heading back to the ranch?" Shane asked.

"No, I'm going to find things to do in town until late this afternoon."

"Why's that?"

"There's someone I want to see, and she doesn't get off work until then." He didn't see any point in telling Shane who the "she" was. How did he explain having a crush on the doctor who would be delivering his twins?

No, there were some things a man didn't discuss even with the best of his friends.

Two hours later, after Alex had hung out in Brighton Valley for about as long as he cared to, he headed back to Selena's office, where he told the receptionist that he wanted to speak to the doctor after her last appointment of the day. Then he took a seat in the waiting room.

This time, when he picked up the *Parents* magazine, he actually found a couple of interesting articles to read.

Apparently, there were plenty of books and periodicals that held a wealth of knowledge for a man wanting to learn about parenting and fatherhood.

Too bad there weren't any easy answers to be had for convincing a woman to give love a chance.

After Selena's last appointment of the day, she took a seat at her cherrywood desk and returned a couple of telephone calls from patients who'd left messages with the nurse.

She'd just hung up the phone when Marge poked her head through the open doorway. "Dr. Ramirez, there's a man in the waiting room asking to talk to you."

"Who is he?" Selena asked.

"The guy who came in earlier today with the new patient, Kristy O'Malley."

Alex? Her heart stalled in her chest. Why would he come back to talk to her? Did he have a question he'd forgotten to ask?

"What should I tell him?" Marge asked.

"That I'll be right with him."

Marge nodded, then turned away, heading for the waiting room.

Selena could have followed right behind. Instead, she opened the bottom desk drawer, where she kept her purse. Then she reached for her makeup bag and pulled out a tube of lipstick and mirror.

As crazy as it was, as emotionally risky, she checked her hair, powdered her nose and reapplied a coat of Matador Red to her lips.

Then she made her way to the waiting room to greet Alex as if it was all in a day's work.

When she walked through the doorway, he stood and greeted her with a heart-thumping grin.

Would it always be like this? Would she struggle with attraction whenever he was near?

Should she have refused to be Kristy's doctor?

"Do you have time for a cup of coffee?" he asked, moseying toward her with a cowboy swagger. "Or maybe dinner?"

Yes. No.

"I need to talk to you," he added.

Did he? Why?

His gaze wrapped around hers, holding her captive, drawing her into his world, to his life. And against her better judgment, she found herself waffling and saying, "There's a coffee bar and newsstand down the street."

Minutes later, she'd grabbed her purse from her office and was crossing the parking lot with him, on their way to The Grind.

"So what did you want to talk about?" she asked.

He paused a beat, then said, "Us."

Her breath caught. He still considered them a couple? When they hadn't dated in months? When she'd told him that she needed to focus on her practice, on her patients?

"I'm not sure I understand," she said.

"I shouldn't have to explain, Selena. What we had together was special. And I'm not buying the fact that your career comes first. I think you're reluctant to date me because of the babies. And I suppose I can't blame you for that."

He thought that she considered his having kids a detriment, and that wasn't true. The fact that Alex had a child or two wouldn't be a problem. But she knew how happy he was to be having Mary's children. And the fact that he was anticipating the birth of the twins was a little...

Bittersweet, she supposed. And a constant reminder of the woman he'd loved, the woman he'd lost. And a reminder of what Selena could never give him.

Her steps slowed, and she turned to face him, her hand gripping the shoulder strap on her purse as if it could tether her to solid ground. "I care about you, Alex. More than I'd like to admit. But..."

God, she couldn't do it. She hated to admit that

it wasn't just Mary she couldn't compete with. She couldn't even compete with his gestational carrier.

"But what?" he asked.

"I'm not ready to take on a ready-made family," she lied. "At least, not at this point in my life."

His gaze searched her face as if he might be able to uncover a lie, as if he knew she wasn't telling the entire truth. But she couldn't reveal more than that.

She refused to be second best or to play the fool again. And dating Alex, helping him parent another woman's children, would put her in that very position.

Everything she'd ever pinned her heart on—the old boyfriend from college, the dream of being a mother one day—had been stolen from her by fate or life or whatever. And being with Alex would only make things worse by subjecting her to more pain, more heartache, more rejection.

"Do you know what I mean?" she asked, realizing he didn't and hoping he'd accept her decision without forcing the issue.

"Sure," he said, his steps slowing to a stop. "I understand."

They stood like that for a moment, at a stalemate, a line drawn in the sand. Then he nodded in the direction of The Grind. "Maybe it's best if we pass on the coffee."

He was right.

There wasn't anything else to say. Not when they had no hope of a future together.

Nearly four months had passed since Selena had stood on the sidewalk near the coffee shop and told Alex one last time that she didn't want a relationship with him, yet not a day went by that he didn't remember their parting, the humbling moment when he'd went to her one last time, hoping for her to reconsider.

That evening was as clear now as if it had only been yesterday. He'd studied her for a beat before responding, hoping that she'd have a change of heart, that she'd hear the finality of her words and offer some hope that time would prove differently.

But she hadn't.

She might care about him, but certainly not enough to consider getting emotionally involved with a single father.

To say that he was disappointed was an understatement. But he'd accepted her decision. And her loss.

It seemed to be par for the course. Over his lifetime, he'd lost everyone he'd ever loved. And yes, he'd come to realize that he really did love Selena. Letting her go wouldn't have hurt him so badly if he hadn't. So even though her decision had been painful, it had been for the best.

As dusk had settled over them that winter evening outside her office, he could have sworn he'd seen her eyes glisten while she'd told him goodbye. And he'd briefly wondered if she might have been feeling something akin to remorse or maybe even a change of heart.

But she'd stood in silence, strong and resolute. So he'd turned and walked away.

At that point, he probably should have looked for another obstetrician for Kristy, but he wanted only the best for his children—and he still considered Selena to be the top in her field.

So from that day on, he'd stayed on the ranch and let Kristy attend her routine appointments without him. And because she always called him afterward, updating him, he was okay with that. And quite frankly, it was easier to not have to face Selena every three weeks.

He had no idea how he'd handle the actual delivery, though. It was important for him to be at the birth, although he wasn't entirely sure why, just that it was.

Still, even though four months had passed since he'd last seen Selena, he hadn't forgotten her, hadn't stopped wishing things had been different, that their feelings had been mutual.

He tried to tell himself that he'd done the right thing, that he'd fulfilled his promise to Mary. And in that respect, he had.

It was too bad Selena hadn't understood why the babies meant so much to him, why he had to go through with his plan in spite of knowing that his decision to move forward had squelched any future he might have had with her.

Sometimes, he'd find himself angry about the unfairness of it all—and angry at Selena for being so...

What? Stubborn? Selfish?

Hell, he couldn't blame her for wanting to raise her own children and not someone else's.

Besides, he couldn't very well stew about things like disappointment and anger when his babies—a little boy and girl—were doing so well.

For a moment, he remembered the day he'd seen them both on the ultrasound screen and learned their sex. He'd almost passed on attending that appointment until he'd learned that Selena was going to be delivering a baby, and that one of her associates would be running the scan.

Hell, if he couldn't even face her, how was he supposed to convince her to give him another chance?

No, he would abide by Selena's wishes, no matter

how tough it was. And the best way for him to do that had been to focus on his growing son and daughter—and on Kristy's uneventful pregnancy.

Now, as he waited for his ranch foreman to return from the barn, Alex watched the sun rise on another beautiful April morning. He breathed in the fresh Texas air. As he surveyed the ranch that had once belonged to his uncle and would one day belong to his children, he watched a new colt frolicking in the corral with its mother. A smile stretched across his face. It was impossible not to count his many blessings on a day like this.

Life was good.

But before he could utter a small prayer of thanksgiving, Lydia walked out of the mudroom and called him to the phone.

"Can you take a message?" he asked. "I need to talk to Jake about the plans for the day. Who is it?"

"It's Kristy," Lydia called out. "And she said it's an emergency. She's already called Dr. Ramirez, who's going to meet her at the Brighton Valley Medical Center."

Oh, God. No. It was still too early for her to go into labor. The babies stood little chance, if any, of surviving outside the womb.

"What do I tell her?" the housekeeper asked.

Alex was already running to his truck, reliving the day he'd gotten the call from the Brighton Valley sheriff's office, telling him about Mary's accident.

"Tell her to call an ambulance," he said. "I'm leaving now. I'll meet her at the hospital."

He prayed he'd make it in time.

And that Selena would be able to help.

Chapter 12

Selena had just stepped out of the shower when her after-hours answering service called, relaying the message that Kristy O'Malley was headed for the hospital in an ambulance.

She gripped the receiver, her knuckles aching, while listening to what few details Kristy had given before hanging up and calling the paramedics. Apparently, she'd been having contractions off and on all evening. She hadn't thought too much about it until they started coming at regular intervals early this morning.

Fortunately, Selena had talked to her about being a high-risk pregnancy because of the twins. And she'd told her not to ignore any unusual aches or pains. In cases like this, it was always better to be safe than sorry.

In cases like this...

Selena's thoughts turned to Alex. Did he know yet? Would he be coming to the hospital?

Of course he would. Those babies meant the world to him, even though he hadn't come to any of Kristy's appointments since the very first one.

As Selena threw on some clothes, she pondered his reasons for staying away. Kristy had implied that he was busy on the ranch, as well as mentioning his involvement in training the horses for the new hippotherapy program at the wellness center. And Selena hadn't questioned that.

Still, a part of her wondered if Alex had been avoiding her for another reason. After all, she hadn't seen him since the day he'd asked her to reconsider dating him—and she'd told him no.

But she couldn't worry about that now. She had to get to the hospital to check on Kristy and the twins. At twenty-six weeks gestation, the babies stood a chance of making it. But on top of the health issues they'd face at birth, they would also be at higher risk for lasting disabilities.

Selena grabbed her keys and her purse, then headed for the door. After locking up the house, she climbed behind the wheel of her car, determined to get to the Brighton Valley Medical Center as quickly and safely as she could. She would do whatever she could to ensure those babies stayed in the womb as long as possible—for Alex's sake.

And maybe for her own sake as well. She'd been afraid to tell him how she'd felt about him, afraid to risk heartbreak. So she'd held back on the truth and had run like a scared rabbit.

For a moment, she indulged herself, imagining that Alex's feelings for her had been stronger than she'd thought they were. That she'd made a mistake by not trusting him to move on from Mary to her. But she shook off the starry-eyed musing, focusing on more important things to worry about now.

By the time she reached the hospital and found a space reserved for physicians, she hurried to the maternity floor and made her way to the nurses' desk, where Sylvia Ramos sat. "Has Kristy O'Malley arrived yet? She should have come by ambulance."

"We put her in labor room 235," Sylvia said. "Gretchen has her hooked up to a fetal monitor."

"Thanks."

Moments later, Selena entered Kristy's room and found her stretched out on the bed, wearing a standard hospital gown.

"What's going on?" Selena asked, as she made her way to her patient.

"I'm not sure. I'd been having some minor contractions last night. I thought they were probably Braxton-Hicks or false labor of some kind, but some of the pains were pretty sharp. And this morning, they were coming at regular intervals. You told me not to take any chances with that kind of thing, so I decided I'd better come in."

"I'm glad you did."

Because Kristy had given birth before, she knew what to expect during labor. So Selena took her worries and concerns seriously.

"Excuse me, Dr. Ramirez."

Selena looked up to see Sylvia Ramos standing in the door way. "Yes?"

"The father of the babies just arrived."

Alex. Selena's heart thumped, and her pulse rate soared just knowing he was here.

"What should I tell him?" Sylvia asked.

"Tell him to go to the waiting room. I'll come and talk to him as soon as I've examined Kristy."

Selena had known that she would have to face Alex again someday. And the next time around, she'd planned to be more honest and up front with him than she'd been in the past.

She just wished their next meeting wouldn't have been during a crisis.

Alex had begun to wonder if Selena would ever come into the waiting room and let him know what was going on.

He probably ought to take a seat because all but two of them were empty. But for some reason, he found himself pacing the floor like the proverbial expectant father.

Yet instead of moving because he was a bundle of restless nerves, he was doing it out of fear.

What was going on behind those closed doors? The nurse he'd talked to at the desk had said Kristy was being examined. Was she in any kind of danger?

He certainly hoped not. And as badly as he wanted the twins, he didn't want to see Kristy's health jeopardized in any way.

Finally, at a quarter to nine, he heard footsteps—a pair of high heels?—clicking in the hall. He turned toward the door, just as Selena walked in wearing a white blouse and black slacks. She looked just as pretty as ever, although she appeared to be a little windblown today, as if she'd hurried to dress.

Of course she probably had. Kristy would have notified her doctor before she'd called him.

Alex strode to the middle of the room, meeting Selena halfway. "How is she?"

"She's doing okay for now. She was having some preterm labor, but she really hadn't started to dilate yet. So I gave her some medication to stave off the contractions, and it seems to be working."

"Oh, thank God." He raked his hand through his hair, then asked, "What caused it?"

"It's hard to say at this point. But the babies seem to be doing fine."

He was glad to hear that, but he was also worried about Kristy. Her husband traveled a lot on business and was gone from home on most weekdays. So who was watching her kids and getting them off to school this morning?

And what if she had to stay in the hospital for an extended period of time?

He was paying her to carry the babies for him—and with twins there'd been a bonus. Yet even though she was being compensated for the inconveniences of the pregnancy, he hadn't meant for her to have to spend weeks or months in the hospital.

Selena placed a hand on Alex's arm, providing a soothing balm without saying a word. The heat of her touch sent him hurtling back in time to the days when they'd first become friends, to the night they'd been lovers.

He covered her hand with his, sealing her warmth, possessing her touch for as long as he could.

"I know how worried you must be," she finally said. "But for the time being, the babies aren't in any danger."

He continued to cover her hand, craving so much more than that. "Thanks for the reassurance, Selena. At times like this, I'm glad you're devoted to your job and your patients."

"At times like this?" She smiled. "You mean there was a time when you weren't?"

Yeah, as a matter of fact there was. Whenever he thought about her and their time together, he resented her dedication to her career, her practice. But how selfish had that been, especially now, when he needed her dedication and skill more than anyone did?

Yet he was tired of pretending that her rejection hadn't hurt like hell. Tired of rolling over.

The babies were a way for him to start a new life. Not that he wanted to give up his ranch and all he'd built there, but it wasn't enough. He needed a home, a family. And he wanted Selena to be a part of it.

For that reason, he'd do whatever it took to make sure that happened, even if it meant taking the chance that Selena would shoot him down once again. So, with his heart still raw with emotion from the fear his children were in danger, he let down his defenses.

"To be honest?" he said. "I'd hoped you'd be willing to become a part of a family. *My* family."

"I…" Selena stiffened and drew back. "We talked about this, Alex. I have a medical practice. And you have a ranch. We live in different worlds."

He knew that. And he appreciated her desire to maintain a career. As far as he was concerned, she could have it all if she wanted to. And he'd support her in any way he could.

Yet as he stood here, baring his soul, she'd retreated into a stiff cloak of professionalism.

She'd been so warm, so loving, so willing that night they'd spent together. She'd been more of a woman than a doctor.

And the fact that she was being so cool, so distant

now, set off something inside of him. Something battered and bruised. And he didn't care who was listening or how vulnerable it made him sound.

"Selena, I love you. I didn't plan for it to happen, it just did. And I want us to be together for life—partners and lovers. If you'd be willing to be a mother to the twins, I'd be more than willing, more than happy to have another baby or two with you."

Selena's lips parted and her breath caught. "It's more complicated than that."

Yes, he supposed it was. So he released her hand and took a step back. "Never mind. There's no need beating a dead horse."

She seemed to chew on that for a moment, then glanced at her watch and let out a sigh. "I really need to get to the office, but that'll have to wait. We need to talk."

Before he could respond, she took him by the arm and led him out of the waiting room.

Alex wasn't sure where she was taking him—or what there was left to say—but he would hear her out.

Selena's heart raced as she led Alex down the hall and into one of the private conference rooms on the maternity floor. But it was time to lay it all on the table—her apprehension, her fear.

As difficult as it would be to lay her heart on the line, to tell him why she couldn't date him, she had to come clean. She'd never given him a reason, which didn't seem fair. Especially now that he'd told her he loved her. And she feared it wasn't enough.

Once they were inside and had some privacy, she

turned to face him. "I haven't been completely honest with you."

His head cocked slightly, but he didn't press her. Instead, he gave her the time to find the words that had to be said.

"I love babies, Alex. That's one reason I chose obstetrics as my medical specialty. And there's nothing I'd like more than to become a family with you, to mother your twins and to give you other babies someday. But I...can't."

"Why not?"

It was such an easy question to ask, but so difficult to answer. Especially when she'd been holding tight to her fears for so long.

"I love you, Alex. More than I care to admit."

"So what's the problem?"

She bit her bottom lip, holding back one last time. But Alex had forced the issue. And her fear of losing the babies he so desperately wanted far outweighed her fear of having her heart broken.

"I can't have children, Alex. I might be able to help bring them into the world for others, but that's as far as it goes for me. I can't get pregnant. And I can never give birth myself."

He reached for her hand and gave it a warm, gentle squeeze. "That doesn't matter to me. If we want more children, we can adopt."

"But there's more," she said.

"I'm listening."

She took a fortifying breath, then threw down the gauntlet that had become too hot to handle. "I'm not willing to be second place in your life."

Confusion splashed across his face. "I don't understand."

She slowly shook her head. "No, not the babies. They'd need to come first while they're so tiny and dependent. I'm talking about Mary."

The confusion in his expression deepened. "What about her?"

Selena took a deep breath, then slowly let it out. "You loved her deeply. And I'm afraid..." Again she paused before going on. "I'm afraid that I'd always be your second-choice wife."

He seemed to toss that around for a moment, facing the truth.

"As a side note," she added, "I hope to find a man like you someday."

His grip on her hand tightened, sending her senses as well as her hopes reeling. "You already have me now, Selena."

Was he kidding? She wanted to believe that, but... "I have you by default. And I need to know that you'd be able to love me as much as you loved Mary."

He reached for her chin, tilting her face and locking his gaze on hers. "You're right. I loved Mary. She was a wonderful woman, a good wife. But that doesn't mean I don't love you every bit or more than I loved her. You're different from her, and I love you in a unique and special way."

She wanted to believe him. Did she dare?

"If a mother has two children," he said, "don't you think she can love them both but in different ways? Her love for one has nothing to do with her love for another."

When he said it like that...

"Give me a chance to prove it to you, Selena."

There was nothing she'd like more.

She glanced at her watch one last time, then back to Alex. "I need to go to the office. But don't worry, I'll be monitoring Kristy from there. I'll give you a call later this afternoon to let you know how things are going. And if they continue to go well, maybe we can set a time and place to meet and talk about this further."

"I'll wait for your call," he said. "And you're right. This conversation isn't over. In fact, I think it's just begun."

She nodded, then dashed out the door.

Did she dare hope that things might actually work out between them? That she might have the family she'd always dreamed of having—and with the man she loved more than anything or anyone else in the world?

By the end of the day, Selena was feeling pretty confident that the medication to stop Kristy's contractions had worked. So she called Alex with the good news as well as an update on the woman's family situation.

"Kristy's mother took some vacation time at work," Selena told him. "And she's going to stay with the kids while Kristy's in the hospital—and for the two weeks of bed rest I'm going to order."

"If this goes longer than that," Alex said, "if there are any other unexpected complications, I'll send Lydia, my housekeeper, over to help out."

"That's thoughtful," Selena said.

"Yeah, well, Kristy didn't plan for this to happen."

"Maybe not, but complications do arise. Family Solutions explains that to their surrogates and gestational carriers. It's one reason the process is so costly."

"Yeah, well…" He paused, as if struggling with his thoughts. "I'm still sorry that she's going through this."

So was Selena. And she was glad to know Alex had such a thoughtful side. After all, he really wanted those babies. Another man with the same dream, the same obsession, might have been too focused on his own concerns, his own worries.

"Do you have any questions for me?" Selena asked, hoping she'd been able to ease his mind already.

"Just one. You mentioned that we ought to talk. And because things seem to be going well, I wondered if you'd like to have dinner with me this evening."

Throughout the day, Selena had thought about the talk they'd had in the conference room, about hope that had sparked after his profession of love. And she was looking forward to discussing the future, to see where their love might lead.

"Sure," she said. "Where do you want to go?"

"How about Anita's?"

She loved Mexican food because she'd been raised on it. And she was glad he liked it, too.

"Another craving for tacos?" she asked.

"I suppose so. But I also feel badly about getting a free dinner there last time."

"The power went out. Remember?"

"I certainly do. So I'd like to patronize the place more."

Alex wasn't just a nice guy, but he was generous, too. Again she thought of how lucky Mary had been to meet him first.

But Selena felt pretty darn lucky, too.

"Okay," she said. "Anita's it is. I'll meet you there."

Twenty minutes later, Selena had run a brush through

her hair and applied a coat of lipstick. Just as she'd done the last time they'd gone to Anita's for dinner, she parked her car at home and walked to the restaurant.

And as she suspected, Alex was standing on the curb, waiting for her. He tossed her a dazzling smile that spun her heart three-sixty.

No, make that one-eighty, because they were both headed in a new direction now.

At least, it certainly seemed that way.

He took her hand, and they walked up the steps together. Then he held open the door for her and followed her inside.

The same silver-haired hostess wearing a red peasant-style blouse and a pair of white slacks greeted them with a friendly smile. She reached for the menus. "Good evening. Two for dinner?"

Alex nodded. "Yes."

"Right this way." The hostess led them across the ceramic tile floor to the carpeted stairway. "You'll be in the library again this evening. But you should feel better knowing our electricity hasn't given us any problems since that night you were here."

"That's good," Alex said.

When they'd been seated and the busboy had given them water and a basket of chips and salsa, Alex said, "First of all, I want to thank you for all you did for Kristy and the babies today. It was a comfort knowing you were in charge."

"You're welcome. Just so you know, it would have broken my heart to see you lose the babies after all you've done to get them here."

He gave a shrug. "It was something I had to do. When I make a promise, I keep it."

"You know," Selena said, "Mary was a very lucky woman." And for once, there wasn't any resentment or envy behind the words.

"I was the lucky one," Alex said. "She put up with all my faults."

Quite frankly, Selena hadn't seen many of them.

After a quiet dinner, Alex paid the bill. Then they walked outside. The clouds darkened the sky, hiding the stars. Yet the evening seemed brighter, more promising than ever before.

"Let me drive you home," Alex said.

"But it's only a couple of blocks from here."

"I know, but I was hoping you'd invite me inside. And I don't see any reason to leave my truck parked here."

"Neither do I," she said with a smile.

She couldn't imagine not wanting to extend their evening together, not inviting him into the house—and into her bedroom. Not making love to him, now that their life together held such promise.

After Alex pulled into the driveway and parked, they walked to the front door. She used her key, then led him into the living room.

She'd no more than turned on the lamp when Alex took her in his arms and pulled her close. She'd missed holding him, touching him, and she lay her head against his.

"Thank you for giving me a chance to prove how much I love you," he said.

"And thanks for hanging in there with me while I was running scared."

"You were worth it." Then he kissed her, slowly, thoroughly, as if they had all the time in the world.

And, as she'd just begun to realize, they really did.

When the kiss ended, Selena remained in his embrace, her heart soaring at the thought of what lay before them. Not just another incredible night of lovemaking, which she knew was just a few heartbeats away. But the birth of the babies, the creation of a family.

"I love you, Alex. And I'm looking forward to whatever the future brings."

He drew her close. "I love you, too."

Selena pressed a light kiss on his lips. "And I want you to know that I'll do my very best to mother the twins and to make Mary proud."

"Let's leave Mary out of this," Alex said. "From this day forward, it's all about you and me and the babies. Agreed?"

She nodded. "All right. It's a deal."

Then he kissed her one more time, sealing the agreement with a heart-strumming, soul-stirring kiss.

Selena had it all—a wonderful career, a man who loved her and the family she'd always dreamed of. She didn't think the future could look any brighter.

Epilogue

Selena couldn't believe all the changes that had taken place in the course of a single year.

Last May, she'd married Alex Connor in a small but romantic wedding ceremony at the Brighton Valley Community Church in front of their closest friends. Then, two months ago, she'd delivered her own newborns—a five-pound nine-ounce son and a six-pound one-ounce daughter—while the happy father, the love of her life, looked on.

It had been a real stroke of luck when Dr. Nathan Blankenship moved to town and joined Selena's medical group. His arrival had allowed her to take eight weeks off while he covered for her.

When it was time to return to work, she would cut back on her hours. Even then, it would be tough to leave the twins, but she knew that Lydia would love and care for them as if they were her very own.

So for the time being, Selena enjoyed the time to rock her babies and marvel in their sweet smiles and the joy they'd brought to her life.

Could any mother love her children more?

"Honey?" Alex called from the mudroom. "Is lunch ready yet?"

She lifted her finger to her lips. "Shh! I just managed to get Jonathon to sleep. He's been fussy all morning."

It was important for Jonathon to nap, just as his sister Caitlyn was doing, because Selena had plans to surprise her husband with some alone time.

Alex entered the kitchen, where Selena sat at the table with little Jonathon wrapped in a blue-and-yellow receiving blanket. He peered at their son, who snoozed in Selena's arms, and smiled.

"But to answer your question," Selena said, her voice lowered to a whisper, "Yes, lunch is ready. But you'll have to wait a while."

"Why? What's up?"

She got to her feet. "Is your horse saddled?"

"Yes, why?"

"Because I'd like you to saddle Sugar Foot for me, too. Just give me a minute. I'll put the baby in his crib and then let Lydia know I'm leaving."

"Where are we going?"

"I thought it would be fun to take a picnic lunch up to Ol' Piney. I also thought I'd bring a blanket along, just in case you had an urge to...nap."

A slow grin stretched across her husband's handsome face. "I'll have those horses ready to go before you can snap your pretty fingers."

He brushed a kiss on her lips. "And it's probably

only fair to tell you that while I'd love to stretch out on a blanket with you, I'm not planning to do any napping."

"Neither am I." She winked, then got up from the chair, careful not to jostle the baby in her arms.

"I love being married to a woman full of surprises."

"You're a fun man to surprise, especially when you're not planning to nap."

Then she tossed him a grin before setting off on a romantic outing, which was becoming a marital habit she had no intention of breaking.

* * * * *

YOU HAVE
JUST READ A
HARLEQUIN®
SPECIAL
EDITION
BOOK.

SPECIAL EXCERPT FROM

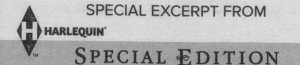

HARLEQUIN®

SPECIAL EDITION

*Cole Dalton thought letting Vivienne Shuster
plan his wedding—to no one—would work out just
fine for both of them. But now not only are they getting
caught up in a lot of lies, they might just be getting
caught up in each other!*

*Read on for a sneak preview of
the next **MONTANA MAVERICKS** story,
THE MAVERICK'S BRIDAL BARGAIN
by Christy Jeffries.*

"You're engaged?"

"Of course I'm not engaged." Cole visibly shuddered. "I'm not even boyfriend material, let alone husband material."

Confusion quickly replaced her anger and Vivienne could only stutter, "Wh-why?"

"I guess because I have more important things going on in my life right now than to cozy up to some female I'm not interested in and pretend like I give a damn about all this commitment crap."

"No, I mean why would you need to plan a wedding if you're not getting married?"

"You said you need to book another client." He rocked onto the heels of his boots. "Well, I'm your next client."

Vivienne shook her head as if she could jiggle all the scattered pieces of this puzzle into place. "A client who has no intention of getting married?"

"Yes. But it's not like your boss would know the difference."

"She might figure it out when no actual marriage takes place. If you're not boyfriend material, then does that mean you don't have a girlfriend? I mean, who would we say you're marrying?"

Okay, so that first question Vivienne threw in for her own clarification. Even though they hadn't exactly kissed, she needed reassurance that she wasn't lusting over some guy who was off-limits.

"Nope, no need for a girlfriend," he said, and she felt some of her apprehension drain. But then he took a couple of steps closer. "We can make something up, but why would it even need to get that far? Look, you just need to buy yourself some time to bring in more business. So you sign me up or whatever you need to do to get your boss off your back, and then after you bring in some more customers   legitimate ones—my fake fiancée will have cold feet and we'll call it off."

If her eyes squinted any more, they'd be squeezed shut. And then she'd miss his normal teasing smirk telling her that he was only kidding. But his jaw was locked into place and the set of his straight mouth looked dead serious.

Don't miss
THE MAVERICK'S BRIDAL BARGAIN
by Christy Jeffries,
available June 2018 wherever
Harlequin® Special Edition books and ebooks are sold.

www.Harlequin.com

Looking for more satisfying love stories
with community and family at their core?

Check out **Harlequin® Special Edition**
and **Harlequin® Western Romance** books!

New books available every month!

CONNECT WITH US AT:

Harlequin.com/Community

 Facebook.com/HarlequinBooks

Twitter.com/HarlequinBooks

Instagram.com/HarlequinBooks

Pinterest.com/HarlequinBooks

ReaderService.com

**ROMANCE WHEN
YOU NEED IT**

HFGENRE2017R